CENTRAL
STATION

CENTRAL STATION

A RAY DELUCA NOVEL

JOSEPH CARIFFE

Bluish, LLC
4030 Wake Forest Road, Suite 349
Raleigh, NC 27609

Bluish, LLC paperback edition July 2022.

ISBNs:
979-8-9863433-0-3 (print)
979-8-9863433-1-0 (eBook)

Printed in the United States of America

Cover design: Jerry Todd
Cover Images: Kevin Schofield, Schofield Images
Author Photos and Images: Peter Thoshinsky, TMAXPHOTO

For Marilyn (Cariffe) Hearns
My loving aunt
My North Star
My muse

CONTENTS

CONTENTS

ACKNOWLEDGMENTS

*T*o *my loving wife Denise* who gave me the inspiration, time, space, love, and support, to write my first novel. To my son Jack who, with love and sensitivity, provided creative direction and important feedback throughout the writing of this book. To my son Nick, who believed in me and taught me the importance of being a dad.

To my dear friends, and relatives, who read early drafts and provided encouragement and critical feedback: Denise Cariffe, Jack Cariffe, Christopher Cariffe, Lori Coombs, Dr. David Padgett, Nola Padgett, and Catherine Fontaine.

To my amazing editors Caroline Tolley and Warren Layberry who humbled me and patiently coached me through the arduous task of editing.

To San Francisco Police Lieutenant Peter Thoshinsky (Ret.) and Lieutenant Kevin Shofield of the Berkeley, California Police Department, both master photographers, who skillfully captured the mood and essence of *Central Station*. Pete and Kevin are an inspiration and helped bring this story to life.

To book cover designer, Jerry Todd, for lending his expertise to this project, creating world-class packaging and book design.

- 1 -

I DO IT TO MYSELF

Exhausted and lethargic, my strength and coordination lost to the fifty-six-degree water, I reminded myself I'd swum in worse conditions, taking gunfire and bogged down with combat gear and weapons. By comparison, this swim was light work. Your basic meat and potatoes open-water swim, and I relished it. Embrace the suck, as we used to say in our SEAL unit.

I joined the Dolphin Swim Club for access to open-water swimming in the bay. It's a fitting spot to swim, a mile west of Alcatraz Island, with its criminal mystique, changing currents, and physical challenges. Early in the morning, the decaying prison presents a ghostly image, shrouded by fog with the Golden Gate in the background.

After years as a Navy SEAL, I'd grown tired of the cycle of deployments and never-ending mission prep, so I completed my last reenlistment commitment and was honorably discharged in September of 2016. After my discharge, I applied to the San Francisco Police Department, but it took almost a year before I was hired. I used the time to decompress from my last tour in Afghanistan and, at thirty-nine, was the oldest recruit in my SFPD academy class that began in June of 2017.

After successfully completing close to a year of required training, I was assigned to a year's probation at Central Station.

As a SEAL, I'd become accustomed to a steady paycheck and job security, so law enforcement seemed like an obvious choice. It was either that, or back to my father's business.

My name is Ray DeLuca, son of Anthony DeLuca. My father's a boss in the Mafia—a *capo* in *la Cosa Nostra*. Before joining the military, all I knew was "the life." Wise guys and mobsters.

For a time, I worked on my father's crew, running errands and picking up packages while I attended junior college. I didn't ask what the packages contained, but knew they were *pittso,* or protection money, and illegal gambling and loan sharking proceeds. I learned collection tactics from the older guys on the crew.

I was being groomed to enter the life, but in a rare moment of conscience, after punishing a girlfriend's father for a gambling debt, I became conflicted and started to rethink my life.

I wanted a challenge and to do some good. I wanted to repent. At twenty-two, the new path I chose was the Navy with the aspiration of becoming a SEAL.

Despite my father's misgivings, he told me he respected my decision.

After I graduated from boot camp, I completed the required SEAL assessment phase and the Naval Special Warfare Preparatory School in Great Lakes, Illinois, before entering Basic Underwater Demolition/SEAL (BUD/S) Training in Coronado, California.

So, here I am, years later, freezing my nuts off at oh-dark-thirty, taking a shower after my swim on the outdoor deck of the Dolphin Swim Club, before reporting for my first day of duty at Central Station. My first day as a proby.

As I looked out at the bay, I wondered if the morning mist and gloomy fog were a foreshadowing of my future.

I abruptly realized I'd lost track of time daydreaming in the shower, so I threw on a pair of jeans, T-shirt, and flip-flops and raced up Columbus Avenue in my black Dodge Challenger to find parking and my assigned locker.

I flashed my police ID at the entrance and was buzzed in. The name tag of the black officer who admitted me read Payne.

"Downstairs," he mumbled and gave me the once-over as I rushed in with my war bag and dry-cleaned uniforms thrown over my shoulder.

SFPD's Central Station is in the heart of San Francisco's Little Italy, next to Chinatown.

Little Italy is also known as North Beach, and an assignment at Central is considered a choice assignment. I'd landed a coveted gig, even if it was only for the next twelve months.

The Central district covers a good chunk of San Francisco's top landmarks and attractions, including North Beach, Chinatown, Russian Hill, Nob Hill, Telegraph Hill, Fisherman's Wharf, Alcatraz Island, and the Financial District.

Central Station is the ultimate throwback. Vintage institutional décor from the 1960s, with all the warmth of a federal prison. As I walked through the squad room, I noticed it was old and dingy, with clutter covering a beat-up conference room table in the main squad room. Most of the chairs around the table were in disrepair, like they'd been supporting tired officers and their troubles for too long.

I ran downstairs and located a battered locker bearing my name hastily written on a piece of masking tape. I wondered how many officers had been assigned this same locker since 1969 and how their stories had played out. Mine was just beginning.

Practically every inch of the locker door was covered with graffiti, stickers, and cartoons from fifty years of cops expressing themselves. Today, much of it would be considered politically incorrect by the woke set.

I rushed to put my uniform on and by the time I was suited up, I was sweating like a racehorse at Saratoga.

I took the worn linoleum stairs, two at a time, and when I hit the landing to the squad room, heard the watch commander barking.

"Dah Looka! Dah Looka! Where the fuck is DeLuca?"

I slid into the back row of the lineup. "Sir!"

The lieutenant sauntered over, squaring off in front of me like a drill instructor, nose to nose. My heart was racing from rushing, but the face-off failed to achieve his desired effect of intimidating me. The more he spoke, the calmer I felt.

"DeLuca," he said in a low voice, "don't sweat on my floor. If you have a handicap, or something that prevents you from reporting on time, you better tell me now. If not, I expect your monkey ass in lineup, on time, every shift. This watch, and your partner, depend on you to be on time. Understood?"

"Sorry, sir. Yes, sir."

A few minutes later the lieutenant was barking out beat assignments.

"DeLuca, you and Lau are the Three-Adam-Fifteen-Boy. Try not to fuck things up or sweat on Officer Lau."

Hank Lau was only about five-eight but broad-chested with arms that moved a lot of iron in his free time. He was excited to meet me, too.

"Hey, Mr. Punctuality, go grab the long guns, and a first aid kit. Don't forget extra rounds. I'm feelin' a little trigger-happy today." He pointed in the direction of the armory. "Over there, numb nuts, let's go!"

I played along and met Lau at our assigned patrol vehicle, carrying everything but a grenade launcher and surface-to-air missiles.

Hank started the black-and-white, chirped the siren, and yelled, "Let's go, turtle. We got a call."

The call was for a report of a missing person. A sleeper of a call. It's a Priority B call and not worth rushing for. They could've dispatched a Cub Scout to handle this one.

Though missing person calls are taken seriously, they frequently have little to no merit. There are many reasons why people break their routines and disappear for a day or so.

I considered the call my penance for posting late for briefing on my first day. I'm an idiot. That was stupid, and I know better.

Hank drove to Café Trieste on Vallejo Street, a few blocks from the station.

"I'm gonna get green tea," he said, "and you can get whatever you want."

That's nice of him . . .

"Of course, you're buying, dipshit. We'll give whoever's missing a few more minutes to get their lying ass home."

I was amused. *So that's how it's going to be?*

Too soon to introduce him to the *other* Ray. I'd play nice for now.

Hank was Asian American with salt-and-pepper hair, worn in a crew cut, military-style. He had a stack of hash marks on his sleeve for his twenty-plus years of service. His boots looked scuffed and fatigued, in dire need of spit and polish.

He was surly and walked with the swagger of a Marine Corps gunnery sergeant.

As we approached the café, I noticed a dark-haired beauty with pale-blue eyes, sunning long, tanned legs at a table by the entrance. She was talking a-mile-a-minute with a girlfriend. They sounded like the women on one of those *Real Housewives* shows, bantering back and forth, so the other can't get a word in edgewise.

Once inside, I turned to Hank. "Dude, did you see that?"

"What?"

"If you miss something like that, you better check your situational awareness, bro."

I got an eye roll, and barely audible ". . . douchebag."

We got our drinks and left for Carmine's, a local restaurant, to take the missing person report.

"Probably some drunk-ass sous chef," I said, "partying all night. Thinks he's the next Anthony Bourdain."

No response from Hank, but at least I was entertaining myself. *Go fuck yourself, Lau.*

The place looked expensive, but anything nicer than Olive Garden impresses me.

Yellow canopy over the entrance, flowers boxes, and a polished brass plaque engraved with Carmine's mounted on the glossy white-painted brick next to the front door. Understated but classy and what you'd expect from a celebrity like Carmine Vaccaro. Carmine is the star of the Food Network's *Mangia with Carmine!* which I admittedly watch for cooking tips.

Like me, Carmine is Sicilian. It was a long shot, but I was hoping we'd get to meet him. Maybe get a picture with him. My mother would love that. She'd make it her Christmas card next year! The place looked closed, so Hank pounded on the door like a Viking.

"San Francisco Police!"

An attractive woman in her thirties unlocked then opened the door. I was impressed not just by her stature but by her grace—she moved like an aristocrat.

"Come in," she said, "I'm the one who called. I'm Gina Vaccaro, Carmine's sister."

We sat and she offered espressos with lemon peel and biscotti on the side, one of the restaurant's specialties.

I accepted. Hank took a pass. Maybe afraid it would interfere with his green-tea Zen state.

It was Wednesday, and Gina explained her brother, Carmine, had been missing since Saturday night.

This guy was a major international celebrity, but I wasn't sure if Hank even recognized the name, let alone had an appreciation for who we were talking about.

"I tried to reach him," she said. "He was off on Sunday. It's not like him to disappear. When he's not here, he still checks on the restaurant.

"Nobody's heard from him. I called the police on Monday, and they said he had to be missing at least seventy-two hours before they could take the report. That's why I didn't file the report sooner."

She reported she checked her brother's apartment in Pacific Heights, including the garage, but came up empty-handed.

"His Lamborghini was parked in his reserved space, so he didn't take his car. It's his baby and had the cover on it. It didn't look disturbed."

"Does he have any enemies?" I asked.

"No. Well, except for the Food Network. They just canceled his show, so he's pissed. He made a lot of money for them."

"What happened?"

"They moved *Mangia with Carmine!* to another time slot and his ratings went down, so they fired him. They screwed up, so they punished him to cover their mistake. Typical."

"Does Carmine date," I asked, "or have somebody in his life?"

"He hasn't dated in a while. Too busy with the TV show and the restaurant. It's not a priority for him."

"Maybe he met somebody and left for a few days?"

She shook her head. "Maybe, but he's not spontaneous."

She mused that living alone and working all the time probably wasn't the best thing for him.

"I think he's been depressed since they canceled his show. Who wouldn't be?"

"I'm sorry," I said, "but I have to ask: Do you think he'd hurt himself? Does he own a gun, or other weapons, or ever talked about suicide?"

"Absolutely not. He doesn't own a gun. I don't think he'd hurt himself, but I can't see inside his mind. I really don't know."

She started to tear up and looked away. "You better leave now. I gotta get ready for the lunch crowd."

I heard a distinct Italian inflection as she spoke. She brushed away a tear, looking grave.

"*Andra tutto bene,*" I said. It's going to be okay.

She smiled, and lightly grabbed my hand. *"Sei così gentile."* You're so kind.

Walking to the patrol car, I said, "She seemed legit to me." Hank was gruff. "You never know with these things. Maybe she's jealous of her brother and put him in the sausage grinder."

"Well, that's a happy thought, Mr. Rogers!"

I guess the cynicism is what twenty-plus years pushing a radio car in a big city gets you.

We went back to the station to make follow-up calls and file the report. We had to find Carmine soon. He was more than a celebrity. He was a national treasure.

- 2 -

TO THE GOOD LIFE!

Carmine *was the happiest* he'd been in weeks as he took in the view from the deck of the *Sicilia*, anchored near the Farallon Islands about fifty kilometers west of the Golden Gate Bridge.

The yacht was the pride of fellow San Francisco restaurateur Vincent Catalano, the host of the day's outing.

Wanting a photo, Carmine reached for his phone, but found it wasn't in his pocket. He thought maybe he'd left it in the cabin with the rest of his things. Content in the moment, he resolved to retrieve it later.

A light breeze off the Gulf of the Farallones swept up over the bow. Carmine savored the aroma of the open seas as he thought about the day's menu Vinnie had proposed.

★ ★ ★

Vinnie was a gifted restaurateur and owned and operated one of the finest restaurants on the West Coast, Trattoria Sicilia in North Beach. Today on *Sicilia*, Vinnie was accompanied by his sturdy sidekick, Frank Bruno, who was useful and could take care of things while Vinnie attended to Carmine.

He admired Carmine and was anxious to get to know him better, especially considering Carmine's notoriety and status as a major celebrity. He'd invited Carmine for a trip on the *Sicilia* weeks earlier.

With his frequent appearances on national TV, you couldn't escape Carmine's celebrity. Vinnie knew that Carmine, the pride of Sicily, was born and raised near Palermo, the very city where he himself grew up.

Carmine, on the other hand, knew nothing of Vinnie before moving to San Francisco and meeting him at a hospitality function and was unaware of his ulterior motive for the day's outing. Vinnie planned to propose a partnership.

As they sat to eat, Carmine thanked Vinnie for extending the invitation. As soon as his glass was full, he raised it.

"*Cin-cin! A te, amico mio.* Cheers to you, my friend."

★ ★ ★

Before the main course, Carmine gorged himself on antipasto and shellfish, using his custom engraved knife—a gift from his father—to shuck oysters for everyone.

As a world-class chef, Carmine could shuck an oyster faster than most people could butter bread. He made working with food look easy. Vinnie watched with envy because he couldn't scramble an egg.

The onboard meal was prepared earlier at Vinnie's restaurant, by his executive chef. The main course was *pasta con i de mare,* made with fresh calamari, which was a favorite of Vinnie's. This was accompanied by fresh fruit, cannoli, and an assortment of gelatos for dessert.

Carmine stuffed his sun-scorched face and crowed with pleasure as he dabbed his mouth and sweaty forehead with a linen table napkin.

"*Bellisimo! Grazie, paisan.*"

Carmine looked forward to this day to escape the pressures of running his restaurant and creating a new TV show.

He found Vinnie interesting and wanted to get to know him better. Vinnie was ambitious, and by outward appearances, successful like him. It was hard to get a read off Frank Bruno, who seldom spoke or smiled.

Both the yacht and Trattoria's Michelin rating stood as a testament to Vinnie's operational and culinary success, which Carmine admired. The fact they were both successful Sicilians was a plus.

Carmine's restaurant was located just blocks from Vinnie's but hadn't yet earned a Michelin rating.

Carmine didn't measure his success by accumulating Michelin stars and believed his food and service were as good as Trattoria's. He knew it was his celebrity that filled his restaurant week after week, and that was *his* measure of success.

Together, Vinnie and Carmine ran the table in San Francisco with two of the finest Italian restaurants in the Bay Area—possibly the entire West Coast.

Vinnie had bragging rights for the Michelin stars, but he knew Carmine's had more celebrity cache and appeal.

Vinnie was envious of Carmine and knew it was impossible to replicate the celebrity vibe at his restaurant.

Carmine was a superstar, a Food Network sensation, but it didn't go to his head, and his fans loved him for it. Reservations at his restaurant were booked weeks in advance, and he enjoyed an enormous social media following, managed by his digital guru.

His genial modesty as they sat at the table seemed utterly genuine.

"Hey, Vinnie, like you, I'm just a guy from Sicily. I've been blessed."

After the meal, Carmine excused himself and returned with a bottle of premium Lucano Sambuca and a rosewood humidor full of Avo cigars—expensive, limited-edition cigars from the Dominican Republic.

He presented the gifts to Vinnie.

"Here ya go, Vin. Amazing day. *Grazie.* Let me tell you about the guy who created this brand and blended these cigars." Carmine retrieved an expensive guillotine from his pocket, and it glistened in the sunlight. "His name was Avo Uvezian. He was a famous jazz pianist. Wrote music, too. I think he was Armenian or some shit like that. He went to Juilliard. He met Sinatra. Long time ago. They were both young. Sinatra was crazy about one of Avo's songs called 'Broken Guitar.' He asked Avo if he could change it up a little, record it, and call it 'Strangers in the Night.' The rest is history. True story.

"Later in life, Sinatra said he hated performing the song. Not sure why." Then Carmine broke unexpectedly into song. "Strangers in the night exchanging glances, doobie doobie doo . . . "

Vinnie and Frank listened intently, leaning in to hear his story. Carmine could spin a tale and had a warm, engaging style all his own. Star power.

"Anyway, Avo sold his cigar company to Davidoff a few years ago for ten mil. Not bad, huh?"

"No shit?" said Vinnie. "That's a great fuckin' story. Let's see if these sticks are any good."

Carmine prepared three cigars, clipping the ends like a pediatrician performing circumcisions.

As a top restaurateur, Vinnie made a comfortable living, but the real money came from his mob activities. Lately, the challenge was hiding and laundering cash from his criminal activities to avoid scrutiny by the feds. He was making money faster than he could find a home for it.

Vinnie generated more income than other Mafia soldiers and was generous with the bosses. Of course, he always wet his beak first before sending the tax back East to the Mafia commission.

The good life had arrived, and nothing seemed out of reach to him. He loved the success but had increasingly become jealous of Carmine's success and his celebrity. For his part, Carmine was oblivious to Vinnie's envy. He handed an Avo to Frank and all three men fired up their cigars.

Everywhere Carmine went, he lit up the place. Fans and paparazzi surrounded him for autographs and pictures. He was used to it and patient with his fans and the press.

He suspected Vinnie had mob associations, but so what?

Carmine had been around mob guys growing up in Sicily. They were everywhere, but his father always told him, "Not our business. Stay out of it."

He learned to peacefully coexist with mobsters from a young age. It was no longer part of his life.

As an entry-level soldier, Vinnie knew it would be tough to achieve the notoriety and celebrity Carmine enjoyed, unless he rose to the level of a capo, like John Gotti and his son years ago, and he had every intention of doing so.

The mob was smaller now, so it could work in his favor to get recognition and move up in the organization.

Maybe instead of the Teflon Don he'd become known as the Restaurant Don. When he thought of it, he chuckled inside.

Vinnie took a puff of his cigar, then stood and man-hugged Carmine. "The Avos are awesome. *Gratzie, mi amico.*"

Vinnie's sidekick, Frankie, chimed in. "Youz fa-fa-fuckin' awright, Ca-ca-ca Carmine. Youz ga-ga-ga got class."

Frankie stuttered since childhood. Sometimes he'd mask the stutter by singing what he was trying to say. *Lah-di-dah, pass the can-noh-lees.*

When he sang, Vinnie smiled and nodded.

That earned him the nickname Stutterin' Frankie, but most didn't have the cojones to call him that to his face. Carmine noticed he didn't say much and thought he looked like he was ready to explode. After the initial introduction, he decided to leave him alone.

That afternoon, the more they smoked and drank, the more outrageous the stories became, and the louder the laughs.

They sipped sambuca, and Carmine lamented about growing up in Sicily.

"My old man," said Carmine, "he was a *bracciante*, a day laborer. I couldn't imagine something like *this* as a kid." He made a sweeping gesture across the deck with his hand.

"My father worked hard. We wuz happy, but we didn't have much. Work for my old man was never steady. We didn't go out to dinner. We couldn't afford anything like that."

As Vinnie and Frankie appeared disinterested, Carmine sensed he was boring his hosts.

"Hey, Vin, I don't mean to get all sappy. I just lost my father."

Vinnie nodded and looked grave. "Sorry about your old man."

They sat quietly, then Vinnie changed the subject, hoping to bring the talk away from death.

"Hey, mi amico, sorry about *Mangia with Carmine.* That was a good show. I liked it."

Carmine nodded but a shadow crossed his face. "Yeah, thanks. We did okay."

Another awkward silence, Vinnie cursing himself for going from one dark subject to another.

"So, what are ya doing now for dough," he asked, "other than the restaurant?"

Carmine sensed what his father used to call *the touch* coming his way. *The touch* is when someone's getting ready to hit you up for money, or a loan.

"I'm good," he said. "Unless you got a couple of bags of Ben Franklin's ya wanna unload."

"No. I'm serious," Vinnie said.

Carmine looked at him, confused.

"I'm good. I'm talkin' to other networks about doin' a new show. This shit happens all the time in network TV. Nothin' lasts forever. Fuck the Food Network. I don't need 'em. I'm already workin' on ideas for a new show."

Carmine puffed his cigar and looked away. His instincts were correct. He wanted to tell Vinnie to mind his own goddamn business. He had plenty of money saved and in reserves from his recent separation deal with the Food Network and had strong cashflow coming in from the restaurant. Money wasn't a problem.

Vinnie motioned for Frankie to step away. Frankie did.

"Hey, Carmine, no offense, but ya probably got a big nut like me. I was only makin' conversation.

"Look, I got a proposition for us to partner on your restaurant, then you can concentrate on your new TV show. I'll take sixty percent, run the joint, and put a couple hundred thou in your pocket. You get some walkin' around money and don't have to worry about the day-to-day stuff. I'll keep your name on the restaurant and you can still be the executive chef."

And there it is, Carmine thought, *the windup and the pitch!* Before Vinnie could continue, Carmine wagged his head from side to side as he exhaled.

"No, thanks. I appreciate it. Not interested. My restaurant. My name. My deal. I've been working my whole life to build my brand, and I don't need a partner, but thanks."

Vinnie bristled. "I can't believe you! I wanna help you out. Why you being an ingrate? That's a great offer."

"Sure, sure," said Carmine, "I know it is and I appreciate it, but I'm not in the market for a partner. I'm doin' fine."

He certainly wasn't going to tell him how good he was *really* doing, especially with the buyout he'd just received on his contract from the Food Network. That would be a mistake.

Vinnie paused, cleared his throat, then went off the rails.

"Who do ya think you're talkin' to, some mutt? You think you're better than me? How do you think I got a Michelin Star and bought this yacht? You think I'm a dope? How 'bout I just take your restaurant and give you *ungatz?*"

Ungatz. Nothing.

Vinnie flicked the fingers of his right hand under his chin and flicked them outward emphasizing the gesture. He clenched his jaw and his face turned red. He walked away and came back with an envelope, tossing it at Carmine.

"Read this. Or don't read it. It's a letter of intent."

"Vinnie, I told—"

"Sign it. We'll be partners."

Vinnie started to pace. Carmine was pissed.

"Where do you get off with this? What the fuck? We're out here havin' a nice day, and I'm not gettin' where you're coming from.

"I thought we wuz friends. Did I do something to piss you off? I just told you I don't need a partner, and my restaurant's not for sale. Why you gettin' so pissed off?"

Carmine excused himself, saying he needed to use the head, the yacht's bathroom, and figured he'd look for his phone in case he needed it.

After using the head, panic set in when he couldn't find his phone. His sense of fear and isolation was exacerbated.

Carmine had dealt with thick-headed Sicilians before. Now, he was pissed. *Who does this? Who acts like this?* When his anger abated and his mind started to clear, he knew exactly who did this: the mob. He knew better. He'd let his guard down letting Vinnie into his life, fooled by his appearances of success.

Carmine wasn't new to the Sicilian way, and as a businessman had experience dealing with difficult people in the food and TV businesses, but he felt like a fool.

With a jolt of adrenaline, his heart started to race. He felt like he'd touched a live wire. He knew he needed to calm down. He looked around and saw Frankie leaning against the cockpit, with that *facia miserable*, that miserable face, glaring at him.

As Carmine's frustration mounted, he muttered, "Fuckin' mook," under his breath.

He felt his face getting hot and didn't give a shit if Frankie heard him.

Another yacht cruised by, heading south, to parts unknown. It gave him a faint glimmer of hope that others were out there, too. It was supposed to be a special day and was turning out to be the day from hell. What happened to all the bonding? He wanted to go up to Vinnie and say, *What are you, a fuckin' psycho?*

He reasoned Vinnie might be testing him, too, as wise guys sometimes do.

Vinnie walked over and sat across from him and with tight lips calmly said, "You need to sign the document."

Carmine's mind was racing. He felt pin-sized bolts of lightning shooting through him, like mini electrical shocks.

At once, he thought of a solution, at least for the near-term and felt some relief.

He'd sign the document and let his attorney get him out of it later. It wouldn't be the first contract he broke, and he could repent and do a *mea culpa* with Vinnie later to keep the peace.

He thought, maybe Vinnie was bipolar, or had a chemical imbalance, or something. Maybe the booze is getting to him.

With his sweaty hand, he scribbled his famous signature across the bottom of the contract and handed it back to Vinnie.

"There. I gotta head back now. I got things to do."

He abruptly stood, ignoring Vinnie's extended hand like he didn't see it, when he attempted a handshake. Vinnie took it as an insult but remained silent.

Carmine felt confident by signing the document it would get Vinnie off his back, so they could sail back to the Berkeley Marina where he could get his feet back on solid ground.

Regrettably, he'd have to call his attorney in the morning.

He felt calmer but continued to sweat. His tongue felt thick, and he couldn't seem to quench his thirst.

He blurted, "Why youz doin' this to me, Vinnie? I thought we wuz friends?"

Vinnie appeared lost in his thoughts as he puffed his Avo, gazing into the horizon.

Frankie lumbered over and put his beefy hand on Carmine's shoulder. "Get up."

Carmine hesitated and instinctively pulled away. "Get your fuckin' hands off me."

Carmine remembered his knife and instinctively reached for it in his pocket, but as he did, Frankie slapped him across the back of the head, practically knocking him off his chair.

Carmine slowly stood, feeling lightheaded and disoriented. He couldn't tell if it was from the smack in the head, the booze, or his fear. The thought of Vinnie or Frankie spiking his drink also crossed his mind.

Frankie stammered, "Ca-ca-ca over there. I wanna talk to you," and pointed towards the swimming platform at the back of the boat.

As Carmine obediently walked ahead of Frankie, he felt for his gravity knife in his pocket and, sensing imminent danger, with the knife cupped in his hand, spun around as if to ask a question, and simultaneously flicked the knife open.

With a fast left to right motion, he delivered a deep laceration across Frankie's cheek and nose. He looked surprised but wiped the blood away like he had a runny nose.

Carmine continued slashing back and forth and managed to cut Frankie's face a second time. He caught his arm, too.

Frankie stepped back and looked at Carmine with bulging eyes in disbelief.

Carmine thought he made his point and hoped it would stop the attack. "Now back the fuck up!"

Frankie's eyes grew larger, and with flared nostrils he charged Carmine like a bull. They landed on the deck with Frankie on top. Carmine gripped his razor-sharp knife, and as he went to slash his face again, Frankie moved his head, and Carmine practically sliced his ear off.

With slippery blood on the deck, Carmine used every bit of his considerable strength to slide out from under him, stabbing Frankie in his side and buttocks repeatedly, like a pin cushion.

Carmine moved to get the upper hand, driving his thumb deep into Frankie's eye socket.

He mounted him and knew what he had to do. It was kill or be killed.

As Carmine went to slash Frankie's throat, Vinnie came from behind, placed him in a headlock, and yanked him off Frankie.

Carmine tried to say *Stop*, but Vinnie's headlock closed his airway, and he was on the brink of unconsciousness and couldn't utter the word. During the struggle, he dropped his knife as Vinnie dragged him the short distance to the swimming platform where he hurled him into the freezing swells.

The icy temperature felt like daggers as he gasped to breathe and stay afloat. He struggled to swim back to the boat, only a few feet away.

You can't un-ring the bell and can't un-burn the toast. That's the way it goes. No do-overs. He knew he'd have to kill them both. But first he'd have to get back on the boat.

He labored against the repetitive surge of the ocean and felt like he was swimming in place, as he pathetically struggled to move his arms and legs in the frigid open sea. That's when panic set in and he started screaming for help. Pleading.

The frigid temperature took his breath away, sucking the life out of him.

He began to hyperventilate and take in water, unable to make an audible sound. He tried to quiet himself and pray.

As he made another attempt to close the distance, he heard the faint sounds of Sinatra singing "That's Life." Something hit him in the shoulder. He looked up and there was Frankie. He stood on the swim platform with a barbed fishing gaff, pushing him away like he was debris, or garbage in the water.

Frankie was unrecognizable, covered in blood like an actor in a horror movie. Even with his ear hanging off and his eye coming out of its socket, it gave Carmine little consolation.

Vinnie started the yacht's supercharged engines and slowly pulled away.

Carmine stayed afloat and with all the strength he could muster, swam hard for the swimming platform, in his coral-colored Tommy Bahama shirt and white linen shorts.

He *had* to grab the swimming platform at all costs.

As they pulled away, he heard Vinnie crowing, "Fuck you, Carmine. You're gettin' *ungatz*, you greedy prick!"

He should have known that for Vinnie, a slice of *Carmine's* would never be enough. He had to take the whole goddamn restaurant.

Carmine's efforts to grab the swimming platform were in vain, and it wasn't long before he gassed-out and went under.

★ ★ ★

Vinnie looked at Frankie in disbelief.

"There's a first aid kit in the galley with butterfly strips. Close those cuts up and tape your ear back on. Put a patch on that eye, too, or you're gonna lose it. Marone, you look like Frankenstein. Get going! Dump the chum in the water too, so Carmine can have some company.

"Fuck! you're dripping blood all over the place. Get movin'! When you're done, get the bleach and start washing everything down. You made this fuckin' mess and you're cleaning it up."

When the buckets of chum were empty, Vinnie blasted Sinatra, as he slowly navigated eastbound for the cruise back to the marina. He smiled as the sleek pleasure craft slid through the swells with ease.

He stood in the cockpit swaying to the music, mimicking the Chairman of the Board, crooning, and holding an imaginary microphone.

"Hey, Frankie," he yelled, "some great whites gonna *mangia* on Carmine's fat ass tonight, huh? *Mangiare!*"

He put the boat on autopilot to help Frankie butterfly his lacerations and pack the stab wounds with sterile pads.

He was more concerned with the mess on the deck than with Frankie's gaping wounds.

Frankie looked like a mummy when they were done, and Vinnie tossed him a worn eighties-style running suit to cover up.

"I'll call Doctor Rosetti from the burner when we're in port. He can meet us at my office to stitch you up. You really are a dumbass. He almost took you out."

As they were navigating into the marina, Vinnie said, "Throw everything out. Your clothes, the bandages, food, cigars, everything goes. Bag it and we'll take it with us."

"K-ka-ka kay, boss."

"And finish swabbing the deck. After Rosetti stitches you up, you got work to do. You gotta burn all this shit to ashes tonight.

"Tomorrow, you're gonna come back and clean every crack and crevice on this boat. Because of you, the boat's a goddam crime scene, fuckin' idiot!"

WHERE'S CARMINE?

Hank and I left Carmine's and Lau notified the watch commander by phone, letting him know that Carmine Vaccaro was the subject of our missing person call. We thought it best not to broadcast that name over the air on any channels, with so many outsiders monitoring police radio traffic with scanners, including news outlets.

"Hey LT," said Hank, "we're gonna grab some sandwiches at Molinari's and be back to the station in a few. What kind of sandwich do you want?"

Molinari's is two blocks from Central Station.

He took the lieutenant's order and a moment later said, "Yes, sir, we'll start on the follow-up when we get back."

By the time we arrived at the station, the reserved parking spaces for police cars were taken by news trucks, so we parked in the alley next to the station. News travels fast and, obviously, someone leaked the information about Carmine's disappearance, or the lieutenant decided to get the information out.

Activity around the station was buzzing, with reporters out front filming live shots and asking for an official statement.

TV news feeds from the major networks, along with the local channels, broadcast the breaking news of Carmine's disappearance across a bank of flat screens in the squad room.

"You two," a sergeant barked, "the lieutenant's office, now."

Lieutenant Flynn leaned back in his chair as Hank tossed his wrapped sandwich on his desk. Flynn pointed to it.

"You remember the peppers?"

"Yeah, it's the way you like it."

He unwrapped the sandwich to inspect it. "Thanks, Lau. So, what's the deal with Mr. Bigshot Car-mine Vah-Car-Oh?"

"I don't know," said Hank, "but his sister seems concerned. Said it's not like him to take off without telling anybody. Maybe he took a dive off the Golden Gate? His sister says he's a saint. No personal problems, except he just got fired by the Food Network."

"Ah, he's probably fine, LT," I said. "Probably back in Sicily attacking some calamari, or scungilli."

Flynn glared at me like I spoke out of turn. He was probably pissed because he didn't know what either dish was.

Flynn looked at Hank. "Get DeLuca going on the report, and no mistakes. It's high profile. Don't fuck it up."

A missing person report is routine, like writing a parking ticket; and even with my short tenure in the department, I had handled a couple of missing person reports when I was in field training.

Usually, the person reported missing got drunk, or high, or they're in jail. Sometimes, they're in the process of a breakup with a spouse, significant other, or staying with a friend, doing a little couch surfing. And sometimes they're avoiding a bill collector, or the repossession of their car, or a probation officer. Most reported missing eventually turn up, hungover and no worse for it. It's life. Shit happens.

It's common, but after interviewing Carmine's sister, none of these scenarios seemed likely.

He didn't have drug or alcohol problems and stuck to his routines. Still, suicide couldn't be ruled out.

Lots of successful people have checked out. He wouldn't be the first celebrity with some dark shit going on. He might also be in jail or in the hospital, so all possibilities had to be explored.

We issued a national BOL (Be on the Lookout) and a regional Amber Alert, knowing how recognizable he is.

If seen, he'd probably be recognized. Within an hour, his face dominated electronic billboards throughout Northern California.

We contacted hospitals, local police departments, the CHP, morgues, and everyone else we could think of, with negative results.

Nick Bay was an inspector with the on-duty SIT (Special Investigations Team).

"I requested a search warrant for his phone records and a cell tower dump," Bay said. "We'll see if there's anything there. The captain pushed this to the top of the priority list. I'm not a big Food Network guy, but I guess this guy's a major celebrity. I wouldn't recognize him if he walked in here, and I wish he would, because I've got a lot of open cases I was just told to put on hold."

A tip and text hotline was created to collect leads, so any minute, the kooks would come out of the woodwork with their crazy theories and sightings.

Video footage from several key areas was being collected and analyzed for clues.

Bay said they were short-handed in investigations, so he asked the lieutenant to release Hank and me from patrol to do some follow-up on the case. The day was slow, and there were enough officers to cover the district, so the lieutenant released us to work for Bay the remainder of the day.

Through a corporate credit card number Carmine's sister provided, we learned Carmine took an Uber early Sunday morning from his San Francisco penthouse to the Gourmet Ghetto area in Berkeley.

I'd never heard of the Gourmet Ghetto, so Hank explained. "It's like Mecca for foodies. That's where you go to burn a lot of money on a couple of shrimps, a piece of broccoli, and a few cherry tomatoes.

"It's worth it, though, because it's *farm-to-table*, whatever that means, and only costs about two Ben Franklins per person. Then you can impress your friends when you tell them you went to Chez Foo Foo."

So far, the trail stopped where Carmine exited the Uber in Berkeley.

We were able to identify and locate the Uber driver and confirmed the date and time of the trip. The driver described his passenger as "stocky," wearing an orange shirt and white shorts.

He handed us an iPhone in a bright yellow case, saying he found it in his back seat earlier that day when he washed and vacuumed his car.

"It was wedged between the back seat cushions. I don't know whose phone it is. I find a couple of them a month. People forget them, or they fall out of their back pocket."

The car smelled fruity like a strip club, with a half dozen tree-shaped air fresheners hanging from the rearview mirror. I'm guessing a collection of air fresheners is a rite of passage for cab drivers and those in the livery business.

The driver confirmed the pickup and drop-off points, so if Carmine did jump from the Golden Gate Bridge, how did he get from Berkeley to the Golden Gate to jump? We were able to review his Uber itineraries, and the last time he used their service was for the trip to Berkeley.

We resisted the urge to tow the vehicle at this point because no crime had been committed.

At this point, we only had a report of a missing person and were optimistic that Carmine would come forward with a reasonable explanation.

We needed to check the cameras on both bridges to see if any jumpers went off the Golden Gate, or Bay Bridge, during the times in question. We also needed to find out why Carmine went to the Gourmet Ghetto in the first place, especially at that hour of the morning.

When we did our canvassing near the Uber drop-off point, none of the chefs or prep personnel working that early reported seeing him.

The Gourmet Ghetto fit Carmine's lifestyle, but not at daybreak.

"He was alone," said the Uber driver. "I don't think I talked to him. I don't watch TV and don't know who he is. I just listen to radio and podcasts, man. I was tired when I picked him up, so I didn't pay much attention. I remember his outfit, though, because he was rockin' an orange shirt and white shorts."

I guess he liked them.

The Uber driver had an unconventional style all his own with face piercings, tattoos, dreadlocks, and large discs in his earlobes. He was wearing a bright, tie-dyed shirt, with baggy pajama-style pants, and sandals. He reeked of patchouli oil and weed and didn't seem fazed by our questioning.

I ran him through wants & warrants, and except for a previous arrest for misdemeanor shoplifting and some traffic violations, he was clear.

I took Hank aside. "This guy's out of it. He smokes too much weed. We probably got all there is to get from his fried little brain."

At least now we had a phone that might end up being Carmine's. And if so, it could provide recent history and direction. We needed a break because, so far, we had next to nothing and there was mounting pressure for answers.

- 4 -

GOT FOG?

After *my shift, I ordered* an anchovy pizza to go from Patsy's in North Beach. I picked it up and drove home to my apartment in Daly City, just south of San Francisco.

The front door to my apartment was chipped and dented and looked like it'd been on the receiving end of its share of domestic violence abuse. It looked like the gateway to the land of sad stories. It was a fitting threshold for an apartment that had all the warmth and charm of Section 8 housing in the Bronx. Unfortunately, it was all I could afford right now.

As you walked in, there was a faint odor of mildew. The stingy bit of dusty sunlight that found its way into the apartment came from the sliding glass doors providing access to a deck. I called it a deck, but it was more like a catwalk. I was on the second floor, and the deck overlooked John Muir Drive facing Lake Merced.

According to the ancient philosophy *feng shui*, used to create balance in an interior space, this apartment had *no shui*.

For someone who spent sixteen years as a SEAL, living in harsh conditions on the sides of mountains, I shouldn't complain, but there were days I'd trade this dump for the mosquitos, rodents, and snakes in the bush.

A package from my mother was waiting when I got home. She'd been mailing me goodies since my days in the military.

No two "care packages" were ever the same. She'd mailed everything from Chapstick, to rosary beads, and Tupperware full of homemade Italian pizzelle cookies.

I teased her when she included church bulletins and prayer cards, calling it Mom propaganda; and whenever I called her Tokyo Rose or Hanoi Hannah, she laughed, but she was Sicilian, and I don't think she knew what I was talking about.

Now, with Amazon Prime delivery, she was on cloud nine. She would one day probably overnight a hot sausage and pepper sandwich or an Italian bride. Both, no doubt, still hot and fresh on arrival.

Today's care package included espresso coffee pods, homemade biscotti cookies, a New York State Mega Millions Lottery ticket, hard Calabrese salami, and a church bulletin. There you go, Mom propaganda.

As I sat and poured a glass of Sangiovese wine, about to devour the pizza, I got a call from my cousin Sal in New York. He was a bookie in the same club as my father.

He likes to check in.

"Yo, cuz. How youz doin'? When youz comin' back to New Yawk?"

When he got to the part about current action and placing bets, he switched to our native tongue, speaking Sicilian.

Sal talked fast naturally, with a lot of local slang, so even other Sicilians had a hard time understanding him. You could have a PhD in Sicilian linguistics or employ CIA codebreakers and still struggle to understand him.

I'm not gonna lie, gambling and numbers rackets were my family's business—it was in my DNA—so I felt compelled to throw a couple of large on the Jets game. Gambling was at least part of the reason I never seem to have much cushion in the bank. It was hard for me to resist sports bets, so the disposable income was always coming and going.

I wagered more than a couple of bucks on the Jets, and it was gonna sting like hell if I lost.

"Get your azz back here to see the famlee and have some fun," said Sal. "Youz work too much. Go see your muddah, then come by tha city. We'll go to Rao's, then hit the clubs, like da ol' days. I'll get it lined up. Just give me da dates."

"That sounds great, Sal. I'll have to figure something out to get back there."

I didn't have the heart to tell him I had too much shit going on.

As a respected earner in the mob, Sal had the keys to the city. I knew it wouldn't cost me a dime.

Hanging with him was like playing a role in the HBO series, *Sopranos,* but he was the real deal and what the writers aspired to capture. I think if Sal ever watched the show, he'd say, *Yeah, so what's the big deal?* From his perspective, it'd be like watching *Everybody Loves Raymond.*

As I finished the call with Sal, Hank called. Now there's a contrast for you.

Hank said he talked to SIT, and the cameras on the Bay Bridge confirmed Carmine's trip to Berkeley.

"Nick Bay and another inspector are going to Berkeley in the morning to look for cameras around the Gourmet Ghetto. Also, the iPhone the pothead found is Carmine's. His sister confirmed it. I mean, who else would put his phone in a bright yellow case."

"I don't know," I said. "Maybe you, *girlfriend?*"

He laughed. "Fuck you, Ray. See ya tomorrow."

I bring out the best in people.

At least now, it felt like we were making progress on the case.

- 5 -

MR. WONDERFUL

Ten days had passed since Carmine's disappearance, and Vinnie helped organize and distribute a missing person flier and leaflets for a mass vigil at Saints Peter and Paul's Church in North Beach.

The leaflet read: "*A mass to pray for our dear friend Carmine, who we hope will be home soon, cooking his amazing food at Carmine's.*" Vinnie made a sizable donation to Saints Peter and Paul's Church to expedite his request through official channels at the church.

Whether Carmine's body, or body parts, were ever recovered, it was Vinnie's intent to deflect and proceed slowly with the takeover of Carmine's restaurant. He was confident he was home free as far as the murder, assuming the body was carried out to sea by currents, or was devoured by some variety of shark or other sea creatures.

The sun was shining, and Vinnie was sipping an espresso at an outdoor café on Columbus Avenue with Frankie. "We need to show sensitivity and restraint. In due time we'll have Carmine's, too."

Intuitively, Frankie lightly touched the still-tender, angry, pink scars on his face.

Contrary to what Vinnie said, he *was* anxious to take control of Carmine's. He wanted the recognition, the cash flow, and needed another outlet to launder money. And as an added benefit, the thought of seeing Carmine's sister Gina each day turned him on immensely.

Vinnie's criminal enterprises were paying off. He was making bank on strip club shakedowns and taking protection money in North Beach and Chinatown, whenever possible. The local merchants in Chinatown feared the Ghost Boys, but many decided to pay the Italian mobsters, too, to stay out of harm's way. In time, Vinnie planned to move into prostitution and sex trafficking as well. It was all lucrative and there for the taking.

He was feeling full of himself and excited with his progress in establishing North Beach as the new West Coast hub for the Mafia.

Later that day, he spoke to his father Carlo on the phone, a capo with his East Coast-based crime family. After giving his father a brief report on his activities, the old man responded.

"I see some progress, but you got a long way to go, *capiche?*"

"*Capiche!* In time."

He yearned for his father's approval but had to hold back some of the cash for himself, or the bosses would increase his taxes. There'd be no end to it. This would include future proceeds from the takeover of Carmine's restaurant. The less they knew, the better.

There *was* no end to the greed with mobsters, and he knew it. It frustrated him because he thought if his father knew the extent of his success, he'd be proud of him, but the cost of telling him was too high.

His father reminded him of how disappointed he was when he was thrown out of the University of San Francisco almost twenty years earlier for trying to bribe Jesuit officials to get college credits he never earned. He never missed the opportunity to rub it in his face.

After the incident at USF, Vinnie returned to New York where his father groomed him several years, before allowing him to return to the Bay Area.

Vinnie loved the Bay Area, so eventually, his father sponsored him with the goal of establishing a West Coast Mafia stronghold.

After all, if his son couldn't get a law degree and become a *consigliere*, this was the next best thing to bring him into the family business.

It was Vinnie's dream to become the next Mafia kingpin and recreate New York's Little Italy in San Francisco, complete with backroom bookies, mom-and-pop restaurants, sidewalk cafés, and espresso bars. He wanted to bring the mob and East Coast Italian culture to North Beach. That would bring him financial success and create a legacy he could show his father.

A social club like the Bergin Hunt and Fish Club, the former Gambino family hangout in New York—and John Gotti's base of operations—wasn't out of the question either. At the rate Vinnie was importing his Sicilian brethren, they'd need a safe place to meet and operate from, anyway.

"The people here are asleep at the wheel," he told his father. "This is the land of opportunity. This is the future."

Using his restaurant to launder money was working out nicely, too. Trattoria Sicilia was thriving since winning a Michelin Star.

Only Carmine's had more demand, and Vinnie knew it would soon be his, anyway.

Vinnie's restaurant, Trattoria Sicilia, catered to San Francisco's elite, including the city's power brokers.

With Stutterin' Frankie standing guard at the front door alongside another doorman built like a D10 bulldozer, their presence was a deterrent to undesirable guests.

Inside, guests were greeted by Nino and Bella, the maître d' and hostess respectively. Both were gracious and handsome and imported from Sicily by Vinnie. He wore a black tuxedo, and she a sequin evening gown. Trattoria Sicilia conveyed all the elegance and accoutrements you'd expect from a Michelin-rated restaurant. The wait staff wore white Eton server jackets with satin shawl collars and red silk bow ties. No detail was overlooked.

Vinnie was a man who believed in first impressions.

As a guest, you were treated to sixties-era Vegas style, and by the end of the night, you wanted your own Rat Pack.

Vinnie bragged to his father that "even Patsy's in New York can't come close to Trattoria. Sinatra would have loved this joint."

Downstairs from the main restaurant, Trattoria boasted a stone-walled wine cellar.

The Cellar provided private dining accommodations for larger groups, offering a five-course gourmet prix fixe menu with a twenty-five-thousand-dollar, hundred-guest minimum.

The sound system played traditional sixties-era Italian favorites like Tony Bennett, Dean Martin, Ella Fitzgerald, Jerry Vale, and, of course, the Chairman of the Board, Francis Albert Sinatra. For an additional cost, live entertainment could be included, with top entertainers flown in from Las Vegas.

The Cellar also featured a separate, enclosed cigar bar offering the finest premium cigars, with butter-soft leather couches, and a state-of-the-art air purification system to keep guests cool and comfortable.

"State of the art," Vinnie bragged to his father. "None better, nowhere."

He also hosted invitation-only, high-stakes poker games in the Cellar to launder cash and to solidify important relationships. In Italian he said, "We use the card games to run the money through. Some of the guys from Vegas fly in and local guys play, too. "I've got union guys, and guys who work for the city, in case we need a favor. You gotta come out and see the operation. You'd be impressed."

His father hesitated. "Yeah, maybe."

Typical response. What a prick. Never happy.

"All the big shots in the city want to be seen here. They love the food, the booze . . . first-class treatment. Nothing like it."

"Okay, Vincent, but don't get sloppy. Make sure you always call me on the special phone, and we only speak in our language. You got a lot to lose. Go slow, be careful. Make sure you got a guy you can trust to check for termites and bugs, too.

"Your house, boat, your car, and the restaurant. Have them exterminate weekly. You wanna be a big-time operator, you gotta act like one. And don't forget to call your mother. She's worried sick all the time."

He considered telling his father about Carmine, but it was behind him now. He had his boat scrubbed and sanitized twice and was there to direct the process to ensure every crack and crevice was deep cleaned.

He knew there was no pleasing his father.

- 6 -

BUONGIORNO, BELLEZZA!
[Good Morning, Beautiful!]

W*ith each passing day*, hope faded that anyone would see Carmine alive again. Reasonably happy people don't suddenly disappear and cease all communication with work and loved ones because they lost their phone in an Uber.

Hank and I drew a choice assignment that day—handling traffic control in front of Saints Peter and Paul's Church for Carmine Vaccaro's prayer vigil. The one Vinnie arranged earlier.

At briefing, Lieutenant Flynn announced the upcoming retirement dinner for Lieutenant Ferarro at Trattoria Sicilia. Despite my short tenure at Central, I knew Ferraro and liked him. I had an earlier interaction with him when I was in field training, and he struck me as a decent guy. I was hoping to be invited to his retirement party.

After briefing, we reported to our posts in Washington Square. The mass service wasn't for another two hours, but as expected, crowds gathered early. It was an unseasonably warm May morning.

News reporters, looky-loos, and paparazzi jammed the sidewalks near the entrance to the church. Like piranhas, they circled for their piece of the Carmine Vaccaro story.

I was controlling traffic from the crosswalk in front of the church when I spotted my dream girl, the Sophia Loren look-alike

I saw in front of Café Trieste on my first day at Central. With those sparkling, pale-blue eyes, she was the most beautiful woman I'd ever seen.

I smiled and said, *"Buongiorno,"* as she passed to enter the church.

She was wearing her hair up, beautifully dressed in a pale-yellow sleeveless dress. She glanced back at me and smiled.

"Buongiorno, Ufficiale," she said with a pronounced accent—Good morning, officer.

I got a whiff of her light, floral perfume as she passed, and knew I'd savor it forever.

I turned to resume control of the crosswalk, when a Vespa scooter, larger than life, struck me head-on. I never saw him coming.

The driver lost control and dumped the scooter on its side. As I lay on the ground, I could hear the engine revving and whining. Apparently, my fluorescent-green traffic vest with large SFPD letters was hard for him to see.

When I fell I hit my head, and when I looked up, dazed and bleeding, I saw *my* Sophia Loren standing next to Hank. She leaned over me.

"The other officers got the guy who hit you. You're gonna be fine, Officer DeLuca."

"Thanks," I said. "What's your name?"

She smiled. "I'm Sophie. Sophie Rossi."

"I think I'm Ray. Nice to meet you, Sophie Rossi."

They loaded me into the paramedic unit, and for a second, I wondered how she knew my name and thought, *maybe she likes me?*

Then again, perhaps that silver name tag on my chest tipped her off? Christ, maybe I should be an inspector!

I was rushed to St. Francis Hospital, Code-3, with lights and siren. Following an MRI and X-rays, the attending physician said it didn't appear I suffered any serious injuries, just a lot of scrapes and contusions.

Later, when Hank picked me up, he asked, "You stepped in front of that scooter to get the Italian princess' attention, didn't you?"

I was infatuated and would have let a garbage truck hit me if it gave me a chance to meet her. But I wasn't going to tell him that.

"Fuck you," I shot back. "It was probably one of *your* relatives who drive like they're in Shanghai who hit me!"

"Nah, probably one of those greaseball Italians driving the *Italian* scooter, trying to pull a mob hit on you. My people drive Japanese bikes, rice rockets. If one of *my* people hit you, they'd be in Daly City by the time you hit the ground!"

The nurse handed me a doctor's note for three days rest, and told me I could return to full duty, absent any complications, after seventy-two hours.

"I'm fine! I don't need to rest."

"Doctor's orders," she said. "I think you'll feel differently tomorrow. You're going to be sore."

I wasn't happy about it but had no choice. I was anxious to get back to the business at hand, finding Carmine.

- 7 -

SUSHI, ANYONE?

I *was sidelined* and there wasn't much I could do about it but sleep.

The next day, Hank called on his way to Linda Mar Beach in Pacifica, a small coastal town fifteen minutes south of San Francisco.

"Pacifica PD called," he said. "They think they've got what's left of Carmine Vaccaro. Human remains were just brought ashore. I'll call you after I see what they've got."

I was banged up more than I initially thought. The nurse was right. I felt like I *was* hit by a garbage truck. My body ached, and I had a major headache, with scrapes and bruises everywhere. I don't remember being hit, but I must have tumbled pretty good and now I just wanted to sleep.

My short rest was interrupted when Hank called again.

"Yeah, it's probably him. Sometimes, when people jump from the Golden Gate, the currents take them south and they end up on the coast in Pacifica.

"A couple of surfers were paddling in and spotted what they thought were fish remains covered in seaweed. When they got closer, they realized it was a torso, so they called the police.

"There wasn't much to identify, but the first officer on scene said he recognized what was left of an orange shirt and white shorts stuck to the torso. He remembered the clothing description from our missing person report and decided to call us. He thought the remains looked like a Creamsicle without the stick. Good cop, funny guy. His name's Lee Tyler.

"The coroner, a guy named Trey, said the body's been in the water for about a week, and that matches our timeline. He was impressed because the shirt and shorts on the torso were both Tommy Bahama.

"Lee thinks the coroner might be a fashionista and said, 'That's a real waste of an expensive shirt. Those shirts ain't cheap, ya know!'

"Anyway, the coroner is pretty sure the DNA tests will confirm it's Carmine. I'll notify his sister after we get confirmation. The way this guy looks, we don't want her to see the body, or what's left of it, unless she insists."

Hank was on a roll and revealed the body had been attacked and partially eaten, probably by a shark. According to the coroner, humans aren't what sharks prefer because we have low fat content. When they attack humans, it's usually out of curiosity, thinking we're something else like a seal.

My head was aching by this point. "Dude, I've gotta sleep."

"They usually make one fast attack on humans," he said, ignoring my appeal. "Sometimes they come back after the first attack, and sometimes they don't. I guess it depends on what they're in the mood for.

"The coroner said human skin absorbs water like a sponge, and eventually, the skin puffs up and splits open. Then the smaller creatures like shrimp and Dungeness crab get a piece of the action and start to feed on the body."

Something to think about the next time I order seafood at Scoma's.

Lau sounded like an episode of *MythBusters* or a narrator on the Discovery Channel. He droned on, so I put my phone on speaker and stepped away to get something to wash down the painkillers.

"I'm telling you, I wish I could un-see the remains because it was disgusting, and it's ruining my appetite. I'll never eat sushi again."

I knew he'd get over it and be back to scoffing down platters of sushi in a matter of days, glopping on soy sauce and wasabi.

We were confident that the medical examiner's identification would be expeditious, which meant Carmine's sister would have some closure and remains to bury. Evidence from what remained of the body and shredded clothing might also reveal how Carmine met his death.

And perhaps the identity of a killer.

- 8 -

GOODBYE OL' CHUM

Mourners lined Columbus Avenue in North Beach, waving small red, white, and green Italian flags as a tribute to Carmine as his funeral procession crawled from the Green Street Mortuary, meandering through the streets of Little Italy to Saints Peter and Paul Church in Washington Square.

It was sunny and warm, the way Carmine would have liked it. A beautiful spring day in May.

The somber motorcade was escorted by at least a dozen SFPD motorcycle officers, known as "four boys," a name derived from the first two letters of their radio call signs, 4-B.

Saints Peter and Paul Church is an ornate, twin-tower church with dramatic belfries and steeples that reach to the heavens. It's known as the Italian Cathedral of the West. It's a majestic, sacred setting for someone of Carmine's faith and standing in the community.

The church was destroyed in the Great 1906 Earthquake that left San Francisco in ruins. The present church was built in 1924.

Recently, it had also become the local parish for San Francisco's Chinese American Catholic community. It was ironic, considering the ongoing turf war between the Chinese Ghost Boys and the Italian mob.

I was still on administrative leave, so I attended the funeral wearing the only suit I own. I call it "the court suit" because on days when I don't wear my uniform to court, this is the suit I wear. My one and only. It's an off-the-rack special I got on sale from Men's Wearhouse.

News organizations, including TMZ and international news teams, were there to cover the services and the story of Carmine's all-too-short life. The mourners included Hollywood elite, local politicians, and celebrity chefs from around the world.

Gina represented the family, none of whom were in attendance because they all lived in Sicily. She planned to have a Celebration of Life service in Sicily sometime in the future.

Today, North Beach and San Francisco were the center of the universe. No bigger story anywhere than the sudden, mysterious death of Carmine Vaccaro.

The outpouring of interest called to mind the deaths of John Lennon, Princess Diana, and other tragedies we mark our time on Earth with.

SFPD was out in force, supported by a large contingent of plainclothes cops and federal agents. Every inch of the church was secured and swept twice by bomb-sniffing dogs and the bomb squad before attendees were admitted to the church.

State-of-the-art video cameras with facial recognition software were installed throughout the church and surrounding areas. Police videographers filmed the crowds as well. Every frame would be analyzed for leads.

Plainclothes officers were dispersed among the throngs of mourners, looking for suspicious individuals or unusual activity.

I pushed through the lines of cops, spectators, and mourners and found a place to stand along a wall at the rear of the church, next to the confessionals. I usually avoid this area as it's a reminder of my sins and transgressions.

I could hear my mother now: *You should have gone to confession while you were there.*

The location offered a decent vantage point to scan the crowd.

I estimated the church was filled with ten percent friends plus Gina, with the rest taken up by reporters, celebrities, North Beach residents, and fans. Sadly, ninety percent only knew Carmine through his TV show and his appearances, but some had dined at his North Beach restaurant as well.

As I leaned against the confessional, lost in my thoughts, my sense of peace and tranquility was interrupted by a sharp jab from behind.

I turned to face Lieutenant Flynn in his Class A uniform.

"What the fuck are you doing here? You're on medical leave! That means *no* police work."

I managed to keep my voice low. "We're in church, watch your language, sir. I worked this case, and I'm attending out of respect for the family."

I wanted to say, *What's your fuckin' problem? Give it a break!*

I got the now familiar side-to-side head gesture, like he was disappointed in a child. What a first-class dick. I started to imagine how I'd take him out and then felt bad having those thoughts in church.

About a minute later, I felt another jab in my side. This time I spun around, ready to break his finger but instead grabbed the delicate wrist of Sophie.

She laughed. "I saw the other cop giving you a hard time, so I thought I'd have some fun."

I broke into a wide grin and instinctively gave her a hug. She smelled other-worldly. How can someone smell that good?

"Sorry for the mad face," I said.

She smiled and waved it off. "No, no, of course. I snuck up on you. I just wanted to see how you're feeling, since the accident."

"A little banged up, but I'm fine. Thanks for coming over. Really nice of you."

With that she said, "Ciao," and returned to her seat.

My heart was beating out of my chest.

The service started, so I focused on the job at hand, looking for suspicious activity. The church was filled with fragrant yellow and white flowers, and heavenly voices from the choir singing "Ave Maria."

A couple of readings were given by close friends with a moving eulogy by Carmine's best friend, a not-so-famous chef from his hometown in Sicily. He fought back tears as he described Carmine as a man of great love and humility. Beyond the food, Carmine was loved for his charity work and his humanity.

With a thick Sicilian accent, he said, "Carmine's celebrity did not change him. He ah used it to help ah others even ah more."

From where I was standing, nothing appeared out of place or unusual, except for the celebrities and plainclothes cops with earpieces.

I caught a glimpse of Hank in his Class A uniform; he was part of the funeral detail. I noticed he might have actually polished his boots, too. Amen brother! I'd catch up with him later.

In addition to celebrities, I recognized local heavies, including the owner of Trattoria who initiated the earlier prayer vigil. I also recognized a couple of other North Beach business owners.

I decided to forgo the graveside service to avoid more criticism by Flynn.

Maybe the service would uncover additional information surrounding Carmine's death. If he *was* murdered, there was a chance his murderer attended his funeral, and I was certain suspect lists would be generated from video.

- 9 -

ON THE NIGHT SHIFT

The morning I was cleared to return to work, Hank called. Early.

"Change your flashlight batteries because we're going on nights. We got rotated to swings. Bring your duty jacket. It gets cold."

Rotating shifts are a part of life for cops and soldiers, and they suck. You no sooner get used to one shift and they rotate you to another. It does a number on your sleep and your body clock.

The number of Priority-A calls and the pace are typically faster on swings, and midway through our briefing, Hank and I were dispatched to a report of an armed robbery in progress in Chinatown.

We ran from the station, threw our things in the trunk and, with lights and siren blaring, arrived on scene in under six minutes. Stockton Street was jammed with traffic and jaywalkers, so I blasted the air horn to clear the way.

"Oh c'mon," barked Hank, "thread the needle, DeLuca!"

Stockton Street in Chinatown is like being transported back in time through a wormhole to Shanghai or Hong Kong in the 1920s—minus the rickshaws. The streets and sidewalks are packed with shoppers carrying stuffed plastic bags and pulling small folding carts to transport their groceries and belongings.

With my window down on the patrol car, I could smell the sweet aroma of roast duck and barbeque pork emanating from the restaurants and tenement kitchens.

Hank dropped into Wikipedia mode. "The population density in Chinatown is more than three times the rest of the city. There's more than sixty-five thousand people living in a twenty-four-block area."

"Okay, thank you, Professor. You ought to be giving sightseeing tours on one of those double-decker buses."

When we arrived on scene, Hank muscled his way through the crowd. "Make a hole! SFPD!"

He repeated the command in Cantonese.

The crowd looked agitated, pointing to the entrance of a jewelry store with a dirty red awning with the name of the store in English and Chinese covering the small entrance. In English, it read Pink Happiness Jeweler.

In the doorway to the store, we encountered an Asian male, about fifty, bleeding from his scalp, eye socket, and mouth. He was a bloody mess and had been viciously beaten.

In broken English, he protested the moment he saw us.

"Go, go! No need you! Everything okay. Go way. Go!"

This as he attempted to shove us back from the storefront.

Hank grabbed him by his upper arms and pushed him into the store, where I locked the door behind us. We escorted him to the rear of the store, awaiting paramedics. Hank spoke to him in Cantonese, and I returned to the front of the store to guide paramedics in.

It looked like every inch of the small store was used to display bright gold jewelry in packed showcases and shelves. Most of the treasures were displayed against bright red backgrounds.

As I waited at the front of the store, it sounded like Hank and the victim were yelling at each other, but Italians do the same thing. A normal conversation can sound like an argument or screaming match. The paramedics arrived and began treating the victim's wounds. That's when Hank brought me up to speed. "His name is Mr. Wu. He said a tall white guy came into the store but didn't seem interested in jewelry. He looked around for a minute, then told him he could protect him from neighborhood gangs."

In broken English, Mr. Wu chimed in. "When I tell man no, he get mad. He yell. Call me name, then hit me in face with pistol, till I fall down. Then he break things and takes jew-ree and money."

He pointed to a shattered display case.

I radioed the vague suspect description to dispatch so they could broadcast to all units. With Chinatown's congested streets and sidewalks, we weren't hopeful.

Too much time had passed, and more than likely, the suspect was in the wind. And based on the victim's defiant attitude, it was doubtful he'd identify the suspect in a lineup or agree to prosecute him anyway.

The victim was transported to St. Francis Hospital, but not before he argued with Hank as to why he didn't need to go.

"Christ, he got pistol-whipped. What's his problem?"

Hand shook his head, exasperated. "Now, I know *why* he got pistol-whipped. He won't shut up! If he doesn't settle his ass down, *I'm* gonna pistol-whip him!"

We canvassed the area for witnesses, but the onlookers scattered, and no one was willing to talk to us. Suddenly, no one in Chinatown could speak English.

"This place is like Vegas," said Hank.

"What happens in Chinatown, stays in Vegas?"

I got the eye roll. "Fuckin' dope."

It was so much fun to break his balls.

"You know they hate us," he said. "They don't trust outsiders, especially the police, and you're both."

"At least you've got the Chinese thing going for you."

"Nah, they hate me, too. Being a cop cancels out the Chinese thing. Chinatown's insulated. It's a different world. I believe half of what they tell me, and I've lived here my whole life."

As we walked back to the police car, loud popping sounds like automatic gunfire exploded around us. I ran for cover behind the engine block of the police car. My heart was racing like I was back in Afghanistan.

I instinctively drew my Sig and heard Hank laughing.

"Kung hei fat choi, gweilo. Probably leftover firecrackers from Chinese New Year."

Gweilo. Ghost man or Westerner.

"They're playin' with us, rookie. They don't want us here. Fuck 'em. Let's go."

What was seen as an innocent prank by Hank was a PTSD trigger for me, but it wasn't something I'd reveal or discuss with him.

When I got in the cruiser, I was irritable and drained. I know from experience that both are common side effects from a PTSD event.

I should be used to it by now. I've lived with it since Afghanistan.

- 10 -

SMELL ME

The next day, I had messages and subpoenas waiting for me when I arrived at the station, including a flowery get-well card from my fantasy girl, Sophie Rossi. I read the card three or four times, like I couldn't understand English. Then I sniffed it and thought, what's wrong with me?

The card read:

> *Dear Officer DeLuca, I hope you get well soon.*
> *~Sophie Rossi.*

A sweet gesture, but could it be any more generic? She could have at least injected a little warmth or put a little spritz of perfume on the card. She'll never get a job with Hallmark with that attitude.

She lives in North Beach, so maybe she's playing me for a favor down the road.

We hit the streets and took our 10-7M, the code for out-of-service meal break, at Sam's Pizza & Burgers near the Broadway Tunnel. It's a tiny dive about twenty feet wide, with a sign announcing, *World Famous Since 1966, Top Three in the World.*

Funny, I'd never heard of the joint.

The owner proudly displayed a framed, grease-splattered photograph of himself standing next to world-famous foodie Anthony

Bourdain. I was told, back in the day, Bourdain featured Sam's as a favorite burger joint on his travel show. Now *that's* street cred.

Sam's Pizza & Burgers was Hank's choice and hands-down the best charbroiled hamburger I've ever had, if you don't mind smelling like wood smoke the rest of the night. The place was the size of shoebox, so we were literally sitting in a smoker while we ate, but it was worth it. I figured, I'm a cop, so who gives a shit what I smell like anyway. Hank felt the same.

"You'll have plenty of time to air out when we walk Broadway tonight," he said. "You don't need to smell nice for these scumbags anyway. They'll think you're soft."

The late-night foot beats are meant to provide a visible police presence along Broadway, known for its strip clubs and nightlife. The department calls it community policing, and I call it boring. Most nights you're freezing your ass off with the damp air coming off the bay.

Broadway looks like most other cities' seedy stretch with neon-lit strip clubs, massage parlors, adult bookstores, and liquor stores. For years, Broadway was home to strip clubs like the Condor, with legendary stripper Carol Doda, and the Hungry I Club. I started to imagine Dirty Harry himself, Inspector Harry Callahan, stepping from the shadows, with hipsters dining on his French onion soup, *al fresco,* at Enrico's Café like they did in the movie *Bullitt.*

Today, you'll see tourists and local dirtbags loiter in groups on the sidewalks, smoking cigarettes, vaping, sipping booze from brown bags, and smoking weed.

The regular clientele converges around eleven o'clock, and party until last call at two a.m. That's when the fun begins.

"This is Mardi Gras *lite*," said Hank, "without the balconies, beads, or boobies."

"Too bad about the boobies."

Whether he knew their real names or not, Hank gave nicknames to the street regulars like Tug, who he said was always either tugging or dragging some drunk out of his bar, or Pimp Daddy and Gummy Bear—a toothless crackhead who was one of Pimp Daddy's prostitutes.

"She gives blow jobs anytime, anywhere, for a piece of crack the size of a booger."

"Hank, you have such a nice way with words."

Maybe he's the one who should be working for Hallmark.

It wasn't long before we broke up a fight in a strip club and told the combatants to leave. We gave the loser a head start before releasing the victor, who no doubt wanted to continue the beating.

"You're both banned from Broadway for thirty days," I said. "If you try to finish the fight in San Francisco tonight, I'll make it ninety."

I don't know where I came up with that bullshit, but it sounded good at the time. My *Judge Judy* moment.

"Perfect," said Hank, and coming from him that was a lot.

Minutes later, we encountered gangbangers known as the Ghost Boys, a notorious local Chinese gang, as they partied in the parking lot next to *Nasty Girls* strip club.

I wondered what marketing genius came up with that name. I'm guessing second choice was *Nice Girls*. I didn't think it would have quite the same appeal.

As we approached the group, Hank whispered, "hands . . ." telegraphing what I already knew—something we'd been told over and over in the academy, namely that *hands kill.*

I asked one of the thugs to hand me his open bottle of Dom Perignon, so I could cite him for possession of an open container in public.

The whole time I'm wondering how this clown could afford Dom, when I'd be lucky to buy a bottle of Korbel for eleven bucks. To make matters worse, I realized he probably bought it in the strip club for the going price of about five hundred bucks, plus tip.

"Hey, big shot, you're not allowed to have an open container in public. Give me the bottle."

As I went to grab the bottle, he yanked it back, to take another swig.

After he emptied it, he wiped his mouth on his sleeve. His voice was slurred but not so much that I couldn't make out what he said.

"Fuck you, gweilo!"

He took up a fighting stance, holding the bottle by its neck.

My first baton strike hit his hand and sent the bottle flying. The second, third and fourth strikes were for good measure. *Not sorry.*

"Who's next?" said Hank.

No takers.

The cowards stood down but continued to run their mouths. It's what they do.

After taking my suspect, who I nicknamed "Dom," to the ground, I handcuffed him. He yelled and continued to resist on the short walk to the patrol car, putting on a show for his home boys.

I could smell the booze, cheap cologne, and stale cigarette smoke emanating from my arrestee and the rest of the crew. Some had stripper glitter on them, which has gotten more than a few husbands and boyfriends thrown out of their houses. It takes just one piece of glitter.

On the drive to the station, Hank turned to my arrestee through the partition in the police car.

"Hey, dipshit, you're in a world of hurt. You attacked my partner with a bottle. That's a felony."

Dom's voice had lost its slur and was tight and elevated now. "I got good information on shit going down in Chinatown, but you need to cut me a break, bro."

"Number one, I ain't your bro, and number two, we'll see what you got."

The suspect babbled on how I had disrespected him in front of his crew, *blah, blah, blah.*

"Go pound sushi, you gangbangin' turd. You give Chinese people a bad name. Do not fuck with the po-po."

During the interview at the station, the suspect's big information turned out to be useless bullshit.

"I heard the guy who beat the dude in the jewelry store in Chinatown was some big-ass white dude with black hair, wearing sunglasses and all black clothes."

"Wow," I said. "That helps a lot. You really narrowed it down for us, Captain Obvious. Even Wu gave us that much. No, you better give us more than that, a name or something, because right now you've got ungatz, you got nada, zilch . . . nothing!"

He took a deep breath.

"Okay, so store owners in Chinatown are being squeezed by Italians offering protection. Goons hassling everybody. They look like the guys from the *Sopranos,* and they ain't fuckin' around. These are some serious dudes."

I admired his powers of observation, but this might have been pure invention—throwing Italian goons back in my face for making him look bad.

"Hey asshole, I'm Italian! You're describing *my* people. You better lighten up on the Italians before I go all *Goodfellas* on ya right here. Got it?"

Ultimately, his information was weak, but we decided to cut him a break anyway. He might come in handy as an informant down the road.

He gave me the stink eye as I pulled him from the holding cell to cut him loose. I asked if the dragon tattoo on his neck was from a Pokémon card. He scowled and flipped me off.

I handed him the citation for the open container violation and told him he was lucky it was catch-and-release day.

"You're also lucky I didn't light you up, motherfucker. If you ever jump bad on me again, you're leaving in a body bag. I don't care about your fuckin' gang. I got my own. You got your one break from Officer DeLuca."

- 11 -

SHAMU

Lieutenant Louis Ferarro was a cop's cop. He earned a reputation for being a first-in-the-door kind of cop. I was told he'd push past other cops to take the door, serving warrants. He was fearless and wouldn't hesitate to put himself in the line of fire to protect his officers.

His retirement party the next day was being held in the Cellar at Trattoria Sicilia, a fitting location for a proud Sicilian with thirty years of service. He deserved to go out classy.

When the subject came up in the squad room, Hank decided to bust my balls in front of a handful of officers.

"The party's invitation only. Sorry, DeLuca."

"Yeah, sure, Lau. I guess it's only for big-time veteran cops like you, huh? The elite?"

I pulled my folded invitation from my back pocket and held it up.

"To be honest," I said, "I'm surprised you got invited. This is a high-end affair. You better go to the big boy's department in Macy's and get yourself some new rags because I'll be styling. I don't want to embarrass you and make you look homeless in front of the brass."

There were hoots and jeers in the squad room. A sergeant tossed me a high-five.

"My man! Smackdown, DeLuca!"

* * *

The following night, I took an Uber to the party to avoid drinking and driving. The entrance looked like a Hollywood awards show with klieg lights, red carpet, and velvet ropes. There were two large muscle heads in black suits on either side of the door. You weren't walking into this place without an invitation.

At the door, I explained I was a Central Station officer and was there for the party. I was told to wait. They wanted me to twist in the wind for a few minutes. The goons eventually found me on the guest list and grudgingly allowed me to pass. Too bad, I was just about to ask them if they knew how to read. My father's a capo, and I've been around wise guys my entire life, so I know when my balls are being busted. I'm not intimidated. Not even a little.

As I was waiting to be admitted, I took a minute to size them up. It came with the job when I worked for my father and also as a SEAL.

As SEALs we dealt with a lot of dangerous foreign actors around the world. Sometimes they presented themselves as friends, and other times they let us know they were adversaries. You learn not to trust anyone. You size people up, so you're prepared to take them out. So, to pass the time while waiting at the restaurant, I thought about what I'd do with the two doormen I nicknamed Tweedle-Dee and Tweedle-Dum.

Years ago, I internalized a quote I read from military legend, retired Marine Corp general, James "Mad Dog" Mattis—and *no*, he doesn't like to be called that.

His advice? "Be polite, be professional, but have a plan to kill everybody you meet."

Some people geek out on their phones while they're waiting and passing time. I think about how I'll put those around me in their final resting place, if necessary.

When I was finally admitted, I walked into the dining area, looking for the entrance to the Cellar. I was greeted by the aroma of garlic and fireplace smoke. You couldn't miss the raised hearth fireplace ablaze in the dining room.

The dining rooms had beautiful reproductions of Old-World Italian frescoes on each wall, softly lit by wall sconces and candles on each table. The frescoes reminded me of ancient murals you see in churches and buildings throughout Italy.

I stopped to take it all in and was gently brushed aside by a waiter carrying serving trays. The place was bustling with tuxedoed waiters and waitresses serving a packed house.

I felt good after a workout earlier and was wearing a new outfit from Nordstrom's. After opening my big mouth with Hank, I had to bring my A-game. I wore a black Cashmere three-button sweater with a dark-patterned Peter Millar sports coat.

A hot-looking stylist at Nordstrom helped me select the outfit and wouldn't stop complimenting me. She said the outfit made me look classy and sophisticated. I lied to her and told her I had a date. What a dope. She was hitting on me, and I should have asked *her* for a date!

My extravagant purchases were yet another reason why I'd be low on cash for the next few weeks, but I had to outclass Hank and punch above my weight class, as they say.

In the dining room, I was surprised to see Sophie Rossi having dinner with a girlfriend, so I stopped by their table.

"Great to see you. I was hoping I'd run into you. I wanted to thank you for the nice card you sent."

After both ladies looked me up and down, she seemed embarrassed in front of her friend, so I asked if she spoke Italian. *Parli italiano?*

She smiled and answered in Italian, *certo*, meaning of course.

I continued in Italian, "Sorry, I didn't mean to embarrass you in front of your friend."

She blushed a little.

"No worries. I didn't expect to see you here but it's a nice surprise. You look nice, Ray. Are you meeting someone?"

"Yeah, most of my colleagues from Central Station are downstairs in the Cellar right now. They're throwing a retirement party for one of our lieutenants."

I should have said I was meeting a lady friend, but again I blew it.

I started feeling awkward taking her away from her meal and her friend, so I asked if she knew where the Cellar was and she turned and pointed to descending stairs past the bar, saying *laggiu.* Over there.

I nodded. "Ciao." And smiled to her friend as I excused myself.

The Cellar was packed when I arrived, so I waded through the crowd to find the guest of honor, Lieutenant Ferraro.

He gave me the big handshake and man-hug. "Hey, paisan, skip the lieutenant shit, and call me Lou. I'm retired now!"

We stood and talked, and he reminded me of one of my earlier shifts working for him, when I was in field training.

We were assigned to a security detail for a World Series game at what was then called AT&T Park and reported to him for the assignment.

My partner and I had been detailed to control access to a secure area behind the stadium where the tactical vehicles were staged for FBI, SWAT, and other federal agencies. The vehicles were ready to deploy if all hell broke loose.

Late in the ball game, I spotted an unmarked Crown Vic inside our perimeter, with the engine running and windows fogged.

In briefing, we were told no one was supposed to be in, or around, the vehicles because most contained laptops with sensitive law enforcement information. Some contained weapons and detection devices for bombs and radiation as well.

My partner and I made a tactical approach to the Crown Vic with our weapons drawn, but at our sides. I tapped on the window, which was fogged over, announcing, "Police!"

After a few seconds and some jostling inside the car, the rear window rolled down a few inches, and an attractive woman in the back seat identified herself as an FBI agent. Unbeknownst to her, her silk blouse was open, with most of the gold buttons down the front undone. So much for the dignified special agent. She was *special* all right!

Standing there, I felt the steam and hormones released from inside the car.

Her male partner was sitting next to her.

"Me, too. FBI. We're just going over some stuff on my laptop." He held it up for me to see, like I'd never seen a laptop before. I recognized both as FBI agents from our briefing.

She also had a case of beard burn around her mouth from her partner's beard stubble. We deduced a case of FBI hoochie-coo and gave them their privacy.

At the time, we reported it to Lieutenant Ferarro on the down low, to be on the safe side. I remember the whole thing seemed so ridiculous, that all of us, including the lieutenant, laughed our asses off. Who does that shit on duty? It was fun reliving the story.

"Those two were a couple of horndogs!" he said. "I remember the two of them were texting and flirting during the entire briefing. I kept thinking, is this what they teach them in Quantico? I guess this is the new generation of today's techno-savvy crackerjack FBI agents."

Some things never change.

Hank showed up late for the party, and when he realized there was no sushi, looked annoyed as he scanned the serving tables.

I guess he'd already pushed what the coroner told him about flesh-eating crustaceans to the delete file in his brain.

All gone! Sushi good now.

He groused and looked like he'd just learned there was no Santa Claus.

Hank is like a whale. He moves through life silent, but deadly, and his whole existence revolves around feeding on krill and crustaceans. In the theater of my mind, I see him swimming through the depths of the ocean with his mouth open, in search of his next meal.

I pointed to the sardines and white beans on bruschetta, prepared Italian style, hoping to settle him down. He had a look of skepticism, but it seemed to have a calming effect. He gave me what my father would call the *faccia miserabile*—miserable face—but appeared less agitated.

Only minutes later, the waiters brought out mountains of shrimp, clams, oysters, and mussels. Hank couldn't get them in his mouth fast enough.

He positioned himself next to the iced serving table like a lion who just took down a gazelle.

His rate of consumption was so fast, I thought, *if he doesn't slow down, he's going to be a candidate for the Heimlich maneuver.* I stationed myself accordingly and was surprised when he didn't eat shells and all.

"Hey, big fella, slow down," I said. "Now I know why you have such a nice, shiny coat!"

My remarks had no effect on him. He was in the zone devouring the shellfish like a starving sea lion.

It wasn't long before the toasts and old war stories began. With more than thirty years—and most of it pushing a radio car—there was no shortage of insane stories about Lieutenant Lou Ferarro.

In SFPD they use the term "pushing a radio car" because by the time you've finished your shift, running your ass off from call to call, you feel like you've *pushed* the radio car around the district.

As tales were rehashed and embellished, I felt the sense of camaraderie I'd missed since leaving the military. This kind of connection is hard to explain to someone who's never been to war or faced death situations in daily life. It's a bond, and it's why soldiers, cops, and firefighters are willing to risk their lives for each other.

I saw the line growing at the bar, so I joined the queue, realizing it would take awhile to get a drink.

For the first time in a long time, I felt contented and had a sense of belonging.

As I stood in line, I was suddenly shoved from behind and turned to see Lieutenant Flynn.

"Who invited you, rookie?"

He was hammered, swaying from side to side. His eyes were bloodshot and watery, "like two piss holes in the sand," as my father would say.

I nodded. "Hey LT . . . " and turned to ignore him.

About thirty seconds later, he shoved me again, but this time harder.

Instinctually, I spun and grabbed him by his wrist. I leaned forward and pulled him to me, pitching my voice low.

"Keep your hands to yourself, LT."

I slowly released him, and as I did, he got loud and belligerent.

"Get thish rookie out of my shight!"

Captain Choo and a sergeant came over.

"Hey Jimmy," said Choo, "what the fuck? What are ya doing?"

The sergeant had Flynn by the arm.

"C'mon, Jimmy boy, let's go." And the two escorted him to a table in the back, on the other side of the dining room.

A few minutes later, the captain came back, and I raised my hands.

"I don't know, Cap. He's drunk."

"No, he's not drunk," said Choo. "He's *hammered!* So, you want to tell me what his beef with you is?"

"I don't know, sir. I really don't."

The captain shrugged. "We'll keep him over there."

I didn't respond because I was hot enough to know to keep quiet.

You don't need to keep him over there. I know exactly how to deal with drunken assholes like him.

Hank walked over to put his two cents in and asked why I was hassling a superior officer.

"Go fuck yourself, moron," I whispered, "and mind your own business."

I walked away and went upstairs to go outside and get some fresh air. The goons let me pass, and had they not, would have found themselves on their asses. Of that I'm certain. I was minding my own business, and just trying to have a nice night out.

What the fuck?

As a SEAL chief, I was used to being shown respect. I earned it on the battlefield. I had a reputation, and few had the balls to fuck with me. Even superiors. These jerkoffs didn't know who they were dealing with, but for now, I had to let it go.

- 12 -

WARRIORS LIKE TO HAVE FUN, TOO

I *sat on stairs in the shadows* next to the restaurant to take a breather. I went into the "Box Breathing" mode I learned as a SEAL to calm down and reset my mental state. The fresh air helped.

I was in a better place when a good-looking Asian woman, who I recognized as a Central Station officer, came over to me.

"You're the new guy at Central. I'm Lily."

"Nope," I said. "I'm the head chef, and I'm on a smoke break. Do you mind?"

Caught off guard, she looked confused, then laughed and offered a high-five.

"Good one. Well, chef, welcome to Central Station!"

"Thanks. I almost didn't recognize you out of uniform. Not that you look bad in uniform, but the dress is definitely an upgrade."

She smiled and shuffled, a little embarrassed.

The ballistic vest and jumble of equipment on the duty belt have a way of hiding any femininity, unless you like flat-chested women with bulging hips. She was striking out of uniform, with a nice smile, curves in all the right places, and a quick wit.

She told me she had been with SFPD for about five years and had been recruited when she was a senior at UC Berkeley. I knew if she attended Cal Berkeley she was no dummy and probably exceptionally book smart. Looks, brains, and a sense of humor: not a bad trifecta.

I could see she was getting cold, as she crossed her chest with her arms and began rubbing her biceps, so I suggested we go back inside. She gave me the vibe she wanted to continue to talk, so at least for now I had somebody to hang with. We got a drink and circulated, and she introduced me to officers I hadn't met before as we worked the room.

Under her breath, she provided color commentary after each introduction, as we walked away, making comments.

"That dumbass has trouble qualifying every time we go to the range. It's a good thing he's best friends with the rangemaster, or he'd be working in the property room. You don't want him backing you up. He'll end up shooting you!"

We joked and hit the bar like a couple of sailors on liberty.

She was getting glances from other cops and was quick to match barbs. I got the impression most had never seen her in a dress before and were suddenly attentive and attracted.

We sat to rest, when a dapper guy in a sharkskin suit with a pink silk pocket square approached us. I immediately knew, not a cop. He gave us a broad smile.

"I just wanted to welcome you and introduce myself. My name is Vincent Catalano, and I'm the owner of the restaurant."

Chest out, he carried himself with an air of confidence and thanked us for protecting the community. *Blah, blah, blah . . .*

"You have an open invitation to dine anytime at Trattoria, no reservation necessary. I appreciate what you ladies and gentlemen do for us, so you're always welcome here."

He looked to be in his late thirties, and it was obvious he was Italian, probably Sicilian. He had the accent and, to put it politely, we know our own.

I'm guessing his suit set him back two grand. He was groomed like a model straight out of *GQ*, and smelled so good, I almost asked him for a date!

He asked my name, and when I told him, he asked where I was from. When I told him Sicily, he smiled. We finished our conversation in Sicilian, which is somewhat different from Italian and other dialects. Later, I would apologize to Lily for excluding her in that part of the conversation and explained what we were bantering about, which was a lot of nothing.

As he excused himself, I stood, and we man-hugged. He gently kissed the top of Lily's hand like she was made of porcelain. I noticed his manicured nails and a garish pinky ring with a large center diamond surrounded by a diamond horseshoe. A real goombah.

He said he would leave instructions with the doormen and maître d' for VIP access, any time.

And the party started to wind down.

"You up for a nightcap?" Lily asked. "There's a place down the street."

It'd been a long time since I'd been in the company of an attractive woman.

"I'm game."

I'd been spending every waking minute studying and working out, when I wasn't on duty, so I welcomed the companionship.

Having been in training for the past year, I'd pretty much given up on a social life, so tonight was nice. We hit the scotch pretty good, closed the bar, and the night of partying began to take its toll on me.

The incident at the party with Flynn was heavy on my mind. I hoped tomorrow the whole thing for him would be a blur. He might have sensed I was ready to snap his wrist in half—because I was. I don't need him exacting revenge on me. I'm not accustomed to *anyone* fucking with me, and I've got no patience for it.

It was late when we left the bar together.

"Hey, I live down the street on Vallejo," she said. "You can crash on my couch if you want, instead of taking Uber all the way to Daly City."

"You sure? Sometimes I snore and fart in my sleep."

"Me too!" she said.

"Now, that's sexy."

We walked arm-in-arm up the steep incline to the top of Vallejo Street like a couple of meandering drunks.

She showed me around her apartment and tossed a blanket and pillow on the couch. She changed and looked amazing wearing a faded UC Berkeley sweatshirt and not much else.

Just when I thought I might get lucky, she surprised me.

"Okay, I gotta hit it, Ray," she said, and closed her bedroom door.

I was disappointed, but relieved. There was always the possibility I could have a PTSD episode, so better I'm on the couch.

As I lay there watching the twinkling lights of the Transamerica Building in the distance, my mind was racing.

I thought about Lieutenant Flynn, Lily, Vincent Catalano, and Carmine's death. I remember thinking, *Marone, I just want a good night's sleep.*

Finally, with thoughts of Sophie Rossi, I reset and felt comforted and at peace.

- 13-

I NEED A BLOODY

*T*he next morning as I was waking up, Lily handed me a mug of steaming hot coffee. As I sat up, she plopped next to me on the couch and grabbed my forearm for closer inspection.

"Easy!" I said. "I'm gonna spill the coffee! They're just henna tattoos. I'm trying to impress my friends."

She chuckled, giving me a gentle shove.

She put her finger on my bone frog ink. "What's this one? What's *Never forget, never forgive* mean?"

"Just what you think it means. I got it to honor a buddy who died. He was a frogman, and the bone frog is a SEAL thing."

Next, she pointed to my trident tattoo and looked surprised when I told her I was a chief petty officer in a Navy SEAL unit.

The other tat was a skull and M-16 rifle with the slogan, *I may walk among the sheep but make no mistake, I am the sheepdog.*

"So, you're a real badass, aren't you?"

I wasn't sure how to answer. "Me? Nah, I'm a snowflake. I like tattoos, poetry, long walks, and pastel colors. Wanna see my nipple rings?"

She laughed and I got another nudge.

"Let's go eat," I said.

We walked to Mama's on Washington Square, and Lily used her charm to get us access through the kitchen, instead of waiting in line for twenty minutes.

"These restaurant guys in North Beach love Central Station cops," she said. "We take good care of them. On holidays, like Thanksgiving and Christmas, they send food to the station for on-duty cops. It's a tradition. So, I look out for them.

"Even when I try to wait in line, if they see me, they drag me inside. It's embarrassing. A lot of them will feed you for free if you're on duty. I wouldn't do it unless you leave a big tip to cover the cost of the meal, to stay off IA's radar. We get paid enough. We don't need free meals."

"Hey, no argument from me," I said.

We nursed our hangovers with eggs Benedict and Bloody Marys. I was glad to have the day off so I could go home and take a nap.

I took an Uber, and as expected, we hit a thick band of fog around the John Daly Boulevard exit heading into Daly City. They should post a sign at the off-ramp that says, *Welcome to Shitsville: The Land of Fog and Drizzle.*

I enjoyed the party but would have to go slow with Lily. I sensed she was interested in a relationship, but it might be my ego talking.

As far as Lieutenant Flynn, no regrets. The problem was his, not mine.

I was reminded of a saying we had in the SEALS: "It's all mind over matter. If I don't mind, then it doesn't matter."

- 14 -

HOLD THE OPIUM, PLEASE

I *went to the club for a swim* and sauna before reporting for duty. I was amped up and re-energized from my three days off. The swim was invigorating, but you never really acclimate to cold-water temperatures. Today, I was beyond goose bumps.

Anyone who says they've acclimated to icy water is usually full of shit, or they grew up in Yakutsk, Russia, the coldest spot on earth. I cold-water swim to maintain the warrior mindset. Pain is good, eat it up. It's a shock *every* time I swim in the bay, and I never know what to expect with changing winds, currents, and visibility. It always sucks, but sometimes it sucks even more.

Our watch was light, with only eight officers to work the district. We're authorized twelve, plus three sergeants and a lieutenant. It's indicative of the difficulty police departments are having with turnover and recruiting new candidates.

With less officers on the street, we'd be running our asses off all night, handling Priority-A calls, with no breaks or downtime.

On shifts like this, you survive on bottled water, coffee, or power drinks and power bars. Fruit if you remember to bring it.

Before we hit the street, I stuck my head in Inspector Bay's office to see if he had any updates on Carmine's death. The homicide inspector was Taggart Yee, but he worked out of another building.

"Well, we got nothing from the Uber driver's car, except for some marijuana seeds and a used condom. No blood evidence at all. They soaked the car in luminol, but nothing. We know Carmine rode in the car, but he didn't meet his fate there. Homicide's been busy serving search warrants. They searched his sister's apartment, his penthouse, his restaurant, and his yellow Lamborghini. So far, *nada!* Matter of time. Somebody, somewhere, knows something."

"Thanks," I said. "Appreciate the update."

For the first few hours of the shift, Hank and I were detailed to work the annual Chinese New Year's parade. An easy detail with support from other district stations.

As we gathered our equipment and drew weapons from the armory, Hank asked, "What's the deal with Lily? I saw you hanging with her at the party."

"What's it to you?"

He grimaced. "Let me show you something."

I followed him down a hallway, where he pointed to a large, framed portrait of a female police officer.

"Do you know who this is?"

"Nope. Should I?"

"That's Lily's mother. She was killed in the line of duty about seven years ago."

An engraved brass plate affixed to the bottom of the frame: Officer May Leung #2104, EOW October 23, 2011.

EOW is an acronym for End of Watch and not something any officer aspires to—unless it's your final shift before retirement. It's often used for officers killed in the line of duty.

"She was killed responding to a 9-1-1 hang-up call. Ambushed and shot in the head down by Geary and Lev getting out of her patrol unit. Never had a chance. Lily was at Cal Berkeley when it happened."

I didn't know what to say, so I shook my head. "Wow. That's fucked up. I didn't know."

"So, Lily is pretty much hands off. She's like a little sister, family. Every cop who knew her mother is protective of her."

I hesitated. "Got it."

★ ★ ★

We worked the parade in a cold, soaking downpour without any serious incidents. The dragon floats, bright colors, fireworks, and marching bands thrilled the crowds and kept spirits high.

My phone rang as we were getting ready to take a break. It was Lily asking to meet at the Vital Tea Leaf, an Asian tea café, about a block from the parade route. I told Hank I'd catch up with him after the meal break.

We sat at a small table in a back corner where Lily gave me a lesson on the significance of tea in the Chinese culture.

She talked about the blends, mystique, and folklore, pointing to glass jars on the shelves.

There was a long wall behind a serving counter with hundreds of blends in airtight glass storage jars, with names like "Dragon Well-Long Jing." A steady line of customers came into the shop.

"Man, this is like voodoo," I said. "Hold the opium, please."

She laughed. "Okay, cowboy," and ordered her favorite for both of us, ginseng oolong.

I was surprised by the high prices, pricier than Starbuck's.

"This is a rip-off. I could buy a box of Lipton's, or Tetley's, for half the price."

"Next time we'll do espressos," she said.

The tea was exotic and unlike anything I'd ever tasted. Hell, I still think brown mustard, siracha ketchup, and chunky peanut butter are gourmet.

"So, I saw you talking to Hank near my mother's portrait."

"Yeah, he told me about your mom. Sorry. I didn't know."

"Hey, Ray, you don't need to be sorry. I made the choice to become a police officer because I realized how much my mother loved her work, and how much the PD loved her back.

"I respected her and what she did and realized what a great family the SFPD is. I've never regretted it. I'm not a charity case. If my mother were alive today, I think she'd be proud of me."

I nodded. "I'm sure she would."

"Some officers are overly protective. It's hard to have a life outside of the job. Hank probably told you to watch yourself with me, but I'm a big girl. I can take care of myself."

"Yeah, that's about the extent of it."

"Besides," she said, "we're just friends anyway. I hope Hank didn't scare you off."

"Of course not. I wish I had known your mother. Our friendship is *our* business."

We left the café and took separate routes to rejoin our partners. When I got to my post, another downpour let loose, with February wind and icy rain blowing sideways.

My duty jacket and uniform were soaked, and I started getting the chills. I stupidly left my rain gear in my locker. The ballistic vest kept the warmer perspiration against my chest and was my only source of warmth.

And my shift had barely begun.

- 15 -

AND JUST LIKE THAT . . .

As the final dragon tail passed, the rain stopped, and we drove the short distance back to the station to put on dry uniforms.

We spent the rest of the shift walking Broadway, talking with shopkeepers, bouncers, and strippers on break. The rain and cold temperatures kept partiers indoors or at home.

The strippers seemed happy to see us and were generous with hugs. Not sure why. Maybe they sensed I needed one. Most wore robes or cover-ups while taking their smoke breaks and talking to bouncers, cops, and passers-by. I'm sure it was in part to get away from the leering jerks, groping, and solicitations inside.

After last call, we headed back to the car to return to the station and finish paperwork. I started to decompress with the end of the shift in sight.

I keyed my mike and no sooner transmitted, "98 to the station, 10-7E," advising dispatch we were en route to the station to finish our watch than dispatch rerouted us to a report of a domestic disturbance at the Ping Yuen housing projects on Pacific Street just a few blocks away.

The Pings, as it was called, was an aging, low-income housing project with several hundred apartments.

According to Hank, over the years gang activity and drug dealing had given the place a bad rap. Most residents were reluctant to call the police because of language barriers and fear of gang retaliation.

A pagoda-style entrance with a bright red gate let you know that if you're not Chinese, you probably don't belong there. Hank said most of the cops knew when you got a call at the Pings, it's usually legit because the residents hated calling us.

We were on scene in less than three minutes and fast-walked to the elevator—they were dark with faded "Out of Order" signs taped to the doors.

We ran up six flights of stairs in the dimly lit, piss-soaked stairwell and found a young, half-naked woman in the fetal position in the corner of an outside balcony that serves as a walkway to individual apartments. She was bleeding from her head and face, with scratches and bruises around her neck.

Barely coherent, she spoke to Hank in an Asian dialect.

Hank said her boyfriend had beaten her and pointed to an apartment door.

"He's in there."

As I knocked and announced, *Police!* the suspect opened the door, pushing past me in a rage.

I went to grab him, but he was swinging and kicking, screaming at the top of his lungs like a mad man. He had foam spraying from his mouth and bloody knuckles. He'd snapped.

He braced himself against the balcony railing and turned to face me, screaming incoherently, as I approached.

The hallway was narrow, so from a few feet away, I ordered him, "Get on the ground! Do it now! On the ground!"

He ignored my commands and screamed, "Fuck you!" from the top of his lungs. He had foam and spittle flying out of his mouth. I quickly moved in to tackle him, but he stiffened like a steel rod, leaning back against the low railing. As he did, he vanished, tipping into the darkness, on his way to the afterlife.

He fell backwards, tumbling six stories into the dimly lit concrete courtyard.

I looked down in disbelief. I remember screaming, *"Fuck! Oh, my God!"*

I ran down the stairs and radioed for a paramedic unit and supervisor to respond. I checked the victim for vitals, but the contortion of his body and condition of his skull made him barely recognizable.

The velocity and impact were fatal. I'd seen enough death and was sure he was gone, but I had to give the appearances of trying to help him.

Within minutes, the watch commander and two sergeants arrived.

A sergeant pulled me aside. "You okay?"

"It was an accident, Sarge. He was fighting like a wild man, and when I went to take him down, he went over the railing. I can't fuckin' believe it."

Ping Yuen residents started to spill into the corridors to see what the sirens and commotion were about.

The sergeant requested additional units to control onlookers and establish crime scenes. Hank requested CSI, Behavioral Science, and the coroner.

The first crime scene was in the apartment where the guy had beat his girlfriend. The second in the hallway where we found his beaten girlfriend, and the third the point of impact in the courtyard.

The sergeant told another officer, "Get DeLuca out of here. Take him back to the station."

In a low voice the sergeant said, "Don't speak to anybody about the incident. That includes other officers and supervisors. If they've got questions, tell 'em to call me. Write out your statement. Do your best to recall this thing from start to finish while it's fresh in your mind. I'll call your union rep, too.

"It's okay for you to talk to BSU, CIRT, and your union rep, but that's it for now. Regardless of what happened, we're here to protect you. Get going."

Central Station was empty, except for the officer on station duty, with every available unit dispatched to the Pings. I felt sick to my stomach and started to sweat. I barely made it to the toilet before I vomited.

I looked in the mirror and saw a ghost with beads of sweat across my forehead. I looked like shit.

I soaked paper towels in cold water and wiped my face and neck, then brushed my teeth and gargled. I laid on a bench in the locker room before going upstairs to write my statement.

As I began my statement, radio traffic became nonstop as units from other district were dispatched to the Pings for crowd control.

Not more than five minutes had passed, when I heard Lieutenant Flynn key his mike. "Code-33! Code-33!" This was to clear the radio frequency for an emergency broadcast.

When radio traffic ceased, Flynn said, "406 at the Pings on Pacific. Requesting emergency backup."

Dispatch repeated his request across all channels.

It was hard to concentrate on my statement knowing all hell was breaking loose a few blocks away. I started to sweat again and felt my face burning up.

Within thirty minutes of the 406 being called, Flynn radioed a Code-4, thanking the units who responded, advising them they were clear to return to their districts.

I don't know why, but I felt in part responsible. I guess I'd add that one to my PTSD mental file, whether I wanted to or not.

- 16 -

I'M FINE. REALLY, I AM

The sergeant came into the squad room and introduced me to the on-call Critical Incident Response Team member. The three of us relocated to the conference room, and when we were settled, she got down to business.

"I know you're going through a lot," she said. "You okay to talk?"

"Yeah. I'm fine."

She glanced at my tats and asked how long I'd been with the department and what my background was. She was giving me the once-over.

"Not long. I just finished field training at Ingleside. I'm new to Central. Before that, I was in the Navy for about sixteen years."

"What did you do in the Navy?" she asked, then after a pause, "Were you in combat?"

"Nah," I said in by best deadpan. "I played the triangle in the Navy band, but we had our tough days. The triangle can be exhausting."

She looked surprised.

"Sorry, I'm just giving you shit. I supervised a SEAL unit. I was a chief petty officer. I saw combat in Iraq, Afghanistan, and a few other places."

"You had me going there for a minute," she said with a smile that suggested I hadn't at all. "Besides, I would have pegged you for the cowbell type."

"Those instruments were above my pay grade, ma'am."

We laughed. "I imagine you've been through this before."

"Yup. Only worse."

She went on to explain that CIRT was there to support members involved in shootings, accidents, and traumatic events.

"Do you have any loved ones you want us to notify?"

"Not that I know of."

Another smile. She explained all the resources available should I want to talk about things further. I listened patiently, not interrupting.

"No, I'm good, Sarge. Thanks for coming by. I'm okay. Sorry I gave you a hard time."

"All good, Ray. We all handle these situations differently."

I resisted telling her when I was a SEAL, if something like this happened, it would have been *too bad, so sad*, and we would have moved on to the next mission.

She handed me her CIRT card and wished me good luck, as the representative from the behavioral science unit walked in and wasted no time explaining he was there for essentially the same reason.

"All our conversations are confidential. Nothing we discuss tonight, or in the future, will be shared with your supervisors, or anyone else, outside of BSU. Most officers involved in traumatic incidents call us to help them process what they're going through and put it all into perspective. It's not about being mentally weak or having mental problems. What you went through is messed up, and we want to help you manage it, so you can stay mentally healthy."

This is nothing, I thought. *If I haven't cracked yet, I think I'm good.*

But the guy was earnest and seemed well-meaning, so it was hard to fault him there. We talked for about twenty minutes, just circling around what had happened before he got the sense that I wasn't really going to open up.

"Y'know, Ray, BSU saved me a few years ago," he said, "when I took a life in the line of duty. After the incident, I second-guessed myself and didn't know how to deal with it. I drank heavily and was out of control. BSU pulled me out of a dark place. I'm not sure I'd be here if it weren't for them."

"Thanks," I said. "Seriously though, I think I'm good. If something changes, I'll give you a call. I appreciate the offer."

I'd rather talk to my bartender, barber, or priest before getting all squishy with another cop.

Despite BSU's assurances of confidentiality, I don't believe it. I reason if you've blown a gasket, somebody's gotta tell somebody to get you help, or send you to the Farm or, worse yet, send you packing altogether. I'm just sayin,' it doesn't add up.

The Farm is a treatment center to help officers deal with stress, substance abuse, and other mental health issues, but you're not supposed to know it exists. Like a black ops thing.

I got up to stretch my legs and escape the conference room for a bit. Minutes later, my union rep arrived in uniform, and I recognized him as a Central Station officer I'd seen around the station.

I was the man of the hour, at least for the night.

As he strolled into the station, he carried himself like a cocksure politician, high-fiving and slapping officers on the back, as he walked to the squad room at the rear of the station.

From across the room, I heard, "Hey Tommy!" And it didn't take long for the insults and jokes to fly.

"Hey, Tommy, you ever take that service hat off? I saw you mowing your lawn the other day wearing shorts, flip flops, and that fuckin' service cap. A little male pattern baldness? Or you just love the department that much?"

He took it in stride, smiled, and shook his head, but I noticed he didn't take his service cap off. He walked over to me

"Let's you, me, and the sarge go in the conference room."

So back we went. He shut the door behind him and took a seat.

"You *are* a member of the POA, correct?" The SFPOA or San Francisco Police Officers Association—our union.

I acknowledged I was and sensed, if I wasn't, it would have been, *Well, good luck pal! Better get yourself an attorney.*

He explained the union was there to protect me, should I be accused of misconduct or a crime. He said they'd provide legal representation free of charge if it became necessary.

He suggested he be present in the event I'm questioned by Internal Affairs, outside investigators, or lawyers.

"In fact, if anyone wants to discuss this with you, I should be there. I'm your new best friend, and I'm gonna help you get through this shitstorm without any problems."

I just nodded.

"Right," he said, "so, what happened?"

"The guy was a fuckin' wild man. I was trying to take him to the ground, and he flipped over the railing, with no help from me."

He listened, nodded, asked a few questions. I gave him straight answers.

"You should be good then," he said.

"Let me get your cell number in case I need to reach you."

We exchanged numbers and as he was walking out, he grabbed my arm. "I got you, Ray. It's gonna be fine."

I finished my written statement incorporating exact times stamped on my CAD (Computer Aided Dispatch log) and turned it in to the sergeant.

He asked if my BWC (Body Worn Camera) was on during the incident and said they'd be reviewing it as well.

"It was on, but I haven't checked it yet."

I unclipped it from my uniform shirt and handed it to him so he could download the video. Naturally, the video would be booked into evidence.

"We're checking all the cameras on-site and around the Pings to corroborate your version of the incident from different vantage points."

They also had Hank's statement and video from his BWC.

As is policy, I was placed on administrative leave, pending the Use of Force findings by Internal Affairs.

Not the kind of vacation I wanted or needed.

- 17 -

RAY'S CHILLIN' WITH RAY

On *the drive home,* my thoughts drifted to two shots of Jameson Irish Whiskey and sleep.

I planned to cook homestyle comfort food the next day. While I'm no Tom Colicchio or Giada De Laurentiis, I am Sicilian and can hold my own. I like to cook—and like to eat even more. While I cook, I usually play Italian favorites like Dean Martin, Frank Sinatra, Ray Charles, and Etta James. Or if the mood strikes me, Italian opera like *La Traviata.*

Tomorrow's menu included antipasto, followed by a steaming bowl of pasta fagioli with hot Italian sausage, fresh garlic bread, and Sangiovese wine. Just thinking about it made my mouth water and took me to my happy place. It's how *this* Sicilian deals with stress.

And maybe to aid in my digestion after this wonderful meal, and strictly for medicinal purposes, I'll have a cigar and sip a glass of Monkey Shoulder Scotch, neat, and listen to Chris Botti or Marc Antoine or some other cool jazz cats.

Screw the shrinks at CIRT and BSU. This is *my* therapy: Italian food, a cigar, music, a little scotch, sleep, followed by a workout the following day. Rinse and repeat.

I might even ask Lily to join me for dinner at Trattoria later in the week for a few laughs and to stay busy. Either way, I've never had a problem feeding or amusing myself. I had time to kill.

The following morning Hank called, sounding sad and forlorn.

"Hey, bro, how ya doing?"

"All good, my man."

"So, the thing at the Pings was legit. The guy you tossed was a Ghost Boy, part of that whole Asian Triad thing. He was a major felon with a four-page rap sheet, so don't sweat it."

"For the record, I didn't *toss* him. He fell back over the railing."

"You missed the 406," he said using the PD code for riot. "Close to two hundred of those assholes were going nuts. They said *we* were fuckin' with their people."

"Well, fuck," I said, suddenly upset, "if the guy hadn't beaten his girlfriend half to death and got on the ground when I told him to, this wouldn't have happened. You can't control crazy or stupid. Fuckin' idiot!"

My heart was racing. He switched subjects.

"The coroner confirmed the torso on the beach was Carmine's, and they think it might be a 187, but I'll keep you posted."

187. The California Penal Code for murder.

"Not suicide, huh? Not sure where he's coming from with the homicide angle."

"The inspectors looked at the video from the Golden Gate and there were no jumpers that they could see. More to the point, there were no pedestrians that matched the guy, and no abandoned vehicle on the bridge. Doesn't look like he went into the water there. Aside from losing his deal with the Food Network, Carmine was in good shape financially and had everything to live for. No problems. No known enemies. No way he committed suicide. I'll let his sister know."

"Let me know if you hear anything else."

★ ★ ★

I texted Lily to ask if she wanted to have dinner at Trattoria later that week, and she hit me back she couldn't, with a sad face emoji.

☹ 10-B in Southern. Raincheck?

I texted back the thumbs-up emoji.

10-B refers to a section of the San Francisco Administrative Code that allows police officers to work off-duty assignments in uniform, on days off, for private companies. Companies submit their requests and coordinate officer compensation through official channels in the police department.

It's basically a rent-a-cop program, and officers wanting to earn extra cash clamor for spots. The assignments are typically easy and boring, but some cops don't mind standing around, or directing traffic all day.

Cops in need of extra cash for Catholic school tuition, alimony, or too many toys like boats and motorcycles, could get some relief working 10-B. And some just use it to save, or fund vacations to relieve the stress and rigors of the job.

Large tech companies like Salesforce spend a fortune for security at their annual conferences, and movie studios shooting on location are required to hire cops for security and traffic control.

I was disappointed Lily couldn't join me but was excited when I finally returned to Trattoria. I went *da solo*, as we say in

Italian, without a date. I was curious to see if I'd get in without a reservation and get the VIP treatment promised.

When I arrived, I was asked to wait on a bench next to the maître d' stand. The hostess explained they were booked, and reservations were required.

I handed her my SFPD business card. "Can you let Mr. Catalano know I'm here?"

Interestingly, on the back of the card it states:

For Business Purposes only. Not a Courtesy Card.

Oh, well, sue me, I'm just trying to get a table.

A few minutes later, Vinnie appeared.

He clapped the maître d' on the shoulder.

"Ray is *famiglia . . .* " and quietly explained I was to be given every courtesy, carte blanche, adding, "Mr. DeLuca doesn't need a reservation, ever."

I thanked him, and we bantered in Sicilian as I was escorted to my table. I scanned the dining room for Sophie Rossi, but no two times lucky for me. I'd have to check the bar later. She's like a ghost.

I had fried calamari with marinara sauce for an appetizer, followed by linguine con vongole, or linguine with clams in white wine sauce, for my entree. When the food arrived, I stopped looking for Sophie and entered *"the mangia zone."*

If she showed up now, I'd have to wave her away and say, "Not now sweetheart!"

The sommelier kept an eye on my glass, so it was never empty, pouring some of the finest wines in the house. I'm no connoisseur, but these wines were better than anything *this* Sicilian ever tasted. With each pour, he'd add a comment about the origin of the wine, many of it from the old country, and how it complemented the food, or the complexities of the nose and the finish.

As I lingered over a glass of sambuca, I thought about Carmine and was mystified that nothing of any consequence had surfaced. Though I didn't know him personally, I'm certain he would have loved this place. I needed to find out why they *now* thought it was a homicide.

Upon the arrival of the espresso and tartufo, Vinnie came over and dropped his hand on my shoulder

"*E sulla casa.*" It's on the house.

"Thanks, Vinnie. The food and wine were great. I appreciate the offer, but I'll pay. I like it here. It reminds me of New York. I love the whole sixties throwback vibe and the *affreschi Italiano*. Makes me think of home. This is a cool joint. *Grazie mille.*"

Vinnie shook his head and made a couple of jokes in Sicilian and invited me to his monthly poker game in the Cellar the following night.

"Sure," I said without giving it much thought. "That sounds great. What time?"

"Come around ten and tell the guys at the door you're my guest."

I played a fair amount of Texas Hold'em in the military. I was hoping I hadn't lost my touch.

I motioned to the waiter to settle my bill.

"No charge, Mr. DeLuca. He's the boss and told me your money's no good here."

"All right," I said. "Thanks very much. The meal and your service were outstanding. Thank you."

I couldn't help but think I was dancing with the devil. When the waiter walked away, I slid a hundred and fifty bucks under my dessert plate. And took a picture of the money on the table as proof I left it. The last thing I need is to be accused of taking free meals.

I laughed when I realized IA could always accuse me of taking the money back after taking the picture. *Stupido!*

My cousin Sal *would* take the money back and ask for more food and wine to go . . . on the house!

I made a quick trip to the bar to check for Sophie, but no such luck.

With a good amount of world-class vino in my system, I took an Uber home and left my car in the garage across from Central Station.

No sense tempting fate.

- 18 -

CHATTY-CATHY

The next morning, after I picked up my car, I stopped by Café Trieste for an espresso on my way to torture myself in the bay at the swim club. I hoped to run into Sophie, but again, not in the cards. I knew she lived locally and hung out at these places but couldn't seem to *accidentally* run into her.

The water in Aquatic Park felt like an arctic storm on the Bering Sea, with cold winds, whitecaps, and fast currents. Biting. I gasped as I got in the water and could feel my heart rate jump, which I knew was not good.

I had to work twice as hard to get my laps in—maybe it was the pasta and dessert the night before. After the swim, I had time to hit the sauna. One hundred and sixty degrees was just what I needed to thaw and relax. I made a mental note to do it more often.

Hank called to pass along what he heard regarding our two pending death investigations.

"Hey, Ray, you didn't hear it from me, but an inspector who knows a guy in homicide said you should be good on the incident at the Pings. Your body cam showed you running at the suspect after he refused to get on the ground. After that, your camera was messed up. The Pings had a camera in the hallway, and the video matched what you said in your statement."

"Thanks, Hank. I wasn't worried, but it's still a relief."

"I ran into Taggart Yee, too. He's the homicide inspector on the Carmine Vaccaro case, and he said it's slow going. There's not a lot there. Not yet. No witnesses, no usable video, and the body was in the ocean too long. Here we are in February, and his body washed up almost eight months ago. Nada!"

He said, "The ocean is never still, and the friction created by currents and waves acts like a washing machine. He said they found traces of blood on Carmine's shirt, but the DNA was too degraded to be usable. He thinks Carmine was bleeding, or had blood from someone else on him, when he went into the ocean. That's why he thinks it was a homicide, but they're still calling it suspicious circumstances for now.

"Also, his phone wasn't much help. They found Vinnie Catalano's number in Carmine's phone contacts, but Vinnie and Carmine's sister confirmed they knew each other and met at a restaurant event.

"According to Carmine's phone records, he did call Vinnie the day before he went missing, but Vinnie told them they talked about a partnership deal they were working on.

"They checked Gina's phone records, too, and she had contact with Vinnie a few months back, but she told homicide she went on a date with him, but that was the extent of it. It was only one date. That was it.

"Taggart said there was an edgy dishwasher working at the restaurant, but they thought he was probably jumpy because he's undocumented, not because he had any involvement in Carmine's death. He had a solid alibi."

Hank was on a roll, so I let him go.

"Maybe Gina offed him, or he had depression or something like that? No ATM or credit card activity. They found his wallet in his apartment and his platinum card in his phone case, so his phone and the one credit card were probably all he had with him, and he left those behind in the Uber. His sister's the only one who'll benefit from his death because their parents are dead.

"His sister stands to inherit about thirty million dollars plus the restaurant. He was one rich dude, so she's inheriting a fortune.

"His sister said he was very generous with her, but she had no idea he was worth so much because he kept financial things to himself.

"Homicide interviewed her a couple of times and said, based on her emotional state and rock-solid alibi, they don't think she had anything to do with it. She and Carmine only had each other, and they were close."

His update slipped into rambling at this point. "I hope nothing like that ever happens to me. They'll never solve the case. Half of Chinatown hates me, and the other half wants me dead. And don't forget my family. They hate me, too. Even the dog. The dog wouldn't come near me if I was covered in bacon. Too many suspects. And what about my enemies in North Beach? That would be one long-ass list of suspects.

"It would be the longest criminal investigation in the history of modern crime, like D.B. Cooper or something."

He wouldn't shut up. I was ready to put the phone down and fix myself something to eat. It was a monologue anyway. If I stayed on the phone any longer, I'd be missing meals, birthdays, holidays, too. He was giving me a headache. Man, that dude can talk!

I finally interrupted. "Hey, chatty-Cathy, I gotta bounce."

- 19 -

SORT OF A GOOD NIGHT

I *arrived at Trattoria at nine-thirty* for the ten o'clock poker
game. I was surprised to see Sophie Rossi and her girlfriend
having a drink at the bar. *Finally*, a Sophie sighting.

The thought she might be gay entered my mind. There's nothing wrong with that, but it would be soul-crushing and probably
eliminate my chances.

As I approached them, Sophie smiled.

"Ciao, Raggio." Hi, Ray.

I grabbed the stool next to them. "Don't want to interrupt,
but what can I get you ladies?"

I ordered them glasses of prosecco and a single shot of Johnnie
Walker for me.

I rushed the conversation and explained I was on my way to
a poker game in the Cellar but wanted to say hello. I downed my
liquid courage and, in Sicilian, asked Sophie if I could call her
sometime.

"Sure. Give me a call."

"For a date," I said and felt like an idiot.

She laughed. *"Sure. Give me your phone."*

I hesitated and handed her my phone, and she quickly tapped
her number into my contacts. I guess the days of writing your
number down on a bar napkin are over. I would have preferred a

perfumed napkin with a lipstick print for posterity, but then I'd be smelling it all the time. Not cool. For all I care, she could have carved the number into my forehead with a pocketknife, and I would have grinned and said, *Thank you. Thank you very much!* I told her I'd call her soon and left for the Cellar. A great way to start the night.

In the Cellar, the other players were seated, and Vinnie introduced everybody around the table. A couple of them looked like Vegas wise guys with thick gold Miami Cuban-style chains around their necks and wrists, with names like Angelo and Nunzio. The other players looked like politicians or businessmen of some sort. One was Joe and the other Nicky. I guess I was the token schlub. If asked, I was prepared to tell them I drive for Uber.

The players had their poker faces on, and the conversation was light, with only a few snarky remarks here and there.

It reminded me of a pack of dogs walking along the sidewalk, and one after the other they take turns pissing on the same bush or fire hydrant. Who can raise their leg the highest? It's amusing and an environment I'm perfectly suited for.

Cigars were offered with a waiter standing by to serve refreshments, cocktails, and wine.

I probably could have ordered a blow job and the server would say something like, *just a moment, sir, while I find someone suitable for you.*

I recognized the logo on the poker table as Akke, builders of the most-expensive poker tables in the world. Why should I be surprised?

Earlier in the day, I watched YouTube videos on Texas Hold'em to brush up on rules and strategy of the game. I found tips from high-stakes professionals, too. After watching the videos for a few hours, I felt like I knocked some of the rust off and was ready to play. I used to do pretty good playing against my SEAL buddies but would soon find out if I could compete with the big boys.

Experts say poker is eighty percent skill and twenty percent luck.

I wasn't going to rely on luck and lose money I didn't have and embarrass myself. I set my loss limit at a thousand bucks, because that's what I had on me. I could always earn the money back working 10-B, if I had to.

I know from previous experience, you've gotta watch your chips closely and know when to quit. Kenny Rogers had it right. The complementary top-shelf booze was tempting, but I nursed three fingers of Johnnie Walker all night and for the most part, drank water.

I enjoyed an incredible Cuban Cohiba Siglo Gran Reserve cigar with my scotch. I was told each cigar was worth about two hundred fifty bucks in the world market. Vinnie explained the Cohiba brand was created for Fidel Castro in 1966, for diplomatic purposes. Nothing but the best.

Most of the players were drinking hard and smoking, and as the night went on, were getting sloppy and glazing over.

I stuck to the fundamentals and only played strong hands. I was quick to fold if the cards weren't coming and watched the card combinations other players were getting, before throwing in my chips.

I was in the zone, as they say.

By the end of the game, I walked away with fifteen hundred bucks. The preparation and discipline paid off, with a little luck. I'm sure no one at the poker table needed the winnings more than me, but I had to control my excitement. To these guys, the loss was entertainment and likely not much more than lunch money.

Seeing Sophie, getting her phone number, and winning poker in the same night felt damn good. Like winning the Daily Double.

I celebrated by having a nightcap with the other players before I walked to the parking garage across from Central Station a few short blocks away.

As I approached my car, I felt confused. The trunk lid was open, and the driver's window was gone with glass scattered below it. For a second, I thought I was in the wrong garage or had the wrong car.

Nope. Across from the police station. *Unbelievable!*

I don't usually leave anything other than gym clothes, a wet suit, or dry cleaning in the car, but I remembered I put my service weapon in the trunk earlier, because I didn't want to carry it into Trattoria. This ought to go over big.

I crossed the street to the police station and went directly to the watch commander's office to report what happened.

I knew the weapon's serial number and model number needed to be entered into the Automated Firearms System (AFS) and reported to Alcohol, Tobacco & Firearms (ATF) immediately.

The theft would also need to be reported to the night captain and up the chain-of-command. Not good. I looked like an idiot. I was praying the watch commander was anyone but Flynn, but my luck ran out.

I knocked on his door and was greeted with, "What are you doing here? Aren't you on administrative leave?"

"Yes, sir, I'm still on leave, but was out for dinner in North Beach. I secured my duty weapon in the trunk of my POV, before going to dinner. It was parked in the garage across the street, so I thought it would be fine. Some piece of shit broke into my car and got in the trunk. I'm sorry, sir."

He wagged his head, as his face turned a familiar shade of mad. When the side-to-side motion stopped, he stared at me. "Not good."

One more reason for Flynn to dislike me. He paged a sergeant to his office.

"What's up, LT?"

"Numb nuts here had his duty weapon ripped from the trunk of his POV, across the street. Get the serial number and let's get this out on an all broadcast. I need you to take charge of the investigation. Let's pull all available video in the garage and on the street, ASAP. The turd who did this is probably still in the area, so let's see if we can ID him and get that gun back tonight before he does something stupid with it. Call every unit in the district and tell them to pat down anybody that's walking like they're strapped or not acting right. Call them on their phones.

"Advise Southern and Tenderloin units, too, that somebody's walking around with an officer's weapon. Extra caution tonight.

"And call the rangemaster and tell him we need to get Officer Dumbass a replacement firearm for now. Ask them to expedite it and let them know I appreciate it."

Then he turned his gaze to me.

"DeLuca, get everything into the system and notify ATF, too. Try not to fuck anything else up while you're on administrative leave."

Condescending prick!

Within an hour, an officer from the range dropped off a replacement .40 caliber Sig.

I left the station after my car was dusted for prints and drove home with the crisp night air in my face and the heater blasting.

A rotten ending to an otherwise good night out.

- 20 -

I REALLY WANTED THAT POPCORN!

As *I approached my apartment*, I spotted a package in front of the door, I assumed from my mother, Rose. This time she sent beef jerky, a Starbuck's card, a St. Michael's prayer card, boot socks for work, Italian breadsticks, and an NYPD hooded sweatshirt.

St. Michael is the patron saint of police officers, and I'm sure the NYPD sweatshirt was a hint to move closer to home. My mother's Italian, so everything she sends has significance and a subliminal message.

I called her right away.

"Mama mia sei troppo," I said. My goodness. You're too much.

She laughed and responded in stilted English. "When-ah you-ah comin- ah home, Ray-Ray? I miss-ah you. I wanna cook-ah for you, and ah-take- ah-you to church."

"I just went to church, Ma. I went to Carmine Vaccaro's funeral."

She responded with the tsk tsk sound she makes with her tongue on the roof of her mouth.

"I been-ah watchin'-ah the funeral on-ah TV. He's-ah one of us. Makes-ah me so sad."

She asked when we were going to figure out what happened to him, and I told her we were still working on it. When I asked about my father, I got a reply I'd heard before.

"He's still-ah bum-ah, still-ah in jail . . . but he's-ah *our* bum-ah."

As we were finishing our conversation, a call came in from Hank, so I told her I had to take the other call for work.

Hank seemed excited. "Hey partner, they recovered your gun. Do you know a meth head who goes by Speedball?"

I didn't.

"Well, they've got the turd on video in the garage busting your window and popping your trunk. A plainclothes street team did a little recon with some homeless dudes and found your guy in the Tenderloin packing your heater."

"My man! That's a relief. I should have known better. You can't leave a stick of gum in your car in this city."

"The good news," said Hank, "is that he's on parole, so they've got him on a Felon in Possession of a Firearm charge, so his parole officer said he'd have him back in San Quentin before you can say Shake & Bake."

"Sounds good to me."

"When you get it back, I'd strip it down and soak it in a tub of gun cleaner. It's probably carrying scabies and every other disease known to man. Speedball is one nasty dude and should be in a leper colony."

He hesitated, then said, "Oh, that's right, he is. He lives in the Tenderloin."

As we were finishing our conversation, I got a text from Lily.

Wud up, Dirty Harry? Let's catch up.

I told her I'd make dinner at my house, and she didn't need to bring a thing.

I did a quick inventory of what I had for food and booze. This would require a trip to Safeway, but I had nothing but time.

Lily arrived at seven, ready to rock, with a big smile and a playful glint in her eye. In the mood to party, as they say.

She ignored my earlier request to refrain from bringing anything and brought wine, fresh cannoli from Mara's, an Italian bakery in North Beach, and a couple of Davidoff cigars to enjoy after dinner.

She was new to smoking cigars but wanted to give it a go. Now that's my kind of girl. The meal and mood were set for what promised to be a fun evening.

As I was preparing the meat sauce for the spaghetti, I put Lily to work making a tossed green salad and garlic bread.

We talked the entire evening, discussing her 10-B gig, the recovery of my gun, the Carmine Vaccaro investigation, the incident at the Pings, and the escalating gang activity in Chinatown and North Beach.

"Until recently," she said, "there was no mob activity in North Beach. This is all new. We haven't had gang activity in Chinatown since the Joe Boys in the seventies. Before our time."

Lily gave me the highlights.

The Joe Boys were a notorious Chinese youth gang founded by Joe Fong. Fong had previously been a member of the Wah Ching Gang. The Joe Boys specialized in drug and fireworks trafficking, and participated in robberies, burglaries, extortion, and murder.

On September 4, 1977, the Joe Boys attacked rival Wah Ching members having lunch at the Golden Dragon Restaurant in Chinatown using a .45 caliber Commando rifle, two twelve-gauge pump shotguns, and a .38 caliber revolver, leaving five people dead and eleven injured. The tragedy became known as the *Golden Dragon Massacre.*

When the gunfire ceased and the smoke cleared, to the surprise of the Joe Boys, none of the victims turned out to be Wah Ching, so it was all for naught and a slaughter of innocent people.

"The original dispute was over fireworks sales. If you include the victims of the Golden Dragon Massacre, by the end of 1977, forty-four people were murdered during the gang war between the Joe Boys and Wah Ching. My mother told me all about it."

That brought her up short, and before I could hop in, she switched subjects.

"Now what's going on with Flynn?"

"I wish I knew. Maybe he's just a hard-ass. I've had good intentions but can't seem to stay off his radar. Shit happens, and now the guy thinks I'm an incompetent asshole. I think he loves giving me shit. I'm still on probation, so this guy can torch my career if I sneeze."

Just the mention of Flynn made me irritable. "Anyway, enough cop talk. Let's go out to the veranda, so we can smoke and sip a little scotch. Try not to laugh when you see the size of the deck. I can hardly squeeze two chairs, a cocktail table and hibachi on it. It's a new trend. *Little is in*, and this is how the rich and famous live in Daly City!"

Outside, she puffed, coughed, and sputtered as she sampled her Davidoff. Laughing, she sipped her scotch as she considered the cigar.

I offered sage words of encouragement like "Come on, Lily," and "Tough it out," and "You can do it," and "Man-up!" This last gem earned me glaring looks and backhanded slaps on the shoulder, in between her hacking and coughing.

We talked about growing up and how different our lives were. She, the daughter of a strict single mom in law enforcement living in Chinatown, and me the son of Italian immigrants, with a father on the other side of the law, living in Newburgh, New York.

She entered UC Berkeley after high school, and I entered the military, and here we sat together, coming from such different beginnings, more than three thousand miles apart. A weird, remarkable, random fate.

The night air became cold and damp, so we moved the party inside to watch something on Netflix. Lily was microwaving popcorn, and I was freshening our drinks when it started.

Pop pop pop . . . pop pop, pop pop pop!

The glass sliders to the deck imploded and bullets sprayed the top of the kitchen cabinets above the sink. We dove for cover.

"Stay down!" I yelled.

I grabbed my cell, dialed 9-1-1, and identified myself to Daly City Police dispatch as an off-duty SFPD officer with shots fired at Lake Merced Arms apartments.

"I heard tires screeching, so they might have left the scene, but I'm not sure. Tell units responding to look for Asian males leaving the area at a high rate of speed, probably en route to San Francisco. Notify CHP and SFPD dispatch, too. These guys could be related to a case I'm working in San Francisco, and they're gang members. I'm with another off-duty SFPD officer and we're armed. We'll stay in the apartment until your units arrive."

We low-crawled into the bedroom to retrieve weapons.

"Tell your units I'm a white male wearing a gray T-shirt and jeans and my partner is an Asian female, wearing a pink sweater and jeans. We're wearing our police ID around our necks."

"Roger that," said the dispatcher. "Responding units are about two minutes out and should be on scene any minute. Stay on the line until I tell you it's safe to answer the door."

Lily and I upended the dining room table and braced it against the front door with a heavy leather chair. We positioned ourselves on opposite sides of the living room behind furniture, in anticipation, should a second assault occur before Daly City officers arrive.

Seconds later, we heard sirens, followed by loud banging on the door with officers yelling, "Daly City Police!"

"Officers are at your door," said the dispatcher. "I'm glad you're both safe."

Officers and their crime scene unit went to work searching the area. They dug badly damaged bullet fragments out of the kitchen cabinets, but beyond that, found no other physical evidence.

A technician looking at the trajectories of the rounds said, "You're lucky they were shooting up from the street into the second story and probably firing from inside their vehicle. We didn't find any shell casings in the street, or along the front of the building, so the casings are probably inside the vehicle. For what it's worth, I'd say the shots were probably meant as a warning."

As the CSI team finished up, they secured the area where the sliders had been shattered with heavy plywood. Lily and I were taken to Daly City PD to make statements.

I called the watch commander at Central Station and told him about the incident and our status. Lieutenant Flynn was off, and the watch commander in charge said he was sending a team from Internal Affairs to Daly City PD to open an investigation. We all agreed more than likely the shots were meant for me as a warning from the Ghost Boys for the recent death of their gang member at the Pings, identified as Stephen Chin.

Lily suggested I stay at her flat for the night as a precaution. We got to her place around three, so I crashed on the couch—again—and she went to her bedroom.

I couldn't help but think this would be one more turd in Flynn's punch bowl that he'd associate with me. How long did I have?

- 21 -

OORAH!

I **drove to the station from Lily's,** instead of directly home, to collect my recovered duty weapon. Word travels fast. I was greeted with high-fives as I entered the squad room where officers were busy typing reports.

One of the senior guys, a leathery motorcycle officer named Simpson, looked up. "Hey, Ray, glad you're okay. Fuck the Ghost Boys. They start some shit with you, they're gonna get all of us."

My stolen Sig was returned, so I took it to the workbench in the station's garage to clean it. When I was done, I was told to report to the station commander, Captain Robert Choo. I didn't know him well, but he had a good reputation and the troops referred to him affectionately as Bobby Choo, or sometimes Choo-Choo.

He asked about the previous night's shooting in Daly City and wasted no time suggesting I relocate my residence.

"You've been getting in the shit with the Ghost Boys, but you've been cleared of any wrongdoing on the Pings incident.

"You're officially off administrative leave and need to check in with your sergeant and partner to see when you're back on the roster. Watch your ass, Ray. If you want to get off the street for a while, I can make that happen."

"Thanks," I said, "but I'm good."

"They want revenge," Choo said, "so keep your head on a swivel. You and your partner need to carry extra magazines and a concealed backup, too. I'll talk to your watch commander and tell the night captain to put the entire watch on alert. We'll notify TAC and put additional units in Chinatown. These assholes could come for you at any time. I can transfer you to another district station, but if they're looking for you, they'll find you anyway. It's up to you."

"Nah, I'm good, sir."

"We've got undercovers working Chinatown trying to nail as many Ghost Boys as we can. For now, don't roll on any calls in Chinatown. Let other units take them unless there's shots fired, or something like that."

With the attacks heating up, I needed to move out of my apartment and ratchet up my situational awareness, on and off duty.

I called Hank to let him know I was returning to patrol, and he said our watch just rotated, so we have the next three days off.

Then he started in on me.

"What happened in Daly City last night? And why was Lily in your apartment?"

"Number one, it's none of your business. Number two, it's *really* none of your business, and number three, you guessed it, it's really none of your fuckin' business."

"Okay, I just—"

"In case you weren't told, we almost bought the farm last night and had six rounds miss us by about eighteen inches, so don't give me any shit. I'm not in the mood. I'll see you in a few days. And by the way . . . *go fuck yourself.*"

I hung up. About a minute later, he called back.

"Don't be a dick. There's stuff going on with the Carmine Vaccaro case, but I can't talk about it on the phone. We'll catch up later. Now, go settle yourself down for a few days and call me if you need me. Say 'Goodbye, Hank. I love you.'"

I smiled. "Goodbye, dickhead."

Instead of going back to the apartment, I drove to SFPD's Lake Merced Pistol Range, down the street from my apartment. I needed to blow off steam and make sure Speedball hadn't damaged my gun. I put close to a hundred rounds through it and was satisfied with its accuracy. I asked the rangemaster to check it as well, and he gave me the thumbs-up.

I returned to my apartment to clean up the mess from the shooting and stopped by the manager's office to discuss the damages.

He followed me to my apartment and said he'd ask engineering to handle the repairs as soon as possible.

When he saw the holes from the rounds sprayed across the kitchen cabinets, he did a double take. I made light of it and explained I was a police officer and told him it was probably job related.

"Either the City of San Francisco will pay for the damages, or I'll reimburse you out of pocket."

He eyed my tattoos and asked if I'd been in the military.

"Yup," I said.

"I'm Mike. Marine Corp. So, I just want to you to know I'll keep an eye on the place while you're out."

Though I was a SEAL and not a Marine, I felt compelled to give him an *Oorah! Semper Fi, brother!*

He smiled, we fist-bumped, and went our separate ways. I know when you're a Marine, you're a Marine for life, and that includes the afterlife.

I'm guessing Saint Peter has a separate intake line at the pearly gates just for Marines, and according to Matthew 5:9 in the New Testament, "Blessed are the peacemakers, for they will be called the children of God."

★ ★ ★

With a few more days off, I got my nerve up to call Sophie for the long-anticipated date. I assumed it was only *me* looking forward to the date, and not her. I figured I'd probably have to jog her memory. I could hear her voice in my head as I dialed. *Ray? Ray, who? Oh, yeah, sure. Ray, the cop? How can I help you, Officer DeLuca?*

I got her voicemail, which was better anyway. That way I didn't put her on the spot. It would give her time to make up an excuse, and though I'd be disappointed, I'd get over it.

I wanted to come off smooth and cavalier.

"Hey, Sophie. This is San Francisco's Finest, your friend, Ray DeLuca. I wanted to see if you're available tonight, or tomorrow night, to go out for dinner, or see a movie, or something. If there's something else you wanna do, just let me know. Hit me back when you get a chance. *Arrivederci.*"

About an hour later, she returned my call.

"Hi, Ray. Let's do something fun and see a movie."

Well, that was good with me, and I didn't care if she wanted to chase squirrels or dig a ditch. I just wanted to be with her on a date. It was a start.

- 22 -

DREAM LOVER

I *picked her up at her apartment,* and she looked younger than I remembered and came off a bit shy. We drove to SoMa, the South of Market district, to a local theater complex.

She looked perfect, dressed in jeans and a sweater and prettier than I remembered. We talked about the upcoming North Beach Italian Festival and parked in a garage about two blocks from the Metreon.

I barely remember the movie, but we held hands during the show and shared a large tub of popcorn with no butter.

Going no butter was her idea.

"Sure, no problem," I said. "I don't eat a lot of butter anyway."

Total lie.

Dry popcorn was a sacrifice, like eating peanut shells, but I'm a SEAL, and I've eaten worse.

I was getting to know her and planned to stop for a nightcap in North Beach after the movie. I was praying for *salted* nuts on the bar, or a salt lick. *Anything* salty!

She knocked me out from the first time I saw her. For me, I was immediately attracted and infatuated.

After the movie, we walked up Fourth Street, talking and holding hands on our way to the parking garage. It was nice. I couldn't remember the last time I held hands with a date.

About a block from the Metreon, I started hearing verbal taunts from about twenty feet behind us.

"Hey, Officer DeLuca, who's that fine piece of ass you're with? Ooh, she fine. We gonna do some evil shit to her tonight. You wanna watch?"

"Ignore them," I said, pitching my voice low and calm. "Just keep walking."

As one was yelling taunts, two others came up, walking on either side of us. The one closest to Sophie put his arm around her waist, then slapped her across the butt.

"Ooh, I'm a do that all night long, baby."

He slapped her again, this time harder, and left his hand there. Sophie was wide-eyed, and quiet. She looked terrified.

I deduced they were the same thugs who shot up my apartment the previous night, but Sophie wasn't aware of that incident. No guns were visible, but I assumed they were armed. They were heavily tatted Asian dudes with GB-SF neck tattoos, so I knew they were Ghost Boys.

I had to react.

I hit the first one who assaulted Sophie across the windpipe with a bladed hand as hard as I could. He collapsed and fell to the ground. I kicked the legs out from under his partner and put the boots to both.

They rolled away from me, covering their heads with their hands and arms. They were gasping and moaning, and as each stood up and attempted to get his equilibrium, I squared off with him.

I broke the first one's nose and hit the other above his right eye, probably shattering his orbital bone. It was important they leave bleeding and marked up for their buddies to get the message.

Both suspects ran across Fourth Street like their hair was on fire. The whole thing was over in about a minute, and I was surprised no guns were drawn.

Still amped up, I grabbed Sophie by the arm. "Let's go!"

She was hysterical, pulled away, and wouldn't let me touch her.

"Jesus, Sophie, it's not safe here right now. *Let's go!*"

By the time we got back to the car, some of her shock had worn off, but she was almost hysterical. "Why'd you have to hurt them? They only slapped my butt."

I tried to explain they were gang members and were serious about hurting her to get to me. I told her about the incident at the Pings and the shooting the previous night.

She sobbed even louder. "Take me home, *please!*"

I walked her to her door. "I'll call you tomorrow."

"Please, don't. I don't want any part of this. I'm scared. Don't call me again. I can't handle this."

I drove to Lily's a few blocks away, but there was no answer. The situation with the Ghost Boys was escalating, and I needed to talk to somebody about it.

My wish came true when my phone rang. It was Lieutenant Flynn ordering me to report to Central Station.

"The two Asian kids you just did a number on South of Market want to file a complaint against you for two-forty-five, so get your ass to the station, *now!*"

Two-forty-five of the California Penal Code (245 PC) is Assault with a Deadly Weapon, usually charged as a felony. I'm fairly certain because I put the boots to them, my shoes and my actions were considered the deadly weapon.

This was the fourth incident with the Ghost Boys in a month. Nasty Girls with my buddy Dom; the death of their comrade at the Pings; the shooting at my apartment; and now this.

And they're filing a complaint against me? I arrived at the station and sat in my car to cool off before reporting to the lieutenant. Five minutes later I was knocking on Flynn's door and stepping into his office.

"Shut the door," he said.

He was in his usual state of high agitation.

"According to these Asian youth, they were teasing you and having fun. What did you hit 'em with, a fuckin' brick? They said you put the boots to them, too."

"With all due respect, that's bullshit, sir. I was minding my own business. I was off duty and on a date. They're known gang members and there's a good chance they're the ones who shot up my apartment and tried to kill me last night in Daly City."

"You don't know that."

"You don't believe me? Go talk to the inspectors and the detectives from Daly City PD. The Ghost Boys have the motive. It's retaliation for their buddy getting killed at the Pings.

"My date and I were minding our own business, walking back to the car after a movie. These punks came up behind us and started with taunts, insinuating they were going to rape my date. Then, one of them put his hands on her and repeatedly smacked her on the ass. I'm pretty sure that's still called battery. How would you feel if it was your daughter who was threatened with rape and smacked on the ass?"

Flynn hesitated. "So, instead of calling 9-1-1, you broke one of their noses and might have cost the other his eye?"

I smiled and flexed my right hand into a fist.

"You're *goddam* right I did. They want revenge. I'll take every one of those little pricks out if I have to."

Flynn sat and stared at me for what seemed like a minute.

"Well, the city's probably gonna get sued for this one, too, on top of the lawsuit for the Pings death. You're talking millions."

I snapped.

"So, this is my fault? Doing my job and defending myself and my date? That's bullshit! You haven't asked how I'm doing, or if my date is okay. I can see this is going nowhere. I'm outta here."

I stood to leave.

"Sit down! I haven't dismissed you."

"I don't need you to dismiss me. Fuck you!"

He jumped up, like he was about to grab me, but I could sense the hesitation as soon as he was on his feet.

"You'll lose," I said through clenched teeth then walked out of his office.

"That's it, DeLuca," he yelled from behind me seconds later. "You're suspended for insubordination!"

Coward. He waited until I cleared his office. He motioned for two sergeants to escort me from the station.

"Get him out of here."

On my way out, I was ordered to surrender my star, my police ID, and gun. I slammed them on the evidence counter, and when I turned to leave, watched as other cops looked away.

At the front door, I paused and turned to my escorts. "Flynn would rather believe gangbangers than one of his own. Can you believe that? How'd a guy like that make lieutenant?"

Neither sergeant was going to rise to the bait. One stayed silent. The other one, Smethurst, at least had the decency to respond.

"Ray, you've been through a lot. Take the time off and get through the suspension and we'll see you when you get back. Try to calm down and relax. It's not worth it."

- 23 -

I HATE TO DRINK ALONE

was enraged and driving the Challenger like I stole it. I thought about Sophie and the job, and by the time I got home, I was in a foul mood.

I sulked for about fifteen minutes, then decided it was time. Time to crack open the Single Malt Glenfiddich I'd been saving, and call Billy. I needed to get my mind off my troubles and have a few laughs.

He didn't answer, so I left him a voicemail. A few minutes later, he called back, and we spent the better part of an hour joking and catching up.

Like me, Billy was a retired SEAL and was now working for an elite executive protection company called Blackhawk in the Los Angeles area. Blackhawk was a world-class personal security agency that handled highly sensitive, and sometimes dangerous, assignments all over the world, and they were paid big bucks to do what others couldn't or wouldn't do.

He'd been training other retired special ops guys and loving his new life; he was a mentor and deserved all the money and good coming his way.

While Billy wasn't a big man, he was hands down the most dangerous human being I knew. Prior to entering the SEAL program, he was a black belt in Brazilian Jiu Jitsu. Later, he trained with the Israeli Defense Forces (IDF) to learn Krav Maga and became a top self-defense and hand-to-hand combat instructor for the SEALS. He taught badasses how to be deadly and was a legend in the SEAL organization and with his peers.

Modest and unpretentious, Billy had a dry sense of humor and Okie drawl. When you coupled that with his smaller, unassuming stature, he could be quite disarming and, truth be told, deadly. Most never saw it coming.

He returned my call after a few minutes.

"Brother Ray!"

We clowned and talked for a while, and toward the end of the conversation, he said, "Hey, cowboy, I got an idea. You're off for a couple of weeks and probably looking for something to do.

"Me and my team are headed to Baja for Escape and Evasion Training. This is gonna be some fun shit in the desert. I've got room for another guy.

"Blackhawk is putting the whole thing on. No cost to you, except plane fare. You can bunk with me. You need to get away from all that cop bullshit and spend time with real warriors."

The training was two weeks away, so I told him I'd think about it.

"You'll like these guys," he said. "All ex-special ops guys and green-face banditos like us. You'll pick up some new skills. I promise you that, pardner."

We finished the call, and I gave it more thought. Considering the new charge of insubordination by Flynn, I could end up losing my job anyway. It wouldn't hurt to brush up on my special ops skills and hang with Billy for a while. Better than sitting around this depressing apartment in the fog.

I knew this type of training requires your full attention, so it could be exactly what I needed. Intense training, sun, fun, and hanging with the boys.

I deliberated and, after a second scotch, called Billy back.

"I'm in. I'll call you in a few days to coordinate my flight and all the details."

Billy laughed.

"You didn't need to waste the call, pardner. I already put you on the roster."

- 24 -

IN THE WIND

I *texted Lily to see if she wanted* to get together and received a response a few minutes later.

Dinner my place. DC not safe. Stay here.

I packed my seabag and booked a flight to New York to visit family. From there I'd fly to San Diego to meet Billy, for the drive south to Baja. I needed to distance myself from the Ghost Boys, the SFPD, and Sophie. It was toxic and dangerous. Distance, time with family, and friends, were the order of the day.

I texted Sophie as I was packing but got no response. I hoped with time she'd get over it.

I told my apartment manager Mike I'd be gone for a while and paid an extra month's rent in advance. I asked him to supervise the repairs on my place and keep an eye out for problems. Then I caught myself.

"I don't know why I'm telling you that. You know what to do. Sorry, man."

I gave him a bottle of Jameson Irish Whiskey for his troubles.

After an *oorah!* and a fist bump, I left for Lily's, anticipating the change of scenery, at least for a while.

Before dinner, we shucked oysters and had them with mignonette sauce and fresh lemons. Lily prepared grilled butter-baked salmon with asparagus, sliced tomatoes, olives, and French bread for the main course. The meal was spectacular, and we knocked off a bottle of chardonnay as we ate and caught up on each other's lives.

Lily outdid herself, and I told her how much I appreciated it. She was an amazing cook. I did the dishes and cleaned the kitchen while she looked for something good to watch on a movie channel.

We sat on the couch with our feet propped up, and it felt good to do something normal for a change. Halfway through the movie, she leaned into me under a warm blanket, and I wasn't going to resist. I hadn't felt a woman's touch, aside from holding Sophie's hand, in a long time, and it felt good.

She kissed me on the neck, and after a steamy make-out session that went on for five minutes or so, I stopped.

"Hey, with me going out of town, maybe we should put this on hold. I don't want to mess things up."

Plus, I was still preoccupied with Sophie.

"I'm going out of town for a few weeks to clear my head and get away from the heat. Let's think about it for the next few weeks and see how we feel when I get back.

"I'm not good with relationships, and I'm not in a good place right now. I don't want to mess with your head. Cool with you?"

She smiled.

"I'm good, Ray. I just like spending time with you. No pressure. I know you're going through a lot."

She got up from the couch and came back with blankets and pillows. "I'm turning in."

She was pissed. I'd developed a knack for throwing ice water on intimacy and romance. After so many years on SEAL missions without intimacy, I lost my confidence and felt inadequate. I couldn't deal with it now, with everything else going on.

I slept restlessly and woke up early for the flight to New York. As I stepped out of the shower, Lily tapped the bathroom door and handed me a hot cup of coffee. Nice.

I called an Uber, and we had a long hug goodbye that ended with a kiss.

I told her I'd check in from the road and asked her to keep my travel plans to herself.

"And that means Hank, too. Nobody needs to know I'm gone or where I am."

"Sure," she said, "I understand."

But something told me she didn't.

- 25 -

GET ME OUTTA HERE!

I *no sooner got in the Uber* to go to SFO, when Hank called. He sounded agitated and told me Flynn was out to fire me. He wanted to know if I really told him to go fuck himself.

I laughed.

"Fuckin-A! And I'd do it again."

I explained the latest incident with the Ghost Boys and told him Flynn sided with the Ghost Boys and tried to make the whole thing my fault.

"He's more concerned with himself and the city getting sued than with the safety of one of his officers. He's been a prick to me since day one at Central. He's a bully, and I don't care what his rank is, I won't take his shit, and he knows it."

"Right, but here's the thing," said Hank. "I heard he also told one of the sergeants he thinks there's a connection between you and the Sicilians in North Beach, and—"

"There is," I said. "We're all from this little island in the Mediterranean called Sicily, and believe it or not, we all share the same language and culture. Maybe you can give him a lesson on geography. Dumbass Irishman."

"Sure, I hear you," said Hank, and I could tell that he had more for me. "Flynn said inspectors have been sniffing around Vinnie Catalano and you seem to be chummy with him. They think he's mobbed-up. He said the girl you were with when you got in the beef South of Market is Sicilian, too. They interviewed her. Bad optics, Ray."

"That's racist bullshit. Just because I played cards with the guy doesn't make us best friends. I met Vinnie at Lieutenant Ferraro's retirement party when he introduced himself to me. We're both Sicilians, so what? And I'll date who the hell I want."

"He also thinks you have it out for the Ghost Boys because they're in a turf war with *your* people. Flynn thinks he's got it all figured out."

"You might want to explain to him that we *are* working in the heart of Chinatown and Little Italy. Fuckin' simpleton."

"Well, he asked me to give you a message. He said he was having trouble reaching you and wanted me to tell you that you're suspended, with pay, pending an internal hearing, which hasn't been scheduled yet. He's also sending the 245 case to the DA, so they can review it for charges against you for kicking the shit out of the two Asian dudes. They might add an enhancement for *Under the Color of Authority*, too. Sorry to give you the bad news, bro."

The 245 case would be Assault with a Deadly Weapon.

"Trouble reaching me? I've been around. The reality is, he doesn't *want* to reach me. I intimidate him, and he's a coward. He's used to cops who are afraid of him. I'm on the right side of this thing, and I'm smarter than he is, so I don't care what charges he brings me up on. He can kiss my ass, but keep that to yourself. But thanks for the intel."

"No problem," he said. "Just so you know, the Ghost Boys gave statements and signed a Citizen's Arrest Form and said you went off on them without provocation. Did you even give Flynn *your* written statement?"

"I didn't, but I explained the whole thing to Flynn and Smethurst when I was told to report to the station. They probably paraphrased what I told them and put that in the report. I didn't stick around long enough to write out a statement because Flynn had me escorted out of the station when he suspended me."

"Well, y'know, Ray—"

"Hey Hank, you know how I know it's Flynn when he walks away? I see your boots sticking out of his ass. That's how far you've got your head up there! Anyway, I gotta jump."

"What the—"

And with that I hung up while he was mid-sentence.

- 26 -

THERE'S NO PLACE LIKE HOME

The flight to LaGuardia was empty with almost as many flight attendants as passengers. I dozed off for most of the six-hour flight with dreams of Sophie from thirty thousand feet.

I wondered how it all became such a mess. I was looking forward to seeing my family and the Hudson Valley.

I sent Sophie a text when I landed, but again, no response. I didn't mention I was out of town. I barely knew her but was intoxicated with her looks and the *fantasy* of a relationship with her. Sometimes we want what we can't or shouldn't have.

★ ★ ★

When I got to Newburgh, I opened the door to my mother's apartment and was hit with the familiar aroma of garlic sautéing in a hot pan of imported olive oil.

She was preparing my favorites. Pasta fagioli with sausage, and a big Italian salad, loaded with cucumbers and tomatoes right from the farm, with olives, and shaved Parmigiano Reggiano.

Local Italian farmers from Marlboro pay homage to my father with produce, homemade wines, and cheeses, so my parents are always stocked up with the best. Old-school Sicilian, Newburgh-style.

This was our tradition. When I came home from deployments, I always asked for the same welcome home meal.

After hugging and kissing, we sat to *mangia*. My mother was loaded with questions. I'd no sooner answer one and she'd load another into the breech.

She asked when I was going to settle down with a nice Italian girl and have some *bambini*.

I laughed, "No time soon. Besides, you're my girl, Ma."

She grinned, grabbed my hand and kissed it.

She told me how she'd been busy with church activities and playing pinochle with her friends. She updated me on her bus trips to the casinos in Monticello and her latest winnings. She was on a winning streak with the slots.

I knew she'd become accustomed to living alone.

With my father in prison, and me on the West Coast, she had no choice but to find happiness her way, and she took life a day at a time. *Sicilian strong!*

She visited my father every Sunday at the Federal Correctional Facility (FCI) in Danbury, Connecticut, about an hour away. She said he was getting along fine, with support and protection from his *other* family.

My mother was no dope and knew my father was a capo. It gave her a measure of peace that no harm would come to him inside any jail. It gave me comfort, too. He wasn't getting any younger.

She said *his guys*, meaning his soldiers, stopped by her apartment on a regular basis to bring homemade food, wine, and cash. She wanted for nothing, and said if she needed anything, they'd get it for her. And she meant it . . . *anything*. Without asking, his soldiers knew, while he was in prison, she was *their* responsibility.

The neighbors were aware of my father's position, so even the local punks stayed away from her apartment building.

"Thanks to your father," one neighbor once told me, "it's safer around here than the grounds of the White House."

God knows where my mother was stashing all the cash, but I wasn't going to ask. She could stack it outside on the front steps, and nobody would touch it.

When she spoke of my father, my mother would lower her voice and speak in Sicilian. Those conversations usually ended with her staring into my eyes and whispering *morte*, as she held her index finger perpendicular to her lips. *Morte* in Italian means death, and the gesture is her way of saying, what she told me is not to be repeated.

A little dramatic for me, but in my family, it means something, so I understand and abide by it. Certain things you don't speak of, outside the family.

★ ★ ★

On Sunday, we drove to Danbury.

FCI (Federal Correctional Facility) Danbury is a low-security prison housing white-collar criminals. It's been the temporary home to celebrities like Leona Helmsley, Teresa Giudice from *The Real Housewives of New Jersey,* and hip-hop artist Lauryn Hill.

Usually, the incarcerated are serving time for things like fraud, tax evasion, and money laundering. FCI is doing time "lite." It's no San Quentin or Pelican Bay.

Kind of like getting lunchtime detention instead of staying after school, which was usually worse. You'd be in more danger shopping in your local mall or doing time in county jail, than being housed at FCI.

In fact, you're probably in more danger walking down the streets of most American cities today. FCI didn't faze my father. It was only an inconvenience.

Punishment at FCI means you don't get nuts and chocolate sauce on your ice cream. But you get the ice cream just the same. Come to think of it, they probably sneak the nuts and chocolate sauce into my father's cell, with fresh whipped cream and a cherry on top.

When we arrived, we were escorted to a private room away from the other inmates and visitors. It seemed like we were given more privacy than the other inmates and were allowed physical contact, but I couldn't be sure.

He looked thinner than I remembered, and his hair was turning gray; but overall, he looked good and was in good spirits. He maintained his fitness and his Sicilian tan. A combination of good Sicilian genes and access to gym equipment.

Or maybe they were bringing in a personal trainer and shuttling him to Miami on weekends. Who knows? His gravitas and influence in FCI were obvious.

He wasn't fazed by his incarceration.

We spoke in lowered voices in Sicilian and the guard smiled and stood several feet away to give us privacy. Obviously, he knew who he was dealing with, and quite possibly my father was taking care of him. *In the pocket,* so to speak.

After we exchanged pleasantries, I asked my father for advice regarding Vinnie Catalano and the turf war in San Francisco. I explained that recently, due to our heritage and some job-related incidents, it was being insinuated I might be connected to the mob trouble in San Francisco.

"I played poker with one of the soldiers and his crew, but I'm not involved with those guys. The soldier is Vinnie Catalano, and his father is a capo here in New York."

He smiled. "Better you stay on the side of the Sicilians than those rotten cops."

I let it slide, and truth be told, he might be right.

He said he'd be out in six months, with good behavior, and he cautioned me to be careful around made guys. He recognized the name Catalano but said he would have to do some checking.

He gave me a name and phone number to memorize, should any problems arise with Vinnie Catalano, or anyone else.

"I think he's somebody in the commission's kid," he said. "Whether you're the police or not, you're still my blood and *famigghia*, and the family will protect you."

My father seldom speaks of these things, but when he does, he's as serious as a heart attack.

We got off the subject and talked about the promise of good food, wine, and good times to come when he got paroled. My mother and I left, upbeat and optimistic.

As my mother says, *He might-ah be a crook-ah, but he's-ah our crook-ah.*

I spent the rest of my time in Newburgh relaxing. I had drinks with high school buddies at Blu Pointe, a waterfront bar on the Hudson, and enjoyed home-cooked meals.

A side benefit to going home was getting the best sleep I'd had in years. I never have PTSD episodes there.

There's something magical when you sleep in your childhood bedroom with the windows open. I think it's the familiar sounds and smells and feeling of security under your family's roof.

When it was time to leave, it was tough saying goodbye to my mother, but since my time in the military, she'd become accustomed to goodbyes. I still got *una acia triste*, a sad face, each time I left.

My mother packed sandwiches, fruit, and goodies for my flight to San Diego to meet Billy.

It reminded me of the hundreds of lunches she packed for me as a kid. My classmates were getting peanut butter and jelly, with Ho Hos for dessert, while I was getting prosciutto and mortadella on thick Italian bread with pepperoncini with oil and vinegar with Stella D'oro anisette cookies for dessert.

The other kids thought I was from another planet.

- 27 -

SOME HA HA IN BAJA!

I *texted Sophie when we landed.*

🙁 How about a do-over?

She was ghosting me, and it was starting to piss me off. Was a response too much to ask?

Billy pulled curbside in a blacked-out Chevy Suburban with a cargo rack on the roof and tote tanks on the back for hauling water.

I tied my seabag to the roof carrier and jumped in to meet the Blackhawk team. After quick fist bumps, they each pointed out the gadgets and toys in the vehicle. This behemoth was like Toyland for warriors. The interior was outfitted with two-way radios, modems, 360-degree cameras, backup phones, GPS, and a FLIR unit (Forward-Looking Infrared Camera).

There were hard cases marked for Kevlar vests, Coveralls, Tools, First Aid/AED, Pyrotechnics, Gas Masks, Protective Suits, and Jaws for extrications. More importantly, it was a mobile armory with AR-15s and H&K submachine guns mounted in custom racks along the roofline.

Loaded high-capacity pistols were mounted muzzle down at a twenty-degree angle, in a steel rack in front of the rear passengers, with concealed quick-release buttons.

"It's designed to survive Armageddon," said Billy. "It's blast-resistant with armored shielding. When we fill it with some of the baddest motherfuckers on the planet, we think it gives us an edge. This sexy thang cost close to a half million to build and has IED protection too, with half-inch steel plating in all the right places, bulletproof glass, and run-flat tires."

IED stood for Improvised Explosive Device. "Shit," I said, "now you got me all hot and bothered."

"That's not all, brother," he said. "It's got Level V armor protection, the highest level you can get. It's been used all over the world to transport heads of state and other security risks."

On the thirty-minute drive to Baja, we used the time to get to know each other. Billy asked each team member to give their brief military bio.

"Tell Ray about any unique specialties or skills, outside the bedroom, and keep it real, or I'll call bullshit."

These guys were modest and I'm sure some, if not all, had received top military honors, including Silver Stars, Purple Hearts, and Medals of Honor. I sensed I was in the company of the best of the best.

A Hispanic guy named Joe said, "I don't want to put the brag bag on, but I did receive the Good Conduct Medal. I'll never forget it.

"It brought me to tears because I know no way was my conduct or behavior ever good. My mother said that's how she knows all my medals are bullshit . . . and that hurts."

Judging from their MOS (Military Occupational Specialties), I was the light bag of chips and would have been on their goon squad with the other lightweights.

Our accommodations were sparse, and I'm being generous. Motel 6 would be an upgrade. The bar of soap was the size of a Thin Mint, and the only danger was losing it you-know-where. At least they wrapped the dirty drinking glasses in wax paper for sanitary purposes.

"When the company is footing the bill for training," Billy said, "they go cheap on accommodations. When it's on the client's dime, we go four, or five stars."

We crashed early so we'd be ready to rock at 0600 to pick up dune buggies. Breakfast would *not* be served, so it was every man for himself.

I woke up at 0500 and devoured a power bar, energy drink, and bottled water I packed earlier. In the military, you learn to plan and always have something to eat and drink with you because it might be awhile before you get something again.

Hell, I've eaten crickets, snakes, and other unmentionables, and washed it down with my own urine. This morning's breakfast was practically gourmet.

We met in the parking lot at 0600 and loaded into a Suburban that the team appropriately named Rolling Thunder.

We rendezvoused with our Mexican counterparts embedded in-country. They loaned us three dune buggies for the trip into the desert. The training was being held in a desolate area north of San Felipe near the salt flats. Billy trailed in our dust in Rolling Thunder.

Training vehicles for Escape & Evasion were on-site, and Blackhawk personnel were sweeping the area with drones and four-wheelers for security, to set up training modules for the day. Our colleagues in-country paid the locals handsomely to stay out of the area.

The training called for Blue Gun exercises before live-fire exercises. Blue Guns are non-firing replica firearms, to eliminate the possibility of a training mishap.

Joe kept things lively with comments like, "Why can't I have a real gun?"

Our instructors included former and retired Secret Service guys, FBI agents, and Department of State types.

We started with classroom scenarios in a pop-up shelter, before heading out to warm up and get acclimated to the training vehicles. As the day progressed, the speeds increased as did the orange safety cones sent flying through the air when we botched an exercise.

"Christ," said Joe at one point, "I wonder if I show them my card from Mrs. Potter's Driving School, I can get out of this?"

We practiced two-point escape turns and driving in reverse at a high rate of speed. If you've ever driven in reverse at fifty or sixty miles per hour, you know it's not for the faint of heart and requires skills and practice.

We spent two days in a "rinse and repeat" mode.

The instructor said, "You'll be required to pass the driving skills test on day four, or you won't get certified. And if you don't pass, the only driving job you'll qualify for will be with Uber or Lyft."

I was along for the ride, so it wasn't critical for me to pass; but I did have my ego and pride, and I didn't want to let Billy down or embarrass him in front of his crew.

On day three we were back in the tent for Vehicle Assault Resistance (VAR) and Attack Recognition & Ambush Avoidance training.

We repeated each scenario and drill until they became smooth and second nature. We trained into the darkness, under limited and no-light conditions, fatigued and ready to drop. Intentional and by design.

If I gained weight visiting my mother, I was losing it in Baja, training in hundred-degree heat with no appetite. Here, it was all about hydration.

Day four kicked off with timed qualification tests for the driving portion of the training. We all passed, but Joe had to go through the driving-in-reverse portion a second time, to take a few seconds off his time and achieve a passing grade.

"Man, it's not natural," he said. "It's like walking backwards. Now, who the hell does that?"

With that he started to do the Michael Jackson moonwalk and had all of us, including the instructors, cracking up.

In the afternoon, we had live-fire exercises. Just the mention of live fire kept the clowning and grab-assing to a minimum.

Every aspect of live fire was under the strict and sober direction of the armorer and rangemaster. The rangemaster looked like he hadn't smiled since his mother tickled him as a baby.

Handgun malfunctions and what's known as Failure Drills were part of each exercise to replicate the things that can—and *do*—go wrong in a fire fight. Failure Drills are when a shooter fires two shots to the enemy's chest and one to the head to stop the attack. That way if the assailant is wearing body armor, and the two shots to the chest don't stop the threat, the head shot will. It's also known as the Mozambique Drill.

The background to the Mozambique Drill is tied to a Rhodesian mercenary by the name of Mike Rousseau when he was engaged in fighting for the Mozambican War of Independence. He was in a gun battle at the airport at Lourenco Marques and from about ten paces, he fired his Browning HP35 pistol and performed a double-tap, shooting his assailant twice in the sternum. When the guerrilla failed to go down, he fired a third shot that hit his adversary in the neck and severed his spine, ultimately killing him.

The mercenary told the story to an acquaintance, who later passed it on to two LAPD SWAT officers, who received permission to incorporate the drill into LAPD firearms training. It was later renamed Failure Drill—to avoid perceived racist undertones.

Both the malfunction and Failure Drill are taught by SFPD shooting instructors and are part of every officer's regular qualification requirement, so that part was easy for me.

When you combine desert temperatures and high-stress live-fire exercises, by 1900 hours we were trashed. Tomorrow would come soon enough, and we'd have final testing then.

Joe continued to whine. "When can we go home?"

Some jokes never get old.

On the way to the motel, the team agreed to drive to San Diego after final testing for a day of R&R before returning to our base camps or respective homes.

When we arrived at the motel, I told Billy to shower first to give me time to text Sophie and Lily.

Once again there was no response from Sophie. No surprise there. Lily texted back, but her response was terse.

10-8, CU later. Busy.

Her way of letting me know that she was on duty and still pissed.

I was hoping for something a little warmer, but who was I kidding? I was the one who pushed her away, and she was giving me what I had coming.

When Billy walked out of the bathroom wearing nothing but a bath towel, I looked up and said, "Billy, you're dead sexy and I could just eat you up like a box of chocolates."

With a straight face he dropped to his knees.

"Ray DeLuca," he said in his Okie drawl, "I've been waiting for this moment forever. Marry me. We'll move to Newburgh and adopt little bambinos."

I laughed until I was about to piss myself, then got in the shower.

Sleep came easy.

The following morning we were pumped, knowing we were in the home stretch.

The final exam consisted of blended scenarios of the previous day's exercises with Blue Guns. The instructors scored us individually, and as a team, and it was a good culmination of the week's training.

We all received Certificates of Achievement, and I made it a point to tell Joe he could frame it and put it next to his certificate for completing Home Economics in junior high.

The insults flew as we packed Rolling Thunder for the drive to San Diego. Homeward bound, as they say.

- 28 -

DON'T TUG ON SUPERMAN'S CAPE . . .

We **were anxious to leave** the arid heat of the desert and return to American soil. Within ten minutes of our departure, as we were leaving the salt flats, we were flagged down by what appeared to be Mexican Federales. They wore some type of paramilitary uniform, but after a closer look, it was unclear who they were. There were four of them, armed, and driving a beat-up Nissan SUV. My instincts told me, *no bueno.*

Billy took control.

"These boys ain't right. Time to go to work. Follow my lead. Joe, you interpret for me."

They immediately ordered us out of our vehicle at gunpoint and told us to kneel with our hands on our heads facing away from them. I understood words like *andale* [come on] and *tus manos* [your hands] and knew there was a sense of urgency. I got poked by the muzzle of a rifle, as they lined us up in firing squad fashion, and that *really* pissed me off.

"Poke me again motherfucker," I said, "and I'll stick that rifle so far up your ass, the muzzle will be coming out of your mouth!"

He obviously didn't understand, but my team chuckled.

I saw two of our captors enter Rolling Thunder and watched as they tried to pillage our equipment. The other two scumbags kept us at gunpoint and seemed to be the junior guys. The JV team, not ready for prime time.

Chaos was needed to bring this thing to an end.

"Heart attack! My heart!" I clutched my chest and feigned hyperventilating. I went to the ground and Billy jumped up to render aid.

In Spanish, Joe told them I was having a heart attack. As one of the captors started to yell and yank Billy off me, Billy turned and hit the guy in the balls and ripped his weapon from him.

Like a scene from *Apocalypse Now*, Billy shot the assailant and fired into the open door of Rolling Thunder, killing both suspects.

The fourth suspect ran for cover on the far side of the Nissan. We pulled the dead banditos out of Rolling Thunder and grabbed weapons to deal with suspect number four.

Before we were able to get in position, Billy grabbed the grenade launcher, hit the gas tank of the Nissan, and flambéed suspect number four, who had taken up a position at the rear of his vehicle.

As the last scumbag incinerated, Billy yelled, "Mount up!" and in a cloud of desert dust, we left the area at a high rate of speed to get back to the U.S. border.

"We're not stopping for *anybody*." he said. "By the time they figure this shit out, we'll be back in the U.S."

I called him the *Terminator* for the remainder of the drive up the coast.

There was a collective sigh of relief when we hit U.S. Route 5 racing northbound from Tijuana.

Our immediate destination was a Marriott Hotel in San Diego, close to the beach. Billy said he'd pick up the tab for the rooms, and I agreed to buy drinks at dinner.

After showers, we wasted no time finding our way to Ruth's Chris Steakhouse on North Harbor Drive. We went big and ordered twenty-two-ounce cowboy ribeyes, bloody, with lots of appetizers and sides.

We started with cocktails and ordered big cabernets to complement the steaks. After five days in the desert, we guzzled water like we'd never see it again and told the waiter to keep it coming.

The wait staff was exceptional and probably worried because we looked more like dine-and-dash types than the upscale clientele they were used to.

Other guests were probably wondering why the restaurant was now admitting pirates. We kept the conversation to a dull roar and skipped dessert in favor of more drinks at a bar closer to our hotel.

We found one on the beach and did more damage before calling it a night.

The next morning, with no texts from Sophie or Lily, I texted Hank to see if I'd get a response. Crickets.

I surmised either Lieutenant Flynn or Internal Affairs had put the word out I was to be avoided at all costs. *Persona non grata.* Or maybe they all decided I was a dick and not worth the trouble, which was a distinct possibility as well.

I felt bad for an instant, then thought *fuck 'em all.*

I gotta do me.

We went to the beach and, after an hour of lazing around, decided to shake it off and have a little fun. We swam to the breakers, had competitive foot races along the shoreline, then rented surfboards to amp things up. Other beachgoers scattered, like a herd of wildebeest had come through.

We wolfed down the cold cuts, beer, and snacks by midafternoon and headed back to the hotel to finalize flight arrangements. Back in the room, Billy approached me.

"Hey, Ray, you made a good impression on the team, and these outcasts don't like anybody. We'd love to have you join us. Fuck the SFPD. I've been authorized to offer you a base of a hundred thousand plus TDY."

By which he meant Temporary Duty Travel; in other words, most expenses paid above and beyond the hundred K.

"You'll make at least a hundred and fifty K year one and won't have to deal with that jerk-off lieutenant or your so-called friends who've turned their backs on you. I want you to think about it."

"Oh, I'll think about it," I said, "but right now I have stuff to deal with in San Francisco. Nobody's talking to me, and I want to get to the bottom of it. I've still got the suspension to deal with, too. I don't like unfinished business."

I reminded him I went through a lot of shit to join SFPD and was trying to salvage my career.

He wasn't one to hide his disappointment.

"Hey, don't worry," I said, "we can still get married, but I want more time to think about kids."

He laughed. "The offer stands, brother."

- 29 -

PERSONA NON GRATA

The flight was short, and we touched down at SFO late morning, landing into a dense bank of fog.

I planned to call Captain Choo at Central Station to see if they'd given me a hearing date yet for my suspension. I also needed to contact Tommy and ask for representation. He was a strong advocate for me with the incident at the Pings, and I was hopeful he'd represent me again with the insubordination charge. My growing reputation at SFPD now included *doesn't play well with others.*

I retrieved my mail after I tossed my seabag into the apartment and opened an official-looking letter from SFPD setting my hearing date for early the next week. No need to bother the captain.

I also received a short, cryptic letter from my fan club aka the Ghost Boys. Two words.

Dead duck.

It looked like it was written by a third grader and signed with Chinese characters. With my Chinese a little rusty, I'd leave it to CSI and the inspectors to decipher. I called Sergeant Smethurst, who'd escorted me out of the station the night I was suspended, and told him what I'd received.

"Try not to handle the letter without gloves," he said. "Put it in an envelope and bring it to the station, and we'll book it with the report about your case. Write out a quick supplemental report to go with it so we can attach it to the insubordination case. Make sure you also reference the earlier case with the death at the Pings. We need it all cross-referenced."

He informed me the Ghost Boys put a bounty on my head. He said an informant told him the bounty was fifty thousand dollars to put me in the dirt.

I laughed. "That's all I'm worth? You can't buy much with fifty K these days. I *was* hoping for a hundred thou, minimum."

My gallows humor was lost on him.

"Ray, we gotta take this seriously. These guys aren't fuckin' around. Everyone's been trying to reach you for the last week. What's the deal?"

"I was out of town and needed some space. Didn't mean to cause a panic. I kept my location confidential for personal safety reasons."

"Well, we sent Daly City PD to your apartment for a welfare check."

A welfare check is conducted to check on someone's well-being. It's not indicative of any need I might have for public assistance.

"The apartment manager told us you were out of town and said he was watching the place for you. He let us in to prove there was no foul play or reason for concern."

"I know. The Daly City officer left his business card with a note. The apartment manager told me about it, too.

"Look, I don't want to leave any breadcrumbs for the Ghost Boys. That's why I'm off the grid. I was ordered to turn in my duty weapon and police ID when I was suspended, so I've been running around with no ID and no way to defend myself.

"With all due respect, if something happens to me and I can't defend myself, that's on SFPD, and I'll make sure my attorney is aware of it."

"I understand. Get the threat letter to me and lay low. I'd suggest moving out of Daly City to someplace remote or stay with a friend or relative."

I wanted to reply, *thank you, Captain Obvious,* but didn't know him well enough, and his capacity for humor seemed a couple of quarts low.

"Hopefully, they'll get your suspension lifted soon. I know you're a good cop, so hang in there; and off-the-record, I'd carry a piece anyway. It's your life. And I never told you that."

"Thanks."

"I'll call Daly City PD when we hang up," he said, "and ask them to help with surveillance outside your apartment. I'll ask Captain Choo to coordinate with them for coverage. If you've got some personal weapons at home, keep 'em close."

He had good intentions, but clearly doesn't know me at all because Ray's gonna take care of Ray at all costs. Always have. Always will.

I'd been packing heat all along.

- 30 -

A COZY COTTAGE BY THE SEA

I **searched apartment rental websites** to find new digs and was excited to find one in Pacifica on the coast. I remembered Lee Tyler's name, the Pacifica officer Hank had mentioned, and decided to give him a call to see if he had information about the safety of the area.

I was able to reach him through police dispatch, and he seemed happy to talk.

"Did you ever catch the Creamsicle killer?" he asked.

I chuckled. "Not yet. It's been a tough case. When we catch him, though, I'll buy you a case of Creamsicles or Fudgesicles. Whatever you prefer!"

He hesitated. "Ice cream sandwiches."

"Right," I said. "Hey, the reason I'm calling is I'm looking at an apartment off Skyline Boulevard in your fine city. If I give you the address, can you see if you guys get a lot of calls for service over there?"

"I'll do you one better," he said. "I've got a buddy renting a cottage, but it's in the southern district, in Shelter Cove, down by the beach. Not everybody wants to live out there because it's remote, but it's a nice setup. If you're interested, I'll give you my buddy's number, and you can use my name as a reference."

I called the property owner and after an online video tour, decided the place would work. I completed the rental application online, and listed Mike at Lake Merced Arms as a reference. I got a call back from the landlord in record time, welcoming me to my new cottage in Shelter Cove.

Safe to assume Mike had my back on this one and conveniently forgot to mention the shooting at my apartment just weeks before. *Oorah!*

The landlord described the cottage as a hideaway in rocky, overgrown terrain. "I hope that won't be a problem."

If he only knew the rocky terrain I've called home.

As a bonus, he told me Shelter Cove had its own beach where I could surf and get a workout in. I could cancel my membership at the swim club and use those dollars for moving expenses.

The one-bedroom cottage was, as advertised, rustic and hidden behind large rocks, scrub brush, and overgrown manzanita trees . . . almost impossible to find without GPS.

The galley kitchen and bathroom were recently updated, and that was a plus. The rest of the place was funky, with the main source of heat a pellet stove. A primitive outdoor shower, with an old surfboard perched against it, completed the cool California beach vibe.

I could smell the salt air and the woody, medicinal fragrance from the eucalyptus trees in the area.

There was also a secluded gravel parking area behind the cottage where I could park my car and motorcycle. I'd yet to purchase the motorcycle but planned to buy a used café racer. The bike would help me avoid detection and flee more rapidly if I was being pursued.

A full-face helmet with a tinted visor and used leathers would make me practically invisible on Bay Area roadways. I'd look like the thousands of other motorcycle riders, lane-splitting and zipping around.

★ ★ ★

I stopped by Central Station to give the threat letter to Smethurst and, as I walked through the squad room, saw Hank pecking away on a report. When he spotted me, he abruptly stood and motioned to follow him downstairs to the locker room.

"You sure you want to be seen talking to me?" I asked. "I'm suspended. *Persona non grata.*"

He ignored the comment.

"Look, Ray, rumors started when no one could reach you. You know how cops talk. Flynn even suggested you'd gone to Italy to bring back more soldiers to take out the Ghost Boys."

I laughed. "If I wanted the Ghost Boys gone, I wouldn't need mob guys to do it. I'd take care of it myself."

Hank gave me a look like he was going to chirp at me—then thought better of it.

"Okay. Well, in other news . . . just a heads-up that I saw your dream girl Sophie coming out of Carmine's restaurant on Vinnie Catalano's arm. All dressed up. Looked like they were on a date. Couple of nights ago. Probably had dinner together."

Now, that was a punch in the gut I didn't expect.

"You sure?"

He nodded. "Yup."

Now I knew why she'd been ignoring my texts.

Before I could digest what Hank said, he added that gang activity was over-the-top with bodies on both sides piling up. There was talk of forming two new task forces: one to focus on the Sicilians, and the other on the Ghost Boys.

"You should be first in line to grab a spot," he said. "You're one of them."

Yeah, I thought, *if you only knew the half of it.*

"So, I can expect to see you on the Chinatown Task Force, Hop Sing?"

He rolled his eyes. "Remains to be seen."

"Well, you're closer to a task force spot than me. I still have the suspension hearing, and because I'm technically on probation, they can fire me if I forget to zip my pants.

"I have the hearing in a few days, and we'll see what happens. There's also a bounty on my head. I'm sure you're aware of that. I've got to be careful, and it's better I'm off the streets now anyway. I gotta bounce."

"Aren't you going to ask about Lily?"

I deliberately hadn't, as a matter of fact. "I gotta go, Hank."

I walked into the sergeant's office and handed him the evidence envelope with the threat letter.

"Go knock out the supplemental report to go with this and you can leave. Thanks."

Fifteen minutes later, I was in the wind.

I donned my government-issued boonie hat and sunglasses and left through the side door of the station into the alley.

I sprinted to my car, checked for the small piece of paper I left in the crack of the driver's door, then inspected the undercarriage for explosives with a small telescopic mirror. So far, so good.

I took a serpentine route through side streets, back alleys, and short stretches of freeway to return to Daly City, keeping an eye out for a tail.

The next day, I rented a truck and offered Mike a couple of hundred bucks to help me move.

I'm a military guy, so I don't own a lot. I'm used to short stays and rapid deployments. We started packing the truck at eight, and by nine-thirty, were on our way to Shelter Cove.

I shed no tears leaving Daly City.

- 31 -

TOO GOOD TO BE TRUE

It *didn't take long to move in* and orient myself to the area. It's the beauty of being a minimalist. I'm like a monk. Give me a room, a blanket, and a hot plate, and I'm good to go. The cottage, not far from the beach, was small and drafty. I could smell the faint odor of mildew and salt air inside the cottage. After unpacking, I drove to a local hardware store to buy weather stripping and a space heater. From there, I made a quick stop at a department store to buy a comforter for my bed and air deodorizers. The place started to warm up, smell better, and come together. It was beginning to feel like home. At least for now.

The neighbors were a good distance away, hidden behind berms of ice plant, eucalyptus, and Monterey cypress trees, which could be defensively advantageous.

I surveyed the area, to find routes in and out of the cove with minimal detection. A couple of large rock outcroppings on the property proved ideal for setting up tactical positions.

I stowed and camouflaged waterproof ammo containers containing loaded AR-15 magazines at those locations.

I also installed trip wires and trigger flares around the perimeter to activate high-intensity strobe lights, should uninvited guests attempt to breach the property at night. No muss, no fuss. Basic SEAL 101 tactics.

The activation of the strobe lights would trigger an alert on my cell and beep in my bedroom. I bought a thermal imaging monocular as well, to detect humans, animals, and other radiant objects in complete darkness. I had fifty thousand reasons to double down on my physical security.

I found a beat-up used Ducati at an independent motorcycle dealer in San Francisco. It was painted flat black and looked nasty but had new tires and ran like a beast. The mechanic knew the bike and assured me the motor was solid.

"Don't judge it by its appearance," he said.

"Yeah, that's what I tell the women I meet."

I bought waterproof camo covers to keep my car and bike concealed behind the cottage.

I drove the motorcycle most of the time and used my helmet with a full-face shield to mask my identity. Old jeans, used leathers, T-shirts, hats, and sunglasses helped complete the disguise.

I looked like any other dirtbag on a motorcycle and got second looks from cops and CHP officers looking for probable cause to pull me over.

I drove the bike to my suspension hearing, wearing my grunge attire. I couldn't risk being spotted by Ghost Boys and needed to blend in.

Lieutenant Flynn, Captain Martinez, and a black sergeant named Rose were behind a table facing me as I entered the hearing room. Each gave me the once-over. I got looks of disgust and disdain as I sat in one of two small wooden chairs facing them.

I started to apologize for my appearance and explain the reason for the getup, but before I could get it out, I got the talk-to-the-hand gesture from Martinez who had a reputation as a by-the-book, tight-ass prick.

Perfect!

He wasted no time explaining that the felony assault charge for the incident South of Market would be taken up separately by Internal Affairs and the District Attorney.

"Our questions today are specifically regarding possible insubordination. Do you understand?"

I wanted to say, *are you fuckin' serious? Do you know who I am?!*

I gritted my teeth. "Sir, I spent sixteen years in the military and was a chief petty officer of a Navy SEAL unit. I'm well-versed regarding conduct and behavior."

He had a look of surprise on his face and paused. "Did you in fact say, 'Fuck you,' to Lieutenant Flynn when you were being questioned about the assault?"

I admitted I did and tried to explain why. They yelled over each other to cut me off and remind me I was *again* being insubordinate. They acted appalled like they'd never heard the f-bomb before, which I found amusing. I wanted to say, *and fuck you, too,* to all three of them.

The captain said if I kept interrupting them, they'd charge me with a second count of insubordination. Thin blue line shit. Unreal. I could feel them closing ranks on me like an illegal chokehold. Their anger and contempt for me were palpable.

My union rep, Tommy, walked in just as the hearing was starting to boil over.

He had a cooling effect. "My apologies, sirs. I was tied up in court. Here's a copy of the subpoena."

He placed the document on their table.

He removed his service cap, and I was right all along. Big time male-pattern baldness. I smiled inside, keeping it to myself.

Tommy listened intently as the captain gave an overview of our discussion prior to his arrival.

He respectfully waited until they were done. "Sir, I'd like to explain both Officer DeLuca's position and that of the POA." The Police Officers Association.

The captain nodded. "Proceed."

"Officer DeLuca was off duty and on a first date with a young lady.

"They had just left the Metreon, when they were accosted by four individuals Officer DeLuca recognized as Ghost Boy gang members. He said he had no doubt who they were. He recognized their gang tattoos. He reported they had GB-SF dragon tattoos on their necks."

The captain started to interrupt, but Tommy gave no ground. "Do you want to hear what I have to say, sir, or keep talking over me?"

Reluctant to take on a union rep, especially one as connected as Tommy, the captain conceded. "Go ahead."

"Officer DeLuca said the suspects started to taunt them, but they kept walking, attempting to get back to their car, trying to ignore the remarks. The suspects wouldn't let up and came up beside them in lockstep. They threatened to rape his date and then physically assaulted her by smacking her repeatedly across the backside.

"Officer DeLuca was outnumbered four to one and took offensive action to neutralize the assault so he could get them out of harm's way. Officer DeLuca was not armed and at no time identified himself as a police officer."

The captain went to interrupt, and Tommy sternly interjected. "Let me finish, Captain!

"Officer DeLuca was contacted on his cell later that evening and told to respond to Central Station. He immediately responded, and when he attempted to explain the situation to Lieutenant Flynn, the lieutenant dressed him down and accused *him* of initiating the fight. The lieutenant also verbalized he was concerned about the city getting sued."

Flynn's face turned red and with a raised voice. "That's total bullshit!"

The captain intervened, "That's enough, Lieutenant. Let him finish."

Tommy continued. "Officer DeLuca said it made him feel like he was the suspect, rather than the assailants.

"It was during Officer DeLuca's frustrating defense of his actions that he said 'fuck you' to Lieutenant Flynn. I think the fact that Officer DeLuca was almost murdered, most likely by Ghost Boy gang members the previous night in Daly City, should be taken into consideration.

"I have copies of Daly City PD's report for you to review, in case you don't have it.

"I hope you'll understand Officer DeLuca's state of mind and the totality of the circumstances, as you review his suspension. It's the union's position that, other than losing his cool with Lieutenant Flynn, he really did no wrong here. He's a good officer, and he's been maligned and was disrespected. He should be reinstated without delay."

The panel grumbled among themselves and said they'd take the matter under advisement.

I knew from experience that taking anything under advisement means you lose.

"Very good," said the captain. "You'll both receive our decision in writing by certified mail within seven days. Dismissed." Tommy and I got up to leave, and I could feel the daggers in my back as we exited the hearing room.

Outside, I thanked Tommy for his representation and told him if the same thing happened again, I'd do it again. "Flynn's an arrogant prick who's had it out for me. He's treated me like shit since my first day at Central. It's all about him and covering his ass. He doesn't give a shit about his troops. Whatever they decide, I'll deal with it. He's a bully hiding behind his rank. Thanks, Tommy."

"I hear ya, Ray. I'll do my best. Technically, you *were* insubordinate; but under the circumstances, they should give you an admonishment, with minimal punishment. Your frame of mind and everything that led up to the incident should be considered."

"And look," I said, "I know the board took my grungy appearance as a sign of disrespect and contempt for the process. I tried to explain why I have the grungy appearance, but they weren't interested. It's that kind of bullshit that makes me crazy. Give a guy a fuckin' chance!"

I'd anticipated today's clown show, so I bought groceries earlier in the day knowing "food therapy" would be in order.

After a steak and salad, I found a spot behind the cottage to build a firepit with rocks. I used an old cooler as a table and put a couple of old Adirondack chairs next to the fire.

Shelter Cove gets cool when the sun goes down and fog and ocean mist roll in. I lit a cigar and texted Lily.

904 Wed. night?

I hit send and took a deep breath. 904 is the code for requesting a meetup with another officer.

After several minutes, she texted back a thumbs-up. I replied with the time and place and was surprised when she accepted the invitation. We hadn't connected in weeks.

Then my thoughts went to Sophie. I was still struggling with her involvement with Vinnie.

She was young and naïve, and at least in this case, not a good judge of character. I was obsessing like a teenager.

I watered down the firepit and walked the perimeter of the property before going inside for the night. The smell of the salt air and tranquility of Shelter Cove were agreeing with me, and I hoped it would stay that way.

- 32 -

THE LETTER OF ILL-INTENT

Months had passed since Carmine Vaccaro's torso washed ashore at Linda Mar Beach, half eaten by sea creatures. His death was still classified as "suspicious circumstances," with strong suspicions of foul play by SFPD homicide inspectors.

His death rocked the culinary world, and the locals in North Beach probably took it the hardest. His fate was debated daily in cafés and bars throughout North Beach.

Vinnie thought enough time had passed to pay Carmine's sister, Gina, a visit at the restaurant. He was anxious to enforce the Letter of Intent and assume control of Carmine's restaurant.

Vinnie originally met Carmine through Gina, who he had a date with a year earlier. He met her at a hospitality event and was attracted to her from the first time he saw her.

When she wasn't interested in sex on the first date, Vinnie thought she was aloof and playing hard to get. He lost interest and wrote her off as a cold bitch, but after seeing her at Carmine's funeral, his interest was reignited. He showed up at Carmine's early on a Saturday morning with two dozen yellow roses. It was widely known that yellow was Carmine's favorite color.

Gina was caught off guard but was cordial, offering him an espresso and pastries to be hospitable.

Vinnie made small talk, asking how she was doing, but soon focused on how things were going with the restaurant.

"We're still mourning," she said. "I'll never get over losing him. He was so creative and had so much energy. Carmine was so proud of this restaurant. He inspires us every day."

Vinnie took her comments as his opening and explained the reason for his visit.

"I didn't want to burden you with this earlier because I know you've been grieving. After you introduced us, me and Carmine became friends. Just before he disappeared, we made a pact and an agreement regarding the restaurant. We wanted to be partners."

She scrunched her face. "What agreement?"

"I know after he lost his deal with the Food Network, he needed to replace some of the lost income. I told him I'd buy into Carmine's for two hundred thousand and handle day-to-day operations to relieve him of the burden. He liked the idea because he wanted to concentrate on the new show he was working on. I'm surprised he didn't tell you. We signed a deal. I take sixty percent of the net profits and you get forty."

"Honestly," said Gina, "this is the first I'm hearing about it. I'm surprised because Carmine usually told me about things like this."

Vinnie produced the Letter of Intent signed by her brother and handed her a copy. It looked like Carmine's signature, but she couldn't be sure.

She noticed only Vinnie dated his signature on the document, but Carmine didn't. He was used to signing autographs, so a lot of times he'd just scribble his signature and forget to date things. The date following Vinnie's signature was prior to Carmine's disappearance.

Vinnie handed Gina a copy of the agreement and a bank check for two hundred thousand dollars.

"Gina, you can show this to your lawyer, and I'm sure he'll tell you it's legally binding. It was Carmine's wish for us to be in this partnership.

"I'm not sure why he didn't tell you, but he probably hadn't found the right time and had a lot on his mind. I waited until now, out of respect for you and your family."

She noticed her hands were shaking. "I need to discuss it with my lawyer. You should leave."

"Sorry, Gina, this is business. After you talk to your attorney, we can get together to work out the details."

There was something about her sophisticated looks, and seeing her in emotional pain and suffering, that was turning him on.

It made her vulnerable and though he was sexually aroused, now was not the time for that. That, too, would have to wait, but he was looking forward to the day.

He quietly stood and left the restaurant without saying goodbye. Gina sat and began to cry.

When she calmed herself, she called her attorney. "Why would Carmine do something like this?"

"I don't know, Gina. Maybe he was worried about money. An infusion of cash would have given him some peace of mind."

"No," Gina said, "I don't think so. He had plenty of money!"

"Maybe there was more to it, and he just wanted to be free of some of his responsibilities? Come in Monday and bring the agreement, and I'll review it."

She stashed the check and the letter in her purse. She was hoping for a loophole in the contract; but either way, having help to run the restaurant *was* tempting, and Vinnie had earned those Michelin Stars.

She'd been working seven days a week since Carmine's passing and felt overwhelmed. But now a sense of dread washed over her. Things were starting to make sense.

She thought, Vinnie had to be behind Carmine's death, but how would they ever prove it? She felt nauseous when she remembered going on a date with him and felt partly responsible because she introduced them. She knew she had to come to terms with it all.

- 33 -

SURFING IN SARDINIA?

With a bounty on my head and nothing to do but mark time, I hopped on my bike to drive south to Santa Cruz to attend a competitive surfing event.

My Pacifica PD buddy, Lee Tyler, mentioned it, so I thought I'd check it out. He's an avid surfer and knows I'm interested in developing my skills. With Shelter Cove only minutes from great surfing, my interest in the sport had been rekindled.

Maybe I'd become the next Italian surfing sensation, like Leonardo Fioravanti or Roberto D'Amico. I watched surfing as a kid in Sicily, and a lot of U.S. surfing enthusiasts aren't aware of the incredible surfing off the coast of Sardinia.

Before I left the cottage, I checked the front door camera, game cameras, and trip wires, to make sure they were live. I also told Lee Tyler about the Ghost Boy bounty on my head. He worked the southern beat and told me he'd keep an eye on Shelter Cove as time permitted during his shift.

He rightfully was reluctant to share the intelligence with other Pacifica officers because if someone innocently let the info slip, it could make its way back to the Ghost Boys. Stranger things have happened.

Years ago, the guns used by the Joe Boys in the Golden Dragon Massacre were, in fact, kept at a house in Pacifica, so gang affiliations and allegiances could still exist there. We both agreed that, when it comes to intelligence, it's safer when fewer people know.

I didn't tell anyone at SFPD about the safe house, and Mike at Lake Merced Apartments was acutely aware of the danger I was in. He'd become a friend, and I was confident he'd be the last one to give up my location. He's a Marine.

I got a post office box to avoid giving anyone my physical address. I locked things down as much as I could. While I wasn't impossible to find, I wasn't going to make it easy; and if the Ghost Boys did find me, I had a few surprises for them.

The ride down Highway 1 is among the most scenic you can take in California, especially on a motorcycle. The highway is cut into the coastal cliffs, and the ocean below glistened with rocks and sandy beaches. While my bike isn't for show, it was made for this kind of winding road. I watched for a tail, but as fast as I was going, it would have been hard for anyone to keep up with me. I was satisfied I was alone.

I grabbed a breakfast burrito at an outdoor café in Santa Cruz and enjoyed the warm morning rays before heading for the beach.

The event was the annual Santa Cruz Longboard Competition, and teams of surfers were vying for prizes. I spent the day watching the competition, eating junk food, talking to other surfing enthusiasts, and visiting vendor booths. As a novice, a lot of it was new to me.

It was a nice distraction spending the day in the sun at the beach. The sights and boardwalk smells of corn dogs, pizza, and sweet treats reminded me of my family's trips to the Jersey Shore as a kid.

I can still see my father wearing a black Ban-Lon polo shirt, dress slacks, and white loafers as we piled into his burgundy 1975 Lincoln Continental Mark IV for the drive to the shore. My father used to say his Lincoln was more comfortable than our living room. At least in the Lincoln, we didn't have plastic slipcovers.

The neighbors used to joke that my father wore dress slacks and shoes whether he was going to church or shoveling snow. The look and style also worked for him as beach wear, and for just about any occasion.

I bought a classic Hobie Surfboards long-sleeved T-shirt with the date of the surfing competition as a memento. I bought one for Lily, too—as a peace offering.

I caught an incredible purple and orange sunset on the ride back up the coast. I couldn't stop thinking about Sophie and Lily. It would have been nice to have one of them riding on the back of the bike to enjoy the day with. I was lonely and looking forward to dinner with Lily the following night.

As I drove into El Granada, I realized I was being followed by a red Pontiac GTO with Asian males in the front seats. They were spinning their tires at stop lights and coming within a few feet of my bike. I didn't recognize them but didn't want to take chances. When they pulled alongside me at a red light, I sensed their stares, but ignored them, and decided to lose them.

I popped a wheelie and ran the light and had the bike up to ninety in a matter of seconds.

I leaned forward onto the gas tank and maintained my speed, passing other vehicles every opportunity I got.

They were nowhere in sight when I pulled into Half Moon Bay, so I slowed down but stayed alert.

When I got to Shelter Cove, I turned the bike's running lights off and approached the cottage cautiously, scanning for signs of a breach. With no sign of trespassers, I was ready to call it a day. Staying vigilant was exhausting.

- 34 -

NO DAY AT THE BEACH!

As *I put my feet up*, my mother called to see if I received the latest box of goodies she sent. I explained I had moved and would need to track the box down with my former apartment manager because they probably left it at my old address. She was disappointed, so I promised to pick it up as soon as possible.

She asked how the disciplinary hearing went.

"Not good, Ma."

Mothers see through lies, even the little white ones, so I had to be direct.

"Every time I tried to explain myself, they shut me down."

I told her I'd probably get a letter about their decision by the end of the week.

When I rehashed how the initial incident happened leading to the suspension, I could hear her sigh on the other end of the line.

In Sicialian she said, "Ray-Ray, you're just like your father. When someone treats him bad, look out. He's got that Sicilian temper. I know you said what you had to to that lieutenant. No matter what happens, your father and I love you and we're here for you. Well, at least one of us is here. Your father is still staying at the resort in Danbury. The one he's not allowed to leave."

We laughed and I told her I had to go to meet a friend for dinner.

She perked up. "Is she Italian?"

"No, Ma. The Italian girl doesn't like me anymore."

Another sigh. This time resignation.

★ ★ ★

It was a quick ride to Half Moon Bay to meet Lily at Sam's Chowder House for dinner. The place was packed, and I was glad I was on the bike. It made parking a breeze in their overcrowded lot. I told her to meet me on the beach side of the restaurant.

As Lily came into view, I watched as she scanned the crowd looking for me. She looked directly at me and past me twice.

I forgot she hadn't seen the stubble beard and the new look. She was surprised when I approached her in biker clothes, sporting a skullcap and aviator sunglasses.

"I've gotta lay low for now."

She smiled. "You're kind of cute with a beard."

I leaned in. "C'mon," I said, "I'm a lot of things, but cute ain't one of 'em."

We sat outside near the heat lamps, by the firepit, and devoured a dozen Kumamoto oysters and both ordered bowls of steaming hot cioppino with garlic bread. Much of their seafood is locally sourced and caught off the coast of Half Moon Bay.

The air got chilly as the fog rolled in, but the food, salt air, and the sound of waves crashing made it worthwhile. A live jazz quartet with a sultry female vocalist set the mood.

Lily updated me on Central Station gossip, including the speculation about my return.

"A lot of guys think you're toast because you're still on probation. They can fire you for anything."

"Well, that's encouraging. Appreciate the vote of confidence."

"Sorry, Ray."

She redirected the conversation back to the gang war.

"I don't know who's winning, but it seems like it's getting worse every day. I heard the Ghost Boys are starting to rebuild old opium dens. Probably the same ones their grandparents and great-grandparents used back in the day. My mother told me they used to transport opium on ships from Vietnam and China."

Lily had an encyclopedic knowledge of Chinatown and explained a lot of opium dens were destroyed in the 1906 earthquake, but some were rebuilt in the 1920s.

Growing up in Chinatown, she knew its history and dirty little secrets her mother shared.

"If you think Chinatown is some quaint tourist attraction with little souvenir shops and cable cars, you're wrong. It's what goes on in the back rooms and basements. Chinese people are secretive, and they don't want anyone to know what they're up to."

She was talkative and always interesting.

"That's why, with the heat in Chinatown right now, they've got surveillance cameras all over the place and lookouts on every block. The lookouts are mostly kids who hold the gang's guns, too. They're wannabes and expendable because they won't do serious time for a gun charge. They're closing ranks to protect their way of life.

"Gambling, drugs, extortion, prostitution, underage sex trafficking, identity theft, stuff like that. That's how they make their living. I grew up there. Most people are decent, but there's always a lot of shit going on behind closed doors and in the alleys and shadows."

I was getting an education, so I didn't interrupt.

"The Ghost Boys have Chinatown on a communication lockdown," she said, "and the smart ones keep their mouths shut."

When I asked where she got her intel from, she laughed.

"You want a bounty on my head, too? Any moves by the Sicilians to take over their action is gonna mean more blood in the streets. Sorry, but Ghost Boys have home-court advantage. Most of them were born and raised here."

A lot had happened since my suspension only a few weeks earlier. We knew the Sicilians had taken sleepy North Beach by storm. North Beach and Broadway merchants were being extorted and forced to pay protection money. The strip clubs had always been fronts for prostitution and drug trafficking, but now the mob was demanding their slice, too.

More guns, more shootings, and an increase in assaults and rapes. It was a lot to take in.

"Okay, okay," I said, "enough cop talk. I've got to ask you: Are you mad at me because I went back East to visit my family and disappeared for a couple of weeks?"

"Ray, I'm not mad at you, but I'm a little hurt. When you left, I thought you'd be in touch more. Before you left, I thought we were headed in the right direction, then you pushed me away. I'm not sure anymore. Maybe we should just let things be. You've got a lot going on, and I don't want to put demands on you right now."

As I was contemplating what she said, I looked up and was startled by three Asian males with GB-SF tattoos on their necks. One of them was talking to the hostess.

"Don't turn around, but there's three Ghost Boys about twenty feet behind you. I'm gonna walk down the beach and circle back to my bike. Can we meet back at your place to finish this?"

Before she could answer, I handed her my credit card and asked her to take care of the bill with the waitress.

"I'll see you in about an hour."

I bounded down to the beach and walked away, pulling my skullcap down over my ears. I turned my face toward the surf and fast-walked away from the restaurant. From about thirty yards down the beach, I did an about-face and sprinted back to the parking lot to make my getaway. It was a close call, but I'm not sure they would have recognized me anyway, but I couldn't risk it.

Sam's is a popular destination, so it was a dumb choice on my part. There are plenty of other out-of-the-way places where we could have met, but Sam's has incredible fresh seafood, with a world-class view of the Pacific.

I parked my bike on Montgomery Street, below the steep hill where Lily's apartment was located on the crest of Vallejo Street. I sat on steps across from her flat and didn't reveal myself until she approached her doorstep. I unintentionally startled her when I came up behind her.

"Sorry. Didn't mean to spook ya."

I sat on the couch as she poured us each two fingers of Monkey Shoulder Whiskey.

She handed me a glass. "I think we need this. That was too close, Ray, and I'm sure they were packing. I wasn't. Were you?"

I laughed and pulled up the hem of my ragged and torn jeans to show her the Kimber Micro 9-millimeter strapped to my ankle. I also had a five-inch Ka-Bar knife stuffed down my other boot.

She smiled.

"Hey. You're not supposed to be carrying. You're suspended."

"Okay. So, I've got these gangbangers who have a bounty on my life, and I'm *not* supposed to defend myself? Well, good luck with that, Girl Scout, because Ray's gonna take care of Ray."

I gave her the T-shirt I bought in Santa Cruz, and she held it up against her chest. "I love it!"

The she kissed me.

I tried to continue the conversation we were having at Sam's, but she moved in close. "Drop it. Let's not talk about it anymore." The smoky smell of scotch on her breath was intoxicating.

She took my hand and led me into the bedroom where we collapsed on the bed and picked up where we left off before I went to New York.

I'm nervous before sex because I've run hot and cold. Too much time in the bush without intimacy. We enjoyed each other and did what came naturally. She seemed satisfied, but who knows? I know we released a lot of pent-up frustration and had no trouble falling asleep afterward.

At about seven a.m., Lily's phone began to vibrate and blink. She grabbed it.

"Hey, Hank. What's up?"

I was tempted to grab the phone and ask him what the fuck he was doing calling Lily. I didn't. She put her phone on speaker, so I could listen to the conversation.

". . . won't believe it. We arrested Vinnie Catalano last night after he slapped his girlfriend outside of Carmine's restaurant.

"The girl was hysterical and signed a C-A. They took him into custody for 243e."

C-A, meaning Citizen's Arrest form; 243e, meaning Domestic Violence with no visible injury.

"Holy shit!" Lily said.

"Yeah, I just thought you'd like to know. When Ray hears about it, he's gonna blow up. She's the hot Italian chick he got suspended for when he beat up the Ghost Boys South of Market. He's crazy for that girl."

After Lily hung up, she turned to me. "Well, there ya go. You heard it!"

"No surprise," I said. "I heard she was dating him. I thought she was smarter than that."

Hank's remarks put more salt in the wound.

★ ★ ★

Lily wanted to go to Mama's for breakfast, but I told her I couldn't take a chance, with the restaurant only blocks from Chinatown and the Ghost Boys.

We made bacon and eggs together, and after I cleaned the kitchen, I got ready to head out. Lily wanted to know where I was living now.

"It's better you don't know. I'm living in a rabbit hole in the woods and need to stay off the grid until this Ghost Boys threat is over. If there's an emergency, and you can't reach me, call Lee Tyler at Pacifica PD. I'll give you his number. He's the only one who knows where I'm staying. He knows how to find me, and, hopefully, I can trust him."

I pulled my beanie down over my forehead and ears and put my sunglasses on to jog to my bike. The only visible part of my face was beard stubble.

I drove up Broadway, past Chinatown, and through the Broadway Tunnel to South Van Ness to get on the Bayshore Freeway for the drive home.

As I rolled into Shelter Cove, I glanced into each car I passed and approached the cottage on high alert. I parked the bike then inspected my security system.

Except for a mangy coyote who skulked in front of the game camera in the middle of the night, I saw no other activity. I did a sweep of the inside of the cottage and checked stash locations for weapons. All good, combat-ready, good to go.

The inside of the cottage was chilly, so I lit the pellet stove, and as I was settling in, my phone rang. Vinnie Catalano. The call caught me off guard, so I let it go to voicemail.

He spoke in Italian. "Hey, paisan, I had a little trouble with some of your officers last night over a misunderstanding with a girl. They arrested me, but I'm out on bail. Call me when you get this. I need your opinion on something."

Inside voice: *You want my opinion? You're an asshole, and I want to beat your ass. If you ever lay a hand on Sophie again, or any other woman, I will come hunt you down like the dog you are. And frankly, "dog" is too good a word for you. I like dogs. Let me see, you allegedly smacked a girl I'm in love with and I'm gonna help you? Please tell me why. Besides, I'm officially suspended and don't have the authority to write a parking ticket.*

I needed to cool off before returning his call; I had to keep him close.

An hour later, I returned his call. He picked up on the first ring. He ranted about how he had an argument with a girl outside of Carmine's restaurant. He claimed she disrespected him in front of an employee, so he slapped her. He said they'd both had too much to drink.

"Hey, I shouldn't have done it. I was wrong. The girl went nuts and got hysterical and somebody called the cops. I don't think it was her. The cops showed up and arrested me. I told the officers I was a friend of yours, and one of them said, 'So what? DeLuca's getting bounced anyway.'"

Vinnie hesitated. Perhaps it was a pause for effect.

"Now, *that* was disrespectful to you! He's the one I should have slapped!"

We both laughed.

"It sounded like they were booting you out. You good?"

"I'm fine. I told my supervisor to fuck off, so they suspended me. The guy's got no sense of humor. We'll see what happens. I'll probably be fired."

"*Marone*," he said. "I tell five people to fuck off before I've had my morning coffee. No big deal! Must have thin skin there."

"Anyway, Vinnie, the department takes domestic violence seriously, and you shouldn't be smacking a woman."

"I know. I know. So, what do you think they're going to do with something like this?"

"I don't know."

And why was he asking me? I assumed he had a good lawyer.

"Here's what I'd suggest," I said. "Send the girl you assaulted an apology through your attorney. You might want to use a female attorney for this. Then, after you apologize, stay away from her, and don't have any more contact with her. Not ever! I mean, the judge is gonna tell you the same thing. No phone calls, no texts, no emails, no flowers, no letters, no contact at all. The judge will grant her a restraining order, so you'll be ordered to stay away from her anyway. If you violate the court order, the judge will put you in jail, so don't mess around."

Vinnie sighed. "Well, I guess that's that."

He thanked me for calling him back. "Even with all this bullshit with the girl, I've got some good news. I made a deal with Carmine before he disappeared, to partner with him on his restaurant. Did you guys ever find out what happened to him?"

"Nah, the investigation's still in progress. To be honest with you, I'm out of the loop on that one anyway."

"I understand," said Vinnie. "I waited a couple of months to tell his sister about our deal, but we worked it out and now I'm part owner and running Carmine's, too. Come down to the restaurant and let me know what you think. You're *famiglia* and always welcome. It's on the house."

A chill ran through me as I thanked him and ended the call.

If I had any doubts about Vinnie's involvement in Carmine's death, they were now gone. The thing of it was I liked him and *hoped* I was wrong. I'd have to tell Hank to let homicide know about the restaurant deal, in case they didn't know already.

I pondered Sophie's situation and struggled to understand her. I didn't understand her choices and her mercurial emotions. I chalked it up to youth and naïveté. I barely knew her, but God knows I wanted to.

She fell apart when I tried to defend her and went crazy when Vinnie slapped her. A lot of wild emotions and drama there.

Fortunately, most young women her age haven't seen the violent side of men. She was a sweet girl, and I felt bad she had to experience any of it. If I could have talked to her, I would have told her to stay clear of Vinnie, but I'm on her shit list as well. That ship has sailed, and I deeply regretted it.

I imagined she was hating all men these days, especially me and Vinnie.

- 35 -

NOW, IT'S FAMILY BUSINESS

I *drove to the apartments at Lake Merced* to retrieve the package my mother sent. Mike asked how things were working out in Shelter Cove. After small talk, I reminded him to deny any knowledge of my whereabouts if asked.

"Like I never lived here," I said. "It could mean my life."

"Roger that. I got you, brother."

I also dropped by the Linda Mar Post Office to retrieve my mail. The clerk had a certified letter from the City & County of San Francisco, which I signed for and stuffed in my coat pocket. I didn't open it there because I expected bad news and didn't want expletives flying out of my mouth in public.

Instead, I tore the official-looking envelope open as I walked into the cottage.

In short order it said, "After careful consideration, your employment and probation are being terminated for cause."

Though I expected it, I was stunned. I guess Flynn got his way after all. Time to lean on the shoulder of the Monkey.

I sat behind the cottage with my Monkey Shoulder scotch and loudly verbalized my anger, as I mentally groused. I was hoping the Ghost Boys would pay a visit today. Any, or all of them. Please, bring it, you motherfuckers, *today!*

I turned my phone off, lit a cigar, and played Andrea Bocelli to soothe my nerves. Despite some mild intoxication, I managed to grill a small filet and make a salad. I couldn't muster up the motivation to open the box from my mother. It would have to wait until tomorrow.

I slept deep, then fitfully, but no PTSD, at least that I remembered. I got up around seven hungover and headed to Linda Mar Beach.

I ran sprints before diving into the cold surf. The ocean temp was in the low fifties and especially numbing without a wet suit. After a quick swim along the breakers, I came ashore, and threw a blanket down to enjoy the rays. The swim, the sun, and Advil were starting to work.

I woke up when someone, or something, started to lick my face. I was hoping it was Sophie, or a bathing beauty, who couldn't resist.

The slobbering English bulldog was accompanied by my cop buddy, Lee Tyler. We had a good laugh as his year-old puppy jumped into my lap. I can't seem to hold on to women, but at least dogs still love me.

Lee said, "Her name is Lola. Isn't she pretty? She thinks she is."

Lee was off duty, out walking his pooch and enjoying the day. We talked for about fifteen minutes, and he asked how the cottage was working out. I told him it was perfect and thanked him for hooking me up. I reminded him to keep my identity and location to himself because the bounty on my life was still out there. I also told him I was just notified of my termination for the incident with Flynn.

He looked disappointed. "Man, I'm sorry to hear that. Sounds like they fucked you good. Any idea what you're gonna do yet?"

"I don't know. I just found out yesterday, so I'm trying to figure that out. I might appeal the decision because I don't want to let this guy off the hook that easy. I may have been insubordinate, but under the circumstances, the penalty was harsh. He cost me my career and it was done in retaliation. I'm sure of that. "I have an offer from a SEAL buddy to join his security team down in SoCal. They mostly do executive protection. They make good money, and he made me a solid offer a couple of weeks ago. Either way, I'll be fine."

"Well," Lee said, "I could put in a good word for you with Pacifica. Less action than you're used to, but good bosses. Good place to work. I think if you explained what happened, they might consider giving you a second chance. It's hard to find good cops, bro. Let me know and I'll talk to my captain."

"Thanks, Lee. I'll keep it in mind as an option. I really appreciate it."

I jogged the fifteen minutes back to the cottage and hit the outdoor shower to knock the sand off, before going inside. I spent the rest of the day with the phone off, laying low. I was in no rush to tell the world I'd been fired.

To keep my word to my mother, I opened the box of goodies she sent earlier to the Lake Merced apartment.

The box contained a gift card for Omaha Steaks, a cooking apron imprinted with "The only thing better than being an Italian, is being a Sicilian," a small statue of Blessed Mother Mary, and a new garlic press.

To try to anticipate, or guess, what she might send next, would be an analytical impossibility even IBM's supercomputer Watson couldn't predict. Bless her loving heart. I called and she was excited to tell me the pastor at Sacred Heart Church, Father Leo, had personally blessed the Mother Mary statue for me.

"He-ah knows it's-ah fa-you."

"That's nice, Ma. I'll put it on my dresser, with the mass cards and everything else you've been sending. I've got more religious stuff in my bedroom than the souvenir shop in the Vatican."

She laughed, then pivoted to the dreaded question.

"So, what's-ah going on with-ah you job?"

I hesitated, then blurted, "They fired me. I got the letter yesterday."

She launched into a tirade of Italian curse words, some of which I'd never heard, putting the hex on Lieutenant Flynn.

Whatever she said, it involved eternal damnation and was probably worse than a voodoo curse. Flynn's days were numbered, and he needed to immediately finalize his plans for his eternal resting place.

I started telling her I might file an appeal, but she cut me off.

She was talking Sicilian now. "I will speak to your father this Sunday. He'll know what to do. That lieutenant will live to regret what he did to the son of Anthony DeLuca."

I didn't want to read into it too much or upset her further. Regardless of what I wanted, I knew there was no changing her mind. She was a hot-blooded Sicilian who you should never cross. To comfort her and make myself feel better, I told her about the job offer from Billy and other things in the works.

"Don't worry, Ma. Like Papa, I got a lot of friends, and they're behind me on this."

We paused and were quiet for a second, then she encouraged me to attend mass and pray to the Blessed Mother. I felt a novena in the works, with nine days of prayers coming my way. Some things never change.

Maybe I needed to warn Flynn not to buy green bananas.

- 36 -

VIOLINS AND THE LITTLE BLACK DRESS

I *ignored voicemails and texts from friends*, deciding to deal with them in the morning. I left the phone off to get a good night's rest but slept restlessly anyway. If that wasn't enough, I got a charley horse in my calf in the middle of the night and bounded out of bed in excruciating pain.

I got up early, tired and limping, and made pancetta, eggs, and melon, before reading text messages and listening to voicemails. Hank called and texted, as did Lily, Vinnie, and Billy. Hank and Lily heard about my termination and weren't surprised but sounded pissed about it. That made three of us.

Lily wanted to get together and said she was worried about me. Vinnie wanted to remind me to have dinner at Carmine's on him. Maybe I'd meet Lily on the sly at Carmine's for dinner. I planned to ask Vinnie or Gina for a private table in a corner, or in a private dining area, when I called to make the reservation.

A voicemail from Billy said he had a few days off and wanted to come up the coast to hang and hit the beach. It sounded like a plan to me. It wasn't doing me any good sitting around bitching and feeling sorry for myself.

I called Hank and he seemed pissed, but who knows. He didn't lose *his* job.

"Hey, Ray, you're a good cop. Flynn's a turd. Anything I can do, just name it."

"I'll be fine, Hank. He's an angry fucked-up dude, so be careful around him. We had ways of dealing with guys like him in the military," I said. "We'd make their life a living hell or we'd frag 'em.

"Anyway, while I have you, I found out Vinnie worked out a deal with Carmine before he disappeared, and now Vinnie owns half of Carmine's restaurant with Carmine's sister Gina."

"You're fucking kidding me."

"I'm not," I said without telling him how I knew. "I'm out of it, so you can let homicide know. I don't think there's any doubt he, or his boys, put Carmine in with the fishes."

Once I got off the line with Hank, I texted Lily and asked if she wanted to grab dinner and got an immediate text back.

Love to.

That's all I needed to hear. I called Carmine's restaurant to make the reservation.

Vinnie answered and seemed delighted I was calling for a reservation, which made me feel a little guilty, as I'd just put the homicide inspectors on him for taking over Carmine's. But for all I knew, they were aware of it anyway. It wasn't my concern.

I spoke Sicilian. "Hey, paisan. I'm taking a friend to dinner tonight. Thought we'd try Carmine's."

He immediately offered dinner on the house, but I told him that wasn't necessary. I did need some privacy though. We agreed on a time, and he said he'd arrange for us to have a private dining area.

Then I called Billy to deliver the news. He sounded incredulous.

"Sorry, bro," he said. "Those guys are amateurs. They had Michelangelo painting their church and focused on a couple of drops of paint on the floor. Idiots! Fuck 'em, Ray. I'd love to have you on my team at Blackhawk."

"We'll definitely talk about it when you come up," I said. "This is San Francisco, so bring your Speedo and some cute outfits."

I took the Challenger to Carmine's and used the valet service. I asked them to have the car ready to roll in a secure area. I assumed the Ghost Boys had the make, model, and plate number of my car.

I met Lily in the entrance and asked for Vinnie at the maître d' stand. Lily looked amazing in a little black cocktail dress and heels. I was hoping my black sport coat, white dress shirt, and black jeans were working for her. I told her earlier, we needed to dress up for Carmine's as per their dress code and to blend in.

Vinnie welcomed us and directed the maître d' to seat us where a private table had been set up in an intimate VIP dining room off to the side.

"Ray is *famigghia*," he told the guy, instructing him to take good care of us.

In an instant, a waiter and sommelier were at our table, with a well-dressed security type in tow. I saw a bulge under his jacket and knew he was armed. He stood like a sentry at the entrance to the VIP area.

The waiter took our drink orders and the muscle introduced himself as Giovanni, and said he'd be close by, ready to assist, as needed. He smiled when I spoke to him in Sicilian. Connection made.

Lily leaned across the table and took my hands.

"I missed you, and I'm really pissed they treated you this way."

I kissed the top of her hand.

"Let's enjoy a great meal and have some fun tonight. I don't want to talk about the job. Shit happens, and I'll be fine. I'm movin' on."

Our cocktails arrived, along with a large tray of bruschetta, olives, meatballs, cheeses, and peppers, so our conversation came to a standstill as the priority switched to *mangiare!*

Lily talked about her academics at UC Berkeley and her passions in life, her violin, and love of cooking. Now, this was news to me. She's a great cook, but at no time did she ever talk about the violin. Now, we were getting somewhere.

She explained that the violin was invented in the sixteenth century in Italy.

"Now I know why I love the violin," I said.

We talked about Beethoven, Bach, and contemporary violinists like Hilary Hahn and Itzhak Perlman.

Lily was full of surprises.

"I used to fantasize about becoming a concert violinist like Caroline Campbell," she said, "and playing in the San Francisco Symphony. But somewhere along the way, I moved on to other interests, but I'm still passionate about it."

After a glass of anisette at the end of the meal, I left two hundred and fifty cash on the table and handed the muscle a fifty. We thanked the servers and security for the great service and hospitality. I asked for Vinnie and complimented him on the amazing food and service, expressing my gratitude.

Using the Sicilian dialect, he said, "We're Sicilians. We're family. I'm here if you need me."

I was conflicted, knowing he probably killed Carmine. I know from experience these mobsters are nice, until they're not—and then it goes bad quickly.

At Lily's insistence, in a moment of weakness, I broke my safe house rule and invited her to spend the night in Shelter Cove. I guess it was the little black dress. We stopped at her flat to pick up a change of clothes, her firearm, and other necessities. I told her, for tonight, stick with the black dress and heels.

"And feel free to bring the violin."

On the drive to the cottage, I explained where the safe house was located and reviewed some of my physical security measures and protocols. I also told her that she was visiting at her own risk.

"Don't worry," she said, "at least you'll have a cop on duty tonight."

I gave her the eye roll. "Yeah, very funny, Officer Leung."

I drove down the Embarcadero to avoid Chinatown and jumped on the freeway from there. Traffic was light, so we arrived at the cottage in record time.

As we drove deeper into Shelter Cove, she said, "You really do live in a rabbit hole."

With only small night-lights on inside the cottage, and the overgrown manzanitas in front, it was nearly impossible to see the cottage from the street. Conversely, it limited visibility from inside the cottage as well. The thermal imaging monocular was money well spent.

Lily thought the cottage was, in her words, "enchanting."

I lit the pellet stove, fixed us a nightcap, and found some classical violin music to take our minds off our troubles. And it wasn't long before we moved to the bedroom, moving slowly to prolong the pleasure. As tough as she was as a cop, she could be just as tender as a lover.

I did my best to concentrate on our lovemaking but was distracted, knowing there was always a possibility of a Ghost Boys attack. These bastards were robbing me of my peace of mind and contentment. I was relatively certain we weren't followed, but you're never sure. Maybe that's why they call themselves Ghost Boys. I hoped I was wrong.

★ ★ ★

We were several hours into a deep sleep when my phone alert activated, and a trip flare illuminated the night sky outside our window. We rolled to the floor, grabbed rifles, and executed an infantry crawl to the back door as planned. I grabbed the monocular as well.

Outside, it was almost impossible to see with thick tule fog drifting inland from the cove. Even with light emanating from the flares and strobe lights, the light bounced off the fog, diminishing the effectiveness of the monocular.

We took up positions with AR-15s ready to let it rip.

I motioned for Lily to hold her fire, as I listened for signs of movement. It was dead still, and I felt like a sitting duck, so we stayed behind cover.

As I scanned the area close to the ground with my flashlight, I suddenly saw movement and a pair of close-set eyes staring back at me. As I adjusted the scope, I realized I was doing a face-off with the mangy coyote I'd seen earlier on the game camera.

I stood and shooed him off and he vanished in thin air, not surprisingly, like a ghost. My heart was still racing when we went back to bed.

- 37 -

THE SNAKE PIT

After breakfast and showers, I drove Lily back to San Francisco on the bike so she could get ready for her shift later that day. She held on tight as we raced up Highway 1 through Pacifica and Daly City into San Francisco. The closeness was nice, and I was ready to do a U-turn and take her back to bed.

I dropped her off and drove back to Shelter Cove to switch vehicles, so I could pick Billy up at the airport later that day.

I met him curbside and felt a sense of relief when I saw him. We had a lot of catching up to do and he'd always been a good sounding board—pragmatic and wise beyond his years.

On the way to the cottage, we stopped at one of my favorite dive bars, the Tattooed Crowbar, off Manor Drive in Pacifica. We had a couple of cold drafts before heading for the lair.

By dive bar standards, we were appropriately dressed and looked as hardened as the rest of the miscreants.

Billy looking, assessing things as we entered: "Nice place, but these women look like they're on parole and smoke in the shower."

"Not at two a.m. they don't!"

We laughed and left after finishing our beers and a bowl of nuts on the bar.

Billy was impressed with the remote location of the safe house and my physical security setup. We walked the property, and he made a few suggestions regarding adjustments to tactical positions. It was good to have another set of trained eyes review the setup. We cooked thick burgers and cowboy beans on the grill for dinner.

We had Buffalo Trace bourbon with beer backs and fired up a couple of cigars. Even with the negative stuff in my life, hanging with Billy—was just what I needed.

He talked about his team's recent assignments and the long days and perks in his new line of work. Most of the travel was domestic by private jet, but some was international. He said the private jet made travel less stressful, as did the five-star accommodations they typically enjoyed. These costs were passed on to the client. He said the team was primarily charged with protecting Fortune One Hundred execs, Hollywood moguls, stars, and sports celebrities.

"We meet a lot of them," he said, "but we don't get starstruck, and discourage non-essential interaction. Most of them are dicks anyway. We're there to protect them and neutralize threats. We're hired muscle providing world-class security.

"Besides, most of them are so self-absorbed, we're invisible to them anyway. They couldn't care less about us. We *don't* carry luggage, pets, or anything else. We're not personal valets."

He explained the guys worked in teams, and one of their biggest challenges was avoiding complacency and boredom.

"We exercise every chance we get and watch what we eat, most of the time. It's a real job and everybody takes it seriously. The offer I made still stands."

I asked if I could sleep on it.

"Absolutely. I want you on the team, Ray, but you've got to have your head in it."

The following morning while I was blasting Italian opera, I heard a sharp knock on the door; but by the time I grabbed a pistol and answered it, the delivery van was driving away.

I carried the box inside and could feel something jostling around. I assumed, with my birthday coming up, it was a gag gift, and my curiosity got the best of me. If I'd given it more thought, I would have remembered no one is supposed to know my location.

I cut the tape with my knife and began to pull the flap back, and in an instant, felt a sharp needle prick on my finger.

It started to bleed, and I thought it was a staple, until I saw a large rattlesnake coiled up on a dirty pillow in a corner of the box. I shut the box, put it outside, and yelled for Billy. He grabbed my pistol, dumped the box over, and unloaded several rounds into the snake's head.

When I showed him the bloody scratch on my index finger, he called 9-1-1 to report a venomous snakebite.

He googled "Treating a Rattlesnake Bite," and was disappointed that he didn't need to carve an X across the wound and suck the venom out. Another boyhood fantasy shattered.

Billy pulled the pillow from the box and discovered large "GB-SF" letters written across the bottom of the box. Now we knew with certainty that my safe house was no longer *a safe house.*

Taking no chances, the paramedics drove Code-3 with lights and siren to the emergency room at Seton Medical Center in Daly City.

It was my good fortune that the emergency room physician, originally from Arizona, did his residency in an ER in Phoenix and had a lot of familiarity with rattlesnake bites. He told me based on my body's reaction to the scratch, he thought it was a dry bite: a bite where the snake fails to release its venom, and explained that twenty to twenty-five percent of all pit viper bites are dry bites.

"Still," he said, "you're one lucky guy."

He cleaned the bite, gave me a tetanus shot and admitted me to the hospital overnight for observation.

Billy explained it was a targeted attack on a police officer and asked the attending physician to request a secure room and to book me as a "John Doe." He also called the watch commander at Daly City PD and requested they assign an officer for protection outside my room. They were very familiar with my case by now.

I felt stupid with all the commotion over a scratch, but so be it. The doctor reviewed the gruesome possibilities, even with dry bites, so it seemed well advised to follow his instructions.

Clearly, the Ghost Boys knew the location of the safe house and were sending a message. They were determined to put me in a body bag.

Billy stayed until a Daly City PD officer arrived. I suggested he lock up the cottage and stay in a hotel for the night. I told him I'd pick up the tab for the room.

We agreed to take extra measures and deal with next steps in the morning, based on my reaction to the bite.

I explained the situation to the Daly City officer, who was familiar with the shooting at my apartment in Daly City.

"It'll be obvious to the Ghost Boys that I was transported here, the closest ER. I'm assuming they know where I'm currently at, and they're not going to rest until they take me out, so I'd stay frosty tonight. If there's a secure room for medical prisoners, I'd be happy to stay there instead, if it gives me better protection."

The officer called his watch commander and reported the updated information.

Within minutes, a second officer arrived. The primary officer contacted hospital security to brief them on the situation, requesting they restrict access to my floor.

I texted Lily to alert her and suggested she stay with a friend for a few days, considering the latest developments.

"I agree," she said. "I'm also calling the watch commander, so she's aware of the situation. This happened because you were doing your job in the Pings as an SFPD officer.

"I'm gonna ask the department to provide security for you because this is all line-of-duty shit, and they need to do the right thing."

"Lily, they fired me, kicked me to the curb, so don't hold your breath. I'm *persona non grata*. Flynn made sure of that."

The nurse gave me a sedative, so I told Lily I'd call her in the morning.

If I make it through the night, I thought.

- 38 -

INCOMING!

barely slept; a nurse kept waking me every couple of hours to check the bite and my vital signs. Early the next morning, the doctor conducting rounds checked the wound and said despite minor swelling, it looked like I was going to live.

"I'm not sure I'd take a bet on that," I said.

He looked at me strangely, but he didn't know there was a bounty on my life.

They released me from the hospital with instructions to rest and keep the wound clean. Because of the attack, a Daly City officer drove me home to what I now referred to as the *unsafe* house, aka the Snake Pit.

Billy and I discussed the current threat, and he suggested, after tonight, we pack things up and stay at his place north of LA until things cool down.

He got no argument from me.

I finally accepted Billy's offer to work for him at Blackhawk, with one caveat: I'd do it on a trial basis for ninety days to see if it was a good fit for them and for me. I had issues I needed to work through with SFPD and needed flexibility with that situation.

Security and protection work can be boring, like 10-B assignments where you're standing around all day outside Moscone

Center, watching trade show nerds with lanyards around their necks, sipping Starbucks and playing with their iPhones. That shit bores me tearless, but some officers love the money and don't mind the slow pace.

We went to the beach with concealed firearms and decided to do the food truck thing for Mexican, instead of packing food. I rested for the most part, while Billy jogged and demonstrated his rough-surf prowess.

My hand was improving. I didn't feel pain, or discomfort, which was surprising. It was still swollen, but that was the extent of it. I was extremely lucky, and had the snake emptied a full load of venom, I might not have survived, or could have had massive tissue damage. There was no doubt in my military mind that these assholes were serious about taking me out, and I had to be prepared to meet them head-on.

We had a quiet evening, and I packed a couple of seabags and tossed them in the trunk of my car for the six-and-a-half-hour road trip south to Agoura Hills, north of Los Angeles, in the morning. I had my personal arsenal ready to go as well.

I called Lily and, without going into specifics, told her I was going off the grid for a while. Another attack by the Ghost Boys was likely.

"This is shitty, Ray. Just when things were looking good for us."

"I know, it sucks. But my priority is to get through this and survive. Being around me is dangerous. It puts you and anybody close to me in harm's way."

"I've gotta go," she said and ended the call without saying goodbye.

She was upset and angry. My mistake was thinking things would blow over and I could have a normal relationship. Billy checked the trip lines, flares, and other security gadgets before we hit the rack for the night. The guns were locked and loaded, and we both sensed a heightened threat.

"The hairs are up on the back of my neck," I said. "They know I survived the attack."

We slept in our camo pants and socks, with our boots ready to go. This was SEAL team protocol, but getting rest was still a priority, so we took turns standing watch and taking naps.

Around three a.m., a barrage of MK 8A flares activated deep into the night sky. We knew immediately our boundary was breached and we were under attack.

Hot rounds penetrated the house, smashing through lamps, cabinets, and furnishings. I threw a couple of flash-bang stun grenades in the direction of the gunfire to disorient our assailants, while we collected our weapons and protective gear. We low-crawled out the back door.

We were both wearing the body armor we acquired as SEALS. Battle-tested and battle-worn, our rigs were the setups we wore on countless missions and provided a sense of familiarity and comfort. We had extra magazines, flash-bangs, pistols, and assault rifles ready to deploy.

We slowly moved to our tactical positions to take cover and identify the targets.

Using hand signals, Billy showed me four fingers, and pointed in the directions of our assailants' positions. He held up his index finger for the one, two, three count, before we opened fire with the ARs.

Billy unloaded his first magazine, then yelled "Red!" as I laid down cover-fire so he could reload.

He reloaded and continued to shoot toward the attackers' gunfire. I reloaded, then resumed my barrage as well. We had done this many times before.

The air was filled with smoke and GSR (gunshot residue), and Billy gave me the sign to cease fire. The quiet was deafening, as we listened for movement, or signs of life. Seconds later, we heard a car start and leave at a high rate of speed.

At the same time, we heard sirens approaching. We found three dead. The rest were gone. The dead all had the familiar GB-SF dragon tattoos on their necks. Two were neutralized by head shots.

I was hoping the Pacifica cops were smart enough to stop all traffic leaving Shelter Cove. Turns out, they weren't. Too focused on running to the gunfight.

Pacifica PD arrived in force, and we tossed our weapons on the ground in front of us.

From a distance, we were ordered to do an about-face, kneel, and interlace our fingers behind our heads. The searching officers removed our body armor and put us facedown to cuff us.

We knew the drill and moved slowly to avoid exciting nervous young officers.

"We're law enforcement, guys," I said as they perp-walked us to the police cars, "and this was a retaliation attack for a gang killing in San Francisco. You can call Lee Tyler to verify it. You can also call Hank Lau, or Lily Leung at SFPD's Central Station. Call Daly City PD, too. It's all documented. They know what's going on. I was using this cottage as a safe house. I'm a former SFPD officer with a bounty on my head."

"If you say so," the sergeant said, "but we've still got three dead, so we're taking you into custody until we find out what happened."

He was disrespectful, wasn't listening or asking questions, and was pissing me off.

"You've got three gangbangin' shitbags permanently off the street," I said, "and you can thank me and Billy for that. Do what ya gotta do, Sarge. By the way, at least one got away, so good luck with that.

"And no, I didn't see the vehicle he left in. That piece of shit is already back in Chinatown. He changed his soiled shorts and is sitting down for a plate of dim sum. You should check with Seton, Zuckerberg, and other local hospitals to see if they've got an Asian male with gunshot wounds and a dragon tattoo on his neck. You can thank me later and send me a fruit basket."

Pacifica's CSI team was setting up their portable crime scene tent and Lentry lights as we were leaving. They had a long night and a full day ahead of them, with more than two hundred rounds exchanged.

I turned to Billy. "Good luck with that, motherfuckers. That's more rounds than they've seen fired in this city in the last fifty years."

We arrived at Pacifica PD and were given VIP treatment that included a complete strip search. Personally, I was hoping for the full body cavity search, but I'd need to upgrade for that, and didn't know if I had enough points on my credit card.

"Always a bridesmaid, never a bride," I said. Billy laughed.

Off duty, Lee Tyler was notified and showed up within the hour. I asked him to call Hank and Lily for me, so they could vouch for us and verify our story.

The detective from Daly City PD made a cameo appearance and confirmed the incidents that preceded this attack.

"You should kick these guys loose," he said after he was done explaining the situation to the Pacifica cop. "They did us a favor."

Pacifica PD was satisfied. By the time the sun was coming up over San Bruno Mountain, Billy and I were OR-ed, which is to say released on our own recognizance, and driven back to the cottage. The Pacifica officers stood by as we finished packing for the drive south.

"So, where you off to?" asked one of the officers.

I couldn't resist. "Our honeymoon."

He shook his head.

At the Pacifica detective's insistence, Billy provided his home address and where we'd be staying for the foreseeable future.

"This is my home address," Billy said, "and you need to keep it confidential. We're under a direct threat from these assholes. Think of my house like a safe house for witness protection."

Billy recorded the conversation on his phone and told them he was recording it.

"Notify the FBI or whoever else you need to, but if my address gets leaked, you're gonna see more bodies stack up, and I'll come gunnin' for you. And that's not a threat. It's a promise.

"Ray and I are professionals, and you and the other cops need to do your fuckin' jobs and get these creeps off the street. If you don't, expect to see the body count go up. And trust me, we won't be in that body count. We do this shit for a living, too, and we're probably better at it than you."

- 39 -

FIRE THE GARDENER

Billy said, *"Fuck 'em all, Ray,"* as we drove south. "If these amateurs even think about another attack, I'll bring the team in, and we'll be done with it, once and for all."

I called Lee, Lily, and Hank and thanked them for coming to our aid when Pacifica had us in custody. I called the Daly City detective, too.

I told Lily I was joining Billy at Blackhawk for now and got no response. I asked her what her plans were, and she said she planned to stay with a friend for at least another week, maybe longer. I apologized for bringing this into her life, but it fell on deaf ears.

"Whatever," she said. "I'm thinking of moving out of the city anyway."

"I'm sorry, Lily. If anything happens, call me and I can be back up in the Bay Area in a matter of hours. Go see Captain Choo tomorrow and let him know what's going on. You should keep him in the loop because these attacks are being planned by the Ghost Boys and they're in his district. If you need protection, or want to get reassigned, he can make that happen. Maybe you should get off the street for a while. If you want, I'll call him and talk to him. Just—"

"Christ!" she said. "Just fucking stop. Don't go all drama queen on me, Ray. I'll be fine."

"I'm dead serious, Lily. Don't be like that."

There was a long silence.

"Look, I gotta go," she said—then hung up.

★ ★ ★

After more than six hours on the road, we pulled into Agoura Hills, breathing a sigh of relief. I texted Lily to let her know we got in safely and eventually got a thumbs-up response.

Ice baby, ice.

Billy's house was a 1920s-era Spanish-style stucco bungalow with a red-tiled roof and a detached garage behind the house. The lawn was brown, scraggly, and overgrown, and Billy was quick to blame the gardener.

"Well, fire him," I said. "Your yard looks ghetto, bro."

"I can't."

"Why not?"

"Because I'm the gardener!"

We unloaded the guns first. Billy had a high-capacity gun safe, weighing more than eight hundred pounds, anchored in the back of his garage, so we stored most of the weapons there.

We set aside six pistols, two AK-47s, and stun grenades that we brought into the house to have at-the-ready. We watched for a tail on the drive down and had no reason to believe we were tailed, but we'd made that mistake before.

The following day, I called Lily to check in. She gave me a quick recap of the major calls she handled the previous night and sounded exhausted. It was her way to deflect. Talk shop, not relationship.

I told her I'd be driving up in a few weeks to put my stuff from the cottage in storage, or at least what was left of it.

"If there's anything you want, go to the cottage and take it. It's yours."

"Nah, I'm fine," she said then switched gears. "The Ghost Boys have been laying low since the attack at your cottage. Chinatown's been quiet. The mob guys continue to make their moves in North Beach, and we don't have good intel, or enough cops on the street to get ahead of it. It's bad. Really messed up."

I couldn't help myself. "Yeah," I said, "I heard they had a Sicilian cop who became friends with the head mobster, so they rewarded him by firing him for mouthing off to his dumbass lieutenant. Clowns. They're more concerned with G.O.s [general orders] than catching bad guys."

She sighed. "You're right, Ray. You have every right to feel that way. I know you need to make money right now, but I'm gonna miss you. If anything happens up here, I'll let you know. I can help you pack the cottage in a couple weeks if you want. I wish you could find a job up here."

"At least for now, I'll be traveling outside of California," I said, "so hopefully, the Ghost Boys thing will die down and investigators can make some progress. I tell you what, though, if any of them come for me again I'm going all-in."

"Alright, Ray."

She sounded tired. We said our goodbyes, and I wished the conversation had ended on a more upbeat note. I shook it off and joined Billy out back where we grilled chicken and hoisted a few cold ones.

Billy raised a bottle. "To the BTFs!"

Big Tough Frogmen. I could drink to that. And did.

As we were relaxing, Billy got an encrypted message from Blackhawk on his company phone.

"We're on. Leaving in twelve hours. Details to follow. They don't tell me anything either, so don't ask. I got nothing. You can't leak what you don't know. I can tell you what to bring and the time and place for departure. Pretty simple.

"At the airstrip you hand over your cell phone, and once we're airborne, we give you the details. This stuff is covert. You know the drill. Welcome to Blackhawk, bro. You're going on your first assignment. Don't fuck it up!"

- 40 -

HOORAY FOR HOLLYWOOD!

We packed light and drove to Station 125 Heliport in Calabasas to board an ultra-long-range Gulfstream G650ER. Based on the type of jet, I was certain our destination was on the other side of the world. No private company's going to burn that much fuel and incur massive operational expenses for a quick trip to Reno.

I would be well compensated anyway, so the destination didn't matter to me. I was content to get paid to sleep on a luxurious Gulfstream.

As we boarded the jet, Billy's team wasted no time resuming the clowning we did in Mexico.

Once airborne, Billy called for a huddle. "Gentlemen, we're on our way to Dubai for an extraction."

He explained a major film studio hired us to extricate a popular Hollywood star known for her rebellious and outrageous behavior. Apparently, after she wrapped up filming in Israel for a soon-to-be-released action movie, she spontaneously jetted to Dubai to party.

"Despite Dubai's reputation for having an exciting nightlife," said Billy, "it's part of the UAE. It's Muslim and governed by strict Shariah law. Western tourists have been arrested for holding hands, drinking booze without a license, and sharing a hotel room with someone other than their spouse.

"Activities that are legal and acceptable in Western societies are sometimes illegal in Dubai, and they practice selective enforcement.

"The actress we're extracting can be a misfit, and she's the wrong person to be in Dubai. She's being held against her will in a private home by a local Emirati who's on our payroll. He'll meet us at the terminal to clear customs and provide transportation. He's a former Dubai police commander, so he's cleared things with airport police as well. He's connected and has assured us he's received the required clearances, but I suggest we move fast and tread lightly.

"Quick in and out. We'll only be on the ground for a few hours. The Gulfstream's got plenty of food, drink, and entertainment for the thirty-four hours we'll spend in the air over the next couple of days.

"There's no booze on board, to stay clear of issues in Dubai, and to avoid problems with our extracted guest. It won't hurt anybody to dry out for a few days."

Joe couldn't resist. "I gotta tell ya, that's gonna hurt. Can we have a light beer? Any beer? An O'Doul's?"

Billy smiled and shook his head.

"We also have no firearms on this jet or anything else that could raise a red flag. We're squeaky clean, and our former Dubai police commander will speak on our behalf if we have issues in-country. Any questions?"

There was plenty of room on the plane, with couches, blankets, and large recliners. Healthy foods and drinks were plentiful, served by an onboard steward. He prepared gourmet meals and snacks and invited us to help ourselves in the galley.

The pilot and flight crew walked the cabin every few hours to check in and stretch during the long flight. Now I understand why flights like this cost ten thousand dollars an hour to charter. As an option, you can buy a jet like this outright, but get ready to write a check for about sixty-five million dollars and spend another thirty-five hundred an hour for fuel costs and maintenance.

We intermittently got up to stretch, each doing our own version of calisthenics. Joe said he preferred hot goat yoga, and since he'd been told to leave his goat home, he was starting to stress.

"Hey, I'm fallin' apart here!" he said. "You can't separate a man from his goat. He's a service animal!"

At the very least, he said he should have been allowed to bring a miniature horse for emotional support.

★ ★ ★

An hour from our destination, the pilot came back to tell us hot lemon-scented towels were heading our way, prior to our arrival in Dubai.

"No gift bags?" asked Joe.

I promised him a ten-dollar Starbuck's gift card when we got back.

As we stood and stretched, we gathered around Billy for further instructions. He took us step-by-step from touchdown to extraction.

He identified the celebrity as none other than Mercedes Cruz, a Hollywood megastar regularly featured on *Entertainment Tonight* and every celebrity newspaper and magazine in the checkout stands.

She was gorgeous, with a reputation for dating Hollywood bad boys and living life with indulgence and abandonment.

"She might require restraints and sedation to get her on the plane," said Billy. "Our police commander described her as loud, disrespectful, and excitable."

"Sounds like my last girlfriend," said Joe.

"We'll have to deal with it once we see what her emotional state is," said Billy. "Our mission is to return her safely to her Hollywood handlers. No more, no less. No judgments. Let's treat her with respect and, hopefully, she won't get abusive. Regardless, she's coming back with us, and we've got to move quickly to avoid any outside interference or attention. I don't want to turn this into an international crisis."

- 41 -

SAY HI TO DUBAI!

We touched down and taxied close to the Jetex VIP terminal. Our police commander met us at the gate wearing a gold Rolex President watch and a custom suit that probably set him back four grand. The weather was sunny and warm, and the Jetex terminal looked more like the Museum of Modern Art than an airline terminal. He escorted us through customs, where we were expedited, and led outside to two black Range Rovers with blacked-out windows.

Billy rode with the police commander and the rest of our four-man team jumped in the second vehicle. Our pilot and flight crew stayed with the aircraft for security, refueling, and maintenance.

We raced through the streets of Dubai to a handsome Mediterranean-style villa in the upscale, gated community of Jumeirah Islands. The commander led us to a room on the second floor. I immediately noticed the heavy-duty steel security door had a multi-point locking system, with heavy-duty hinges.

"I think he's done this before," I whispered to Billy.

"She's wild," said the commander, "so get ready to restrain her."

As we slowly opened the door, the commander stood back, and we realized the room had no windows and appeared soundproofed. Mercedes was handcuffed to a bed rail and looked different than how I imagined her, probably due to stress and captivity.

She went into a tirade and screamed profanities, yelling, "Are you here to gangbang me?! Well, fuckin' get it over with, you pigs!" She kicked her legs wildly and spat at me as I got closer. Billy grabbed her arm and injected her with a load of barbiturates to calm her down.

After a few minutes passed, I asked the others to leave the room. I sat and introduced myself and told her why we were there.

"Miss Cruz, we're not here to hurt you, assault you, or disrespect you. My name is Ray, and we're going to take you back to Los Angeles."

She looked at me, suddenly very angry. "The fuck you are! Nobody tells me what I can do! You're fuckin' nobody, so fuck you!"

"With all due respect," I said, "you're not in charge here, Hollywood, so calm down, because if you don't, you'll leave here with a gag in your mouth bound like a fuckin' mummy. You have ten seconds to tell me how you want it to go, and I'm not known for my patience."

The shot seemed to be taking effect, as she slurred her response. "Get me out of here."

I replaced the handcuffs with flex-cuffs for the ride to the airport and escorted her to the waiting Range Rover.

The commander obtained clearance for us to drive on the tarmac next to the waiting Gulfstream.

"Okay, Hollywood, I'm gonna walk you to the plane. Just keep quiet and don't make a fuss because if you do, we'll probably all end up in some Third World prison."

I threw my jacket over her shoulders to cover her bound hands and completed the ensemble with my Yankee hat and large sunglasses.

She was out of it.

"I'll put my arm around you and walk you up the stairs to get you on the plane. You can lean on me. You're doing good. Just stay calm. We're getting you out of here."

She mumbled what sounded like profanities, but at that point, we needed to board the plane and take off. Joe and I propped her up and practically carried her up the airstair into the cabin of the plane. We laid her down on a couch, as the crew prepared for takeoff.

Joe lightened the mood. "Not sure, but I think she's hot for me."

"I think you're right, Joe," I said. "Like a honey badger and a house cat, and you're the house cat!"

In less than two hours, we had completed the extraction and were thundering down the runway on the return flight to LA.

Billy gave me a high-five.

"Good job, Ray. This one was a cream puff. If *Miss Manners* sleeps off the sedative, we may need to give her a second shot. We don't need her acting out at thirty-five thousand feet."

I cut the flex-cuffs off while she was sleeping, hoping it would make her more comfortable and sleep longer.

She was covered in a cashmere comforter as well, but if she slept, I couldn't. I was the self-appointed lead on this one and needed to do the over-watch until we landed in Calabasas.

About four hours into the flight, she began to mumble and stir.

"You're okay," I said. "Go back to sleep."

She sat up, covering herself with the comforter, trying to focus.

"My name is Ray, and you're on a flight to Los Angeles from Dubai. Me and my buddies are here to make sure you make it back safely."

She glared at me. "Well, fuck you, Ray."

"Bless you, too, Mercedes. Are you hungry, or thirsty? Can I get you something?"

"Water."

I got her a bottle of water and a plate with some fruit and snacks.

"Thanks," she said begrudgingly. "Why don't you sit next to me?" patting the cushion next to her, like I was a lapdog.

"No, thanks. I'm fine where I am."

I got a nasty stare back. "Like I said, fuck you, Ray."

I put my headphones on and went back to watching the action classic, *Terminator 2: Judgment Day*. I looked around and the rest of the team were asleep. The lights were low and before long, I couldn't fight it and started to drift off.

I awoke and Mercedes was next to me, leaning in to me, with her head on my shoulder covered with a blanket.

"What are you doing?"

"Ray," she said, "you know I'm in movies just like the one you're watching. I'm a star."

"I know that, but you need to go back to your seat and relax."

She angrily stood and slapped me across the face. "He's trying to feel me up!"

I grabbed her by the wrists and in my softest voice said, "Listen, Hollywood, if you assault me again, it won't be good for you. Do it again, and I'll put your ass in restraints and shoot you full of sedatives. Now sit the fuck down."

I got the impression she hadn't been talked to like that, at least not in modern times. She had a bewildered look. Two of my colleagues applauded. For some reason, she had zeroed-in on me.

"Yeah. Be careful with Ray," said Joe. "He tried to feel me up, too."

Once things settled down, my thoughts drifted to Sophie. I was still surprised she dated Vinnie Catalano and found me too angry and aggressive. Me, aggressive? Are you kidding? Sophie, meet Mercedes!

I thought about Lily but couldn't decide if there was a future there. She wanted more from me than I could give. I was starting to think it wasn't my time for a relationship. Too much time in the military, self-absorbed, sexually inactive, and insecure, *always* in survival mode. Or maybe I'm not a real grown-up yet.

Over the past two weeks I'd been fired from the SFPD, hunted by Chinese gangbangers, shot at, bitten by a rattlesnake, and I just signed on with a team of special ops guys to take on high-risk international security assignments. And now I'm escorting a famous Hollywood actress from Dubai to LA on a Gulfstream.

I started to think, *What's James Bond got on me?* And if that wasn't enough, I was an Italian immigrant, born in Sicily, with a father who's a capo in La Cosa Nostra, serving yet another prison sentence for racketeering.

You couldn't make this shit up. Who was I anyway?!

My mind was racing, but eventually I fell into a deep sleep. In a dream, I was lying naked next to Sophie, holding her, and kissing the back of her neck.

When I awoke, I realized Mercedes was nuzzled next to me, sound asleep, lying against my arm. I couldn't bring myself to wake her, so I sat and watched another movie. Not one of hers.

Halfway through the movie, I pried her grip from my arm so I could use the restroom and get something to eat. This was one long-ass flight.

The flight attendant offered to prepare a late-night snack of chicken breasts, pasta, and a salad, and it didn't take a lot of convincing on his part.

I sat at a small table near the galley, waiting for the meal, and was soon joined by our guest of honor who slid in the seat across from me just as the flight attendant was putting the food on the table.

"Good timing," I said. "You hungry?"

She sleepily nodded. "Yeah."

I asked the attendant to bring a second plate and utensils. I gave her one of the chicken breasts and half of the pasta and salad.

"Mangiare," I suggested.

She smiled the movie star smile she's famous for. "I like you, Ray. You're sweet."

I smiled back. "If you only knew. I'm a lot of things, but sweet ain't one of them!"

"You're Italian. Say something in Italian!"

I laughed. *"Le belle donne sono guai!"*

She bit her lower lip. "What's that mean?"

"I'll write it down and you can google it when you get home."

She asked if I had a girlfriend.

"Of course! My mother, Rose."

I excused myself to get back to my movie. She followed and sat next to me. I resumed the movie and she tapped me. "He's a friend of mine. Arnold's the best."

"Shush."

She punched me in the arm. I ignored it and soon she was doing the cuddling thing and fell back asleep on my arm.

As Billy and the guys began to stir and move around the cabin, the jokes and comments started to fly about "Ray's new girlfriend."

"Better she sleeps," I said. "Don't wake her, or she's yours."

"Oh, Ray," said Joe, "I hate to break it to you, but she's just using you to get to me."

Eventually the pilot announced. "We're now entering U.S. airspace, ladies and gentlemen, and we're about two hours from Los Angeles. Almost home."

Mercedes moved in her seat but kept hold of my arm.

About an hour out, Billy called us over to brief the team on the final leg of the operation.

"When we land, we'll have two vehicles waiting on the tarmac.

"They'll drive up to the airstairs and everybody, but Ray and Miss Cruz, will deplane. We'll complete a quick sweep of the area and advise Ray when he's clear to deplane with our guest. They'll get in the back seat of the lead vehicle. Both vehicles will have preloaded weapons in the usual places.

"We'll be given an address in Beverly Hills and we're on our way. We'll deliver the package, and our work is done. Once she's delivered, we'll drive back to the airport on the 405 to the 101. All-in, it should take about an hour. We don't anticipate paparazzi unless someone in her camp leaked information. We're only using encrypted communications on our end. Let's get everyone ready for a fast exit, so we can put this one behind us."

As planned, when they completed the security sweep, Billy gave us the signal to deplane, and I took Mercedes by the arm and we hustled down the stairs and into the back seat.

About ten minutes out from the airport, Billy typed an address into the vehicle's navigation, and fifteen minutes later we arrived at a gated mansion. As we pulled around the circular driveway, our team exited the vehicles to again complete a security sweep.

Mercedes put a small slip of paper in my chest pocket.

"Call me."

We fast-walked into the residence, where a handsome couple in their fifties came down a curved staircase and rushed to embrace Mercedes. With that, our job was done, and we left for the short ride back to Calabasas.

Back in the SUV, Billy turned to me.

"So, what did you think about the assignment, Ray?"

"Cake run. I've had more stress deciding what to have for dinner."

- 42 -

HEL-LO, GUNNY!

While *I was away* on my first Blackhawk assignment, I left Lily a key to the cottage and asked her to check on it while I was gone.

She said she brought Hank for company and was glad she did. When they approached the house, they saw "GB-SF" spray-painted across the front of the house in Day-Glo orange.

"We backed off and called Pacifica PD. They went through the entire cottage and couldn't find any signs of forced entry, or damage, beyond the graffiti. They're doing a report, and we notified the inspectors at Central, too. The suspect probably didn't go into the house because he thought it was booby-trapped. After the light show and carnage you treated them to the night of the attack, they're aware of your capabilities. They came the day after you left for LA, because the video's time-stamped, and you can see a guy dressed in a dark hoodie with a distortion mask walking across your property. This dude was tiptoeing, but I think he knew you were gone. You're lucky he didn't burn the place down. It looked like he was looking for trip wires, or booby traps, as he approached the front door.

"The video shows him spray-painting the front of the house, and as he turned to leave, his Ghost Boy tattoo was partially visible. It's the only identifying marks we saw in the video."

"Obviously, don't go back there," I said. "I'll call Lee Tyler with Pacifica PD and ask him to keep an eye on the place. If it's not too much to ask, can you drop the key off to Lee at the PD?"

"Of course, in my free time. That's what I'm here for."

"Sorry, forget it," I said. "My bad. I've got it."

"I've gotta go, Ray. I guess I'll see ya when I see ya."

I had too much to focus on to get sidetracked with relationship drama.

I called the landlord to tell him what happened and said I'd be back in a week to move out. I apologized for the trouble and told him I'd pay for damages and give him an extra month's rent.

I didn't want to burn Lee Tyler, who helped me get the cottage in the first place.

When we returned from the trip to Dubai, Billy and I sat outside by the garage to down a few beers after I finished making phone calls.

I said, "I think I'm tired of feeling bad. I'm constantly apologizing to Lily and everyone else all the time. Things are a mess, and the last thing I need is a relationship. Sophie thinks I'm a violent psycho, and Lily wants what I can't give. It's a fuckin' mess."

Billy laughed. "Don't know about Lily, but I think I have to agree with Sophie, you are a psycho."

I shook my head. "I've got too much unresolved crap going on. The Ghost Boys, the pending assault charges, and to make things worse, I owe my cousin Sal a grand for a bet I lost a few weeks ago on a Jets game. And by now, with the vig, it's probably up to fifteen hundred. If we weren't cousins, I'd be in a body cast by now."

"Rough," said Billy.

"But aside from the pending criminal charges, being rejected by women, owing the mob money, getting fired, and having a bounty on my head . . . everything else is *really* good."

Billy stared for a few seconds. "Well, princess, I don't know how I can compete with that. Let's just go to the mall and buy you somethin' pretty."

He tossed his empty beer bottle into the tall weeds on the side of the garage.

"What's that," I said, "hillbilly recycling?"

★ ★ ★

About an hour later, we were sent another Blackhawk assignment with a planned departure for the following morning.

We returned to the airport in Calabasas to board a Learjet for parts unknown.

We were told to pack business attire and artillery for this trip.

There were four of us on this assignment, and I was glad to see Joe at the airport. We turned our phones off and tossed them in Billy's seabag, per protocol, before takeoff.

As Joe turned his off, "What if I just use it to play Candy Crush?"

Billy smiled. It wouldn't be Joe if he wasn't popping off.

After we were airborne, a high-tech executive who I recognized from TV commercials and business news reports stepped out of the cockpit and introduced himself as Günter Becker.

Billy explained there was a credible threat against Mr. Becker, so we were flying north to San Jose Airport to protect him and take him to a private residence in Los Gatos Hills. He'd been staying in Malibu with his own security team but needed to attend a board meeting and handle other business in Silicon Valley.

"Look," said Becker, "I'm not overly concerned, but the FBI is taking the threat seriously and suggested I use Blackhawk while they're focused on their investigation. They recommended my personal security detail provide a secondary layer of protection with Blackhawk as the primary. Knowing what I know about you guys, I'm in agreement.

"I only ask that you treat this assignment with the strictest confidence and refrain from sharing any of this with anyone, including spouses and significant others. And that includes after we conclude our business as well. Of course, you'll all need to sign non-disclosure agreements.

"As I'm sure you know, these situations can have a far-reaching impact on things like investor confidence and stock prices.

"Your supervisor is now free to share details with you, *after* you each sign an NDA."

For a moment, I thought, threats? He doesn't know the half of it—not until the Ghost Boys bring their welcome wagon to *your* house.

As Mr. Becker walked back to the galley kitchen, Joe whispered, "Do you think it's okay to call him Gunny?"

Billy laughed and poked him in the side. "No bueno. Knock it off. Now, listen up. These CEOs regularly get threats, but this one stands out because, beyond weaponizing social media against him, the suspects were dialed-in to his personal habits. They launched a ransomware attack on his company costing them millions, and they've threatened his life if he doesn't step down as CEO. This guy's high profile, so the FBI has stepped in with their cybercrime unit to try to flush the creeps out.

"Our mission is straightforward. We're gonna be glued to this guy for the next few days to make sure he gets through his meetings. We'll utilize all executive protection protocols. When we move him, everybody wears body armor, *including* him. "I made it clear to Mr. Becker that we're in charge, not him, so he's got to follow our instructions. He doesn't get to weigh in. If he gives you any pushback, let me know."

"Now you're talking," said Joe. "I like when you talk tough, Billy."

That brought some levity to the briefing, and a bad-boy smile from Joe.

"He's paying for the best," said Billy, "so let's give him his money's worth. We're not here to be his friend or to investigate anything. We'll let the bureau handle that."

When we touched down at the airport, we kicked it into high gear to load up vehicles and get Mr. Becker safely off the plane.

His security detail met us at the plane, introduced themselves, and led our convoy to a large, gated residence set back at least a hundred yards from the street.

"After we get him situated inside," said Billy, "we'll discuss assignments for the overnight watch. We'll need overlap surveillance inside and out, taking turns to get sleep. The client provided a private chef to keep everyone fed. He'll keep us in fresh coffee, too. The mission is simple—keep Mr. Becker alive."

- 43 -

SOME VINDICATION

We *spent the next three days* protecting Günter, and the time moved at the speed of a glacier. Death by a thousand cuts. I tried to remain positive, but it was difficult. At least we ate decent chow.

On the flight back, Joe captured the team's sentiment.

"I've had more fun in the lobby of a tire store waiting to get a flat fixed, and that was *after* they told me I actually needed four new tires."

I told Billy I needed a week off to move out of the cottage and tie up loose ends. I had to pull things together and set a new course. I was approaching my fortieth birthday without a home, significant other, or long-term plan.

He gave me the green light, so the next morning, I hit the road with apples, power bars, and a thermos of coffee to minimize stops.

Just north of Santa Barbara, I was stopped for speeding by a CHP motorcycle officer, and luckily had registered my car "c/o San Francisco Police Department," instead of using my home address. It's done for confidentiality reasons and alerts officers running my plate that I'm a law enforcement officer. It's encouraged for personal safety reasons.

The motor officer was off her bike and tapping my passenger window in an instant.

"Nice ride, speed racer," she said. "You an officer?"

"San Francisco PD," I lied.

She asked if I knew an SFPD motor officer by the name of George, who she attended motor officer training with.

"Sorry, I don't."

I went to hand her my license and registration, and she waved them away. "Just slow your roll a little."

"Will do."

She smiled, gave a thumbs-up, and left in a cloud of dust like her bike was propelled by rocket launchers. I was relieved she didn't ask to see my SFPD ID because, like my career, it was gone.

I later stopped in Salinas for a quick bite and bathroom break and was back on the freeway in less than thirty minutes for the final stretch back to the Bay Area. To avoid staying at the cottage, I got a room in Half Moon Bay just south Shelter Cove.

I'd been following Bay Area news online, and the gang violence in North Beach and Chinatown were the lead stories.

News reporters were starting to draw analogies between the Joe Boy's violence in Chinatown in the seventies and the Mafia activity in New York City around that same time.

It reminded me of the Chinese takeover of Little Italy in New York City many years ago. Today it's more of a tourist attraction, with less than a thousand Italians living in the once-thriving home to thousands of Italian immigrants. Ironically, Little Italy in New York is largely Asian now.

As I was getting situated in my hotel room my phone rang, and when I picked up, the caller identified himself as Lieutenant Mark Mahoney from IA.

"Well, Mr. DeLuca, I've got some good news for you. The DA has investigated the assault incident you were involved in South of Market and has decided to dismiss the case in the interest of justice. I'm glad you were cleared. I think justice was served and I wish you the best."

I thanked him and we ended the call.

"Yeah, baby! Fuck you, Ghost Boys, and fuck you, Flynn."

I was relieved to be vindicated. I could scratch that one off my to-do list. Had the case gone to trial, I'm confident I would have won, but I would have had the expense of hiring a lawyer, which I couldn't afford, and the hassle of the trial itself.

I decided not to call Lily on this trip, as she'd probably think I was using her to help move—then it would be yet another stop on the apology tour.

I called Mike and offered him a few bucks to give me a hand. I had a hot cup of joe waiting for him at the cottage, and we wasted no time emptying the place out. I gave him food and cleaning supplies I no longer needed and a couple of lamps he liked.

"Anything you see," I said, "if you want it, it's yours."

We drove to a storage unit in Pacifica and had everything salvageable secured by midday. I planned to store my motorcycle in the unit the following day.

I bought burgers at a spot by the beach, and we talked about life in the military. I insisted he take money for the help he gave me, but he declined, so I tossed the bills on the front seat of his pickup when he wasn't looking. He was the real deal, and friends like that are hard to come by.

I went back to the hotel room and phoned Hank. He didn't answer, so I left a voicemail telling him the assault charges were dismissed. I knew he'd spread the word around the department faster than Perez Hilton, the Hollywood gossip columnist.

As soon as I finished the voicemail, my mother called. She scolded me in Italian for not calling, then her voice went soft.

"Ray-Ray, I worry when I don't-ah hear from-ah you. I told-ah your father what-ah happened and all about-ah that sonofabitch-bastard lieutenant. Your father's-ah gonna handle it."

I love when she doubles up her curse words. It's a lost art.

"Ma, that's not necessary," I said. "Besides, I'm out. I was fired."

She laughed and switched to Sicilian. "Well, you don't know your father very well. He has ways of making things right, and he wanted me to tell you that you would be contacted by a very important lawyer in San Francisco. Hang on, let me get his name."

A second later, she was back on the phone.

"His name is Gianni Lentini, and your father said he owes him a big favor and he'll handle your situation. Your father said to tell you that Mr. Lentini is one of us and you can tell him what happened. He knows everybody, and he's a powerful man in San Francisco. He'll take care of it."

"Okay, Ma, I'll see if the guy calls, but I'm not gonna hold my breath. It's over. I was fired."

We switched subjects, and I told her the District Attorney dropped the assault charges against me.

"It's about time," she said. "You shouldn't have been charged in the first place!"

I explained I was living and working with Billy in Southern California for the time being.

"So, where should I send your goodie box?" she asked.

"Ma, better hold on to it for now. Billy's got to keep his address confidential because of his job. He's like Secret Squirrel."

She failed to see the humor and didn't know who Secret Squirrel was. "Just wait until I get situated. It'll give me something nice to look forward to."

I could tell she was a little hurt, so to get her off the topic, I told her I was looking for a nice church near Billy's house, so I could light a candle, or attend Mass. That earned me a pass, and I was able to get off the phone unscathed. The art of deflection.

To celebrate my vindication, I thought I'd treat myself to a nice meal somewhere local. The hotel recommended a seafood restaurant close by where I enjoyed a salad, oysters, and some breaded artichoke hearts.

With the artichoke capital of the world only ninety minutes away in Castroville, artichokes were becoming my new passion.

As I savored the meal, I wondered what my father had in store for SFPD and Lieutenant Jimmy Flynn. I smiled, knowing Anthony DeLuca is not someone you mess with. *Not ever.*

With my father, things aren't over until he says they're over, and if you hurt his family, all bets are off. Right or wrong, he *will* exact his revenge.

- 44 -

SORRY, AIN'T GOOD ENOUGH

Later the same day, I received a voicemail from Gianni Lentini.

I called him back and he reviewed what he'd been told by my father and volunteered a few more details.

"Well, Ray, I'm a labor lawyer, and I work with unions and this whole thing sounds unfair and punitive to me. Can you meet me at my office in San Francisco this afternoon?"

He spoke in a low, almost reverent tone when he spoke of my father and concluded in Sicilian.

"I owe your father everything. I look forward to meeting you this afternoon."

On my drive to San Francisco, I was caught off guard to see an incoming call from Sophie.

"Sophie . . ." I said when I picked up, not knowing what else to say.

"Hello, stranger. I was thinking about you and thought I'd call to see how you're doing."

I hesitated. "Well, after ghosting me for the past couple of months, I'm surprised to get a call from you."

"I'm sorry. After what happened outside the movies, I was scared and didn't know what to do."

"Well, you probably know by now the assault charges against me were dropped."

"I know. The district attorney called me yesterday. I'm glad it worked out. I told them you did nothing wrong and were only trying to protect me."

"Unfortunately," I said, "the whole thing cost me my job. I was fired and moved out of the Bay Area."

"I didn't know," she said. "I hope we can still be friends and see each other if you come back. I'm sorry, Ray, I really am."

"I heard about the incident with Vinnie Catalano. Aren't you seeing *him* now?"

"No. It didn't work out."

"Well, I've got to get to a meeting, but if I come back to visit sometime, we can grab coffee. Take care of yourself. I gotta run."

I was glad she called but pissed she'd kicked me to the curb in the first place. I was still feeling the sting. It felt good to blow *her* off for a change.

I arrived at the attorney's office and was escorted to a conference room decorated with high-end ultra-modern Italian furniture and a built-in espresso machine.

He had a large watercolor of the Sicilian Coast on the wall opposite the floor-to-ceiling windows, with a view of the San Francisco Bay. Every inch of this place said money.

I was offered espresso and fresh Italian pastries, which I gladly accepted. When he entered the conference room, he reminded me of the actor Sean Penn but taller at about six-three. He appeared confident and had a big presence. When I mentioned the resemblance, he laughed.

"I guess I'll take that as a compliment. I've heard it before."

He took his suit jacket off and sat down.

"Relax and start from the beginning," he said. "I wanna know how you did in the police academy, and in field training, before you were assigned to Central Station. Then tell me about your relationship with this supervisor, Lieutenant Flynn.

"Your father loves you, and he's very proud of your service as a Navy SEAL. I want to hear about that, too. Your father says you're a man of great courage and character. Now is *not* the time to be modest."

His assistant took notes like a court reporter, and periodically he stopped to redirect me or drill down further.

He also wanted the details of the accidental death at the Pings and the shooting at my apartment in Daly City the night before the incident with the Ghost Boys South of Market.

"These things are important," he said, "because they speak to your state of mind when confronted by the Ghost Boys outside the movie theater and how you reacted when Flynn confronted you later that night."

It was apparent he was constructing a case to call into question the ongoing disrespect and treatment I'd received after a long-distinguished career as a SEAL and then as a new police officer and subordinate of Lieutenant Flynn's.

He said he'd also look at SFPD's disciplinary policies and procedures to make sure they were lawful and administered equally, without bias or prejudice.

"Sounds like this Flynn doesn't like Italians."

"Maybe," I said. "The latest rumor he's spreading is his belief that I had something to do with the recent influx of Sicilians into North Beach. It's fantasy, ridiculous."

We concluded after a couple of hours.

"Ray, based on what you told me, your termination lacked sufficient cause. This lieutenant has a vendetta against you and went over the top pushing for your termination when a warning or suspension would have been sufficient. In the next few weeks, I'll prepare a case and formally appeal your termination. I'll work with your police union officials to straighten this out.

"I've got relationships with city leaders and some of the guys who run the POA (San Francisco Police Officers Association). No guarantees, but I'll see what I can do. Don't get rid of those uniforms just yet."

He quickly stood and retrieved his jacket.

After a firm handshake, he said, "Give your father my best. I owe him more than I can ever hope to repay."

- 45 -

WHY NOT?

I *called Billy to check in* but didn't tell him about my visit with
the attorney. He said there were a couple of assignments in
the works but nothing too exciting.

He said Blackhawk corporate called him and wanted to forward
an email to me from a client, so Billy told them to send it to my
Blackhawk email address, which I rarely check.

After we hung up, I brought the email account up on my
laptop and was surprised to see a message from Mercedes Cruz.

Hi, Ray. I don't have your cell but wanted to invite you to
a party at my house in Bel Air next Saturday. Come solo
because I'll be your date. We'll have fun! Xoxo, MC.

I was about to delete the message when I came to my senses.
Why not?
I emailed her back.

Sure. As long as I don't get a work assignment before then.
OK if I bring Billy? Maybe you've got a friend for him?

I included my cell number in the email and hoped I wouldn't
live to regret it.

I drove the six hours back to Agoura Hills with a sense of relief, putting miles between me and the Ghost Boys. I had some trepidation about involving an attorney but was glad my father called in the favor. Still, I didn't want to get my hopes up.

Billy and I barbecued by the garage, and after we ate, fired up cigars to enjoy with our bourbon. I needed to explain to him in-person the situation with the attorney and the police department.

"Hey, bro, I've gotta update you on the situation with the PD. My mother told my father I was fired, and he went off the rails. You know, he knows everybody, and they all owe him favors, so he called in a marker with this high-powered labor lawyer in San Francisco to get me reinstated. Normally I'd say I don't have a chance in hell, but with my old man, if you're told to get something done, you get it done. So, I met with the lawyer while I was up there."

"Aw dude, don't do this to me. I love having you around."

I exhaled and looked down. I knew I let him down.

He took a pull off his cigar then sent a plume of smoke skyward. "But if that's where your heart is, you gotta go with it. I got your back. You've got a job with me as long as you need it."

I felt a sense of relief. "Thanks, bro. We'll see what happens. The whole thing might fall apart."

I wanted to get off the subject, so I told him about the party invite from Mercedes on Saturday night and he lit up.

"You know she's got the hots for you, so why not? She's obviously nuts like the rest of Hollywood, but she's smokin' hot, and you're not tied to anybody, so go for it. Live a little!"

"Well, you're going with me," I said, "so let's see who she's got in mind for you. Just another adventure, my man."

We toasted and called it a night.

The next day we took an assignment in LA picking up ballots for Oscar nominees and delivering them to Price Waterhouse Coopers to be tallied for the Academy Awards. It felt like a silly assignment, but I guess somebody's got to do it. Funny how you never think about who handles these types of things until it's you.

Mercedes called while we were driving around, and when I told her what I was doing, she was giddy and asked me to write her name in for Best Actress. We laughed and she texted me her address and told me to bring Billy. She said she had a beautiful actress friend that was excited to meet him.

"These parties go late, so plan on staying for the night," she purred. "And don't bring your PJs!"

I laughed and asked what we should wear for the party.

"Surprise me! This is Hollywood, Ray."

We took a couple of short assignments that week, flying an executive to Los Cabos and helping complete a threat assessment for the Oscars. Interesting work. Not a lot of action.

With time to shop, Billy and I hit a high-end men's store in mid-Wilshire to take our game up a little. Getting Billy to shop for clothes was like asking him to walk into a lion's cage wearing pork chops around his neck.

"Aw c'mon, cowboy!" he said in his Okie drawl, "I don't need fancy clothes. I already got boots and jeans!"

I explained the idea was to look good without looking like we're trying to look good.

He scratched his head. "Now dammit, Ray! Don't confuse me like that!"

"Well, we don't want to look like hipsters. I just want to look presentable, so they let us in, and we don't look like Lloyd and Harry in *Dumb and Dumber*."

- 46 -

OH, WHAT A NIGHT!

It *took thirty minutes* to drive to Bel Air. Mercedes lived closer than I realized. It was a warm night, a typical June evening in LA. Billy and I were amped up like a couple of high school freshmen on our way to a school dance. Billy told me my new outfit made me look muscular and accentuated my blue eyes. "I *am* muscular, you clown." I looked him over. "You, on the other hand, look like that country music star Kenny Chesney, but ya need a hat! Maybe some cattle, too!"

I'm glad we haven't matured since the age of fifteen.

Billy had grown accustomed to seeing the over-the-top Hollywood lifestyle through his work with Blackhawk, but this was new to me, and I was going to enjoy every second of it. Why not?

The Cruz estate was gated, and after we cleared security, a valet parked our car, and we were escorted through a side gate into this amazing resort-type setting with an enormous infinity pool. A firepit was blazing in the center of the pool, surrounded by lush gardens, fountains, cabanas, and oversized couches and chairs.

I looked at Billy and said, "Unreal. It's like the Four Seasons or the Ritz."

As we looked at each other I thought, *maybe we are Lloyd and Harry?*

About a hundred guests and servers mingled around the pool. Billy and I grabbed a drink at a covered pavilion and thought we'd do some celebrity-watching while we waited to greet the hostess and star of the party, Mercedes Cruz.

It was like sitting in the stands on the red-carpet runway at the Golden Globes. Most of the guests were recognizable celebrities and rock stars. We assumed the guests we didn't recognize were producers, directors, agents, and others in the business who make the magic happen.

"Man, Billy, why do I get the feeling someone is going to call security on us?"

He laughed. "Ray, they're all just people who try to imitate real people like us. Just make believe and enjoy."

As we toasted the evening, Billy broke into a wide grin—that's when I felt a full embrace from behind. I let it linger for a second before I turned to return the favor, giving Mercedes a long kiss. It was impulsive and even I didn't see that coming. That being said, she certainly kissed back.

"Wow!" I said, "I guess it's officially a date!"

She flashed her movie star smile. "I'm so happy to see you, Ray. And I'm glad Billy could come, too."

I had seen her at her worst in Dubai. Tonight, I was seeing her at her best. She was gorgeous, and I was having a hard time controlling my stare.

She gave Billy a long hug, too. "I've got someone fabulous I want you to meet."

Arm-in-arm the three of us walked to the far side of the pool where Mercedes introduced us to a striking brunette I recognized from television.

"Billy, this is Danielle."

She was a bit taller than Billy, even in his cowboy boots, but he didn't seem to mind, and they both looked awestruck as their eyes met.

"Beautiful lady," he said, "can I buy you a drink?"

She smiled. "I'd love that."

They locked arms and walked toward the bar.

I looked at Mercedes. "Wow, no chemistry there. Does she know Billy's *not* in show business?"

Mercedes laughed. "I told her Billy was casting for the next Scorsese film. I told her you and Billy were my heroes and next to you, Billy's the baddest dude I know. Danielle adores strong men. She's gonna love getting to know Billy."

We drifted around the party and shared a plate of hors d'oeuvres.

As we strolled, she introduced me to a "Who's Who" of Hollywood celebrities. We stopped along the way to pose for pictures. Some of the photographers were, no doubt, paparazzi friends of hers.

"I feel like I'm at the prom and we're the King and the Queen!"

She laughed and stayed glued to my arm.

I suddenly realized some of these pictures would be in the tabloids, probably before the sun came up. Mercedes' action thriller was set to be released in a few weeks, so paparazzi were all over her.

My mother would get a kick out of it if she saw me in a supermarket rag. I can hear her now, *Mama mia!* She'd buy the entire newsstand.

On a serious note, I was concerned I'd be recognized by one of the Ghost Boys if they saw me in the tabloids. While a picture wouldn't necessarily tell them where I am, it could put a target on Mercedes, if the dopes put two and two together. They might try to get to me through her.

I decided not to get ahead of myself and enjoy the rest of the night.

I kept an eye out for Billy and saw he was getting along fine without me. He was the last guy I needed to worry about.

Later that night a deejay, who Mercedes said was one of the top deejays in the world, played a high-energy EDM mix. She talked about the whole international club scene and how deejays like "Diplo" and "Marshmallow" make millions for an appearance.

"I saw him at a club in Brazil last year and asked if he'd play for a party at my house. Done deal, so here we are. Do you like him?"

"It's not what I listen to," I said, "but it's fun. Maybe he'll play something a little more chill in a while so we can slow dance."

She kissed me, left, and came back smiling.

"You better not step on my toes."

We slow danced to two or three songs, and I had to resist the temptation to take the intimacy too far. Mercedes was less disciplined and steamier. I could feel her heat.

I tried to keep her in check.

"We've got a lot of eyes on us. I want to protect your image and reputation. You're a big star. But if all these people weren't here, we'd be doing a lot more than this."

She kissed me again. "You're sweet."

I was seeing an entirely different side of her, and she was nothing short of intoxicating.

I caught up with Billy as the party was wrapping up.

"Hey, cowboy," he said. "I'm heading into the sunset with Danielle for a little nightcap. I'll see you tomorrow at the house, or I won't."

"You're staying with me," said Mercedes, "so let's disappear."

Out of sight of the guests and paparazzi, we wasted no time retreating to her room to strip down and take a shower. Then, using a bedside remote, she changed the lighting and mood in her suite to a sunset with the sounds of waves crashing.

"Let's take our time, Ray."

We made love until the sun came up. Then we did it again, just to make sure we did it right the first time.

She asked what I liked for breakfast. "Lucky Charms or Count Chocula if ya got 'em?"

It was fun being silly with her, and she seemed to enjoy my stupid, immature humor.

- 47 -

LIFE AIN'T FAIR

We had breakfast by the pool where Mercedes pulled up the Hollywood gossip websites on a flat screen in the pavilion. From TMZ to Perez Hilton, she—or should I say *we*—dominated the news cycle. The only good news in all this was most of the stories were on celebrity websites, and it's doubtful the Ghost Boys had any interest in them.

As Mercedes looked through the pictures and stories: "Everybody thinks you're hot, and they're writing about you more than me. You're stealing the show! They're calling you the new mystery man who came out of nowhere."

"Yeah, well, let's keep it that way."

"Don't be surprised if you see pictures of us on magazine stands and stuff."

Wonderful. I felt a momentary wave of panic.

"On a serious note, there is something I need to tell you about."

She gave me a serious look. "God, you're not hooked up or married, are you?"

"Of course not. Like I told you before, I became a cop in San Francisco after I left the military. I had a few serious incidents with a Chinatown gang called the Ghost Boys. It's not important how it happened, but I ended up killing one of them after he almost beat his girlfriend to death. It was accidental, and I wasn't trying to kill him. I was exonerated of any wrongdoing, so I'm not in trouble for it, but the Ghost Boys put a bounty on my head and want me dead. That's why I left the Bay Area and came here to work for Billy. I needed to get away from them. They've made several attempts on my life."

"That's terrible, Ray. Now I'm gonna worry about you all the time. I don't want anything to happen to you!"

"I'm hoping the police department will eventually arrest enough of them, but I can't be sure, and now I'm worried about you. With you and me all over the press, if they find out I'm seeing you, they may come after you to get to me."

She looked away and was silent for a minute. "We're just starting out. This is so unfair."

"I'm sorry, Mercedes, maybe I should stay away so there's no more publicity. Trust me, you don't need this in your life."

"Ray, I'm crazy about you. You're my hero, and nothing is going to keep me away from you. I've been thinking about you since the moment I met you in Dubai. I have a lot of money and can protect myself at home, on the set, and when I go out. I always have armed security with me. Nobody's a hundred percent safe anymore anyway."

I held her.

"You're amazing. Just so you know, a labor lawyer in San Francisco is appealing my case with the city to get my job back. I plan to go back to SFPD to clean up this Ghost Boys mess. After that, I don't know."

"But what about us?"

"There is no us. Is there?"

She embraced me. "I want there to be."

I was starting to think, I felt the same way.

"I'm sure you're away all the time making movies. Right?"

"Yes. I'm gone a lot."

"Well, I can come down when you're not working, and we can be together. I only work four days a week, so we can spend time together, if things work out. But let's see how things go."

- 48 -

MOB MONDAY

I **phoned Hank on my way back to Billy's** and told him I had a big favor to ask. I felt a sense of urgency to reach him. When I got him on the line, I said, "I know you're gonna think I'm nuts, but I need a favor. I need you to go to every supermarket and corner store within ten blocks of Chinatown. Go to their magazine stands and look for any gossip magazines or newspapers with pictures of me or pictures of me with Mercedes Cruz. When you find them, buy all the copies.

"I'll reimburse you. It's a long story, and I can explain later, but I don't want the Ghost Boys seeing my picture, especially with Mercedes Cruz. It might give them the idea to go after her to get to me, and I have to protect her."

There was a long pause on the line.

"Mercedes Cruz? What the fuck are you talking about? Is this a joke?"

"No, it's not a joke. I'm seeing her, and like I said, I'll tell you about it another time. Just do me this favor, and I'll reimburse you for your time and any expenses, too. I just need your help with this."

"Okay if I ask Lily to help me?"

"No! She'll go off the rails, and I don't want that. It'll be a lot of quick stops. If you can hit Daly City and Pacifica supermarkets

247

and corner stores, too, that would be great. Like I said, I'll pay you for your time, and expenses. Take somebody with you and I'll pay them, too. Just hit the obvious places where the Ghost Boys might go to get smokes, buy gas, and whatever other shit they buy. C-stores and places like that. Think like a punk-ass Ghost Boy and hit the stores in the areas where they might hang out."

"Ray, you never cease to amaze me. You are one mysterious motherfucker."

"Yeah, sure . . . you don't know the half of it."

Billy got home about twenty minutes after me and looked as happy as a man can be. He looked like he'd been rode hard and put away wet.

"Talk to me!" I said.

"That's one fine lady," he said in his okie drawl, emphasizing the word fine.

"Oh c'mon, don't give me that gentlemen don't kiss and tell bullshit."

We laughed and he said, "Pretty amazing. I think there'll be a second date. Probably more after that. I think we're *sim-pat-ico!* Did I say that right?"

"Well, get yourself a pair of those lifts for your boots. She's a tall glass of water."

"Pardner," he said, "height is overrated."

★ ★ ★

The following day, I got calls from Vinnie Catalano, my attorney Gianni Lentini, and my cousin Sal the bookie. Now that's a mob hoagie.

First Vinnie.

"Hey, paisan. I just wanted to let you know you were right about the problem I had with the girl outside Carmine's. My attorney got the whole thing dismissed, and I agreed to stay away from her. I need that shit like a bad haircut. Where you been?" "Just a little vacation. I'm glad it worked out for you." "Come by Carmine's or Trattoria when you get a chance, and I'll buy you dinner. Bring a date."

How about I bring that chick you slapped the shit out of? "Thanks, Vinnie. I will. When things free up a little. I appreciate the offer."

I had a hard time not liking this guy. No doubt he wasn't aware I'd been fired from the police department, or he'd be recruiting me for his crew, with promises of the good life. Just as well.

I no sooner finished the conversation with Vinnie when Gianni called.

"Hey, Ray, I've prepared your case and want to review it with you for accuracy before I submit it to the union and civil service commission. Do you have time in the next couple of days?"

We set a time and I made plans to fly up from SoCal and return to LA the same day.

As I was hanging up from the call, I saw my cousin Sal was trying to reach me, so I called him back.

"Hey, cuz," he said. "What the fuck? I'm pretty sure youz owe me a coupla large for the Jets bust.

"The vig is growing and now youz up to two g's. Youz *famigghia* and I been covering for you, but youz need to get dat paid before they make me release the hounds."

"No, you're right. I got it, cuz. If you can cover me for forty-eight hours, I can send the money Western Union, or Venmo, or something. Text me what you want me to do. My apologies. I've got a lot going on. I'll get ya paid."

"I got it, Ray. Now get back here, so we can party."

If all that weren't enough, Mobster Monday ended with a late-night text from Mercedes.

She sent me a provocative picture, making sure her face was obscured, with a string of hearts.

Miss you, Ray.

I guess a girl can't be too careful.
I texted back:

Me, too.

Me + U go to premier for my new pic?

I hit her back: Want to. Call U tomm. Sweet dreams.
Things were getting interesting.

- 49 -

SO, YA THINK I GOT A SHOT?

Gianni was laser-focused and needed to verify everything we discussed earlier. He was meticulous and had to get it right, especially for Anthony DeLuca's son. After very few clarifications and modifications, we were done. He invited me to lunch, but I explained I had to fly back to LA for another commitment.

Before I left his office, he said, "No promises, Ray, but I like our chances. Hang in there. I'm working every angle."

When I stepped into the elevator on Gianni's floor, I was surprised to see Carmine's sister, Gina, standing behind other passengers. After I exited, I waited until she stepped out.

"Hi, Gina. I don't know if you remember me. I'm Ray DeLuca."

She smiled and extended her hand. "Of course, I remember you. You were so kind when Carmine went missing. Funny running into you here. My attorney's in this building."

"Mine, too," I said.

"So, how are things with the police department?"

"Long story, but I'm kind of on a leave right now. Not sure if I'm going back."

"Well, come by Carmine's anytime. I'd love to see you again."

I was surprised she was being so forward, but like a lot of guys, I tend to flatter myself thinking any pleasantries from a woman means they want to have sex with me.

"Sure. I've been out of town a lot lately, but the next time I'm around, I'll call for a reservation."

"No. I meant to have lunch, or dinner *with me*, and it's my treat. "She handed me her card. "Really, Ray. Call me."

We had an awkward handshake that turned into a hug, and I told her I looked forward to it.

And I did. Especially after that nice hug.

I think my initial thoughts were correct.

Feast, or famine. A few weeks ago, I couldn't get a look if I pranced buck-naked through a female prison, and now I'm getting propositioned daily.

I checked newsstands at a couple of San Francisco C-stores and delis before I caught a ride to the airport. Nothing yet.

At the airport, I got a text from Lily.

Mercedes Cruz . . . really?

Here we go.

I don't know why I was surprised. She felt used, but that was never my intention, and I never expected Mercedes to come into my life. I felt awful. Why am I always feeling bad about someone, or something? Sometimes being me can be miserable.

I texted back.

Met through new job. Just friends. No big deal.

Crickets.

I glanced at newsstands in the airport but didn't see any pictures of Mercedes or me. Good news there.

Hank must have told Lily. That guy gossips more than a high school cheerleader.

I boarded the plane for the flight back to LA, keeping an eye out for Ghost Boys. I wore a SF Giants baseball cap and sunglasses in the airport and on the plane, until I was confident no assassins were on the flight.

THIS WASN'T SUPPOSED TO HAPPEN

t felt good to get back to Billy's and the smell of barbequed chicken and beef on the grill. He was making fajitas. Maybe I *should* marry him? (We don't swing that way, but if we did, it would be a marriage made in heaven.)

Billy looked like he just won the lottery, just short of gushing over Danielle. I'd never seen him happier.

"I can't believe it, Ray. It's all I think about. Man, I'm in tall cotton! I was with her again last night. She left for Canada today to film something for the Hallmark Channel. She'll be gone for a couple of weeks. That parts a drag."

I made light of it.

"So, which one do you have a problem with, eh? Canada? Or all those happy endings on the Hallmark Channel?"

"You know what I mean, cowboy. I'm thinking like a teenager."

As Billy took the meat off the grill and walked into the house, gunfire erupted from a hedge row on the side of the house.

I dove into the garage and grabbed an AR-15 from Billy's open gun safe. He'd been cleaning guns that afternoon and luckily hadn't finished the project.

Billy tossed a smoke grenade into the hedges and made a run for the garage. I heard rounds hitting the side of the cinder block walls. He busted through the side door and ran to the safe and grabbed an AK-47.

He looked at me. "You're hit. Where'd they get you?"

I glanced down and realized I was bleeding on my left side and was dripping blood on the garage floor.

"I'm fine. This is going to end, right here, right now."

We quickly grabbed our body armor and spit-balled a plan to toss flash-bangs and pepper both sides of the house along the hedge rows with automatic gunfire.

The AK was incredibly loud, so the neighbors probably called the police, so we had to move fast to take them all out. We had no idea how many assailants there were, but estimated at least five, based on the number of incoming rounds.

Billy took the north side, I took the south, and after we tossed the flash-bangs, we went full auto with our weapons and doubled down with second magazines, firing more than a hundred rounds into the hedges.

After about a minute or so, Billy yelled, "Cease fire!"

We tossed smoke grenades and cautiously moved along the hedges to check for additional suspects, the dead, and any survivors.

Billy called 9-1-1 and was told officers would be on scene within a minute. I heard a parade of sirens, probably responding from Los Angeles County Sheriff's Department and California Highway Patrol.

I heard the slapping of rotor blades of an LASD airship overhead and recognized its green, yellow, and gold markings.

We put our weapons back in the garage and prepared to "assume the position." The deputies didn't disappoint.

I overheard one on his portable radio requesting the coroner. "10-85, six Asian males," indicating a coroner was needed for six.

TV news trucks and stringers were on scene as we were handcuffed.

A paramedic looked at the wound on my left side and confirmed I'd been shot. They loaded me into the EMT wagon after I was handcuffed to the gurney to treat the wound.

I was only grazed but had a good-sized divot in my side. It looked worse than it felt, especially after they injected me with morphine, to take the edge off.

I watched as a deputy perp-walked Billy to an awaiting police vehicle.

Another deputy who accompanied the paramedics read me the Miranda Warning, explaining my legal rights to representation, en route to the hospital.

I gave him the number of the lead SFPD inspector on the Ghost Boys case, and as I was waiting to be treated in the Trauma Unit, he confirmed my story and uncuffed me from the gurney.

"Sorry, bro. You know the drill."

"No problem," I said. "Did you get a look at the suspects' neck tattoos?"

"They were dragons with large initials. CB, or GB, or something like that."

I asked the deputy to call the unit who had Billy in custody to release him as well.

He told his colleague, "Ongoing gang investigation. They've made death threats and have a bounty on my vic who was shot. He's a former San Francisco cop."

After treating me, they admitted me to the hospital overnight for observation. They also sent two fresh deputies to sit outside my room for the night.

After settling into my room, I turned on the TV to pass the time. The story was being sensationalized on most of the LA news channels, with news chyrons that used terms like *SF cop, gun battle, Agoura, six dead, Asian gang members.*

By the following morning, pain was setting in, so they administered more pain meds and changed the dressing. I was feeling pretty good.

I channel-surfed morning shows like *Good Morning America* and *CBS This Morning*, and the headline on the updated story was *Mercedes' Hero Kills Six Gang Members.*

Billy came to visit.

"Hey, princess, you only got a scratch. I've had bigger boo-boos falling off my Big Wheel!"

"You know me," I said. "I'm gonna milk this thing."

"Listen, pardner, thanks for telling those deputies to kick me loose last night. I came to the hospital, but you were sleeping, so a deputy drove me to the house. They put two deputies outside my house all night. It wasn't as good as having you home. Neither of them would spoon with me."

We needed the laugh.

We watched the news and Billy said, "I think Mercedes just hijacked our fifteen minutes of fame. She already called this morning, freaking out. I forgot she has my number. Danielle, too."

"My phone's dead," I said. "Let me use yours. I've got to call Mercedes and my mother to settle them down. My mother probably saw it on *Good Morning America* and is in a panic."

He tossed me his phone and said he was going downstairs and would get us espressos from the coffee bar in the lobby.

"Take care of the deputies, too," I said.

I called Mercedes, but got her voicemail, so I left a message telling her not to worry and texted her I was fine and would check in after I was discharged. Then I called my mother.

My mother went into a stream of Sicilian obscenities before I could get much out. Lots of double and triple curse words. The triples are the best.

"Ma, this was like falling off a bike. It's a little scratch."

She asked about Mercedes, but I downplayed it. "She's just a friend I met through the job."

"Your father's worried sick, too," she said. "I'll call him and let him know you're okay. Your father is very upset with these attacks and said he's got his own gang, and if this doesn't stop, he's going to take care of it."

"Ma, I appreciate that, but for now I need to handle it. If it gets worse, I'll let you know, and he can deal with it his way."

As I was getting dressed, preparing to be discharged, I heard a commotion outside my door and heard Billy explaining to someone that Mercedes was a friend, so it was okay for her to visit.

Her security guys were told to wait outside the room, as nurses approached to get a look at her.

Mercedes walked in and hugged me around the neck, covering my face with kisses. We comforted each other.

"Billy said it looks like a mosquito bite," she said.

I got a snicker out of her as she told me how worried she was. "Come to my house. You can recuperate there. I'll talk to Billy about hiring more security from your company while you rest. You'll be safer there and I can keep an eye on you."

She was probably right. It was best to avoid Billy's house for now.

"I don't want to leave Billy alone. Okay if he stays at your place, too?

"Of course. I've got lots of room, and I love having Billy around. I always feel safer when you two are with me."

The nurse entered the room with a wheelchair. "Sorry, regulations."

She looked at Mercedes and gasped. "Oh, my God! Well, would you like to push him out to the car?"

"Of course," she said and flashed her mega-star smile.

As we exited the hospital, paparazzi and news crews were there like a swarm of locusts.

As she pushed me to her waiting SUV, she whispered, "Smile . . . you'll get used to it."

The deputies gave us an escort to her estate, and Billy said, "I'll go to my place first and grab some things and meet you there later. I'll grab your stuff, too."

It was good to be out of the hospital, and Mercedes and I sat by the pool to relax and catch up. She asked her chef to prepare lunch and refreshments.

I knew the events of the past twenty-four hours hadn't hit me yet; I was foggy with pain medication.

After lunch, I took my phone off the charger and turned it on for the first time since being admitted to the hospital. As anticipated, there were at least a dozen texts and phone messages from family and friends.

As I was checking my messages, Mercedes watched the news on the flatscreens in one of the pavilions.

I texted Lily and Hank.

Six more.

I got a text from Gianni Lentini, my attorney.

You OK? Negotiated settlement.
Good news. Call me.

As I was about to call him, Mercedes let out a blood-curdling scream like I'd never heard. She was hysterical. As I went to grab her, she pointed to the TV screen that had a live shot of the exterior of Billy's house, with the headline *BREAKING NEWS. Another Gang Attack in Agoura.*

They showed aerial shots with cop cars stacked up for blocks outside of Billy's house.

"Oh, my God," I said. "I've got to check on Billy. Can your driver take me there?"

She nodded.

"Stay here," I said. "Until I know what happened."

Her driver, Pete, helped me to the car. He was retired LAPD, so he knew shortcuts to get there and wasn't concerned with speeding or being stopped.

He got us through the roadblocks using his LAPD ID, just in time to see them carrying a body bag out of the house to the coroner's van.

An investigator escorted me to his car.

"I'm really sorry. Your friend's gone. I'm sorry for your loss."

I felt faint, so he asked a deputy to bring cold water, as he helped me sit on the curb.

"As far as we can tell, the shooter was inside the house, and shot him as he walked in. Our units cleared the scene a couple of hours ago after doing the forensics on last night's shootings, so the house was unattended.

"I'm guessing after our units left, the suspects broke in and waited for you to come home. They fired on your friend as he came in the back door. He was lying in the doorway when we arrived. Never drew his weapon. Never had a chance. Head shot and another hit him in the throat. Instantaneous. He never felt a thing and probably never saw it coming."

"I need to see him."

We walked to the coroner's van, where they unzipped the body bag so I could see him. I confirmed it was Billy and wept. Those bullets were meant for me.

As I turned to walk away, Pete came over. "I'm sorry, Ray. Let's get you outta here."

After we cleared the scene, as we were leaving the area, Pete opened the glove box, grabbed a flask and handed it to me.

"Drink this. I'll drop you off at Mercedes' and call the sheriff's department. I've got friends over there from my days at LAPD. I'm going to ask them to provide round-the-clock security at her estate until things quiet down. I'll call Blackhawk to notify them. I'm sure they'll send some guys over to help."

"Thanks," I said. "I'll need to go back to Billy's later to get my things and secure his weapons in the safe. Can we go back in a couple of hours?"

"Sure, no problem, Ray."

Mercedes' personal physician was leaving as we walked into the house. "I just gave her a sedative, so let her rest for a while. She's extremely upset."

That's when he took a better look at me. "Sit down. Let me check you. You don't look good."

I talked him out of giving me a shot and he handed me a few sedatives.

"In case you need them later."

I walked back to the pavilion and turned the flatscreens off. I called my attorney and updated him on the latest assault and Billy's death.

"Ray, I'm very sorry to hear about your friend. You've been through a lot. Let's do this later."

"I'm okay, Gianni. Now is fine. It'll take my mind off the other thing."

"Alright," he said. "The police department has agreed to reinstate you and provide back pay. You'll show no break in service as part of the agreement. Reinstatement is very rare in the police department. It's like putting the toothpaste back in the tube. You really caught a break here, Ray, but I think we made a good case; and aside from the insubordination, supervisors said you were doing a good job. They said you're a good cop.

"Part of the agreement also calls for you to apologize to Lieutenant Flynn. I think it's worth it, Ray, to get your life and your career back on track. You can go back to Central Station, or any district station of your choosing. They've got a lot invested in you, and they're glad you're coming back.

"The lieutenant who harassed you has been admonished, too, and he's been transferred from Central to another district station. I heard he wasn't too pleased with that, but at least you don't have to see him every day. Avoid him. It's a big department, but sooner or later, you'll cross paths. Just be respectful and stay cool."

"Gianni, I don't know what to say. I'm distracted right now, so I apologize. Thank you! This is beyond anything I thought was possible. Let's talk tomorrow so we can review it again. I'm in a fog and I'm not retaining anything right now."

"Alright, Ray. Call me tomorrow and we'll hammer things out."

I said, "Grazie amico mio," reiterating my gratitude.

I no sooner hung up than Pete came over.

"Let's run to Agoura and get your stuff before we're out of daylight. Four deputies are here, and your boys from Blackhawk just pulled up, too. Give me five minutes, and I'll get them situated and we can go."

The guys from Billy's team walked in and we formed a circle with our arms around each other and cried.

"It's fuckin' awful," I said. "This wasn't supposed to happen. Those bullets were meant for me."

Joe shook his head. "Don't say that, Ray. Billy would have taken a bullet for any one of us, and you would have done the same for him. We all know the risks. This is who we are. Those motherfuckers are gonna pay."

Just then, Mercedes shuffled into our group hug, and we all embraced, releasing the waterworks again.

Pete gave us our time and space, then came over. "C'mon, let's roll, Ray."

"If you guys don't mind," said Joe, "I'm going, too."

The deputies and the rest of the team stayed back to guard Mercedes and the estate, and the three of us drove to Billy's house.

"Ray, you and Joe grab the guns in the garage," said Pete, "and I'll grab your things in the house. Seabag, right?"

"Yeah."

"I'll check for other valuables, too."

I realized Pete didn't want us in the house where we'd see the crime scene carnage. I'm sure the hazmat cleaners hadn't arrived yet, to handle the cleanup. This was something Pete had a lot of experience with as a former D-3 detective for LAPD's venerable Robbery-Homicide Division, or RHD, as it's called.

A real pro.

- 51 -

TOO YOUNG

The following day, Mercedes and I were finally able to reach Danielle, Billy's new sweetheart, who was traveling to Canada for the Hallmark production when tragedy struck.

She went from disbelief to breaking down. Between tears, she said, "He was the most gentle and sweet man I ever knew. My heart's broken. We were falling in love. This is awful."

Through her tears she said, "He always wanted to talk about me and build me up. He was so modest. He would make jokes about himself, like he was nobody special. But I knew better. He was so strong and courageous."

We listened and let her pour her heart out. It was painful to hear.

"I'll get a flight out tomorrow morning," she said.

"Hang on, Danielle," I said. "Sit tight for now. We know how much this movie means to you, and there's nothing here for you to do. Honest, there isn't. Billy was crazy for you and told me right before you left, how deeply he was falling in love with you.

"He never talked about a woman the way he talked about you. He was like a teenager and told me he couldn't stop thinking of you.

"He adored you and wouldn't want you going through this. He'd want you doing what you love, making a movie."

"But—"

"Think about it, and Mercedes will call you in the morning."

The next morning, I called my mother and broke the news about Billy. She never met him but felt like she knew him through me.

She wept.

"I gotta tell your father about this. Ray, I'm so sorry you lost your good friend. I know how much he meant to you. This craziness has got to stop, *Marone!*"

Marone is an Italian expression of frustration and an appeal to the Blessed Mother.

"I know, Ma. I'm being careful and working on some things to put a stop to it. I'm getting my job back with the police department, and that will help, too. Tell Papa, Mr. Lentini has been great, and I really appreciate the help he's giving me. I love you both. We can't discuss this on the phone. I have to go and deal with funeral arrangements for Billy and track down his family."

I called Billy's boss at Blackhawk corporate and, like the rest of us, he was dealing with his own grief over the loss. Blackhawk had already called Billy's emergency contact and beneficiary in his personnel file. He had a brother, Jess, just outside of Tulsa.

Billy told me his brother had been struggling financially, so I was sure he'd appreciate any proceeds from Billy's life insurance and the sale of his house in Agoura. He said he had a young family and was working two jobs.

The exec from Blackhawk said, "We'll pay to fly his remains to Tulsa and pay for the funeral. I'll give you the dates once I have them, and if you'd like to accompany him on his journey home, we'll cover your expenses and any of the team members, too. I know you guys want to be there to honor him."

"I appreciate it," I said. "We'll give him a hero's sendoff with an honor guard. If you can, text me his brother's phone number, so I can call him and help him deal with things."

After getting his brother on the phone, I learned there wasn't much of a family, just Billy and Jess. Billy was older, and Jess put him on a pedestal.

He laughed. "I guess I don't have to worry about paying him back the grand he lent me two weeks ago."

Then he started to cry, and it broke my heart.

I made a list of things he needed to handle as Billy's next of kin.

"Jess, just deal with your grief right now, and when you're ready to deal with the other stuff, I'm here to help. He wasn't just your brother. He was mine, too. So, that makes you and me brothers, too."

- 52 -

TENDER AS SHE GOES

We escorted Billy's remains to his final resting place, a small, grassy cemetery outside Tulsa. The team sat together for the three-hour flight, took an oath, and plotted our revenge. The remaining members of this evil, ruthless gang had to pay for what they did and be expunged from the earth. Every one of them.

We made a simple, but elegant plan.

"They'll be no peace," I said, "until this is done, and once it's done, we'll never speak of it again. Not ever."

We had a modest service for Billy at a local Episcopal Church Billy attended as a kid. Jess and his wife and kids were there, as well as some childhood friends still living in the Tulsa area.

We wore our Class A military uniforms and took our positions as pallbearers. I couldn't remember when I'd seen more "fruit salad" on military uniforms. They each had stacks of campaign ribbons, as well as other awards and citations, including a Bronze Star, Silver Star, and Navy Cross.

In addition, each member had received at least one Purple Heart. These guys were as good as I thought they were.

Joe did the readings for the service, and I gave a brief eulogy. Joe abandoned his sense of humor. I'd never seen him so stoic.

The honor guard met us at the cemetery, where they played Taps, performed a twenty-one-gun salute and presented the flag that was draped on Billy's coffin to Jess.

We hired a local bagpiper to play "Amazing Grace" from atop the hillside near the burial site. It was a cool, drizzly day for June, and the haunting sounds of the bagpipes permeated my soul and reflected the depths of our sadness.

Following the graveside service, we took Billy's family to a local steakhouse to celebrate his life.

We enjoyed hearing about Billy's youth and the things he never told us. Billy was notoriously private and humble, so there were stories we'd never heard before. Like his love of rodeo and a failed attempt to ride bulls professionally. His first car was an old Corvette that broke down more than it ever ran, but Jess said he still loved that car. We also learned about his deep faith, and his interest in joining the seminary as a younger man.

We took a red-eye back to LA and were picked up by Pete at LAX for the ride back to Mercedes' estate.

The team went their separate ways, and Joe explained he'd be the acting team leader until they were able to conduct interviews and select Billy's successor as team leader.

"You interested?" he asked.

"Sorry, bro, I'm leaving Blackhawk. My attorney negotiated my reinstatement with SFPD. Plus, I'll have more access to intel on the scumbags who killed Billy."

He hung his head, closed his eyes, and looked forlorn.

"Well, bro, we still have unfinished business with them, and you're one of us, so we'll be in touch. Any future discussions about this should only be on a secure line or use burner phones."

"Agreed. Let's table it for now, and I'll call corporate tomorrow to give my two-weeks' notice."

Pete told me he dropped Mercedes off at her agent's office in Beverly Hills for a lunch meeting, and he'd be picking her up at two.

"Thanks, Pete," I said. "I'm fried. I'm taking a nap until she gets here."

"Well, we've got Blackhawk guys here and a couple of deputies," said Pete, "so everybody should be fine."

"Right, and I'll have my hardware close by."

I closed the blackout curtains in Mercedes' suite and dozed off. The room was cool and dark.

I dreamt recurring dreams I was being chased by thugs but kept getting lost and couldn't seem to get away from them. I awoke soaking wet, so I stripped to take a shower. I was rinsing off when I sensed and smelled Mercedes as she lightly stepped into the shower. She turned the lights low and put on ambient music, and neither of us said a word.

We generated a lot of steam and barely made it to the bed where a chilled bottle of Dom Perignon in an ice bucket was waiting for us. We opted to forgo the champagne in favor of comforting each other.

We had dinner next to the pool, enjoying the views of the hills and canyons.

As we sipped our spritzes, Mercedes said, "I had lunch with the studio execs today, and they've got a new project they want me to star in."

"Congratulations. That's great news. I'm happy for you. Your fans are going to be excited. You're a superstar, and they can't get enough of you. This is your time."

I walked around the table, leaned over, and kissed her.

She hesitated and then took on a serious tone. "Here's the issue, Ray. It's going to be filmed in Italy, and I'll be over there for at least a year."

I hadn't considered that, so it was a surprise.

"Well, baby, this is how you make your bones. We both have unique careers that can separate us at times. We'll figure things out."

She brightened. "You can live here and come see me in Italy. You can teach me the language. I'll pay for everything."

"Sweetie, I've got news, too. My attorney is getting me reinstated with the police department. I thought I'd rent a small house in Marin County, then come to LA on my days off, but it sounds like you won't be here anyway."

She got up, sat on my lap, and put her arms around my neck, with her head on my chest. We held each other for what seemed like an hour, but I wasn't complaining. This was painful, and I felt an ache in my heart and knew she did, too.

"I think I'm going to accept their offer," she said. "My agent likes it, and it's the most I've ever been offered for a picture. You can come to Italy when you have time off, and we can be together. I don't know what else we can do. We both have our lives, and our work is important to us."

My heart continued to sink, but she was right. Besides, she'd be safer over there, until the Ghost Boy threat was eradicated anyway.

I spoke to Gianni the following day and reviewed the terms for my return to duty. He negotiated back pay as well. That would come in handy and help me set up new living quarters.

"I'll tell them you can report for duty in two weeks," he said.

"I appreciate it. Just let me know when it's final, so I can resign and give Blackhawk my notice."

At dinner the following night, Mercedes blew me away with the gift of a platinum Rolex Yacht-Master watch. I was speechless.

I'd never been given anything like that before. Anything that expensive. I could tell from her loving smile she was as excited to give it, as I was to receive it.

"Even in uniform," she said, "people will know how special you are. You're my hero and every time you look at it, you can think of me."

I know she had a sense of guilt over leaving for Italy, and I think she was trying to make up for it and show me she was serious about our relationship.

We both needed to move on for a while and get on with the business of life.

- 53 -

ADDIO DOLCEZZA

[Goodbye, My Sweet]

As my time with Mercedes waned, there was a growing sense of emptiness, sadness, and distance. The feelings were inevitable and unavoidable. In a matter of days, I was moving back to the Bay Area, and Mercedes would be leaving for Italy to throw herself into her upcoming role.

I wanted the aching in my heart to stop.

I packed my car the night before I left for San Francisco to avoid a long, drawn-out goodbye in the morning. I avoided staying for breakfast and told her I needed to get on the road early. Saying goodbye to Mercedes was the hardest thing I'd ever done, even though I planned to see her one more time before she left for Italy.

"It's *not* goodbye, Ray," she said. "You're my hero and I love you. We just need to go back to our jobs for a while. Call me when you get to San Francisco."

Mercedes had agreed to continue with Blackhawk's security detail until she left for Italy. Pete said he'd travel with her to help her get situated but wasn't sure how long he'd stay.

"Sometimes, it's boring as shit," he said. "I'll go for a while and see what the deal is. I've never been to the Amalfi Coast, so I'll do some sightseeing when Mercedes is working."

Pete and I had become friends.

"I'll keep my ear to the ground with the Sheriff's Department," he said, "and let you know what I find out on Billy's investigation."

We agreed that future conversations would only be on secure lines, which meant burners or encrypted phones.

A real estate agent in Marin County showed me some small houses and bungalows off the beaten path in Fairfax. The location was close to work, on the other side of the Golden Gate Bridge.

I picked a cottage that was isolated, knowing at some point, a Ghost Boys attack could occur.

Once again, my Marine buddy Mike came through to help me move.

I avoided talking about the job and Billy's murder in Agoura. I took him to dinner after we finished to thank him and catch up on things in his life. He had a new girlfriend and that had him pumped.

At dinner he said, "I saw *you* on the news and in magazines in the supermarket. I thought, holy shit, that's my friend Ray! Are you really dating Mercedes Cruz?"

"Yeah, we've been hanging out for a while. I met her when I was working in LA."

I didn't want to give out too much information. "She's off somewhere filming her next movie, so it might be awhile before I see her again. Hopefully, I can introduce you at some point."

We finished the meal, and I left cash in the visor of his truck when he was distracted.

The next day, out of the blue, I received a call from Deputy Chief Potente, the head of investigations. He congratulated me on my return to SFPD and wanted to know when I was going to personnel to sign my reinstatement papers.

"Tomorrow, sir. At ten-hundred hours."

"Do me a favor, don't broadcast your reinstatement just yet. No need to worry. Everything's fine. I assure you."

My heart sank.

"After you sign the papers," he said, "I'd like to meet with you at my office. I've got something I'd like to talk to you about. No need to worry. It's all good."

I met Gianni in the personnel office in SFPD headquarters on Third Street the next day to sign the reinstatement papers. He wanted to be present to avoid any problems. I was also given a check for back pay.

As we were waiting for the administrator, Gianni admired my Rolex with a smile. "They must have been paying you pretty good at Blackhawk. Maybe you should have stayed there?"

"No way, Gianni. This is a gift from my rich girlfriend."

"Oh, yeah. I know who she is. I love her movies. You've done well, Ray, and look terrific. Things are coming together for you. Consider me your *consigliere* for anything. It's been great meeting you."

"By the way, how much do I owe you?" I asked. "I might have to pay in installment payments."

"Not on your life. You've seen my offices. None of it would have been possible without Anthony DeLuca's help. You're pre-paid with me for a lifetime, and if you ever need my services again, I'm here for you. *Capiche?*"

After signing the documents, we shook hands, and went our separate ways.

As instructed, I reported to the DC's office. His call was heavy on my mind and gave me a restless night's sleep. What did he want to meet with me about? To admonish me? What was I walking into?

His assistant escorted me into his office and shut the door. After a quick exchange, he told me to sit and relax.

Yeah, right!

I apologized for my grungy biker appearance, but he smiled.

"Don't change a thing. It might come in handy."

I glanced around as he got situated. Situational awareness, I guess. Lots of plaques, awards, family pictures, and posed photos with dignitaries.

I'd never met him in person, but he was larger than I imagined. I'm guessing six-foot-four, fifty years old. He was a dark-complected Italian, with a full head of salt-and-pepper hair and a seventy-five-dollar haircut. Reasonably fit, too. Women would probably find him attractive, and some men might find him intimidating. I didn't. He had a large scar across his chin.

He sat facing me in a trendy upholstered chair that was too small for his frame, in front of his desk. He was in a crisp uniform, no gun belt, with a .40 caliber Sig Sauer pistol in a black pancake holster with handcuffs looped through his belt. Ready for business.

He proceeded to speak to me in Sicilian and asked if I signed the reinstatement papers.

I answered, "Si signore."

He smiled and continued in Sicilian: "Congratulations and welcome back. The reason I wanted to see you is we've got a major problem with some of our countrymen terrorizing North Beach and Chinatown. I know you're aware of it. I think you're also aware that Vincent Catalano is behind a lot of this, and I know you've been friendly with him. Correct?"

Like all good Italians, his speech was accompanied by hand gestures.

"Yes, that's correct."

I explained that Vinnie introduced himself at Lieutenant Ferarro's retirement party.

"I like his restaurant," I said. "On occasion I eat there, and I've played a little poker with him and his friends. We're not best friends, but he's Sicilian, and he's been decent to me. I don't accept free meals from him or anything like that. It's all on the up and up."

Potente said, "You know he's mobbed up, right?"

"Of course. By the way, my family is, too, and I'm sure you know that from the investigators that did my background before I was hired. I was completely upfront about it.

"But remember, sir, I've been far removed from it all for a long time. I spent sixteen years as a Navy SEAL and only came home when I was on liberty. It's my family. I'm not embarrassed about it, it's just a fact. I grew up in the life, and so did my father, and it supported our family."

He showed no emotion. Just listened and gave me the steely stare. After I finished answering his question, I returned the stare.

Just cut me loose, I thought, *so I can grab some lunch and get out of here. I've got things to do!*

I didn't know what he was getting at. I'm not known for my patience, and I was hungry to boot. *Hang-gry.* I was worried any minute I'd tell *him* to go fuck himself and be marched out again for insubordination. This time for good.

He sighed, then said, "I'd like to make you a proposition. We're creating an Organized Crime Task Force, and I'd like you on that team. There's nobody in our ranks who knows La Cosa Nostra firsthand better than you. You'd be undercover and would not return to Central Station.

"At least not now. You'd have to disavow any connection to SFPD and stay off the grid. Of course, you're one of us, but we think it would be better for you and this operation to limit knowledge of that to myself, the chief, and personnel. You'd have to tell everyone that the reinstatement didn't work out and you've decided to move on. Tell them you're still doing stuff for Blackhawk."

He let me digest it, then asked for my thoughts.

"Sir, what's in it for me? Why would I do this? I'm not going to use my family to get information. My father's still in prison, for Christ's sake."

"What's in it for you . . . " He let it hang in the air for a few seconds. "DeLuca, right here, right now, this opportunity would be *your* best purpose where you could do the most good for this police department. Help us clean up the Central, and you'll be recognized for it and get on the fast track for promotions, if that's in your plans."

He pointed to his large leather chair behind his desk.

"Might be you sitting back there someday. Maybe. If you take advantage of the opportunities in front of you."

I thought about that.

Potente said, "Look, you'd be a founding member of the task force. We plan to add two or three more undercovers. Central's become a shit show, and CompStat has our homicide rates four times the other districts. The locals are calling the mayor, supervisors, and the chief's office daily. They're fed up. Who wants to ride the cable cars or shop in Chinatown when gangbangers and mobsters are on every corner? How are people supposed to enjoy an espresso on Columbus Avenue with shootings and wise guys everywhere? We're getting killed in the press, and it's pretty much shut down our tourism, which is the lifeblood of this city."

"What if I say no?"

"It's up to you. You can go back to patrol in the Central, or you can really make your mark and help us solve a major problem."

I sat silent for a moment. "I appreciate the offer, but I'd like a day to think about it."

"No problem. Take twenty-four hours. Until you've decided, don't communicate with anyone about this, including other members. And don't go to Central Station. Strictly confidential."

He handed me his card. "Let me know by tomorrow."

I was dismissed and left the public safety building with my head spinning.

I had to reconstruct what he said, in my mind, in Sicilian, because our entire conversation was in our native tongue.

- 54 -

IT'S WHO YOU KNOW

I *left the public safety building* and drove my motorcycle to King Street en route to the Embarcadero to meander into the Central district. Per the DC's request, I'd avoid Central Station, but felt drawn to drive the district and reflect on his offer. I missed the pulse of the city and pushing a radio car. The smells of roasting coffee beans and baked bread when I was cruising up Columbus Avenue brought it all back.

I parked next to Washington Square and took a minute to watch dog walkers and Asian women performing Tai Chi in the park across from Saints Peter and Paul's Catholic Church.

As I zipped around the district, the earworm of Steely Dan's classic hit "Dirty Work" played in my head, especially the chorus, "I'm a fool to do your dirty work, oh yeah . . . "

Maybe an omen.

I was starved, so I got a sandwich to go from Molinari's Deli and raced home to my new hideout in Fairfax.

After I devoured my Renzo Special Italian sandwich—with marinated artichoke hearts and extra pepperoncinis—I called Mercedes.

"Hey, baby, you're going to love my new digs. It's nicer than your place, but a little smaller. In fact, your walk-in closet, just the part for your shoes, is bigger than my entire cottage."

She laughed. "I miss you so much, Ray. I've been crying all day. Come home. I don't think I can do this."

"Of course, you can," I said, "and you *will*. I miss you, too, baby. Pete and the security guys are there, right?"

"Of course. I'm doing everything you told me to do."

"Next time we'll FaceTime."

"I'd love that because I want to see your handsome face."

"Me, too, beautiful."

We kissed goodnight. "We're gonna be fine. Sleep tight."

She was crying. I had a lump in my throat.

★ ★ ★

The next morning, I called DC Potente.

"Chief, while it sounds like a great opportunity, I think going back to patrol in the Central would be my preference right now.

"I appreciate your offer, but after being on the bench for a while, I miss working uniform in a radio car. That might change down the road, but right now I think that's what's best for me for reentry to get back to old routines. I hope you understand."

There was a pause on the other end of the line.

"I've gotta say I'm disappointed, Ray, but I understand. It's a tough job and you've gotta be up for it every day. I know that. If you're open to it, I'd like to sit down with you again and pick your brain about recruitment for these positions. As I said when we spoke yesterday, no one in the department has your insights and experience in that world, including me. Would you be available for that? I can talk to Captain Choo so you can do it during your shift. That would be helpful."

"Of course," I said. "Just let me know when."

"Very good. I'll ask my assistant to coordinate a time with you in the next few days."

I was relieved he seemed to understand my position and was flattered that he wanted my advice.

I hadn't done any serious grooming in a while, so I made an appointment for later in the day at a high-end salon in San Rafael before going to Central Station to avoid scaring my fellow officers. I opted for nicer clothes as well and drove the Challenger to the station instead of the bike.

At Central Station, I was immediately buzzed in by the station keeper, Officer Payne, who smiled and offered a high-five.

I went directly to Captain Choo's office, as instructed, and apologized for not calling the previous day. I made the excuse that I was waiting on some final paperwork.

"Christ," he said, "you look good, Ray. Where you been, at a resort?"

"Nah, just that warm LA sun."

He unlocked a desk drawer, then handed me my star, ID, and duty weapon.

"Welcome back. Just a word of caution," he said. "The scumbags who've made your life hell are still out there, so when you come back from reentry, operate accordingly. We'll have extra officers on your shift, and you'll be working the five-car, but don't go into Chinatown unless all hell breaks loose. Just lay low and let's not poke the tiger yet."

I put my star and sidearm on. "I understand, sir."

Regardless of my intentions, there was nothing else to say.

I walked into the squad room to a standing ovation. I turned around to see if they were clapping for somebody else.

My union rep Tommy was there. "Hey, Hollywood, welcome back!"

A female officer said, "Whoa. You clean up nice."

Lily walked in and hugged me. That was a surprise.

"Did someone take you to the groomers? You look like you've been on the beach in St. Tropez."

Another officer yelled, "Where'd you steal that watch? You ain't buying a watch like that on a cop's salary. Somebody better run the serial number on that bad boy."

Another said, "We heard you're driving a *Mer-sayyy-dees* now."

I smiled. "Have your fun. I've got to go through reentry at Taraval Station, so you won't have me to kick around for a while. If one of you can come to the range with me and shoot some holes in my target, I might have a shot at qualifying and getting back here."

I grabbed a few uniforms and equipment from my locker and drove to Taraval Station to drop things off.

At Taraval, I was welcomed like a foster child released from juvenile hall and introduced to my FTO (field training officer) for reentry.

She introduced herself and said, "I'm Mary Quinn."

She had short red hair and came off as masculine and tough. She stood about five-four, and what she lacked in height, she had in girth. In a word, sturdy. No judgments, though. I planned to be respectful and follow her lead, to get through this.

She was nice enough. "I heard Flynn jammed you up. Sorry to hear that. We just need to make sure you're still 10-8."

The code 10-8 communicates that you're in-service and available for radio calls; but in this case, was used to ascertain if

I was fit for duty and squared away. I was assigned a temporary locker and told to report for day watch the following morning. As I was leaving, an officer in the squad room called after me . . . "Hey, aren't you the guy who's dating Mercedes Cruz?"

Choosing to divert, I said, "That's me. I'll see you guys tomorrow."

The following day was awkward until I learned the training officer was a *huge* fan of Mercedes and her movies, so she quickly became more interested in Mercedes than re-qualifying me.

The news of my arrival at Taraval traveled fast, and there wasn't much I could do about it. They printed pictures of me and Mercedes from gossip pages and posted them around the station with the caption, "Taraval's New Celebrity Officer."

After a week with the training officer, she took me aside. "Look, Ray, you obviously know your shit. You should be training me!"

"Thanks, Mary."

"Take your three days off. I'm releasing you to Central, but you have to promise me an autographed picture from Mercedes, and I want to take a picture with you before you leave Taraval."

"Done and done," I said. "Thanks for kicking me loose. I enjoyed meeting you and working with you."

- 55 -

CHILLIN' AND GRILLIN'

I *got high-fives and pats on the back* the next morning in lineup at Central, with a hug and kiss from Hank.

"You're buying lunch today," he said. "Scoma's."

"I better call ahead and make sure they've got enough sushi and fish on hand. They may need to send out another trawler before we get there."

That earned some hoots and jeers from the watch.

Hank and I were partnered once again. "I'm driving," I said as we headed out. "And you can carry your own shit to the car."

He had a look of surprise. "A little bitchy, huh?"

After we loaded our unit and went in-service, Hank looked over at me.

"There's something different about you. I can't put my finger on it. Did you have Botox or something down in LA? I think your lips are fuller and you just got cuter. I'm terribly attracted to you!"

"Nope. But I have been taking better care of myself, watching my diet, taking my vitamins, and I did switch to a new shea butter body lotion. Oh, hot yoga, too. Maybe that's it? Where you buying me coffee, shitbird?"

Hank sighed and shook his head in resignation. "Café Trieste."

It was déjà vu, pulling in there, but I didn't see Sophie—not that it would have mattered if I had.

Mercedes called to check in on my first day back. I'd told her she could and that I'd answer if I wasn't tied up. I picked up.

"Hey baby, say hi to my other partner, Hank."

I passed him the phone.

Hank wore a huge grin. "Hi Mercedes . . . yes, it's good to talk to you, too . . . Of course, I'll look out for him. He's my partner . . . Nah, he's tougher than anybody out here."

He covered the phone. "Don't let it go to your head."

He passed her back me, and Mercedes and I talked for a few minutes before a call came over the radio, and I had to cut things short.

"I gotta go," I said. "I'll call you later . . . Okay. *Ciao, bella.*"

Hank seemed a little starstruck. "Dude, was that really her? Wait until I tell my wife and kids. Holy shit!"

"Nah, wasn't her, just some chick from a bar in Daly City."

Hank was on cloud nine.

"Next time we'll FaceTime," I said, "so you can see her, and she can see what *I* have to look at every day."

The calls were routine, and we rolled on three individuals cooking on one of the old piers behind Scoma's Restaurant.

On scene, we approached three large Samoan males guzzling beer and grilling fish on a rusty hibachi. They looked homeless— or "displaced" as they say—with shopping carts full of personal belongings and random items.

I conservatively estimated each of them weighed between three and four hundred pounds.

"Gentlemen, I hate to spoil the party, but you can't have fires out here on the pier. You're also not allowed to have open containers, so finish what you're drinking. The piers are old and it's a fire hazard. It's all rotted wood. You need to put the fire out and move on."

One of them mumbled something, but they kept sipping and grilling.

Hank got ID from one of them, and the others said they didn't have any, but provided their names and dates of birth.

I ran their names through Wants & Warrants, and they stared at me the entire time as I was waiting for the returns. It's usually a sign that one, or more, have an active warrant for their arrest and they're getting ready to resist, or run. When the names came back, I turned to Hank and pitched my voice low.

"The big one is 10-30 for a 459 warrant out of our city."

So, we had one of them with a confirmed felony warrant for burglary. I couldn't pronounce his name, so I said, "Kahlua-Lua over there. He's the biggest one with the brown blanket around him. He's going."

"Go hook 'em up, ace," he said. "He kinda looks like an angry Shrek. You got flex-cuffs or leg irons? You'll never get handcuffs around those fuckin' wrists."

As we reapproached them, Kahlua-Lua said, "I ain't goin' witcha, brah."

He stepped back as I advanced, then one of his friends piped up. "He the dude! He wid dat girl in the movies!"

They started to laugh and banter in Samoan, and Kahlua-Lua smiled. "Awwrigh, I go witcha, brah."

I looked at Hank. "I'm glad I didn't have to hurt him. You better call a wagon for this one. He'll never fit in a Crown Vic."

We extinguished the fire and told his posse to leave, as we waited for the wagon.

His compatriots came back clear in the system.

Kahlua-Lua was surprisingly mellow and compliant, but I'm sure if you pissed him off it would probably take an entire SEAL team to take him into custody.

Loading him into the wagon was like moving a piano. They'd need help in the sally port at the Hall of Justice to extract him from the wagon, but our work was done.

"Next time you see a herd of buffalo like this," Hank said, "it's okay if you wanna flip a bitch or drive past them."

- 56 -

FINDING NEEDLES IN A HAYSTACK

I *met with DC Potente* early the next morning while on duty. The sergeant told me to take an unmarked car for the meeting with the chief at SFPD headquarters.

The new headquarters was officially opened in 2015. It's strikingly ultra-modern and austere. The cavernous common areas gave it a cold and unwelcoming vibe. I wanted to leave as soon as I arrived.

The chief was prompt and smiled, seeing me for the first time sans the beard stubble and grunge look. I took extra efforts to wear a fresh uniform, polish my brass, and spit shine my boots.

"Looking sharp, Ray," he said. "How about a cup of coffee?"

"Black, sir."

We sat at a small, round conference table in his office with yellow legal pads and pens ready to go.

He grabbed a pad. "Okay then, let's get to it. I'd appreciate hearing your ideas on how we can recruit for these unusual positions. It's not every day we recruit and search for officers with organized crime expertise."

"I've given it some thought," I said, "and I think you need to begin by identifying the specific characteristics you're looking for. These jobs will be highly specialized and call for experienced officers who are tough, incorruptible cops. They'll need to be

Italian, obviously, and speak the language fluently. Sicilian would be preferred. They'll need to come off as the real deal."

Potente nodded.

"Also," I said, "it would help if they grew up around the life and are knowledgeable about the mob and the mob culture. Guys like me from New York, New Jersey, Philly, or even Italy. Even if our local mobsters make them for cops, they'll get more out of them when they realize these cops are the real deal and not far removed from who they are."

The deputy chief said, "That's a tall order."

"Chief, I'm talking best-case scenario, so they can blend in and won't be intimidated. Maybe you recruit from the feds, like the FBI's Joint Terrorism Task Force, or agencies like NYPD, or Newark PD in New Jersey? There's also DIA, the Direzione Investigativa Antimafia unit in Italy. I don't think there're a lot of guys like me on the West Coast. I think you'd have better luck recruiting from agencies in the northeast. For the right individuals, it would be good if you could offer them a signing bonus and moving expenses. Cops in the northeast are paid a lot less than we are out here, and that should help you recruit them. A lot of them only make half of what we make."

"All good points," said Potente.

"I'd also suggest that you interview them in Sicilian, or Italian, but don't tell them that beforehand."

"This is good, Ray. I'll talk to the chief and see if he agrees. We'd probably have to hire a headhunter and do some independent networking on our own."

"Okay then. Anything else, Chief? I probably need to get back on patrol."

"Would you be open to sitting in on the interviews? I have a feeling you'd smell bullshit a mile away."

"Of course, Chief."

"You sure you don't want to reconsider?"

"I'm good, sir."

- 57 -

GOODBYE, HOLLYWOOD. HELLO, FAIRFAX

I spent my first day off working on the physical security of the bungalow and ordered blackout shades and replicated the security setup I had in Shelter Cove. I had plenty of firepower with Billy's HK submachine gun and the rest of my arsenal.

With Mercedes leaving for Italy in a few days, as promised, I flew to LA to take her to dinner at Nobu, her favorite sushi restaurant. Pete helped me with arrangements and drove us to the restaurant. We hit the usual swarm of paparazzi coming and going.

I suggested we keep the mood light and enjoy our time together, which we managed to do.

A few Hollywood A-listers stopped by our table to say hello. Mercedes made it a point to introduce me as her significant other, which I appreciated. Before dessert arrived, I gave her a diamond rope-style bracelet I bought from a high-end jewelry store. The salesclerk said the style was the latest thing, and I fell for it. With a little luck and working 10-B, I'd probably pay it off in a few months.

Mercedes beamed. "It's gorgeous, Ray. I'll wear it all the time."

At that point she started to tear up.

"Let's just enjoy the rest of the night," I said.

The next morning, I helped Pete load at least ten suitcases, makeup cases, and a wardrobe into Mercedes' SUV. Pete had a small duffel bag.

I accompanied them to the private jet terminal at LAX to say goodbye. The Blackhawk guys planned to drive her SUV back to her estate to garage it, while she was out of the country. The security team followed us in their SUV as well.

At the jet terminal, valets handled the luggage while Mercedes and Pete cleared TSA and customs.

After a tearful goodbye, I left with the Blackhawk guys, who dropped me at the Southwest terminal before driving back to her house.

As I waited for my flight, I could still taste and smell her, and my heart ached. I had to get my mind off Mercedes, so on the flight to SFO, I daydreamed about taking out what was left of the Ghost Boys. Avenging Billy's death and stopping these attacks was a top priority.

We had to get it done quickly before they took me out, too. I was certain they knew I was back on the job. They always seemed to have the inside track and intel on my whereabouts. Somebody wanted me out of the way.

Wearing my skullcap and sunglasses, I bought cheap burner phones for cash at a bodega in South San Francisco and FedExed one to Joe for untraceable conversations. Then I remembered Blackhawk phones were also encrypted, so we had even more communication options.

I called Joe on a burner. "I'm getting intel now and will be in touch. LASD said two shooters took Billy out, so let me start there and see if I can get names. Once I have that, we'll decide on next steps."

"Sounds good," he said. "We can handle stragglers, too, if we need to."

"Give me a week."

"Stay frosty."

I dropped my things off at the bungalow and walked to downtown Fairfax. I got a recommendation from a local to eat at Sorella Caffe, a local favorite for Italian food.

The food was amazing, and I met the owners, sisters from Brazil, raised by an Italian mother and Korean father. One of the sisters recognized my accent, and got wide-eyed when I told her I was from Newburgh. Ironically, her husband, John, was from Newburgh, too.

They lived five minutes away, so she called her husband and asked him to come to the restaurant to meet a surprise guest.

After a brief introduction, I said, "I've been trying to get away from Newburgh my entire life, and now this."

We high-fived. "I'm your new best customer," I said.

After the meal, John bought me a drink, then I walked the meal off and buttoned up the bungalow for the night.

It gave me a sense of comfort, knowing John and his family and Sorella Caffe were right down the street. New friends and a taste of home.

I sat up sipping too much Buffalo Trace Bourbon and was having second thoughts about taking out Billy's killers.

The whole thing was unsettling.

- 58 -

SHAKIN' HANDS, KISSING BABIES

The briefing that morning focused on recent gang activity, and the lieutenant asked Nick Bay, the SIT inspector I met awhile back, to address our lineup. He glanced at me when he walked over to address our watch.

"Welcome back, Ray," he said. "Okay, while we're seeing things a bit calmer in Chinatown, there's still a fair amount of extortion and sex trafficking. We have undercover teams in place to monitor the activity.

"Feel free to let your presence be known. Get out of your cars and do some community policing. Let the citizens in Chinatown and North Beach see our physical presence.

"As far as our Sicilian friends, well, these guys are growing their operation by leaps and bounds. They've got their hands in everything, including the unions. When you see a new face, stop, and welcome them to our fair city, and make sure you complete an FI card. Please send a copy of those FI cards to me as well."

The FI, or field interview card, was used to provide detailed identifying information about individuals detained, with the location, date and time of the stop, and anything else the officer feels is important. The information on the cards is entered into the CDW, or Crime Data Warehouse, system for investigative purposes and future audits.

"Even if you don't have probable cause for a detention," said Bay, "nothing's stopping you from being friendly and talking to people. At least you get a look at them and can find out if they speak English. Let 'em know we're out there. Walk Broadway. Go into the strip clubs. You might find 'em shaking down the club owner or doing something else nefarious.

"Walk Columbus Avenue and Green Street. Anyplace you see them mingling. Stop and say hello wherever you see them congregating. Washington Square and restaurants like Trattoria and Carmine's. The sidewalk cafés, the bars, coffee shops.

"It goes without saying, watch for the 221s [guns] as well.

"When you're not handling calls for service, be out there making new friends. Let them feel the pressure. These guys look different than us and dress sharp with a continental flair, if you know what I mean. They're easy to spot.

"Ray, I know you're Sicilian and you know the language and the culture. You know a lot more than any of us. Anything you'd like to add?"

"Sure," I said. "These guys are associates and some are soldiers. Just assume they're packing. Even without a gun, these guys are dangerous and they're not afraid of you, or me, so be careful around them. When you meet them, smile, and say, *Vaffanculo!* Welcome to San Francisco."

A couple of officers were writing that down. One asked how to spell it.

"Okay, no, no scratch that. I'm kidding. *Vaffanculo* means go fuck yourself. Save that one for later."

The room erupted in laughter. We had our marching orders to ramp up community policing in North Beach and Chinatown.

When we were dismissed, Hank felt like stirring the pot. "Can't your people behave?"

"My people? What about *your* people? Next time we're in the locker room, remind me to show you the chunk of flesh one of *your people* took from me in LA. I'm just glad the asshole wasn't a better shot."

We stopped by Trattoria, but Vinnie wasn't there. A server said he might be at Carmine's, so we went there.

At Carmine's I told the person who answered the knock, "We're just dropping by to say hi to Vinnie or Gina if they're here."

Gina came out, gave me a hug. "I'm so glad to see you. With everything I've been hearing about you and Mercedes, I thought we lost you to Hollywood."

"Thanks, Gina. No, same ol' Ray, just walkin' the beat trying to keep the lunatics from killing each other."

"Vinnie's not here," she said. "Would you like some coffee, or espresso? Stay and talk a minute. *Per un minuto!* Have some biscotti. We just baked it."

"We'd love some coffee, but I'm gonna pass on the biscotti. I gotta watch it. But my partner would love some. You know I'm Sicilian. *Amo troppo il cibo!* A little too much, especially the food that comes out of this place. *Marone!*"

I explained to Hank, "I told her I like their food too much."

We kept the conversation light, and it was obvious she was reluctant to say much in front of Hank and might have been paranoid about Vinnie showing up. But she was flirtatious and enjoyed dropping in our Italian expressions. I hadn't seen that side of her before and was enjoying it. My mother would adore her.

When we said our goodbyes, she joked in Sicilian and told me she still wanted to have a nice dinner together.

"We will," I said. "No worries."

As we were walking to the car Hank asked, "What was she saying to you in Italian?"

"I'll tell ya," I said, "but don't repeat it."

"Okay."

"She said, 'I wanna eat-ah you up like sweet panna cotta.'"

He looked at me like he half-believed me then said, "You're an idiot."

"Don't knock it till you've tried it! Let's cruise around *your* hood for a change."

"Not happening, bro. I wanna go home in one piece. I don't know who the Ghost Boys hate more, you, or me, and they still have a contract on your head. Choo Choo and the watch commander told us to stay out of Chinatown."

"So, what's the word on the street? You live there, don't you?"

"It's been quiet, and with you taking out at least ten of their top guys, I think they're laying low."

"So, who's left?"

"Why? So, you can go gunnin' for 'em?"

"Hank, they're gunnin' for me, and I wanna know who I need to watch out for, okay? They just killed my best friend. I got nothing against the good people in Chinatown any more than I do the good ones in North Beach. My problem is with the gangbangers and mobsters. We need to eradicate these motherfuckers, and the sooner the better. This shit can't continue. *Capiche?*"

He nodded. "I'm hungry."

"So, what else is new? You should have had more biscotti."

I had a feeling no names would be forthcoming from Hank. Not ever. I wouldn't ask again. I was starting to understand my father's loyalty to our people, but I was conflicted because Hank and I were supposed to be partners, and that meant no secrets. He was hiding something, and I was starting to wonder if he was the source of the leaks.

- 59 -

QUID PRO QUO

The phone startled me around midnight. Mercedes checking in. With Italy's local time nine hours ahead, this was going to be tricky.

She said she was having breakfast on the veranda of her private estate in Positano, courtesy of the movie studios.

"Ray, I miss you, baby, and can't wait until you can come see me. I'm wearing a bikini and my gorgeous new bracelet, and I'm thinking of you."

"You stop that, young lady," I said, "or you're gonna make me crazy. What's the bikini look like?"

"Well, what are *you* wearing, Ray?"

I hesitated. "Hair shirt and a loin cloth, what else?"

She liked that, and the conversation got a little raunchy for a minute. I switched topics to put it on a low simmer. I asked her how she was doing over there.

"I settled in, thanks to Pete, and some friends in wardrobe."

"Are you studying your lines?"

"You know I am. Like it's my first part."

"Good girl. Remind them why you're worth all those euros."

We talked a bit more, then she had a call waiting for her.

"Hey, do me a favor," I said, before letting her go. "Ask Pete to call me in the next few days on a secure line. No rush.

I just wanna catch up with him. I like him. He's become a good friend."

"He likes you, too. I'm glad you two get along."

The next day when I got to the station, a tall black inspector known as "Big Dee Washington" told me he had "one of the greaseballs" in custody for extortion but was having trouble communicating with him.

"Well, Inspector," I said, "how about this: I won't call you a *melanzana*, if you don't call my people greaseballs." Melanzana is Italian slang for blacks, meaning eggplant.

He looked surprised but not offended. He shrugged. "Fair enough. Sorry, man. I apologize. Can you help me interview this guy?"

"Sure. Give me fifteen minutes. I've gotta suit up and get ready for my shift. Tell the LT I'm helping you with an interview and won't be in lineup."

What I later learned was that Inspector "Big Dee" Washington, with his fancy suits, fedora, and cowboy boots, hoped to emulate the late, great, SFPD inspector Napoleon Hendrix, also known as "Slim." In his twenty-one-year career as a homicide inspector, he cleared more than eighty-five percent of his more than five hundred murder cases. At six-foot-five, even without his famous ostrich cowboy boots, he was an SFPD legend and San Francisco's most successful homicide cop ever.

Salvatore Caruso was hands down the most immaculate, best-smelling guest in our holding cell that day. In fact, he was probably the only one in the cell who had bathed in weeks. The stench inside the holding cell would make a barnyard pig hold his nose.

The suspect smiled when he realized we were from the same tiny island between the Mediterranean and Tyrrhenian Sea: the island of Sicily. As I carefully placed his expensive Italian loafers on the floor to let him slip them on, he seemed grateful, smiling and nodding.

I escorted him to the interview room where Big Dee asked me to read him his rights in Sicilian.

He waived his right to have an attorney present and agreed to speak to us. After introducing myself, I asked him specific questions about a shakedown at a local strip club. It was obvious this wasn't his first sit-down with the *polizia*, and he denied pressuring the club owner for payment.

In Sicilian, he said, "He owed me money. I was just collecting what he owed me."

After a few go-arounds, I motioned to speak to the inspector outside the interview room.

I told him, "This is a reach, bro. He's not giving anything up. I'd suggest kicking him loose, and at least now you've got him ID'd.

"Let's get him on something bigger down the road. Something with some meat on the bone. I'll tell him we're doin' him a big favor, but he's gonna owe us one. He knows how the game is played."

"Okay, but let him know we're looking for payback soon, or we'll keep pullin' his chain."

"Done. Let's go back in there and finish the interview and turn off the recorder."

After the recorder was off, I asked where in Sicily he was from.

"Palermo."

"Nice," I said. "I love the fish markets there."

He smiled.

"Look," I said in Sicilian, "we're both Sicilians, and I want to do you a favor and get you out of here, but I need something from you."

"Name it," he said.

"You've got competition with the Ghost Boys in Chinatown. Those little pricks with the dragon tattoos on their necks."

He smiled and nodded.

"A group of them killed my friend in LA a few weeks ago. I wanna know who they are. I want names. Maybe a 'friend' can talk to them. Get me names and then we're even. *Capiche?*"

He gave me a long look. "*Si, capisco.*" Yes, I understand.

I returned his personal property from the booking envelope but put his passport in my pocket.

"Get me that information, and I'll give you back your passport."

The inspector didn't notice I swiped the passport.

"Thanks, Ray," he said. "I appreciate the assist."

- 60 -

KEEP YOUR ENEMIES CLOSE

After the interview—and with Hank already on the street handling a call for service—I asked the sergeant if I could run solo for the day as a SAM unit. The sergeant was already ass-deep in problems, so he waved me on.

"Yeah, sure. Advise dispatch you're the Three-Adam-Five-Boy."

As soon as I went in-service as 3A5B, Hank called.

"What are you doing? Who authorized you to be a SAM unit?"

"Chill. Maybe I'll get some real police work done today. I've gotta go. Have a nice day, cupcake."

It promised to be a great day. Places to go, people to see, without Hank yammering in my ear. I planned to do a slow roll through Chinatown and drop in on Vinnie at Trattoria.

I owed Gina a visit at Carmine's because the last time I saw her she was stressed and probably holding back with Hank there.

I was feeling frosty, so first, I parked on Stockton Street in Chinatown and walked a block, hoping to draw attention. The streets were crowded, and I didn't think the Ghost Boys would shoot me in broad daylight in uniform. I talked to a couple of Ghost Boy lookouts and had them scattering like cockroaches. One ran like he was being chased as I approached him. Probably carrying a firearm.

"Run! Run like the wind, you little turd," I yelled after him.

For fun, I stopped and asked a merchant in a firecracker shop if he knew where the Ghost Boys' clubhouse was.

"No, no! Why you ass me dat?!"

I smiled, settled him down. "I'm just kidding. Relax."

I got my point across, so I cruised out of the district into North Beach, sure by now half of Chinatown knew I was back. Point made.

Next stop Trattoria. I caught Vinnie as he was walking out.

"Hey, goombah!" he said. "*Come stai?*" How are you? "Christ, you look good, Ray. Glad you're back."

"Yeah, back in the saddle. Gotta make a livin'. How you been? What's new?"

"Keepin' busy with the restaurants. Come by and *mangia!*"

"Yeah, kinda watchin' the weight, but I'll come by for some *pisci.*" Meaning fish.

"Such restraint! Anyway, I gotta go," he said. "I'm late for an appointment. Come by and *mangiare* soon."

I watched as he drove off in a new Ferrari Roma coupe with temporary plates. He drove in the direction of the Financial District, so it was safe to assume he wasn't going to Carmine's.

Activity was light, so I cruised to Carmine's to see if I could catch Gina.

★ ★ ★

"Let's go down the street to Nino's Café," she said, "my treat."

I told her that sounded good to me, and after we left Carmine's, she said, "Too many cameras and spies. They don't need to know everybody I talk to."

We walked a half a block to a small outdoor café.

"So, how's things?" I asked.

"It's been a little slow. Aside from the great food, Carmine was the main attraction. That's why people came in. Everybody wanted to see him, get an autograph, or a picture with him. His absence is still felt by customers, but they're slowly coming back."

"Sorry to hear that. It'll pick up. How's the partnership with Vinnie?"

"The partnership's fine so far. I'm okay with it. I don't have a choice, and I make the best of things. I never mentioned this before, but I introduced my brother to Vinnie. We went on a date awhile back, but it didn't work out. Not really my type. He and my brother apparently hit it off, and Carmine let him buy into the restaurant, to get some cash and get out from under the daily grind of running it. I can't say I blame him."

"He's been nice to me, so far, so I guess that's good."

Gina dating Vinnie caught me off guard, and I wondered why she didn't tell me sooner. I theorized it was probably an oversight, or she didn't want me to know because she was interested in me.

She seemed embarrassed. "It's no big deal, Ray."

I smiled. "Is there anything else you think I should know?"

"I don't think so. You know he's got a boat, right?"

I didn't. "Where's he keep it?"

"Not sure. I've never been invited."

We sipped our espressos.

"So, enough business," she said. "When am I going to have that dinner with you?"

"Gina, we can have dinner as friends, but right now, I'm in a committed relationship, so the timing's not good. I'm trying to make it work. I haven't always been good at doing that."

"Of course, I understand. I don't want to interfere with that. We'll just keep it friends. Two friends having dinner. I'm working all the time, so I don't get a chance to meet nice guys like you and would enjoy the company."

"That's nice of you to say. No reflection on you. I think you're great. I've got to make this relationship work. Maybe we can have dinner in the next couple of weeks."

She smiled. "I'd really like that."

"I better get back to my police car before somebody starts stripping it."

We left the café and stopped in front of my patrol car parked near the restaurant.

"Thanks for stopping by, Ray. If it's okay, I'll call you next week for our friends' dinner."

"Sure, no problem."

I felt guilty even entertaining a casual dinner with a friend, but I figured she was lonely and probably just wanted companionship; and truth be told, with Mercedes gone, I could use some company, too.

- 61 -

BACK TO DALY CITY

I *called Mike in Daly City.*
"Hey, bro, do you have a small furnished apartment? A short-term rental?"

"What about the bungalow in Fairfax—you blow it up already?"

"No, not yet. Those gangbangers are still after me, so I'm trying to stay one step ahead. Keep 'em guessing. I don't want to be a sitting duck, no pun intended."

"No worries," he said. "I've got a studio apartment in the back that's furnished. It's been vacant forever. It ain't fancy. It's tucked away and a slight upgrade from a room in the barracks."

"That'll work. I'll pay whatever the going rent is."

As we finished our discussion, the blackout shades for the bungalow arrived, so I installed them, or I'd never be able to sleep during the day.

I called Mercedes for a quick good night. She was jazzed with the leading man, a rising star out of the U.K.

"He's like a young Russell Crowe, and he's been great to work with. You'll like him."

"Great. Just make sure he doesn't get too carried away with the love scenes because, if he does, he's gonna have to prove he's as tough as he thinks he is on screen."

She laughed.

"No, baby. Don't be crazy. You're my guy. He's an actor, not a badass. Now c'mon, what's up with you?"

"Just started back on patrol. It's like I never left," I said, "and I got a second place to sleep, away from the love shack, to keep the bad guys guessing."

She got serious. "Ray, I'm worried. When's this gonna be over? It's bad enough you're a cop."

"Soon. Real soon. Before I forget, is Pete around?"

"I'll have to find him and tell him to call you."

"Tell him to call me using our arrangement," I said. "He'll know what you mean."

"Don't know what that is, but okay."

About thirty minutes later, he called on a burner.

"Hey, buddy, any news yet from our friends in SoCal?"

"Good timing. I'll text you what I got."

"Thanks. So, how's the Amalfi Coast?"

"Freakin' amazing. When I'm not standing around on the set, I've been taking in the local scene."

"Well, enjoy. Keep an eye on my girl, and I'll talk to you soon."

About an hour later, I got an encrypted and coded text on another phone, using the protocol we had agreed on. It took another ten minutes to decipher the names of the killers, and none resonated with me. No prior contact with any of them.

I called Caruso, the mobster whose passport I was holding, and asked him for an update on my request.

"What are the names?"

"*Domani,*" he said and hung up. Tomorrow.

I was off work the following day and called my mother. She was anxious that I was back with the police department, still worried about the gangbangers.

Eventually the talk got around to Mercedes.

"*Marone ah me.* Marry her, Ray. She's ah-big-ah movie star. Then-ah you get-ah divorced and-ah lots ah-money. Then-ah you marry a nice Italian girl to give-ah me and-ah your papa *nipoti.*" Grandchildren.

"Don't you ever give up? None of the Italian beauties want me, and you're already taken, Ma."

She was excited with my father's parole date coming up.

"When-ah he gets-ah out, I want-ah you to come-ah home and we can-ah pick-ah him up-ah together, like ah-*famigghia.* He'd-ah be so happy, Ray-Ray."

"Get the date of his release and I'll book a flight. I'll be there."

She was getting emotional; I could hear it in her voice.

"I'll take you and Papa out for dinner, wherever you want to go. Maybe sushi?"

There was a pause, then she burst out laughing.

I pulled the blackout shades down and drove my bike to Daly City to see the studio apartment and give Mike the rent. The apartment was as advertised.

"Now you know why it's vacant," he said.

"Beats the side of a mountain in Afghanistan in January."

- 62 -

BUY ME SOME PEANUTS
AND CRACKER JACKS

The next day, I got a call from Caruso. He wanted to know where we could meet.

We set up a meet in the parking lot of the San Francisco Yacht Club. I drove the bike and wore my biker getup and caught him by surprise as he waited in his black Escalade. He handed me a piece of paper with two names on it, and I handed him his passport and motioned for him to leave.

In Sicilian I told him, *Tell no unu.* Saying, tell no one, gesturing with the universal throat cutting motion.

I abruptly left.

The names matched those Pete sent me from the investigator at LASD, Michael Ng and Nester Fong.

We'd identified Billy's killers.

I sent a text to Joe at Blackhawk to call me.

Twenty minutes later, he called on a burner.

"I'll explain face-to-face."

He previously told me a trusted friend from Blackhawk would contact me with the specifics regarding their trip to the Bay Area.

They were driving from LA to avoid airport cameras and flight records and had local contacts to help with recon.

About an hour later, I received another call on a second burner from an unfamiliar, artificially modified voice.

"We'll be in your neighborhood next Tuesday to deliver."

"Message received," I said and hung up.

I got to the station with time to spare, so after I suited-up I went to the SIT office.

"Did you guys know that Vinnie Catalano has a boat?"

"Yeah, *The Sicilia*.

"We served a search warrant on it in the Berkeley Marina and found trace blood on the deck at the back of the boat where Vinnie said they fish from. We also found traces of blood from his gangster buddy, Frank Bruno, who said he cut himself fishing, along with traces of fish blood. "Interestingly, Bruno has a roadmap of fresh scars on his face and looks like he was used as a knife sharpener.

"The entire boat had been sanitized, including the deck. Every crack and crevice had been powerwashed and cleaned professionally. We checked with the company who cleaned it, and they said they routinely sanitize the boat. They said the owner's a clean freak."

At least now I knew Vinnie had access to a boat.

"Ultimately," the inspector said, "it's a lot of circumstantial evidence, but nothing he can't easily refute, or beat in court. If charged, he'll bring in a team of attorneys that would rival OJ Simpson's Dream Team. What we need is somebody to talk."

I thought, especially in arguably the most liberal major city in the country. The case had to be airtight, bulletproof, and *beyond a reasonable doubt.*

Hank and I spent most of our shift detailed to a San Francisco Giants game. I don't know what we did to deserve the assignment, but day games are about as easy as life gets for a cop. The biggest danger is indigestion—or heat stroke on sunny days. A nice break from shucking calls.

To avoid Hank's third-degree about my reinstatement or questions about Mercedes and Lily, I stayed occupied talking to fans and passersby and eating ballpark food. I went with ballpark dogs and garlic fries and found fresh ahi tuna for Hank at a small vendor cart.

Hank is what they call a *piscivore*, a carnivorous animal that primarily eats fish. I shared that fun fact with him, but he wasn't amused.

A brief call from Mercedes was the highlight of my day, and Hank's, too, because I passed him the phone and told him to say hello. He did and handed her back after a moment.

"Oh my God," she said, "I can hear all the fans cheering. Did someone just get a hit?

"Sure did! Hunter Pence just got a double."

"You're making me homesick. You didn't have hot dogs, did ya?"

"Ah, well, a couple. I had to have one for you, too!"

She sighed. "Aww."

She sounded forlorn.

"Well, it must be getting late for you. Are you filming tomorrow?"

"Of course," she said. "This director puts in long days. I've got to be on set by seven tomorrow, so I better get some sleep."

The timing was good because, as I hung up, Hank and I were dispatched to a fight in the stands. It was in the next section over, so by the time we arrived, other officers had a bloodied fan in custody.

As we approached, one of the officers held up four fingers, signaling Code-4, indicating they had things under control.

I looked at Hank. "Too bad. I wanted to work off those hot dogs."

Later, on the way back to the station, Hank said, "I heard you were cruising around Chinatown the day you worked as a SAM unit."

"Yeah, I drove down Stockton on my way to Union Square. I was a rover all day, so I was checking the entire district. So what?"

"Right, but I thought you were told to stay out of Chinatown. I'm just sayin', you're playing with fire."

"They don't intimidate me. Fuck 'em! I'm a cop in this city, I'll go where I want. They know where to find me."

We got off work on time, so instead of going directly home, I drove the long route up Highway 1 to Stinson Beach, to check out the sunset. I had to avoid predictability.

It was overcast, so I grabbed a quick dinner at an outdoor seafood joint and went home.

The bungalow was undisturbed, so I watched some local news and drifted off to sleep.

At about two in the morning, a flare activated, so I did the tuck and roll and grabbed the machine pistol and night-vision monocular.

From the rear window, I saw a figure, but couldn't tell anything beyond that. My heart started to race. I went out the front to circle around and take up a defensive position. I soon realized it was a vagrant tossing my trash. A common problem in Marin County and the Bay Area. Probably looking for something to eat or steal. I told him to stay put and came back with a couple of beers and a twenty. He looked confused when I handed them to him.

"Hey, buddy, don't come on this property again. I could've shot you. Go somewhere else and enjoy the beer and buy yourself something to eat in the morning."

He grumbled something that sounded like thanks, but I couldn't be sure.

I replaced the flare and went back to bed.

- 63 -

BOBBING FOR APPLES AND
THE HONEYBEES

B*efore leaving for work*, I packed a knapsack with a change of clothes and planned to spend the night in the barracks in Daly City. Last night was a reminder the Ghost Boy threat was still very real.

On patrol, I was surprised by an unexpected text from Sophie.

Just saw you. Glad you're back. Coffee?

I texted back. When? Where?

2pm @ Café Trieste?

I texted back a thumbs-up emoji.

I took my meal break at the café, and Hank drove the few blocks back to the station to eat his lunch.

I admit, there was still part of me that lusted for Sophie, but with Mercedes in my life, and our history, I'd be asking for trouble. She was still beautiful and looked like she went through considerable effort to look and smell good for me—but I resisted.

"You look so good, Ray," she said when she saw me. "Like you've been living at the beach, or something."

It was flattering.

"Thanks, Sophie. I guess the Southern California lifestyle and sun must have agreed with me."

She sat and brushed some loose hair back from her face with her delicate fingers.

"So, tell me what you've been doing. I know you've been dating Mercedes Cruz. That's amazing. I see your pictures with her all over the place."

"Not a big deal," I said. "I think she's desperate." I'm not sure why I said that.

She smiled. "Desperate? I don't think so. I think she could have any man she wants, and she knows exactly who she wants. You!"

"You're making me blush. Enough about me. How about you? What have you been doing?"

"Well, I switched jobs and I'm working at Apple now. I'm working on an AI team, and it's interesting. I'm finally getting to use the data science stuff I learned at UCLA."

"That's fantastic. I'm happy for you. Does that mean you can upgrade my iPhone for free?"

"Of course! Give it to me."

I handed her my iPhone, and she typed a message in my Notes app. "There. You've been upgraded. The instructions are in your Notes. You can read it later."

As she was talking, I got a text from Hank.

Code-7 over. Out front.

I held up the phone. "My partner. Gotta go. He's out front."

We stood and hugged for what seemed like an extra-long hug. I got the full embrace.

"I want to do this again," she said.

"Sure," I said. *Me, too.*

I could still smell her on me after I got in the patrol car. These women. It's how they mark you, and I've got a nose like a truffle pig. Hank, too, apparently.

"Ooh, you smell yummy."

"You do, too, Hank. Like a barrel of fish. Now let's drive by Trattoria and Carmine's so I can keep an eye on Vinnie's whereabouts. He likes to park his new Ferrari out front like it's an Oscar award."

I looked at the note Sophie typed in my phone: Maybe we should try again? I blew it.

My heart skipped a beat. I was flattered and confused.

We saw Vinnie's Ferrari parked a couple of blocks from Trattoria. As we approached, I could see a head bobbing up and down on his lap. Obviously, he was in some type of danger.

"Hank, I gotta make sure he's safe."

Hank rolled his eyes. "You're a real dick, Ray. At least let the guy have a happy ending."

"No way," I said. "He doesn't deserve it. He's mine."

I exited the patrol vehicle, and when I tapped on the passenger window, the woman quickly sat up.

Vinnie turned to see who had interrupted his tryst, and it took him a second to recognize me. I think he was glazed over in ecstasy, losing all sense of space and time.

"What the fuck, Ray?"

"Sorry, Vin. I just wanted to make sure you're okay."

"Okay? I was on my way to great!"

In Sicilian I said, "I couldn't resist. And put that thing away. It looks dangerous."

He laughed. "Payback's a bitch. Now, let me finish in peace." "It's the middle of the day, Vinnie. Take her somewhere private. Now you two lovebirds enjoy each other and have a nice day."

I recognized his date as Bella, his hostess at Trattoria, and wondered if this would affect my VIP status in a good way.

We left and drove to a pier off the Embarcadero so Hank could introduce me to a buddy of his, a supervisor in charge of the SFPD Marine unit.

"You'll like this guy," he said. "I think he was a Navy Seabee, or something like that. He's a real badass. I worked with him a few years ago at Mission Station."

"Didn't you serve with the Honeybees and the Honey Nut Cheerios?" I asked.

He laughed. "Nah. I was Cocoa Crisp."

His buddy seemed solid and seaworthy, with arms like Popeye the Sailor Man. We compared duty assignments, which for him included Kabul in Afghanistan. He proudly showed us around the SFPD patrol boat and invited me to ride along at a future date to get some time on the water.

"Just clear it with your supervisor."

"But I don't swim," I said.

He looked surprised, as Hank started to cackle. "He was a fuckin' Navy SEAL. He swims like Michael Phelps, only faster."

The guy laughed and said, "You're starting to grow on me, Ray."

As we continued to bullshit, we were joined by a guy he introduced as a friend and pilot boat captain.

"This is *the* guy. He knows every contour, every inch of the Bay. He's one of a handful of captains licensed to guide cargo and cruise ships in and out of the Bay."

The pilot boat captain brushed it off. "A child could do it, but don't tell anybody and screw up my gig."

He, too, was retired Navy, so Hank was the odd man out, but I stuck up for him.

"Hank wasn't Navy, but this sonovabitch knows fish. He's half sushi and half sashimi."

We had a good laugh. I asked about the currents and tides near the Golden Gate Bridge.

The sergeant and pilot boat captain argued about tides and currents but agreed it's seasonal and complicated. Currents regularly flow in a southerly direction, which would have transported Carmine Vaccaro's body south to Linda Mar Beach if he jumped from the Golden Gate bridge—or if he was tossed from a boat west of the bridge.

I'm a sailor and this stuff matters.

- 64 -

ENDANGERING ENDANGERED SPECIES

It *was August, and the days and weeks* were flying by as we neared my father's release from incarceration. I called my mother to see if she had a parole date, so I could make flight reservations. She did but forgot to tell me.

She said she'd been busy helping the church plan their annual Feast of San Gennaro supper, complete with a spaghetti dinner. And there was the bus trip to the Catskills with her friends to do a little gambling.

"Ma," I said, "get me on the committee for next year's dinner. Spaghetti? Really? Maybe next year you can have hot dogs, or fish sticks? *Marone!*"

She laughed. "Oh, Ray-Ray, we have-ah lots-ah other food, too. Salsiccia and-ah meat-ah balls. A nice-ah salada and ah-cannolis and ah-biscotti. Homemade-ah vino, too."

She gave me the date for his release, and I told her I'd book a flight, as promised. It didn't take long for her to shift topics at that point.

"I keep-ah seeing-ah Mercedes on-ah TV with ah-handsome man she's-ah makin' ah movie with."

"Ma, they have to publicize the new movie, so people go see it when it comes out, so they take pictures of the stars together all the time. They *want* you to think somethings going on between 'em."

"I don't-ah know, Ray. They look-ah too close-ah to me."

"I can trust her, but you never know. Don't worry about it, Ma. I'm fine."

Still, after I hung up, I called Pete to see if I was missing something.

"Hey, somebody in the States told me that Mercedes is getting cozy with her co-star. Is there something going on that I should know about?"

"Man, nothing I'm aware of, Ray, but I don't really look for that sorta thing. I mean, the actors hang out together, so I don't know."

"Can you keep an eye out and let me know?"

"Ray, I work for Mercedes and the studio. I gotta stay out of it, plus I'm flying back to California the day after tomorrow."

"I understand. Don't worry about it."

After we ended the call, I got an uneasy feeling. Pete seemed like he might be avoiding the issue.

I'd have to pay attention to TMZ and the Hollywood reporters, which I didn't typically do. It was Pete's job to be loyal to Mercedes and the studio.

As I was waiting for lineup and briefing, I called Mercedes to check in. She was sweet but hurried, and said she had to leave for dinner with the film crew and other actors. I was put off, but figured I was starting to read into things too much anyway.

We handled a few low-priority calls for service in the morning and stopped by a corner market, so I could buy gum. As I waited in line to pay, I spotted a tabloid in a newspaper stand with a picture of Mercedes and her new co-star, coming out of a restaurant, with the caption, Romance on the Amalfi Coast. New Beau for Mercedes?

I felt my face flush as my mind raced. I've never been the jealous type, but the potential was there. I reminded myself celebrities like Mercedes have no privacy. She was hounded by the paparazzi wherever she went, so innocent behavior could be misconstrued. In fact, it was the paparazzi's *job* to use pictures to make something out of nothing.

I was in the mood for seafood and needed to take my mind off Mercedes, so Hank and I went to Scoma's on the wharf and used the kitchen entrance in the back.

"It's on me," I said.

Hank laughed. "Ooo, big spender. Seeing how they're gonna comp us anyway."

The restaurant kept a table set behind the kitchen for cops to have privacy and eat, away from other patrons. They served us huge portions and, of course, as we were getting ready to go . . .

"Complimentary. We love San Francisco's Finest."

We thanked the waitress and chef, and as we left, I put a couple of twenties under my coffee cup.

"See Hank, it *was* my treat, dickhead."

He didn't answer, but I could tell he was content, as he got quiet with a belly full of fish. He was purring like a kitten when we got in the car.

"You did pretty good in there," I said, "and probably added at least one class of fish to the endangered species list. Meow. I'll drive, so you can take a catnap?"

He groaned. "I went easy on 'em. I know they need enough for the dinner customers, too."

Touché!

We stopped and parked near Fisherman's Wharf to walk off lunch and do a little walk and talk.

I almost pissed myself when a street performer known as the Bush Man leapt from the side of a trash can, where he'd been lying in wait behind a leafy branch to prank me. He got lots of laughs and support from tourists and passersby out for a day of fun in the sun.

It was doubly funny for tourists to see him prank a cop. I had to laugh, and Hank was busting a gut.

A citizen approached us and pointed to a couple arguing at the entrance to Pier 39. It looked like they were ready to go to blows. We sprinted over and separated them.

I ran their names through the system, and the husband had a prior for domestic assault, and his wife had an outstanding misdemeanor warrant for Failure to Appear on a traffic ticket.

I pulled the husband aside.

"Hey man, you're here with your kids. What are you doing? Knock it off. If you lay a hand on your wife and I get called back here, you're going to jail, and that's after I kick your ass. I see you've got a prior for domestic assault. Not good."

I forgot to turn on my BWC, body-worn camera. Probably a good thing.

Hank told the wife she had an outstanding warrant, and if not for the kids, he'd be marching her off to jail. He spoke out of earshot of the kids.

"You need to take care of the warrant within a week. I'm writing your information down and I'm gonna check with the court in a week. If you haven't taken care of the warrant by then, I'm gonna pay you a visit. If you can't pay the fine now, work something out with the court and maybe they'll let you make payments. And stop arguing in front of your kids. That's not right. If we come back, you're both going to jail."

I nicknamed them *the Bickersons.*

I got a call from Gina as we were heading back to the patrol unit.

"Ready to have that friends' dinner?"

"Sure. How about tomorrow night?"

"Works for me."

"Great," I said. "How about meeting me at a place in Marin. Maybe Mill Valley? You pick. Anywhere you want to go. We'll meet there. Text me when and where and I'll be there, okay?"

"10-4."

"Cute," I said.

I ended the call and Hank gave me a side-eye.

"*Another* lady friend?"

"Jealous?"

"I'm starting to feel less and less special to you, Ray."

"Well, that's a relief."

We went back to the station to complete our reports, in anticipation of our three days off. I planned to get takeout from Sorella's that night and chill.

The following day, Gina texted me.

Buckeye Roadhouse, Mill Valley 7pm?

I acknowledged and after that, as luck would have it, Mercedes called to tell me she was sad because Pete left to return to LA.

"I don't blame him," she said. "I'm sure it's boring standing around a movie set all day, watching the same scenes over and over. When are *you* coming to see me, baby?"

"Probably not for a while. I've got to go home to see my parents. I promised I would, and I already bought the ticket. I don't have a lot of vacation accrued yet."

"Anything I can do? I miss you so much. I want to be with you."

"Oh c'mon, I see your picture with your co-star all over the place. It doesn't look like you're missing me *too much.*"

"That's not fair, Ray. It's my job, and the paparazzi are like horseflies. No matter how much you swat 'em away, they never stop. I love you, and I'm sorry if those pictures hurt you. I never want to do that."

"No, I'm sorry. I miss you, too, and I don't want to act like a jealous jerk. I guess I need to remind myself that it's your job to be seen living it up."

"We'll get through this, and I know everything's gonna be fine because you're my hero, and I love you. Don't ever forget that."

Now, I was feeling guilty about having dinner with Gina that night. But I hadn't misled her. I told her the dinner was only as friends.

I had a sense of relief after my conversation with Mercedes. I'd have to be careful not to send Gina mixed signals tonight.

- 65 -

LIGHTS, CAMERA!

I *avoided wearing cologne or primping* too much because I didn't want to give Gina the wrong idea. I didn't need to look like I was dressing to impress, like I would for Mercedes. To Gina's credit, she was casually elegant, but not over the top, which I appreciated. Very light on the makeup and perfume, too. Not that she needed it. She was a beautiful woman and smartly put together, but I couldn't bring her into my life for more than friendship, and I hoped she understood that.

It was an unseasonably cool night in September, so it was nice to be seated at a table for two next to a blazing, stone fireplace. The setting was rustic like a hunting lodge, with dark paneling and hunting and fishing trophies mounted on walls. I liked the warm masculine vibe. A nice surprise.

I looked around. "Had I known, I would have worn a flannel shirt!"

She laughed as we ordered cocktails.

"I spend too much time at Carmine's," she said. "It feels good to get out. Since I came to San Francisco a year ago, I haven't made too many friends because I'm working all the time. And then I lost Carmine, and it turned my life upside down, so it's nice to get a change of scenery and spend time with a friend."

"Before I met Mercedes, I spent a lot of time working, or training, and the rest of the time, I was alone, so I understand.

"Most of my friends are Navy buddies, and they're scattered all over the place, so I don't get to see them either."

We shared a dozen chilled oysters on the half shell and ordered wine. There was no shortage of things to talk about as we got to know each other. She had a sharp wit I enjoyed.

We talked about growing up Sicilian, and at least half the time spoke our native language. I enjoyed going back and forth. Aside from speaking Sicilian and Italian with my parents, I don't get too many opportunities to do that, so I was enjoying it.

She understandably asked about the progress with Carmine's investigation. I had to be careful.

"Well, I've been off for a while, and I'm not the inspector on the case. I did hear that there's not a lot of solid evidence yet. But I'm not really in the loop on the case. They keep things tight-lipped. These guys will stick with it until they find out what happened. It takes time. I wish I had better news for you. It's a matter of time before someone comes forward or more evidence is uncovered."

I got the sense she was fishing a little, but it is her business, so I let it slide.

She excused herself to use the restroom. As she stood and strolled away, I watched as she took short steps and was awestruck with her goddess-like figure and graceful walk.

I knew I could never tell my mother about her. She'd be all over me to marry her. Gina was *exactly* who my mother had in mind. A Sicilian beauty with style and brains who could give her those little *bambinos*. *Marone!*

But I made my choice.

After the meal, as we were sipping our espressos, a young woman came over to our table.

"Are you Mercedes Cruz's boyfriend?"

"Well, I . . . " I was caught off guard. "Yes, I am. I'm Ray, and this is my friend, Gina."

"I'm a huge fan and see you and Mercedes in a lot of magazines and on TV, too."

We shook hands.

"I hate to ask, but would you mind if I got a picture with you?"

"Sure."

She handed Gina her iPhone and politely asked if she'd take the picture.

After the picture was taken, I said, "Well, Mercedes is filming a new movie and it should be released in about a year. I hope you go see it. She would love that."

"Thanks," she said and walked away like she was walking on air. I smiled at Gina. "Sorry about that."

"No problem. Having Carmine for a brother, we had a lot of interruptions over the years by his admirers. It comes with the territory, and Carmine used to tell me that you had to be nice to your fans because, without them, you've got nothing."

I insisted on paying for dinner and walked her outside to wait for the valet to retrieve her car. I was surprised when the valet pulled up in Carmine's yellow Lamborghini.

"I always wanted this car," she said, "so I can't part with it."

I thought about her on the drive home, and wondered why she'd keep the Lamborghini, but I'm no psychologist.

- 66 -

UNTRACEABLE

Joe called on a secure line.
"Let's meet somewhere you're not associated with. I'll be alone. We don't need to socialize. We've got business."

Joe was somber. Billy's death took its toll on all of us.

"Call me when you're an hour out, and I'll give you the coordinates."

He called late in the morning, and we met in a wooded area near the Lafayette Reservoir in the East Bay. We both intuitively dressed in camo with skullcaps and sunglasses. He came up behind me and, without speaking, motioned me to follow him. He startled me. I never heard him coming.

We walked to an area off the dirt path and found a small, secluded spot under a canopy of trees to avoid cameras and drones. We used hand signals and turned off our phones before we uttered a word.

I'd dreaded this meeting for the past few days, but what I needed to tell him had to be said in person.

After looking around for unexpected onlookers, I pointed to a large tree stump to sit and talk.

I pitched my voice low. "Sorry, brother, but I've done a lot of soul-searching, and I can't do this, or be a part of it, even if I'm at arm's length. My conscience and gut, right down to my core, tells me to let it take its natural course. I know how angry we all are over Billy's death, and there's still a bounty on me and a target on my back, but I just can't take them out that way. Eventually, they'll come to me.

"It's a matter of time before they'll be killed, or in custody. I'm a cop and plan to deny any knowledge of this. As far as I'm concerned, it was just drunk bravado talking."

Joe looked disappointed, but he nodded. "I understand. You're out. We never had this or any conversations about this, other than drunken angry talk. You're good with me, Ray."

With nothing else to say, I waited until he left and was out of sight and walked in the opposite direction.

A man's got to have a moral compass, or he's got nothing.

- 67 -

THREE OLIVES. NO MORE, NO LESS

I **woke up startled, soaked in sweat,** to the sound of gunfire. Luckily it was coming from the surround sound speakers in my bedroom. I had fallen asleep with the TV on, and the gunfire must have triggered my PTSD while I slept.

I was awake, so I hit the shower and thought I'd call Mercedes to catch up.

After several rings, she answered.

"Come stai?" I asked. How are you?

"Ti amo, ti amo!" I love you! I love you!

She was really starting to grasp the language. She was sharper than some people gave her credit for.

"Molto bene."

She explained she was in Monaco with an actress friend, enjoying a couple of days off. She sounded relaxed and pleaded with me to visit.

"We wore scarves and sunglasses to avoid attention, and so far, so good. It's a gorgeous, sunny day here, but I miss you every day. I'm obsessed with you."

It was good to hear.

"I promise, I'll see what I can do to put a trip together. It won't be long, but I'll only be able to come for a few days. I don't have a lot of vacation time accrued. Remember, I'm just a humble public servant!"

She dropped her voice. "Nobody is better than you. I need to taste you and smell you."

"Hey, now!"

Things got intimate at that point, but not for long because, a minute later, I got a call and told her I needed to take it. My cousin Sal, and just when I was getting hot and bothered.

His call was like getting ice cold water poured over my head. "Hey, cuz! The betting gods have not been with you, and now you're into me for another fifteen hundred. I need to collect, cuz. I got guys I gotta take care of!"

"No sweat, cuz. Give me a couple days, and I'll get you your money. You know I always come through."

I was slowly depleting the back pay I received when I was reinstated. Not good.

I'd have to hit the 10-B assignments hard when I returned to maintain some reserves and not get sideways, especially after promising Mercedes I'd visit her in Italy.

I had dinner at Sorella Caffe then walked home to relax for the night.

Gina called around nine to see if I was up for a late dinner and a drink. I told her I already ate and had an early flight in the morning.

"I thought of you today," she said, "and just thought it'd be nice to see you and talk. You help me keep things in perspective, and to be honest, I just need someone to talk to tonight."

"No worries. Everything okay?"

"Absolutely," she said. "Just a little lonely."

"I understand. Can we catch up on the phone? Let's each grab a cocktail and we can have our very own virtual Happy Hour."

She cheered up. "That would be so nice."

We set our phones down, got our drinks, and resumed the conversation.

She said, "I made a Spritz Veneziano with a nice orange slice, just like home in Sicily."

"I hate to disappoint," I said, "but I'm having Tito's on the rocks with three Vermouth-brined olives. The olive count is *very* important."

She laughed, then got serious. "I think Vinnie wants to pick up where we left off."

"Well, that's a personal decision."

Maybe she was saying that to make me jealous.

"Ray," she said, "what if he had something to do with my brother's death?"

"But you don't know that."

I didn't want to take her to a dark place emotionally.

"You're right, and the restaurant's doing much better now, and we're getting along fine. I guess I have to focus on that and let things run their course."

We bantered back in forth, going from English to Sicilian, with no rationale for doing so, except it was our little bond.

We talked for about ninety minutes, and after my third vodka, I told her I was starting to fade, plus I was overdosing on martini olives.

"When you get back, let's have dinner again," she said. "It'll give me something to look forward to. This time I'm paying. Thanks for being there for me, Ray. I always feel better after talking to you."

"*Non è niente,*" I assured her. It's nothing.

- 68 -

THE SMELL OF FREEDOM

I *was hungover and slept* most of the flight. We landed at Newark Airport, and I felt a little better after getting some sleep. I picked up a rental car at the airport and drove the ninety minutes to Newburgh.

My mother was as excited to see me as I'd ever seen her. She had stocked the house with food in anticipation of my father's homecoming and my visit. She'd made baked zitis, lasagna, and pizzelles, some of my father's favorites.

The minute she opened the door to her apartment, I smelled garlic and olive oil wafting through the air. My customary coming-home meal was almost ready to be served.

She was cooking up a storm and joyfully dancing around the kitchen with her colorful cooking apron imprinted with "All the stunads give me agita!" A funny way of saying all the idiots aggravate me.

If I were ever on death row, my request for my last and final meal would be her pasta fagioli with sausage. But only if *she* makes it. (Maybe a cigar and a little scotch after, too. Is it too much to ask? Hey, I'm dying here!)

My mother and I talked into the night and had a big day ahead with my father's release at eleven the next morning. She was overcome with excitement.

I was exhausted from traveling, the time difference, and homemade wine. I opened the bedroom window and could hear the local traffic and smell the streets. I fell asleep when my head hit the pillow.

We arrived at the Federal Correctional Institution in Danbury in record time. After waiting for close to an hour, my father was escorted to a waiting room.

The guards came over and shook my father's hand, wished him good luck, and handed me a brown bag with his personal effects.

Outside, as we walked to the car, my father stopped.

"Do you smell that?"

"No, what?"

"*That's* the smell of freedom."

I suggested lunch at Cosimo's, one of my father's favorite local restaurants.

My parents were arm-in-arm, enjoying the moment, but my father's ears perked up at the mention of food.

"Sounds good, Ray."

We drove along Route 300 with the windows down because my father wanted to take in the fresh air. Understandable.

At lunch he asked, "So, what's with this beautiful Hollywood actress you've been seeing? All the guys in the joint seemed to know about it and asked me about her. I didn't know what to say. I saw pictures of you two on TV."

"I met her when I was working in LA, and we hit it off. Not at first, but that's a long story. She's filming a new movie in Italy right now, and I'm going to see her as soon as I can schedule more days off. In a couple of weeks, I'll fly over there for four or five days. You'll know when I'm there because the paparazzi will have it all over TV and the Hollywood gossip papers."

My mother laughed. "You're-ah famous, Ray-Ray."

"Not me, Ma. She's the famous one. I couldn't care less about it."

"Are you-ah in-ah love-ah with her?" she asked.

"Yes. I am. She's beautiful inside and out."

"Does-ah she-ah love-ah you, Ray?"

"Yeah, Ma. She does."

"Well, that's-ah good enough-ah for us. If you two-ah love-ah each other, then-ah we love-ah her, too," she said, then paused. "Even if she isn't Italian."

On the way home, my father wanted to stop at his local hangout, a small bar on Williams Street that serves as the Italian American Social Club, with Italian flags adorning the old, battered entrance. It was his Ravenite Social Club, the home of New York wise guys for close to seventy years. There were always a few wise guys smoking and joking in front of the place. Centurions, I guess. No "civilians" would dare cross *that* threshold.

My mother said she was tired and wanted to go home. She wanted no part of it, but my father already knew that.

We dropped her off at their apartment, and he invited me to join him at the social club. In Sicilian he said, "C'mon! Say hi to the crew."

My father, the capo, was reverently kissed and greeted by every wise guy in the place. Several whispered in his ear. A guy I recognized as Angelo Borelli, known as "Ang," walked back into the small kitchen and came back with an envelope I presumed was stuffed with cash, handing it to my father. My father stuffed it into the front pocket of his dress slacks.

Ang left and returned with two glasses of homemade red wine and a couple of Toscano Cigars. They're the original Italian cigars first made in Tuscany. They've got a nice, sweet taste to them and look like crooked, dark-brown twigs.

He seated us at an old, wooden table. "We got some sauce and meatballs coming out in a minute."

He left and returned with a loaf of Italian bread, a bowl of Italian olives, and a wheel of Parmigiano Reggiano cheese.

We sat, intermittently smoking and snacking, as club members stopped by to pay homage. All warmly welcomed me as well, many knew me since I was a kid.

When our sauce and meatballs were served, the guys left us alone to eat. They left the old, dented pot with more sauce and meatballs on the table, for us to help ourselves.

As we were finishing up the meal, he said, "By the way, I talked to your cousin Sally, and he said you're into him for a few dollars. He didn't want to tell me. I had to pull it out of him."

He took the envelope from his pocket and pushed it across the table next to my plate. "Get him paid and be done with it."

When I resisted, he said, *"Non preoccuparti!"* No worries. And I knew from experience, you can't argue with him.

A guy I didn't recognize came over and asked to speak to my father alone. He frowned and was flexing his hands. I got up and walked to the other side of the small room to talk to some of his soldiers.

As my father's conversation continued, I heard the pitch of their voices go up until they were in a full-blown argument. I tensed and got ready to start swinging, when my father flipped the table over on the guy, pasta sauce and all, and began banging him over the head with the aluminum pot yelling *"Fottuto idiota,"* or fucking idiot.

A couple of soldiers grabbed the guy, stood him up, and tossed him out the door like yesterday's trash.

My father shrugged it off and mumbled, *"Idiota,"* as Ang righted the table and wiped up the mess. My father went into the kitchen and came back with a large chunk of the Reggiano cheese, more bread, and another carafe of the homemade wine for us to sip and nibble on. Ang tossed two more crook cigars on the table.

We picked up where we left off and my father acted like it never happened.

He asked if I was good with going back to the police department and the gang attacks. I told him we killed most of the attackers, and I was being careful in my dealings with both the Asian and the Italian mob.

"You don't want to get in the middle of it," he said. "Let them sort it out. I met Catalano's father once on the golf course, but don't know his son. He's in another family. Be careful with him so we don't end up with more problems."

- 69 -

LIFE IS GOOD

The next day we went to church as a family. My mother insisted, saying we hadn't attended Mass together in years. As we sat in the pew, I could feel parishioners glancing our way, some staring.

The pastor, an Italian priest named Father Leo, made it a point to approach us after the service and welcome my father home. A small crowd gathered at the entrance to the church as we were about to leave. There was a line of friends and neighbors with hugs, handshakes, and greetings, paying homage to *il capo*. My father. The boss.

A couple of ladies I went to high school with approached me to say hello.

"Oh, my God, Ray," one said. "You're so handsome. I should have gone after you in high school. I see you on TV and in magazines with Mercedes Cruz. That's unbelievable. You're a celebrity. I tell everybody I know you."

I smiled. "You two are silly, but thank you for your nice words. I'm still just Ray from Newburgh, and it's great to see you both. You look terrific, too. Thanks for coming over to say hi."

With that, I gave each a hug.

I gathered my parents up, and as we walked to the car, my father said, "Hey, Ray, you're almost as popular as me."

"I'm trying."

After Mass, we went out for lunch, and while we were waiting for our food, I called Mercedes on the phone and introduced her to my parents. They were surprised and took turns talking to her. When our food arrived, I said, "Thanks, baby. We're gonna *mangia,* so I'll call you later."

My parents were beaming.

"Ray-Ray, she's-ah so-lovely and-ah I can tell how she-ah talks about-ah you, that she-ah loves you. A mother knows-ah these things."

My father smiled and nodded. "You done good, Ray. I'm proud of you."

After we finished eating, we dropped my father off at a clambake hosted by the local chapter of UNICO in New Windsor. UNICO is the largest Italian American Service Organization in the U.S., and my father's a former chapter president and a big supporter.

When we dropped him off, I got out of the car and asked if he thought he was safe at an event like this.

He waved it off. "I'm fine. These are my people, my friends. I'm good. I'll stay for a while and get a ride home."

When I got back in the car, my mother reached over and patted my knee. "Don't-ah worry about-ah your father. They know-ah who he is."

When we got home, I made online arrangements for my trip to Italy.

In anticipation of the flight back to San Francisco in the morning, my mother made a beautiful meal, with enough food to feed a platoon of Marines.

It was a short trip, but I had to be there for my parents.

- 70 -

SHARP DRESSED MAN

Dead. *One Nester Fong and one Michael Ng* by unknown assassins. One shot in Daly City, the other in San Leandro thirty miles apart. No details beyond that.

In briefing, the lieutenant kept things professional.

"The two of them were the head of the snake," he said as he wrapped up, "and it's expected to have a devastating effect on the Ghost Boys."

I wanted to yell, *Fuck 'em both! I hope the assholes rot in hell! I'm just sorry I didn't get to drill 'em myself!*

I thought better of it and stared eyes front.

Hank was conspicuously absent, and the lieutenant told me to see him after the briefing. I was assigned to work a SAM unit solo that day, so I surmised Hank was out sick. I enjoyed working alone anyway. It was quieter in the car, easier to concentrate, but more intense with just one set of eyes and no immediate backup.

I walked in the watch commander's office after briefing.

"Close the door."

I thought, *here we go again. What have I done now?*

"Hank is out on bereavement leave for a few days. One of the Ghost Boys assassinated was Hank's cousin, Michael Ng."

I sat, dumbfounded. "Are you fuckin' kidding me?"

"Easy, DeLuca."

"Sorry, sir. I don't know what to say. He never mentioned his cousin was a Ghost Boy, and he knew they were trying to kill me." The lieutenant said, "I know. Nobody knew. I'm not making excuses, Ray, but we don't yet know what Hank did or didn't know. The inspectors will deal with him when he comes back from bereavement leave. It'll be fully investigated."

"Sonovabitch," I muttered.

"Look, DeLuca, Michael Ng was a violent piece of shit with a rap sheet six pages long, so good riddance. It's a *good* news story. You'll be working as a SAM unit until Hank gets back. You good with that?"

"I prefer working as a SAM unit. For the record, I'll never partner with that motherfucker again. His cousin killed my best friend. I better get out there, sir. We're short-handed."

I needed to get some distance to avoid popping off again.

I was stunned. Hank's disloyalty was beyond comprehension. He was either in denial, a conspirator, or chose to look the other way.

None of these possibilities were acceptable. I planned to request a move to another watch. I never wanted to lay eyes on him again.

I went in-service, and to get my head straight, grabbed a large espresso at Café Trieste, and drove to Aquatic Park to watch the swimmers and take in some salt air before the shift got busy.

I had to get my mind off fantasies of killing Hank.

As I sipped my espresso, my thoughts turned to Carmine Vaccaro and how he lost his life in the Bay and ended up on the beach in Pacifica. Time to check in with Gina. She didn't know I was back from Newburgh and would probably be glad to see me.

As I approached Carmine's, I saw Vinnie's Ferrari parked in front. As I was exiting the patrol car, he appeared on his way out.

He gave me the man-hug and asked how I was doing. *Come stai?*

"Just checking in to see how Gina's doing."

"That's nice of ya. I gotta run. When you comin' back to Trattoria to play poker?"

"Call me. I'm up for a game."

Just what I needed, to drop more money I didn't have.

Gina was wide-eyed and smiled as she came over to hug me.

"How about some nice fresh *frutta*?" she asked. "They just cut it up, and I'll get you an espresso."

She was back in minutes with a tray full of scones and fruit. She looked happy and energetic.

"*Minchia!* [pronounced "minka," an expression of gratitude and joy] You look great, Gina. New man in your life?"

She laughed. "No, Ray. I'm just happy to see *you*."

She had nothing new to report about Vinnie and didn't seem interested in talking about him.

"Yeah. I talked to him before I came in. I let him know I was checking up on you."

"Thanks, Ray," she said. "He's been fine."

After a few more minutes I made moves to get up. "I better get back on the street before they send a search party."

"Friends' dinner next week?" she asked.

"Sure."

★ ★ ★

Late afternoon, I got a message on my CAD (Computer Aided Dispatch) screen to call dispatch.

The dispatcher said, "Possible dead body in a hotel on Geary. Said it's a guest. Probably natural causes. I didn't want to put it over the air and have ambulance chasers pick it up on a scanner."

"I appreciate that. I'll roll down there and advise. Let's keep it off the air."

I checked in with the front desk manager who escorted me to a room on the fifth floor. He unlocked the door, pushed it open and stepped back.

As soon as I laid eyes on the guy, I immediately thought of the ZZ Top song "Sharp Dressed Man."

The guy was wearing a starched white dress shirt, a colorful silk tie, gray dress slacks, and freshly polished black shoes. He was groomed to perfection with a cigarette in one hand and a red BIC lighter in the other.

He was sitting at the foot of the hotel bed, and it appeared he'd laid back to rest for a minute before going outside for a smoke, probably before a big night out.

The only problem was, he was dead.

There were no signs of a struggle or trauma, at least none that were obvious to me.

I taped the area off and called dispatch to have a supervisor respond to the scene. I'd wait for the go-ahead before tossing the room for evidence.

In the meantime, I spoke to hotel guests and staff, and none reported hearing loud voices, a disturbance, or anything unusual.

According to my personal hotel rating system, I'd rate this hotel as a Motel 5, no higher. It was located on Geary Boulevard, just a couple of blocks north of the Tenderloin, in a neighborhood known for cross-dressers and transgenders. I was aware that some of the local hotels had private dance clubs in their basements and catered to hourly customers in their rooms. My victim didn't appear to fit the environment.

A female sergeant by the name of Torres arrived on scene and, after checking the body without moving it, gloved up and began to open dresser drawers.

About thirty seconds into the search, she held up a pair of men's crotchless underwear and a handful of capped hypodermic needles.

"Who knows," she said, "maybe he's diabetic and goes both ways. Not a crime."

She carefully rolled up a sleeve of the victim's dress shirt and revealed an expensive-looking watch and track marks—the kind you see with recreational junkies. We tossed the room but didn't find illegal drugs. He did love his kinky underwear, though, and there was more of that in the dresser drawers. *Par-tay!!!*

The sergeant removed a wallet from his back pocket and found a good amount of cash, credit cards and his driver's license. He was out-of-state with no criminal record locally, statewide, or through NCIC, the National Crime Information Center.

I checked LinkedIn and learned he was an executive for a technology company in the Midwest. Maybe in town for a little sex, drugs, and rock'n'roll?

I had ZZ Top playing an endless loop in my subconscious.

As we waited for the coroner to arrive, Torres stared at the body inquisitively and strangely began to unbutton the victim's shirt. I was taken aback.

Her curiosity and intuition paid off revealing a string of elegant white pearls around his neck.

I looked at the sergeant. "Pearls. Perfect for any occasion. The symbol of elegance and impeccable taste."

She smiled. "I can't argue with that. I love white pearls with a white cashmere sweater, too!"

"Here's what I think," she said. "This guy is dressed like a Brooks Brothers model, and I think he came here to fly his freak flag. He's here to cop some dope and meet up with some like-minded cross-dressers and tranny types. Maybe he can't do that back home. It looks like he got ready to go out for the night and had a heart attack, either that or something he shot up earlier killed him. He's got a fresh injection site still oozing on his arm. I saw a spot of blood on his crisp white sleeve.

"He planned to go outside and have a smoke when he felt something coming on and sat on the edge of the bed. Whatever it was, he laid back and it was lights out. I'll tell you, though, even in death, this guy was one sharp dresser. That's the way you wanna go out. Lookin' sharp!"

"Yeah," I said, "he looks better dead than I do alive."

The coroner arrived and agreed with the sergeant's theory. It was a natural or at least *accidental* death—probably due to heart attack, a drug overdose, or some combination of the two.

He rolled the guy over and confirmed no gunshot or stab wounds. With lividity setting in, the coroner estimated the time of death to be four or five hours earlier.

I planned to add "Sharp Dressed Man" to my Spotify playlist, but the song would take on a new meaning.

- 71 -

DON'T GO THERE!

For the first time in weeks, I drove my Challenger to work, feeling a sense of relief with Billy's assassins dead. Things were moving in the right direction.

As I walked into the station, Sergeant Torres approached me. "There are detectives from the LA County Sheriff's Department, Daly City PD, and another from San Leandro PD, waiting for you in the interview room. Do you want me in there with you? Should I call your attorney, or union rep?"

"I'm good for now. Thanks, Sarge. I'm sure it's about the Ghost Boys that were killed. I got this."

As I walked into the room, the LASD detectives stood and shook my hand. I recognized both as the detectives investigating Billy's murder. The others stayed seated and nodded.

The lead LASD detective said, "Hey, Ray, you probably heard the two suspects in Billy's murder were killed here in Northern California. These detectives, along with my department, are investigating the homicides. We wanted to find out what you might know.

"To protect you and to keep this on the up and up, we're gonna read you your Miranda Rights and record the conversation. You okay with that? Or you wanna call your attorney, or somebody else?"

"Everything I know I already told you when I was in LA," I said, "but if you have other questions, go for it."

After waiving my rights, the questions focused on my familiarity and knowledge of either suspect. I had none. That was followed by questions regarding my whereabouts when the subjects were assassinated.

"I was in New York visiting family. You can verify it with the airlines, my parents, and the guards at the Federal Correctional Institution in Danbury, Connecticut."

The last comment earned me a second look.

The San Leandro detective asked, "Did you say you were at the Federal Prison in Connecticut?"

"I did."

He looked bewildered. "Can I ask what for?"

"My father was just paroled," I said, "and I wanted to be there for his release."

"What was he was in prison for?" he asked.

"None of your business. If you want to find out, do your own research. It's my father, and what he does is *his* business, and he just finished paying the price for it, so I suggest you mind your *own* fuckin' business. I'm a cop, just like you, so don't give me that look, or you'll be picking yourself up off the floor."

The room went silent.

"I lost my best friend to those maggots who were just killed, so I don't give a fuck about them, or your investigation. Unless you've got something else to ask me, I've got lineup in twenty minutes. I gotta go."

"I think we're good," said the lead LASD detective as I stood. "Nothing against you, Ray. You know we're just doing our jobs. If you hear anything, let us know."

"Yeah, sure."

With that behind me, in between radio calls, I phoned Mercedes to give her the dates for my visit.

"Oh, my God!" she screamed into the phone. "We're gonna have so much fun!"

"It's only for five days," I said, "and two of the days I'm in transit, so we'll only have about three days together, but it's better than nothing, right?"

"I'll need to work with the director on the production schedule," she said, "but we'll make it work. They can shoot around me for a few days. You're my priority, baby, and I can't wait."

It felt good to have that to look forward to.

- 72 -

I NEVER KISS AND TELL

Gina called a few days before my trip to Italy, and true to my word, I met her for our friends' dinner. At her suggestion, we met at a new Asian fusion restaurant in Burlingame, south of San Francisco.

She was dressed sexier than our last dinner, and her scent and aura were emanating sex. She was taking her game up a notch. I had to keep things platonic, but it was going to take every ounce of willpower. She looked stunning.

The food was fantastic, and they had us sitting close in a candlelit setting on a terrace. The owner of the restaurant recognized Gina from Carmine's, so all the goodies, adulation, and extras came pouring out of the kitchen.

"I hope she doesn't have me confused with some food critic," she joked, "because we're getting major VIP here, and I'm not sure why."

"Gina, your restaurant is a big deal, and you and your brother have a lot of fans. She's just showing you the professional courtesy and respect you deserve."

She blushed and nervously reached across the table to grab my hand, and I let her. We held hands for about ten seconds too long. It was the most intimacy we'd ever had, and I liked it.

The paparazzi would have fun with a picture like that. That's a homewrecker.

I felt guilty, so I changed the conversation to my upcoming trip to see Mercedes in Italy. I learned long ago, the best way to throw cold water on a steamy situation is to mention another woman. We awkwardly broke contact, and I excitedly talked about seeing the Amalfi Coast for the first time. Gina had been there, so she made some foodie recommendations that I tapped into *Notes* on my phone.

Ironically, as I opened the app, I saw Sophie's recent note about getting back together and felt even more confused.

Gina asked for updates about her brother's death, and it seemed like she was more interested than usual about any new developments.

I repeated what I'd told her earlier. The investigation was now in the hands of homicide with some help from our local SIT inspectors. I'd certainly let her know if something came up that I could share.

I explained I was keeping an eye on Vinnie and keeping my ears open in the department and on the street for new information.

"I know they've served several search warrants of houses, cars, your restaurants, and Vinnie's yacht, but haven't found anything yet that's strong enough to get an arrest warrant. There was blood on Carmine's shirt, but the origin is unknown, because the DNA from the blood was degraded from the ocean water. Our inspectors feel the blood on his shirt points to foul play, and that's why we remain committed to finding out what happened."

"Thank you, Ray."

"Trust me, he's not forgotten."

As we waited for the valet to get our cars, she glanced up at me, with a devilish smile.

"Nightcap?"

"Sure. Where?"

"Follow me."

A yellow Lamborghini shouldn't be too difficult to follow in traffic, if she keeps it under eighty.

I followed her northbound on U.S. 101 to South Van Ness Avenue and a tree-lined residential street in Pacific Heights where she signaled and pulled into a black stone driveway, which was the entrance to a parking garage. She motioned me to follow. The garage provided parking for a stunning glass-and-steel building about ten stories high. It was brightly lit with a uniformed valet, enormous containers of exotic plants, and brightly painted walls with commercial-grade carpeted walkways. Most of the parked cars were high-end vehicles neatly tucked in their spaces, including Ferraris, Porsches, and Bentleys. Some had car covers to protect expensive paint finishes.

She greeted the valet. "Hi, Louis! I'm in for the night, and Mr. DeLuca is my guest and will retrieve his car later."

We left our cars and I naively asked, "Is there a bar in here?"

She laughed. "Of course. Follow me."

The lobby looked more like the Ritz Hotel with polished black stone floors, a long ultra-modern rectangular fireplace, tall, fresh floral arrangements, and a concierge.

Gina gave the concierge a smile and nod as we entered the elevator.

We got out on the top floor and stepped directly into an enormous residential penthouse. My jaw dropped.

"Who lives here?"

"My brother Carmine. At least he *did*." She paused, then said, "I do now."

"Wow."

"Sadly, he didn't live here that long. Let me fix you a drink." She lit the fireplace, softened the lights, and asked me what I'd like to listen to.

"I think a little Chris Botti or Marc Antoine might be nice." She'd heard of neither, so I helped her find them on Spotify.

I avoided sitting on the couch near her and chose an over-stuffed chair with an ottoman across from her.

She kicked off her shoes and tucked her long, tan legs under her on the couch.

"Relax, Ray, you look tense. *Madone!* Get comfortable."

I took my shoes off as well and put my feet up. She was right. I felt enormous guilt for being there and was tense. I needed to relax.

Conversation came easy. It always did with her. She kept the drinks coming, with bowls of mixed nuts and popcorn.

The snacks increase your alcohol consumption, and it's why bartenders put salted nuts and pretzels on bars. She may have had an agenda beyond snacking.

I excused myself to use the bathroom, and when I returned, noticed the lights had been dimmed even more—or was that my imagination—and I was fading fast. I was relaxed, mildly intoxicated, and felt the stress leaving me.

I thought about Mercedes partying it up with her co-stars and friends, realizing it wouldn't hurt for me to do a little relaxing, too. This was fun. I spent too much time amped up and on edge.

The mix of classical and contemporary jazz artists set a nice mood. When trumpeter Chris Botti broke into the slow Irving Berlin classic "What'll I Do" with vocalist Paula Cole, Gina advanced, and took my hand.

"Dance with me," she said, her voice soft.

She extended her soft hand and gently helped me up from the chair. I couldn't resist. A strong attraction had always been there. We broke the Bible's distance rule for slow dancing, and she immediately folded herself into me. I could feel her heat and sexuality through her silky dress, and her warm breath, and soft lips gently kissing my neck.

We continued to embrace and slow dance for what seemed like an hour as Spotify seemed to take control, rotating through an elegant mix of slow torch songs. Neither of us wanted to break the embrace and the physical connection. Was it a longing we both felt or just loneliness? No words were spoken or needed to be.

On my way to the point of no return, I said, "I better go," and gently kissed her cheek.

My head was spinning as I exited the garage, but as my thoughts cleared, I thought about Gina driving Carmine's Lamborghini and living in his penthouse. It's like she took over his life. I knew she'd been grieving with the loss but couldn't help but wonder if she had anything to do with his disappearance or death. Maybe she knew about the letter of intent when Carmine was alive, and was promised something in return from Vinnie. Maybe she didn't realize ultimately Carmine would be murdered.

I hated myself for thinking that way, but I couldn't help it. Moments earlier, I held her in my arms. It gave me the creeps, but she certainly had inherited a considerable fortune with her brother's death.

I questioned my character for tempting fate and for having let things happen, but life had gotten complicated. I now had four beautiful women: Mercedes, Sophie, Lily, and Gina trying to have a relationship with me, and I was feeling lost, like a rudderless ship at sea. I felt like I didn't deserve any of them if I couldn't commit. Maybe I'd spent too many years alone, trying to survive.

I got an icy nod from Hank in briefing and looked right through him. I had to control my anger and resist thoughts of killing him with my bare hands.

After lineup, I walked over to him.

"You're on your own. Get yourself a new partner."

He looked at me with dead eyes, expressionless.

I walked into the watch commander's office and shut the door.

"What do you want, DeLuca?"

"A new partner or make me a SAM unit. I will not partner with Lau."

"I'm aware of the situation. Let me figure out a long-term solution. For now, you can roll as a SAM unit until you go on vacation, and by the time you get back, we'll have something more permanent figured out. I'll let the sergeants and captain know."

I spent the shift snagging as many calls for service as possible. Within days I'd be on vacation and wanted to stay busy to pass the time.

I couldn't go to Italy empty-handed, so I stopped by Tiffany's and bought Mercedes a stainless steel watch with the Tiffany Blue dial and lots of diamonds, spending way more than I could afford.

It was sparkly and elegant, like her. I asked them to engrave it and told them I'd pick it up the following day.

The salesperson recognized me. "Is this for Mercedes Cruz?"

I smiled.

"I never kiss and tell."

She smiled as I wrote down the inscription for the back: "To my star. Love, Ray."

I went back in-service, and within minutes, a call was broadcast reporting a man beating a dog on a sailboat docked in the marina by Pier 39. Units wasted no time answering up on the radio to take the call, regardless of their assignment in the district.

If the call was a man beating another man, it would have taken longer, or worse yet for a car break-in. The dispatcher would grow old waiting for a unit to take an auto burglary call. To save a kid or dog, we go in like the cavalry.

As I came on scene, two other units arrived as well. We jogged down to the dock, and as we approached the vessel, the RP, or reporting party, met us and pointed to a dirty, beat-up-looking sailboat tied to the pier. The reporting party was a woman in her thirties dressed in jeans and a hoodie.

"He's drunk and blasting his music," she said. "When I called, he was beating his dog. The guy's a monster. I heard the dog yelping and crying. I think it's a black Lab. I hope the poor thing's okay."

I talked to the other officers on scene. "If this guy goes nuts, he could toss one of us overboard and you might not survive in that water wearing boots and thirty pounds of equipment."

I started removing my gun belt and the rest of my equipment. I quickly unloaded my pistol and handed it to another officer.

"Just watch my stuff. There's a lot of spectators watching."

When I was down to my boxers and tee shirt, I announced myself as a policer officer and boarded the boat. I had plastic flex-cuffs ready to go. The suspect was below deck, so I opened the hatch to start a dialogue.

Empty beer cans littered the hull of the boat, and I could smell the booze emanating from the suspect from ten feet away.

Curled up in the corner, the dog barked and whimpered. I ordered the suspect to come up on deck. I told him I was a police officer and was taking him into custody for abusing the dog.

The woman who reported the animal cruelty signed a Citizen's Arrest Form allowing us to arrest him without witnessing the crime ourselves.

The guy didn't move.

"Come up topside," I said. "You're under arrest."

His response was a drunken slur. "Fuck you! I'm the captain. You have no authority on this boat!"

"Last chance, before I come down to get you. Get moving!"

I stepped down into the cabin and quickly restrained him. I took him topside and handed him over to another officer on the pier.

I went back into the cabin to get the dog. I gently coaxed him and picked him up to carry him off the boat. The poor thing was skin and bones and shaking like a leaf. As I stepped onto the pier, I got applause from onlookers and gave a thumbs-up.

Animal Care and Control officers took the dog from there.

"Just promise me the dog won't be released to this asshole or be euthanized," I said.

They assured me he'd be well taken care.

"If there's a problem," I said, "call me and I'll adopt him. My name is Ray DeLuca. I work out of Central Station."

- 73 -

NICE BOXERS!

As *I walked through SFO* to the international terminal for my trip to Italy, I spotted a front-page picture of me carrying the dog off the sailboat with the headline "Mercedes' Hero Saves Dog."

I bought a copy because I knew Mercedes would get a kick out of it. I was glad when the woman at the cash register didn't recognize me.

On board, after a couple of scotches, I settled in for some serious napping for the sixteen-hour flight to Naples, with a stopover in London. I brought a book, and music, and would look for a movie with my favorite action star if I could keep my eyes open.

The crew lowered the cabin lights for a good portion of the flight, so sleep came easy.

We arrived on time, and Mercedes sent her driver to pick me up. He was holding a sign that read Welcome Home, Hero!

Very cute. The driver holding the sign recognized me and shook my hand. He asked if I preferred to speak English, or Italian.

"I'm from here, so I'm fluent in both. Whatever you prefer is fine. I appreciate you coming to pick me up."

He insisted on carrying my bag to the curb where a valet retrieved a Mercedes-Benz G-Class SUV, also known as a G-wagon, which had become *my* Mercedes' trademark.

I could hear her now, *Of course, it's a Mercedes. They named the car after me. Why would I ride in anything else?*

The driver offered bottled water, energy bars, and fruit for the hour and twenty-minute drive up the Amalfi Coast.

As we walked in the entrance to the villa, Mercedes came bounding down the stairs and into my arms. I think she kissed every inch of my face and neck.

When she finished, I said, "I think you missed a spot."

She devilishly smiled. "Oh, don't worry, I'm just getting started."

She introduced me to the house attendants and asked them to take my bag up to her room.

We followed and promptly locked the door behind us, wasting no time stripping to take a hot shower together.

We made passionate love like it was the first time ever.

We had dinner by the pool overlooking the Salerno Gulf on the Tyrrhenian Sea, and talked nonstop, kissing between sentences. She told me all about the filming and how excited she was because they were using her in so many action scenes.

"That's what stunt doubles are for," I said. "So don't get carried away. You're too delicate."

I asked for it and got a punch in the arm and a loving headlock.

After dessert, I excused myself and came back with the newspaper I'd picked up at SFO and her gift.

She loved the headline and found it hilarious that I stripped down to my boxers and T-shirt in preparation for the arrest and rescue. Carrying the big scrawny dog was the topper.

"You think of everything, Ray," she said. "That's why you're my hero. You're the best and know how to take care of business."

She lit up when I handed her the box and screeched when she opened it. She immediately put the watch on her wrist.

"I love the light-blue face. It's beautiful!"

After she read the inscription, she got up and sat on my lap and started to cry. They were tears of joy—sadness, too.

She composed herself and said, "I gotta make a quick call."

I heard her speaking to her agent Ari.

"Yeah, something big, so we can cruise with a full crew. I want it first class with a nice suite. It's gotta be perfect. Yes, the day after tomorrow. Thanks, sweetie."

"So, what was that all about?"

"I told Ari to rent us a big-ass yacht the day after tomorrow so we can celebrate being together. I hope you brought your swim trunks, otherwise we'll have to skinny-dip."

It was a heady, joyful day I knew I'd never forget.

- 74 -

A FAMOUS NOBODY

We *stopped by the movie set* in the morning. Mercedes introduced me to her co-stars, the director, and the production crew.

The director shook my hand. "Aren't you the hero?"

I shook my head and smiled. "No hero here. Just a lucky guy."

We drove about forty-five minutes up the coast to Positano for lunch and sightseeing. The beach was rocky, with dark sand, unlike the white sandy beaches in California, but the views of the rocky cliffs and ocean were breathtaking.

We had a few paparazzi in tow, so I asked them to give us a little space and we'd reward them later with a photo op. They agreed and backed off.

We had lunch on a private terrace overlooking the beach and enjoyed some of the best seafood and risotto I've ever had. Everything was fresh, probably mere hours out of the Mediterranean. We walked off our lunch and, as promised, posed for a few pictures for the paparazzi.

As much as I encouraged them to take pictures of Mercedes by herself, they wanted me in the photos, and so did she. I'd be getting some serious heat for the publicity when I got home.

I kissed her on the forehead. "I'm becoming the world's most famous nobody."

"Don't you ever say that, Ray DeLuca."

The yacht was about ninety feet long and owned by a friend of Mercedes' agent, who was co-owner of one of the largest talent agencies in Los Angeles.

The crew of six stayed busy with navigation, food, and beverage service, catering to our every need. We set anchor in a private cove, not far from shore, and dove in for a swim. The water temperature was about eighty degrees and a far cry from the frigid Pacific I'd been swimming in.

"I love watching you swim," said Mercedes. "You're so strong."

I said, "I know. I don't even need the water wings anymore."

She swam to me and hung around my neck.

"I like this," I said. "Let's move here."

We ended the swim with a splash fight.

After drying in the sun, we disappeared to the master suite with some Dom Perignon for some private time and a nap.

We toasted "to us," and to her new movie. She thought it would rival movies like some of Schwarzenegger's and even *The Matrix,* which was one of her favorites.

"But we've got at least another six months of filming. The movie won't be released for at least a year, but I'm going to be so proud of it when it's done. The worst part is being away from you. I want you to come here every chance you get. I'll pay for everything. I just want to see you."

"I know," I said. "I feel the same way, but I've gotta pay my own way. The only thing I'm using my vacation time for is to see you and visit my parents, but I've used a lot of it recently, so I don't have much left. We'll have to make the best of things for now, and I'll come back when I get more time accrued."

We had a candlelit dinner on the deck of the yacht and enjoyed a bright orange-and-blue sunset over the water.

We decided to sleep onboard and enjoy half a day on the water the following day before I had to head back. My flight was scheduled to leave later in the day. Our time together was flying by, and it pained me to think about leaving again and saying goodbye.

After making love one last time, we showered and said our goodbyes from her suite in the villa.

Her driver rushed me to Capodichino Airport in Naples, and I arrived with little time to spare. I asked Mercedes to hang back at the villa to avoid a prolonged goodbye.

I read for the first couple of hours on the plane to take my mind off things and tire myself out. I reminded myself we'd be together soon enough and, eventually, forever. There was no doubt in my mind.

- 75 -

WAGGING TONGUES

After the watch commander welcomed me back, he held up a copy of the now infamous "Mercedes' Hero Saves Dog" newspaper headline for the entire watch to see.

Following the catcalls and snarky remarks, he said, "The Ghost Boys have dialed it back since two of their top mutts were killed. No one's in custody yet for doing the deed, but nobody's losing sleep over it, either. Our local mobsters are very active. Two were found dead last night in a car two blocks from the station, at Union and Stockton. Both shot execution-style, close range, back of the head. There was spatter and brains everywhere. I'm surprised it didn't hit the side of the station. Both had their tongues cut out and placed in their hands. We'll never get any of them to talk now. I'm sure they're part of Vinnie Catalano's crew, and that was a message to the rest of them. They're killing their own.

"DeLuca. Stay close to these guys. I know there's some trust because you're Sicilian. No offense. Just see if you pick up any chatter on the street."

"No offense taken."

After briefing, I drove to Carmine's restaurant to say hello to Gina and see if I could get an update on Vinnie and his activities while I was gone. I got a long hug and knew she was happy to see me. I hadn't seen her since the night we slow danced in her penthouse.

She gave me a searching look. "We good?"

"Of course, we are. Why wouldn't we be?"

"Vinnie is showing up less and less, like he's got other things to do," she said. "I don't know what's going on."

She leaned in and whispered in Italian. "Mama mia, Ray. All these Sicilian mob guys are getting killed in North Beach. It's awful."

"I know. That's what I heard in briefing today."

She changed subjects. "So, how was Italy? I see pictures of you and Mercedes everywhere. You two look so good together. So happy."

Knowing how Gina felt about me, I kept it short, avoiding details. Before I left, she handed me a bag with a sandwich, fruit, and biscotti prepared by her chef while we were talking.

"Here. In case you get hungry."

"Boy, you can take the Sicilian out of Sicily, and you know the rest. You're too much, Gina. *Marone!*"

I hugged her and kissed her on the cheek and left. I cruised by Trattoria Sicilia and stopped when I saw the Ferrari parked out front in a loading zone. I couldn't resist, so I wrote him a ticket for being illegally parked. I had no intention of turning the citation in for processing, but a cop's gotta have a little fun.

His goons were milling about, so in my best official voice, I told one of them, "Go find Vinnie before I tow his car."

It's fun to break balls now and then.

He came out yelling. "*Cosa stai facendo?*" What are you doing?

"You're illegally parked!" I barked. "I can't let that go just because we're friends. Wouldn't be right."

As he snatched the citation from under the windshield wiper, I burst out laughing. He made a big show of tearing it up.

"When's the next poker game?" I asked.

"This Thursday. Can you make it? Or do you have to go to the Oscars, or something?"

"C'mon, Vinnie, don't be like that. I'm in."

The lieutenant asked me to stay close, and I couldn't think of a better way than to hang out and play cards with the boss and his goombahs. Of course, any wins, or losses, were on me.

- 76 -

SPLAT!

Naturally, *I lost big-time*, but took it like a champ. I recognized two of the guys I played with previously, and the other two looked like fresh imports from Sicily.

The Sicilians spoke poor, heavily accented English. I limited my verbal interaction and use of Sicilian and Italian languages intentionally. Instead, I listened, and it's probably why I broke my concentration and had my ass handed to me to the tune of about a grand.

I think Vinnie felt bad, but I waved it off.

"No worries, Vin. Nobody twisted my arm. I just gave back what I won last time!"

I reported what I observed to the lieutenant the next morning. Unfortunately, there was nothing of any consequence other than the influx of more Sicilians. I explained they were cautious in front of me, and I'm sure it was on direct orders from Vinnie. I omitted the part about my financial setback.

Shortly after going in-service for my shift, I was contacted by phone by the watch commander, who told me to call DC Potente's office Code-2, which means without delay.

I pulled over and called him immediately. His assistant got him on the phone.

"Hey, Ray! We've got three finalists for our open positions for the new task force. They'll all be here tomorrow for interviews.

I've cleared it with Captain Choo for you to join me for the interviews. I want your opinion on these guys and, as you suggested, plan to conduct the interviews in Sicilian. All candidates said they were fluent during the initial phone interview and screening by the recruiter. On paper, they all look good, but we'll see who passes muster. The candidates selected will spend the rest of the week completing all other phases of testing, including physicals and a psychological. We created an Expedited Testing plan. If selected, we'll start backgrounds right away. They'll have a quick turnaround if they pass all phases and start an accelerated lateral academy in about two weeks to give them the chance to go home, resign from their agencies, and return."

"Sir, that sounds great," I said. "I'm anxious to meet them. I've gotta jump. I just got an A-priority call, so if you can text me the time and location I'll be there."

With that, I hit my lights and siren to proceed to a call of a possible jumper from the roof of the Hilton Hotel across from Portsmouth Square on Kearney Street. Security personnel led me to an alley on the north side of the building where the body of a male lay splayed and splattered. After requesting a supervisor and the coroner, I asked security personnel if anyone witnessed the incident. It was early in the morning, so it went undetected until a dog walker went into the hotel to report it.

The victim appeared to be a middle-aged, dark-haired man, lying facedown, shattered, and contorted, with goo oozing from his fractured skull.

The coroner confirmed my suspicions with identification from his wallet that identified him as Salvatore Caruso of Palermo, Sicily. I recognized his expensive Italian loafers laying several feet from his body. This was the same guy Big Dee picked up weeks earlier for extortion.

I surmised that he might have been "encouraged" to take the dive by an individual, or individuals, from the warring gangs— either the Ghost Boys or by fellow mobsters.

I requested security camera footage from the hotel for the last twenty-four hours. It could certainly provide us with possible suspects.

A SIT inspector arrived and agreed to take the investigation from there. I shared my suspicions and what I knew and told her I'd complete a preliminary incident report later that day.

77

SFPD'S ANSWER TO THE MOB

T he first candidate wasn't hard to spot as I walked into the waiting area on the first floor at SFPD Headquarters. I was in uniform and introduced myself, escorting him upstairs to another waiting room outside the conference room we were using to conduct the interviews.

Candidates were scheduled every two hours, with a short break for lunch. It would be a full day of interviewing, but for me, something a little different.

DC Potente was prompt and had the interview room set up with water, coffee, and writing materials. When we were both settled, he leaned back in his chair.

"Think of this like you're recruiting for a SEAL team," he said. "We want the guys to be cohesive and work well together. Also, think of them in the SFPD environment. All three candidates we're interviewing today are finalists. They were screened and had an initial interview with Sergeant Amato, who's been chosen to lead the task force. You have resumés and other important background information on each candidate in the blue folders. The first interview is with Jack Gerard. As you can see, he's currently a special agent with the FBI's Joint Terrorism Task Force in New York City.

"Let's bring him in, and remember, we speak only Sicilian to see how he does and to take him off guard. If he struggles with it, then we know and can remove him from the list of candidates. We don't have to hire them all, but I'd like to get at least two of the three."

Gerard was born and raised in Staten Island and started his career in law enforcement as a beat officer with NYPD. His parents emigrated to the United States from Sicily just before he was born and only spoke Sicilian in their home. He had incredible experiences with both the NYPD and FBI and was highly decorated. He held a master's degree in criminal justice from John Jay College of Criminal Justice in New York City. He was divorced with no children and wanted to move to a warmer climate and make more money in a respected organization large enough to offer good resources and opportunities for advancement.

The second candidate's name was Stefano DiNardo. He was outgoing, friendly, and clearly comfortable in his own skin. Nardo, as he liked to be called, was born and raised in Trapani, one of the most beautiful cities in Sicily and home of some of the most spectacular beaches the island has to offer. He was raised on the island in what sounded like a warm, wonderful family, and his father was a high-ranking police official with the Police Provincial Command Trapani. Police work was in his DNA, and currently Nardo served as an undercover officer for Direzione Investigativa Antimafia. Their main task was fighting organized crime in Italy. Ironically, he, too, attended a John Jay study program, Lorenzo de' Medici in Rome. Nardo was energetic and animated with a great sense of humor. I later noted he had a unique ability to quickly change his tenor, tone, and intensity when talking about operations he'd been a part of in Italy. Obviously, as an undercover, he used these gifts to emotionally react and survive. Playing the part is a big part of undercover work and survival in the underworld.

The third candidate, Luca Provenzano, a police detective from Newark, was straight out of central casting.

He was tall and heavyset and wore an inexpensive, tan linen blazer that was wrinkled and at least a size too small. He had black slacks and a black dress shirt unbuttoned for the first three buttons, exposing his chest hair, a heavy gold Cuban link chain, and a gold Italian horn necklace. To complement the ornate jewelry on his chest, he wore a large diamond pinky ring and heavy gold bracelet on his enormous wrist. He came into the interview chewing gum, and about thirty minutes into the interview, apologized and removed the gum from his mouth.

He attended Rutgers School of Criminal Justice in Newark, New Jersey, but hadn't yet completed his studies.

For me, it was love at first sight. His swagger and resumé said it all. This guy, if not for his appearance, probably would have been made Newark's chief detective. He was sharp, had a major case clearance rate higher than anything I'd ever seen, and for him, wise guys were like catnip he liked to play with.

He had my vote two hundred percent.

After we excused the last candidate, I turned to Potente with a smile on my face.

"Chief, it doesn't get any better than this. Hire 'em all!"

78

THIS WASN'T SUPPOSED TO HAPPEN

That night, I woke up just past three, soaked in sweat, with my heart racing. I didn't know why, but assumed it was another PTSD episode. I rarely remember what I dream, so I don't always know what triggers the episodes. I got up, took a shower, and called Mercedes but got her voicemail. She was foremost on my mind, and I needed to hear her voice.

She turned her phone off when she was working and sometimes left it in the trailer to avoid distractions. I'd have to try later.

I don't usually make a big breakfast, but since I had the time and appetite, I cooked bacon and eggs.

At about six a.m., I received a call from an overseas number I didn't recognize. At first, I thought it was a spam call, but with Mercedes in Europe, I figured I should take the call.

It was a woman's voice.

"Is this Mr. DeLuca?"

"Yes, that's right."

"Mr. DeLuca, my name is Dr. Moretti. I'm the studio physician for Thunder Pictures filming in Italy. We met briefly when you were recently here. Are you somewhere private where you can talk?"

My heart sank. "I am, what's going on?"

"I'm sorry, but I have some very bad news. You should sit down. Mercedes Cruz was killed today in a helicopter crash."

She gave me a minute to comprehend what I'd just been told.

"I am so sorry for your loss, Mr. DeLuca."

I had difficulty breathing and immediately started to sweat and feel lightheaded and nauseous.

"Are you sure it was her? What was she doing in a helicopter?"

"They were flying from Amalfi to Positano to shoot scenes, and the helicopter collided with the side of a mountain. Everyone was killed on impact. The crash is being investigated by the National Agency for the Safety of Flight, *Agenzia Nazionale per la Sicurezza del Volo.* They may have run into some visibility problems.

"I'm so sorry. She was a beautiful person, and we all loved her. Is there someone I can call for you?"

"No. Thank you. If you, or the director, can call me with the phone number to reach her family in Los Angeles, I would appreciate it. Have they been notified?"

"Yes, we called them first. I'd recommend you wait a day to call them."

With that, she gave me a phone number to reach Mercedes' parents. I hung up and ran to the toilet to vomit. I cried, screamed, and pounded my mattress until any strength I had was gone.

How could this happen? I remembered, only days ago, swimming in the cove with her. How she hung around my neck, kissing my face, telling me she loved me. I'd never felt so loved and I never loved a woman so much. *Dear God, how could this happen?* I was angry with God and beyond grief-stricken.

I called Central Station to notify the watch commander I'd be out on bereavement leave. He had just seen the news and offered his condolences.

"Ray, take the time you need and let us know if you need anything."

I felt lost in an alternate universe. I called my mother who had just seen the tragedy on the news, and we cried together on the phone. My father cried, too. He told me he knew I loved her.

"I'm deeply sorry, son. She's up there with the angels now. We'll pray for her and for you."

As I finished the call, I got another. This time from an area code I recognized as LA.

"Raymond, this is Antonio Cruz, Mercedes' father. I'm so sorry. We wanted you to know how much our beautiful daughter loved you. When we spoke to her, if she wasn't talking about the movie, she was talking about you. You were the center of her universe. She adored you. Even though we haven't had the chance to meet, we feel like we know you through Mercedes."

We both wept and I offered him my condolences. I told him I'd be happy to fly to Italy to bring her home to Los Angeles. He said he was in touch with a representative from Thunder Pictures, and they wanted to fly her back to LA on their company jet. They also offered to pay all funeral expenses.

I told him I wanted to help as well.

"I'll fly to LA," I said. "I want to be there when she comes home. Can I call you later to update you?"

He thanked me.

"Of course. She loved you and loved making movies, so we know she died happy. She was doing what she loved, with the man she loved. We'd see pictures of you and Mercedes, and you both always looked so happy together."

We started crying again, so we ended the call and I promised to call later. I was emotionally and physically drained, so I lay on the bed feeling empty.

I dozed fitfully for a couple of hours and awoke disoriented, thinking it was a bad dream. When I realized it wasn't, I lay there for what seemed like an eternity, reliving every second Mercedes and I had together.

I sat up when the phone started to vibrate, hoping it was Mercedes and it was all a mistake. Maybe it was her stunt double that died?

When I answered, an unfamiliar caller with a heavy Italian accent spoke.

"Raymond, this is Monsignor Celauro from Saints Peter and Paul Church in San Francisco. I know you've just suffered a terrible loss, and I want to stop by to see you and give you my blessing."

I thanked him. "Not necessary. I'm fine, Monsignor."

"I insist, Raymond. Please give me your home address, and I promise not to stay long. It's a nice day for me to take a drive."

He arrived an hour later and encouraged me to grieve. I think he tried to give the tragedy perspective, talking about heaven, parables, and the afterlife. It did little to ease the pain. I probably heard ten percent of what he said.

We knelt and prayed God would take Mercedes in his loving arms and welcome her home.

When we finished praying, I offered the monsignor a scotch. He smiled and accepted. He may have done this once or twice before because, before I could ask him how he liked it, he said, "Neat please."

Only minutes after he left, I got a call from Gina, offering her condolences.

"I need your address to bring food."

"Not necessary, Gina, I'll be fine."

In Sicilian, she admonished me. "Ray, this is how we grieve. You know that. You can't stop me from doing what I have to do. Text me your address."

I did and an hour later, she showed up with boxes of prepared food from her restaurant sealed in foil containers. She had meals for breakfast, lunch, and dinner.

"Freeze what you don't eat."

She also had a bouquet of white roses and lilies she set on the table.

I poured us each a scotch and we sat, held hands, and cried. We talked about Mercedes. Then talked about her brother Carmine and my best friend Billy, too. Beautiful souls. Unfathomable losses. I struggled to imagine how I'd carry on without them. The world would never know the likes of their humanity and special gifts again.

"I'm here for you," she said, "like you've been there for me. You've always given me a shoulder to cry on. Let me do that for you. We both lost beautiful, loved ones. Let me know what I can do."

Just as she left, I got a call from DC Potente, who in Sicilian said, "Ray, I'm so sorry for your loss. If there's anything I can do, or the SFPD, we're here for you. God bless."

I went to Saints Peter and Paul Church the following day to light a candle for Mercedes and give Monsignor Celauro a cash donation and a gift of Johnnie Walker scotch and cigars.

"In case you have some wayward friends who drink and smoke," I said.

We spoke Sicilian and I thanked him for his visit and asked him to say a Mass for Mercedes.

"That's a very generous donation, Raymond. We'll be saying Masses for Mercedes for the next six months. Keep that up, and she'll get a stained glass window, too."

We both smiled.

79

IT SEEMS LIKE A LIFETIME AGO

I *drove to LA for the funeral services,* hoping the six-hour drive would give me time to think.

I checked in to the Beverly Wilshire and called Mercedes' father in Glendale, where he and his wife were living in a beautiful home their daughter bought them a year ago.

They invited me for dinner, but I declined.

"Instead, let me take you and Mrs. Cruz out to dinner."

They accepted the invitation and we met at a local restaurant.

"You're family now, Raymond," said Antonio. "We want you to sit with us at the funeral services because that's what Mercedes would have wanted."

"Of course," I said.

"The studio has been wonderful," he said, "and sent a funeral director from West Hollywood to work with us on arrangements. It's helped a lot, and the studio is covering the entire cost."

"If they don't," I said, "I'd like to pay."

I didn't know where I'd come up with the money, but I'd find a way.

"Not necessary, Ray, but it's generous of you to offer. I do have one request, though. There'll be lots of paparazzi, and we're not up for making any statements. If you can be the spokesman for the family, that would be helpful and give us our privacy.

The studio has hired your friends from Blackhawk to provide security for us."

"Of course. I'd be honored."

"Our family is Catholic, so the services will be held at the Church of the Good Shepherd in Beverly Hills. So many people have sent flowers and plan to attend the services, it's probably the best location for everyone."

After we said goodnight, I called Joe and Pete and invited them to join me for a nightcap at the Beverly Wilshire. It was early, so both dropped by.

We toasted Mercedes and Billy and made it an early night with the funeral the following day. If Billy hadn't given me the job at Blackhawk, I would never have met Mercedes.

"From the moment you two met in Dubai," Joe said, "the sparks flew, and I knew you two would either kill each other or fall in love."

"A lifetime ago," I said.

★ ★ ★

I arrived at the church early to be there for Mr. and Mrs. Cruz and to avoid the paparazzi. I parked a block away and entered through the sacristy at the rear of the church. I apologized to the priest, who had just arrived and explained the situation.

Thinking like a good Catholic, Joe and his team escorted Mr. and Mrs. Cruz through the same sacristy entrance. The priest suggested we wait in the rectory for the next half hour to make things easier.

We had coffee and sweet rolls, until the service was about to begin.

I stood with the immediate family in the first pew and watched as they slowly guided the casket down the aisle.

Antonio and I comforted Mrs. Cruz. Aunts, uncles, and cousins mourned with us. Mercedes had a beautiful, loving family. A lay person for the church made an announcement for all phones to be turned off and asked that paparazzi remain outside during the service.

"This is a private funeral service, and out of reverence and respect for the deceased and her family, we ask for everyone's cooperation.

"No phones, audio recording, or pictures, please. Please turn your phones off."

Several Beverly Hills PD officers were there as well. I saw Joe and his team coordinating logistics with them. Hollywood came out in force. I recognized the leading man from Mercedes' latest project, with the director and production crew.

A couple of her cousins read passages from the Bible, and the film's director gave a heartfelt eulogy, at times stopping to compose himself. He knew Mercedes well, having worked with her on several pictures, and he invited the crew from her current project to join him at the lectern. It was emotional but respectful and reserved, and local floral shops must have been seriously depleted with this outpouring of love.

Death at any age is difficult and sad, but when it's unexpected and tragic, it amplifies the grief.

At the conclusion of the service, the family escorted the coffin to a waiting hearse.

The paparazzi kept their distance and used telephoto lenses to get their shots. Mercedes was known for treating paparazzi with respect, so today, they returned the courtesy to her family by keeping their distance.

As the hearse departed for the cemetery, as agreed, I gave a statement on behalf of the family.

I kept the statement brief and thanked the media for their respectful coverage of the tragedy. In memory of Mercedes, I asked them to give the family time and distance to grieve.

One reporter, out of either ghoulish curiosity or sheer half-wittedness, wanted to know if she suffered.

I stepped forward to hit him, but a Beverly Hills officer behind me pulled me back. A sergeant brought the press conference to a close, and a detective volunteered to drive me to the cemetery for the graveside services.

I felt the same aching in my heart when Mercedes left for Italy, but the permanence of this loss would be with me forever.

- 80 -

WORLD TURNED UPSIDE DOWN

I *don't recall much about the return trip* to San Francisco. I wanted Mercedes back. I wanted to touch her again and hear her laugh. I wanted to hear her call me hero again. There were moments when it felt like it never really happened. It was just a dream.

I was technically still out on bereavement leave, but thought I'd stop by the station to check for messages and get caught up.

As I walked toward the modest entrance to the station, I spotted a large Missing Person poster taped to the glass by the walk-up window. It was a picture of Sophie Rossi with a ten-thousand-dollar reward for information leading to her whereabouts.

My heart sank.

My mind was racing, and I suddenly felt disoriented. I was in another world and startled when officers extended their condolences. The watch commander came out of her office and offered condolences, too.

I asked her if she knew about Sophie's disappearance, and she explained how, a few days earlier, Sophie's girlfriend came to Central Station to report her missing. She hadn't been seen in about a week. The lieutenant gave me the inspector's name handling the case—Nia Thomas, working out of our SIT office.

I immediately went downstairs to investigations where Inspector Thomas gave me a quick rundown of what they had so far.

"She told her girlfriend she met a guy on an online dating website and was going to meet him for a first date. It was described as a quick call, and the girlfriend told us that was the last time she spoke to her. Sophie was last seen getting into a vehicle in front of a bar on Green Street, a vehicle we later learned had stolen plates. Somewhere out of sight of video cameras, her phone was tossed. We recovered the phone but still haven't unlocked it yet. We've also submitted a request to get her phone records, so everything is speculation right now. The whole story sounds *off*, and even her girlfriend was puzzled as to why she'd go on an online dating website. She's a beautiful girl with no shortage of suitors, but who knows."

"Believe me," I said, "I know. She's got no issues meeting men. She's a beautiful woman. Any recent contacts with the PD?"

"Only the restraining order that's still in effect, ordering Vinnie Catalano to cease all contact. I'm worried about this girl. We've got fliers all over the city and an Amber Alert was activated. I don't have a good feeling. No one's come forward with anything usable. Catalano was interviewed a couple of days ago, and he swears he knows nothing about it."

"I know her personally and she's young and naïve. I'll do some poking around North Beach and let you know if I hear anything. If *you* hear anything, let me know."

My theories included Vinnie having her kidnapped so he could have her to himself, regardless of the restraining order—but perhaps she *did* go on an online date and met with an evildoer and,

God forbid, was now dead. That seemed far-fetched. I decided I'd keep my theories to myself until I had something to go on. It was hard for me to collect my thoughts and think straight.

I was in a panic for Sophie. Too many losses. Everything I loved in my life, everything good, was being taken, or leaving me.

I spent the better part of the night with a drink in my hand.

BEWARE THE HIGH AND MIGHTY

H*ungover, I returned to work* the following day with dry-cleaned uniforms thrown over my shoulder. As I was walking past the alley next to the station, I noticed a stocky Asian guy in civilian clothes mashed up against a female cop in uniform, making out with her with his thigh between her legs, grinding on her. It was unexpected, and it took a second to realize it was Hank and Lily.

I looked away, hiding my face with the uniforms.

World gone mad.

I dropped by the investigations office where Inspector Nia Thomas apologized and told me they had nothing new to report.

"We've interviewed friends, family, and co-workers," she said, "and pulled a lot of video. The security video outside these businesses is crap. I think most of the cameras were installed twenty years ago. A lot of them don't work at all. Also, I've been jammed up on a Use of Force investigation involving Lily Leung. You probably know her."

"Of course, I do. What happened?"

"She knocked the shit out of some dude resisting down on Broadway. It's her second Use of Force in less than a month. She's on a tear." Thomas took a deep breath. "I've said too much. Forget I told you that and keep it to yourself. I'm sorry."

I shut the door to the tiny office. "I think she's having an affair with Hank Lau. Hank was my partner for the past year, and I know Lily, too. These guys are friends of mine. As I was walking into the station a few minutes ago, I saw them in the alley making out and grinding on each other. Hank's married. Can't be good. It might have something to do with why Lily is so jacked up."

"Okay," said Thomas, "if we're sharing secrets, you're not supposed to know this, but they're forcing Hank into retirement over the Ghost Boys thing. He's out, so he's spun out of control, too."

"I heard Internal Affairs was looking at him," I said, "and I'm glad to hear he's gone. I'm not sure I wanna know more because I'm afraid of what I'll do. He fuckin' cost me a lot and almost cost me my life."

"Well," she said, "I'm sure IA will want to interview you to get more details. I know you've been out on bereavement leave, and I'm sorry for your loss."

I thanked her and we sat quietly for a minute.

"I'm working a day watch SAM unit this week. When I'm not tied up on calls, would you mind if I did a little snooping around on the Sophie Rossi case? I'll ask the LT to clear it first and let you know. If I find anything, I'll do a supplemental report and turn it over to you."

"Of course, be my guest. Just, Ray, be sure to stay objective. I know there's a connection there."

"Focused and professional," I said, but what I felt was that my life was unraveling before my very eyes.

- 81 -

STROKE, STROKE, STROKE

I **read the original Missing Person Report** regarding Sophie's disappearance and found no fault with it. Inspector Thomas did a thorough job, by the book. The LT agreed to let me do some follow-up, so I decided to reinterview her girlfriend, employees at Trattoria and Carmine's restaurants, and her parents.

I also planned to drop by her supervisor's office at Apple as well. Somebody might remember something they forgot to report earlier or something they felt was insignificant at the time.

I had a sense of dread and darkness, especially with Mercedes and Billy fresh in my mind. I didn't want to lose Sophie, too, even though our relationship never got off the ground. I know from the recent note she tapped in my phone, she had her regrets, too, and wanted to give things another try.

The restaurant employees who knew her as a customer, and as a friend of Vinnie's, had nothing new to report. Sophie's girlfriend had mail piled up by her apartment mailbox, so I assumed she left, or was out of town. I knocked on her door, but there was no response, or signs of forced entry.

Sophie's parents were gracious and invited me into their apartment. They were Sicilian immigrants, and her mother immediately broke down.

Her father was stoic and composed. Not unusual for Sicilian men. He looked familiar, but I couldn't recall where I'd seen him. Probably just strolling around North Beach, as the locals do.

Sophie was off the grid, and her parents hadn't received any communications from her, which was highly unusual. She had never gone dark before. The family was loving and close. I could see the deep worry in their faces as her mother wept.

I handed her father my card and asked them to call me if she contacted them or if they received any information whatsoever that might aid us in the investigation.

Next stop was Apple on Second Street, South of Market. The security guys escorted me to her boss' office, a middle manager with Apple Machine Learning and Artificial Intelligence. I expected to meet a guy with two heads, or a robot, but was pleasantly surprised. He was friendly and what I'd describe as the typical geeky software engineer.

He was shocked by Sophie's disappearance but had no usable investigative information. He was unaware of any issues she had in the workplace and offered to help us in any way they could.

"Can you crack the security code on her iPhone for us?" I asked.

"I can," he said, "but I won't. Sorry, sir. That's a no-no and above my pay grade."

Well, that wasted the better part of a day and I got nowhere.

I drove by Trattoria and spotted Vinnie getting into his car. I stopped and told him I was passing by and wanted to say hello. He was surprised to see me driving an unmarked car, so I made light of it and told him I had a stakeout earlier in my shift.

"So, you haven't seen Sophie since she had you arrested, right? I mean, you been keeping out of her way I assume."

I channeled my best Lieutenant Colombo from the old TV series.

That touched a nerve.

"On my mother's grave. I haven't fuckin' seen her! I'm concerned, too! She's a good kid. Do you guys know anything?"

"Nothing," I said. "Ungatz. You *sure* you don't know nothin'?" He gave me the stare, obviously pissed.

"What's wrong with you?" I said. "I'm just bustin' your chops."

My instincts told me he knew about Sophie and knew what happened to Carmine, but I had no proof.

"Hey, enough doom and gloom," I said. "So, how's everything else?"

"It's all good. It's raining money." He crossed his arms and leaned against his new Ferrari. "Can't get outta the way of the money."

"Man, you're amazing, Vinnie. I don't know how you do it."

I'd pissed him off, but by the time I left, I had him feeling good. I knocked him down, then built his enormous ego back up. So much so, he probably had an erection by the time I left. Stroke, stroke, stroke . . .

I was reminded of the old Muhammad Ali saying: "Float like a butterfly, sting like a bee!"

- 82 -

NO MAS! NOT ON MY WATCH

When *I came in from patrol* at the end of my shift, Sergeant Smethurst caught my attention.

"Deputy Chief Potente left a message. He wants you to call him, and I'm not going to ask why."

I laughed, "Well, Sarge, DC Potente and I are pretty tight. That's all I can say."

He smiled and nodded. "DeLuca, you're a man of many talents. You never cease to amaze me."

He handed me a scrap of paper with the chief's cell number, so I must have been kicked up a notch on the trust thing.

The chief answered right away.

"Welcome back, Ray. Again, I'm so sorry for your loss. Are you working tomorrow?"

"Yes sir, I am."

"Okay, good. I've got the new team for the Organized Crime Task Force coming to headquarters tomorrow to meet with me, Chief Castillo, and Sergeant Amato. I'd like you to join us for that meeting. Eight a.m. sharp, chief's office. You've given us good insights, and if you don't mind, I'd like to keep you in these conversations, as we ready this team to go 10-8."

"Sure, sir. I'll need to clear it with my LT."

"Already done, Ray. Captain Choo will be joining us as well." The candidates all passed backgrounds and all phases of testing, so they'll be starting an accelerated lateral academy next Monday. Per your suggestion, we put them in temporary housing in the apartments near Lake Merced. Good choice."

"Thank you, sir."

"See you tomorrow, Ray."

Life is who you know, and it couldn't hurt to have a friend on the command staff.

My night was wrought with demons. Some were of my own doing, and some came uninvited. I sat and listened to everything from jazz to Italian opera, while I made love to a very smooth bottle of Buffalo Trace bourbon and an Arturo Fuente cigar.

Sleep came easy, but not for long. My dreams were haunted by Mercedes and Billy. After I finally got back to sleep, a bout with PTSD left me an emotional wreck in a puddle of sweat, so I got up and made coffee and breakfast. That night the demons won.

I sat and pondered Sophie's whereabouts. All possibilities led back to Vinnie Catalano. I'd have to speak to Inspector Thomas again, after the meeting at headquarters.

I arrived early for the Organized Crime Task Force (OCTF) meeting and got a few minutes alone with Chief Castillo, who I'd yet to meet in person. He was cordial and knew more about me than I thought he would.

He offered condolences for my recent loss and thanked me for the work I'd done thus far with Deputy Chief Potente.

"Maybe when the time is right for you, you'll join OCTF as well."

"We'll see, Chief. Right now wouldn't work, but we'll see what the future brings. As you know, I just went through some personal setbacks, but I never say never. I'm glad I can help out behind the scenes."

When I spotted a shadow box with Army Ranger patches, ribbons, and medals, and a folded flag with the thirteen folds, I figured I'd just met a kindred spirit.

As we assembled around the conference room table in his office, the chief shook hands with each of us and made sure we all had coffee before starting the meeting. A good host.

He started the meeting with a short speech:

"Thanks for being here. As I'm sure you've been told by DC Potente, this task force is top priority and mission critical for our police department. This city has been terrorized by La Cosa Nostra and the Ghost Boys for too long, and our community deserves better. Tourism, the lifeblood of this city, has come to an abrupt halt because of this violence, and we're getting killed in the press because of it."

He paused and met each man's eyes in turn.

"This is not going to happen on my watch. I'm here to say, *no mas!* Enough is enough! This is *our* city, not theirs, and with your hard work, your courage, and skills, we'll take it back. That's why you're here. I'm also here to tell you time is of the essence. Today, we'll talk about where we're at, and how we'll bring a sense of safety back to the City and County of San Francisco, so buckle up. We're going to move fast and expect you to keep up. You were carefully selected because of your unique backgrounds and skill sets. I'll use an analogy Officer DeLuca is very familiar with—this is like a special ops unit, like a SEAL team.

"I've asked Sergeant Amato to give you a quick snapshot of his background."

Amato stood.

"Great to meet you guys. I'll be brief. Like you, I'm one hundred percent Sicilian and speak the language fluently. My parents are both Sicilian, but I was born in San Jose, California. I'm coming up on ten years with SFPD; and prior to this department, I was with San Mateo Sheriff's Office for seven years, and much of that time, I worked undercover narcotics and sex trafficking. I've worked patrol, mostly out of Southern and Mission stations, since I joined SFPD. With only four of us, this will be a formidable task, but I'm familiar with your backgrounds, and it's truly an honor to serve as your leader.

"I know I'll learn a lot from each of you, and I'm also excited to have Officer DeLuca work with us as a consultant. He's got a very interesting background and a unique skill set as a former Navy SEAL. We're going to learn from each other."

DC Potente chimed in. "Officer DeLuca, anything you'd like to add?"

I took a sip of coffee to wet my throat. I stood.

"First, I'd like to thank Deputy Chief Potente for his confidence in me. I'm not a supervisor, and I joined SFPD less than two years ago . . . *and I was already fired once!*"

That brought surprised looks and an expletive from Nardo, *Minchia!* That essentially means *fuck!*

We all laughed. "Then you must be doing something right!" said Luca.

I shrugged. "In fact, I just came off probation, working patrol out of the Central District, which is ground zero for the mob and gang activity. My father is a capo in La Cosa Nostra in New York, so I probably have a better understanding than most about the organization. I was born and raised around wise guys."

These statements stopped the OCTF team in their tracks and got everyone's attention.

"I'm not claiming I'm an expert, but if I can help the unit in any way, that's what I'm here for."

DC Potente projected a map of the Central District from his laptop onto a screen and brought up an overlay with Uniform Crime Reporting (UCR) Part I offenses in the Central police district; the ones that include criminal homicide, forcible rape, robbery, and aggravated assault. He also displayed the CompStat statistics for each of the ten SFPD district stations. For the first time in years, Central District now had the highest incidence of Part I crimes and crime overall in the city.

DC Potente said, "Captain Choo is the commanding officer of Central Station. He's here for obvious reasons. The Central police district is ultimately his responsibility, and I know he's anxious to see you complete your training and begin to build cases against these thugs."

"Gentlemen," said Choo, "this can't happen soon enough. Our residents are afraid to go outside, and our resources are tapped. I've seen your backgrounds, and my money is riding on you. Together, we're going to do this. You'll have my full support, and I'm grateful to Officer DeLuca for all that he's brought to the table."

"After you finish the lateral training course," said Potente, "we'll team you up with the FBI and U.S. Attorney's Office to bring you up to speed and make you experts on how to build RICO cases. It is a process, and you'll be able to take advantage of the

Feds' expertise, utilizing the Racketeer Influenced and Corrupt Organizations Act. Ray, we'd love to have you attend the training as well, on the off chance that someday you may choose to join us. Special Agent Gerard is probably ahead of us on the RICO training, as a former bureau employee and terrorism expert."

Jack Gerard was reserved but smiled and nodded.

Chief Castillo said, "You'll also receive additional training with the Department of Homeland Security to learn about immigration holds and how to deport those with temporary visas for criminal activity. You guys better be good students and absorb things quickly because with the body count climbing, we need you to catch on fast and start making cases so we can take control of the district again. The mayor has us under a microscope and needs our help to make this city safe again and bring back tourism."

I added, "I hope you're finding your accommodations at Lake Merced apartments acceptable. The manager's a Marine and a good friend of mine. If you need anything, ask for Mike and feel free to drop my name. Also, if you're *truly* Sicilians, you know how to cook, so I'll be anxious to see your mastery in the kitchen. Any of the Sicilian favorites like *pizzolo* [unique pizza native to Sicily], or something like *Zeppola di riso* [delicious, deep-fried sweets invented by the Benedictine nuns] will do."

There were smiles around the table.

"I'll be looking forward to a team dinner, as soon as you're done with your training, and I'll bring something special as well, including cigars and a brown adult beverage to drink."

★ ★ ★

- 83 -

DON'T LEAVE TOWN

nspector Thomas called and had a hard time controlling her enthusiasm.

"Ray, I think we've got her on video. She was a passenger in a silver or gray Ferrari, coming out of an alley behind Trattoria restaurant. We ran the plate, and it comes back to Vincent Catalano. This was about eighteen hours before she was reported missing. This girl could still be alive. We're gonna pick him up and rattle his cage. He's probably behind this."

"I'm gonna stand down on this one," I said, "because I don't want to spook him or show my hand. Let me know what you get out of him. He'll probably lawyer-up and won't tell you a thing, but grab him and let's see what he's got to say. Make sure you record the interview. He's gonna shit himself when he sees you've got video."

"We're gonna mess with his head," she said. "We're gonna tell him about the video and that he's in violation of the restraining order to stay away from Sophie Rossi. I'm also gonna tell him we're looking into the Letter of Intent that Carmine signed, essentially giving up control and sixty percent of his very successful operation for a paltry two-hundred grand. We'll let him know we think Carmine was coerced and the document was signed under duress."

"I like it. He's gonna freak."

"I may tell him we're gonna get more search warrants but won't tell him for what," she said. "We'll mind-fuck him a little and let him squirm."

"That's beautiful, Nia. Keep him off-balance, and he'll be running around trying to figure out what we know."

Hours later, they picked him up and brought him to Central Station to be interviewed. When he asked for me, the inspector shook her head. Luckily, I was able to see it all from the comfort of the next room.

"Ray's off. He's on vacation."

"Fine, so what is it now?" he asked.

That's when she unloaded on him.

"It's a matter of time. We've got video of you with a missing person and in violation of a restraining order, I might add. It doesn't look good for you."

"So what?" he snapped. "She had too much to drink so I gave her a ride. I told you, I have no fuckin' idea where she is."

"Funny you didn't mention that when we questioned you the first time. Why is that, Mr. Catalano?"

He sounded amused. "Funny, I don't remember being asked about it."

She let that pass. What he was or wasn't asked was all on record. She wanted to jump ahead and put him off-balance.

"We're also looking into the Letter of Intent you coerced Carmine into signing before he was killed. We're making progress, Vinnie, so as they say, 'Don't leave town.'"

He sneered. "I got nothin' to say. Arrest me, or I'm outta here. I'm a successful businessman. I ain't listening to this shit!"

The inspector stood. "Don't get too comfortable. This ain't over by a long shot."

When he left the room, Vinnie looked guilty as hell to me.

I'd already left an outgoing voicemail message on my phone saying I was away on vacation, with no access to email or cellular. That would discourage him from trying to call me. I anticipated he'd flee, so I asked Captain Choo if I could take a week off to travel before the OCTF team finished their training.

"Sure," he said. "Do it now because it might be awhile before you get time off, between working patrol and helping them out. Where you going?"

"I dunno," I said. "Maybe visit relatives in Sicily."

- 84 -

WHERE WERE MY MANNERS?

I *couldn't stop thinking about Mercedes* and Sophie on the flight to Sicily. It was a long flight, with a stopover in Lisbon, but I spent extra money for a seat upgrade, so I could sleep.

I didn't know what I'd find there, but I had three goals in mind: first, to get a change of scenery and to unwind; second, to be in Sicily if Vinnie fled there or brought Sophie there; and third, to immerse myself in La Cosa Nostra culture in Corleone, historically home base to most of Italy's Mafia activity.

In my extra role consulting SFPD's new OCTF, I needed to take it all in and understand the current environment in Sicily. I looked at the trip as market research.

I rented a cottage in Menfi for a week, close to Corleone. Menfi is known for its beaches, restaurants, and wineries, and it fit the bill for the relaxation part of my trip.

The first day, I slept on the beach, swam, and hit a couple of local restaurants. I ate outdoors and enjoyed fresh seafood and local wines. The only thing missing was Mercedes.

I rented a Vespa scooter and did some sightseeing in Corleone. Back in the sixties, the town became the hub for the Sicilian Cosa Nostra. During that time, one of the kingpins was Salvatore "Toto" Riina, a ruthless murderer who reportedly ordered the killing of local magistrates and a hundred and fifty others. Nice guy, that "Toto."

Corleone was later featured in Mario Puzo's 1969 bestseller *The Godfather* as the adopted surname of the fictional Corleone family, who in the story emigrated to the U.S. from the town of Corleone in Sicily.

There were no outward signs of mafioso today, but I'd been told it was the birthplace of the Mafia and many still reside in Corleone. None today have the power that Riina once had. Riina died in prison in 2017, while serving consecutive life sentences.

In 1992, the Italian government sent five thousand military troops to nearby Palermo, following the car bomb deaths of anti-Mafia magistrate Giovanni Bruno, his wife, and three police escorts.

Two months later, their colleague Paolo Borsellino was killed by another bomb, along with his five bodyguards, as he approached his mother's house.

For the next four years, there was a heavy military and police presence in and around Palermo, the likes of which hadn't been seen since World War II.

The unprecedented number of arrests and prosecutions during that period weakened the Italian Mafia in ways from which it's never recovered.

There were lessons to be learned here.

Despite this weakening of the Mafia, the legacy, memories, and traditions live on through some of their families that hope for better days and future organized crime opportunities.

Vinnie Catalano fell into that category and hoped to recreate and profit from some of those same activities in San Francisco.

I visited the *Museo Antimafia,* the Anti-Mafia Museum, and took a guided tour of Corleone. The tour guide was captivating and explained how the massive resistance movement by its citizens, along with the military, police, and brave prosecutors, defeated the Mafia in the nineties. The history and tragedy have been well documented by the museum curators, along with pictures and paintings that brought it to life.

The guide called it a great tragedy for the people of Sicily and described it as quite different from the romantic version you see in American movies and television.

I noted that, according to their archives, Bernardo "The Tractor" Catalano succeeded Salvatore "Toto" Riina as Cosa Nostra's *capo di tutti i capi*, or boss of all bosses. Likely, a relative of Vinnie's.

Catalano changed the paradigm of the Mafia from high levels of violence to a more reserved approach, dialing back the violence. He still raked in cash, however, from protection rackets and contracts for the construction of public buildings.

Catalano was eventually arrested in what was described as a crude cottage in the hills above Corleone.

Aside from the Mafia, Corleone is also known for its many churches, so I made it a point to visit the most famous of them all, The Mother Church, dedicated to Saint Martin and built in the late fourteenth century, with paintings dating back to the 1700s.

I'd rack up points with my mother for visiting the churches. It couldn't hurt.

I walked the streets and sat in plazas people-watching and enjoying the sun. There were lots of old men sitting in caffès and on benches in threadbare suits and wearing berets, so I asked a group of them about the Mafia.

All but one ignored my question as they continued to talk among themselves.

One old guy turned to me, very serious. "You shouldn't ask questions like that."

"I'm a tourist. I was just curious. Are there still a lot of mafioso here in Corleone?"

I guess he didn't find the question—or my persistence—polite, so he stood, excused himself, and walked away.

- 85 -

STRANGE BEDFELLOWS

The following day, on a suggestion from a waiter, I drove to Palermo to attend *Festa di Santa Rosalia*, or *U Fistinu*, to honor the patron saint of Palermo. It's an annual celebration with fireworks, Sicilian music, and street food and drink.

Interestingly, I caught a glimpse of a woman from a distance who reminded me of Sophie. I realized it was probably a combination of imagination and too much wine-tasting in the sun. There were a lot of beautiful women in Sicily, and many with similar coloring and looks.

About an hour later, I saw her again, from about twenty feet away. This time I was sure it was her. Either that or she had a twin.

I pushed through the crowd and as I got closer, I called out to her.

"Sophie! E Raggio!" Sophie, it's Ray!

She turned, looked at me, and had a look of panic on her face. She turned and pushed through the crowd, fast-walking away from me.

"Sophie, vieni qui!" Come here!

She started to run through the crowds of festival-goers, out for a day in the sun.

I lost her along the way but could smell her perfume. Her scent was unmistakable, so I knew for certain it was her.

I drove back to my cottage in Menfi and called the lead inspector on the missing person case, Nia Thomas.

"It's Ray DeLuca and I'm calling from vacation in Italy. You better sit down for this one."

I gave her the background and then let her have it.

"I don't know where she is now. But I can tell you, with absolute certainty, it was Sophie Rossi I saw today here in Palermo. It's late here, and I want to see if I can find her tomorrow in the daylight.

"She's Sicilian, and I don't know why she left San Francisco without telling her parents, her employer, and her best friend. I know she was thrilled with her new job at Apple, so it's hard to imagine she just walked away and left her family and her life in San Francisco behind. There's gotta be a Vinnie Catalano nexus in all this. He may have threatened her life and the lives of her family if she didn't leave and go with him to Sicily. Maybe he sees her as his possession. His *goomah*."

"A *goomah?*"

"It's East Coast slang for a mistress or kept woman."

"No, of course. Sorry, I've heard the term. It just feels . . . I don't know."

"Colorful and Italian? I'd start getting used to it if I were you."

"I guess so," she said. "Anyway, if you can find her and positively ID her, we can at least shut down the Amber Alert and pull the Missing Person Bulletins."

"At some point," I said, "we'll ask for help from the Italian cops, the Carabinieri, or local polizia, but my fear is Vinnie may have them on his payroll. This could get dicey, but we just hired a former undercover, Stefano DiNardo from *Direzione Investigativa*

Antimafia who may be able to help us if we get jammed up. Right now, he reports to Amato and Potente.

"I'll let you know if I can locate her again for positive ID. I'll get back to you tomorrow one way or another. I promise. When Sophie saw me today, she looked scared for her life, so I'm guessing Vinnie Catalano is here in Sicily."

I hung up and called Gina.

"Hey, stranger," she said when she picked up. "Where you been?"

"I took some vacation time to get a change of scenery. How you been?"

"Busy, but I've been worried about you with everything you've been through. You okay?"

"I'm coping. Just getting used to this new life without Mercedes."

"You know I'm here for you, Ray. Let me know when you're up to it and we can have dinner."

"Thanks, Gina. I appreciate it. Everything good with the restaurant? Business good?"

"It's been good. Vinnie's been gone, so I've been handling everything."

"Really?" I said. "Where'd he go?"

"Not sure. It's been a few days. Maybe he took a trip, or went back to Sicily for a visit? He doesn't tell me. He'll show up sooner or later, because this is where a lot of his money comes from."

So, now I knew both Vinnie and Sophie were MIA. Sophie was here in Sicily, probably with Vinnie, who she had a restraining order against in San Francisco. It had to be against her will. A kept woman, an unwilling *goomah*.

Sophie recently indicated she wanted to try a relationship with me again, so the likelihood of her hooking up with Vinnie seemed remote, especially after he assaulted her.

I was on Vinnie's home turf and needed to stay sharp-eyed. If he was in Palermo with Sophie, he likely knew I was here, too.

- 86 -

NO FREE BREAKFAST; NO FREE LUNCH

I got dressed and was sitting on the side of the bed, enjoying the sounds of the ocean and sea birds, when I was startled by a knock on the door.

A bright woman's voice. "Room service. Breakfast."

"I didn't order breakfast."

"It's complimentary, sir."

Without further thought, I opened the door and was shoved back and held at gunpoint, while an intruder covered my head with a black hood, and another put my hands behind my back and bound me with flex-cuffs.

"Don't say a word," one of them said, "or make a sound, or you'll be dead."

They put me in the back of a vehicle and drove for at least thirty minutes. It sounded and felt like we transitioned from pavement to a rutted dirt road and were going up an incline for at least half the trip.

No one spoke. The vehicle eventually came to a stop, and they escorted me into a damp, musty room and sat me in a hard, straight-backed chair.

"Why am I here?" I asked.

No response.

"Where's Vinnie?"

Still no response.

"What do you want from me?"

Crickets.

As a SEAL, I had extensive SERE (Survival, Evasion, Resistance & Escape) training. My years of training meant I knew I needed to remain calm and stay situationally aware.

I knew there were three of them, and I had caught a glimpse of one weapon, a submachine gun, possibly an HK MP5. I memorized the route we traveled while we were in transit and tried to figure out where they were holding me.

I felt a draft coming into the room from an open doorway or window, and because we didn't climb stairs, I knew we were on the first floor of a country house or outbuilding. I heard no other sounds, so my best guess was we were in a remote, rural area.

I only heard two sets of footsteps in the room, so one of the captors went elsewhere, probably to report in. They only conversed from a distance, making it difficult for me to hear what they were saying.

I decided I'd cooperate within reason and try to ascertain their endgame. I sensed the abduction was hastily planned and ordered by Vinnie and knew, from experience, additional threats and torture were imminent. If they were going to kill me, it probably would have happened by now.

But you never know.

After some time passed, unprovoked, one of the captors began backhanding me. I was relatively sure he was wearing weighted tactical gloves, like police sap gloves, to protect his hands and inflict maximum damage. I smelled the leather. The blows were heavy, and it felt like he was slapping me hard with the back of a wet catcher's mitt.

The attack caught me off guard and knocked me to the floor. I could taste and smell the iron in my blood. I was stunned and dazed. "*Codardi!*" I spat. Cowards! And was rewarded with a kick to my ribs.

The other captor told him to stop, so they righted the chair, stood me up, and sat me back down.

"What do you want with me?" I said in Sicilian. "I'm a beat cop from San Francisco."

I suddenly heard soft footsteps, like the sound expensive loafers, and smelled a familiar musky cologne. Vinnie had arrived.

He removed the hood.

"Ray, I thought we was friends. What the fuck are you doing in Corleone and Palermo? You got no business here, and now you're chasing Sophie."

"Fuck you Vinnie, I'm from Sicily, too, remember? I'm here on vacation. I saw Sophie at a street fair. I wasn't looking for her, if that's what you think. When she saw me, she ran. What am I supposed to think? She's a missing person in San Francisco. It's no big deal. I can tell them she's been located and she's safe and sound. They'll take her out of the system. Case closed."

He hesitated, as if in deep thought.

"You got one shot to leave here alive. You can be our guy on the inside. Your own father's one of us, for Christ's sake. You need to swear an Oath of Omertà, or we'll cut you up and feed you to the pigs."

"Vinnie, I can't do that. It's not for me. Nothing against you or anybody else, but it's not what I want. It's not gonna happen."

"You think you're better than me, don't ya?"

"I'm nobody," I said. "You're the guy with the famous restaurants and all the toys. I'll stay outta your way. Cut me loose."

He spat in my face, put the hood over my head, and began punching me for all he was worth, knocking me off the chair. As I hit the ground, he kicked me until he ran out of steam.

In the fetal position, I did my best to tuck my chin to my chest to avoid getting my teeth kicked in or ribs broken. My mind was racing, and I knew he meant what he said. He had every intention of killing me if I didn't do what he wanted. He was a sociopath and egomaniac.

His thugs dragged me to a room close to where I'd been beaten. I'm not sure why I wasn't dead already, but assumed he was weighing his options, and the benefits of keeping me alive.

And he had another thing to consider. My father. That was probably the only reason I was still alive to breathe the musty air.

In my mind I thought, *Go ahead. Kill a capo's son—and the fury and wrath that will be rained down on you won't stop until my father's killed your entire family.*

I was increasingly concerned because I knew he'd made a hasty decision. He backed himself into a corner and didn't know what to do. The beating was a sign of his own frustrations with that decision. I presented a real problem.

I laid back and asked myself, *What would General Mattis do?* and remembered his mantra: "Be polite, be professional, but have a plan to kill everybody you meet."

They locked me a room, and I sensed the day was coming to an end. I eventually fell asleep on a filthy, stained mat on the floor. I'd slept on worse.

- 87 -

MEET THE *OTHER* RAY!

In the morning, I knew there'd be a visit from my captors, so I planned to introduce them to the *other* Ray. I keep the *other* Ray hidden, but he's always prepared for these types of situations. *That* Ray you only meet once, and typically the meeting is brief.

When the guard entered the room, I asked him to check the circulation in my hands. I was in the fetal position, with my hands behind my back against the wall, hidden from his view. I had easily broken the flex-cuffs earlier. A simple maneuver I learned in SERE training.

As he stood over me to check the restraints, I yanked him to the ground by his hair and broke his nose with the heel of my hand. I hit his windpipe full force, crushing it. It was fast, violent, and effective. I ripped his pistol from his holster and shot the backup guard in the face as he rushed into the room. Meeting adjourned.

I wanted to say, *Congratulations motherfuckers! You've officially met the other Ray!*

I took their pistols, ammunition, and phones and sprinted from the building for cover and to get my bearings to locate an escape route. I ran through a field toward a stand of scrub brush and small trees. I needed to keep moving to put distance between me and Vinnie and his crew.

Orienting myself, I ran in the direction of Mount Etna, which I recognized in the distance, knowing there'd be opportunities to snatch backpacks and supplies from tourists. Vinnie would expect me to return to the cottage in Menfi, and it was why I wouldn't. They'd be all over the airports, too, and probably had cops and airport workers on the payroll.

My goal was to stay hidden and go into survival mode. Food, water, and shelter. Then, develop a plan to rescue Sophie. I couldn't leave her behind.

I turned off the phones as I approached the woods and removed the SIM cards and batteries. I threw them down a ravine to avoid being tracked by GPS. Both phones were locked and of no use anyway.

After walking for hours, I was dehydrated and knew I had to find water soon.

Beside a trail, I noticed horses tied up near a grove of shade trees and riders, probably tourists, sitting by an open fire. It looked like they stopped to eat lunch and rest their horses.

I spotted a large rucksack close to the horses, so I snatched it and ran into the woods. I waited until I was a good distance away before I opened it to find two large water bottles, a Swiss Army knife, binoculars, first aid kit, iodine tablets, waterproof matches, sunscreen, a couple of large moisture-wicking shirts, a waterproof poncho, trail mix, and energy bars.

This was the mother lode, and whoever stocked it was an experienced survivalist. Most likely, it belonged to the tour group leader.

The backpack was a reset and increased my chances for survival. My plan was to stay close to small villages and tour groups to take advantage of available resources, until I figured out what to do.

As the sun set, I found a small cave in an outcropping of rocks, to protect myself from the wind and hide for the night. I used the poncho as ground cover to keep dry and layered on the shirts from the backpack and covered myself with leaves and branches as barriers from the cold.

It helped, but it was still bitter cold when the sun went down and hard to sleep. I used Wim Hof methods to control my breathing to help get warm. Wim Hof, known as the Iceman, is a Dutch extreme athlete, known for his ability to withstand freezing temperatures.

I thought my cold-water workouts should help me adapt as well, at least mentally. Making a fire was out of the question.

I woke up stiff and sore from sleeping on the ground and from the beating I took the previous day. Somehow, I'd made it through the night. I knew I'd warm up with sunrise and physical activity and needed to get on the move.

I remembered I failed to call Inspector Thomas as promised. I told her I'd seen Sophie and was trying to find her again. Hopefully, she'd become suspicious that I hadn't called back and notify Captain Choo I was MIA, Missing in Action. In turn, he would notify DC Potente, who would probably ask Stefano for advice regarding DIA intervention in Sicily.

I spent another night hidden away, at times shaking with my teeth chattering from the dampness and cold, in a mossy, wooded grove providing little shelter from the cold and wind. Early the next morning, while my mind was fresh, I made a new plan. I'd descend the mountain and find my mother's relatives near Messina at the base of the mountain. I knew there's a lot of them and that they live in a small village called Savoca. I'd never been there. My mother used to brag that some of the scenes in *The Godfather* movie were shot in her hometown. With less than two thousand residents and relatives that have lived there since the Stone Age, they shouldn't be hard to find.

If family could give me shelter and access to a cell phone, I'd call DC Potente and suggest using Stefano DiNardo's DIA connections for help locating Sophie for a rescue.

By ten a.m., I arrived in Savoca, and through the owner of a local bakery found my mother's brother, Nunzio, who I recognized from family pictures.

He asked, "Have you been living on the street?"

I explained the reason for my disheveled appearance, and without further questions or hesitation, he offered a shower, fresh clothes, and the use of his home and cell phone.

When I finished showering and was dressed, I wandered into the kitchen, where my uncle had prepared a charcutier plate with cheeses, meats, peppers, bread, and olives. He also set out a carafe of homemade wine.

Uncle Nunzio called my mother while I sat there. After they chatted it up, I briefly told her everything was fine, downplaying my capture. I was doubtful she believed me.

"I'm having a wonderful time, Ma!"

Uncle Nunzio rolled his eyes. *"Madone!"*

Even *he* could see through my bullshit.

I called Inspector Thomas who was working the Sophie Rossi case, and DC Potente, and apprised them of the situation. Potente said he'd ask Stefano to contact me immediately and request DIA support.

"I'll call the U.S. Attorney's Office for guidance on getting warrants issued for Vincent Catalano and the U.S. Marshalls as well. At a minimum, he's wanted for Violation of a Restraining Order, and for Federal Kidnapping, transporting Sophie Rossi across state lines and out of the country. When you speak to DIA, tell them U.S. warrants are in progress and they can verify that with me, if necessary.

"I'm sure DIA can take your statement and get EU [European Union] arrest warrants as well."

I called Stefano, and within fifteen minutes he called back with his former DIA boss, Valentina "Val" Andresini, conferenced in.

She recorded a statement from me and said she'd get an EU arrest warrant issued for Vincent Catalano for his attack on me and the assault and kidnapping of Sophie Rossi. Stefano emailed the Missing Person Bulletin to Val and said he'd forward the U.S. federal warrants to her as they're issued.

Val had DIA undercover associates in Palermo and dispatched them to begin the search for Sophie.

"Give me a number where I can reach you and let me get things underway," she said in quick, forceful Sicilian. "I'll get a ride to the island to meet you, probably with Carabinieri, and coordinate the search for Miss Rossi."

Stefano explained that Val was an attorney and former public prosecutor with *Pubblico Ministero* before she joined DIA, so she was knowledgeable, well-connected, and highly respected.

"She's also a martial arts expert. Some form of jujitsu. She's fierce. I think you'll like her. A natural blonde, too. Not so common in Italy. We give her a hard time about it."

A half hour later, Val called, saying they'd be airborne in five leaving for Sicily and would land near Messina on the coast. She added, "After we land, I'll have a DIA investigator pick you up."

I insisted I participate in the mission to rescue Sophie.

"We have good undercovers in the area familiar with the Catalanos. They assured me they'll locate her whereabouts by the time we land. They have a good intelligence network."

I received a call from a DIA investigator late afternoon, and moments later there was a knock on my uncle's door. His name was Aldo Moretti, an old friend of Stefano's.

"Officer DeLuca?"

Moments later I was introduced to Val Andresini. She was tall and slim, wearing black BDUs (fatigues), and as reported, was very blonde.

She extended her hand. "Are you the SFPD guy who stole Stefano, one of my best undercovers?"

We laughed, then her voice took on a serious inflection. "We think this young lady is close by in a village outside of Messina."

She was holding a copy of the Missing Persons Bulletin in her hand and brought up an aerial view of the house on an electronic tablet, where they thought Sophie was located.

"At dusk, we'll set up a perimeter," she said, drawing a bright yellow line around the neighborhood with a stylus.

She marked locations where officers would be positioned and told me Aldo and I would accompany her to take the front door. Aldo had an old-school Enforcer battering ram to breach the door and make a tactical entry.

Val handed me a Beretta 92 in a holster, a favorite of the Carabinieri, with two spare magazines.

"It's not a gift," she said. "I *will* need that back!" Then she tossed me a ballistic vest. "That too!"

"What are *you* carrying?" I asked

She held up an HK MP5 submachine gun and gave me a wry smile. "Rank has its privileges!"

"As it should."

"If Mr. Catalano is there," she said, "we'll take him on the EU warrants. We're not sure of *his* whereabouts, but an informant said the girl is there and that's our top priority, so gunfire will only be a last resort."

As darkness set in, Val ordered everyone to don their balaclavas and move into their assigned tactical positions.

She pointed to a rusted-out, unmarked van and said, "We're going in that. We'll jump out when we get to the house."

If we don't fall through the floorboards first! I thought.

I was glad I recently got a tetanus shot.

We mounted up. I was anxious to rescue Sophie, but in my gut had a sense of dread.

- 88 -

KNOCK, KNOCK!

Val *yelled unintelligible commands* to the driver, and after a few minutes, we skidded to a stop in front of the house. "Out!" shouted Val.

We ran to the porch and Aldo proceeded to slam the fifty-pound ram into the jamb of the beat-up door near the locking mechanism. The door offered no resistance, and the inertia of the ram almost took him to the ground.

Val yelled, "*Polizia antimafia!*"

There was no gunfire, no resistance, no Sophie, and no Vinnie Catalano. We cleared the small two-story house in record time.

"I can smell her perfume in the air," I said. "They just left."

As we regrouped in the entry, Val was furious.

"*Vaffanculo!*" Fuck off! She slammed the heel of her hand into the doorframe.

Someone tipped them off.

"No surprise there," muttered Val.

They were on the move, and we needed to move *faster*.

Val keyed her mic and with a taut jaw said, "Find her, now!"

We got updated intelligence moments later, advising Sophie was forcibly taken in an older, red Fiat 500.

We were probably only minutes behind, so Val ordered road-blocks, positioning units north and south. Aldo, Val, and I drove west from the coast toward Scala.

About fifteen minutes later, we received a radio report of a major accident, with at least one fatality, in a busy intersection east of Scala on *Viale Giostra*, the road we were on.

Aldo increased his speed and activated the lights and the siren, the kind with the high-low tone you hear in foreign movies.

Val asked dispatch for a description of vehicles involved. They answered seconds later.

"Dark-colored Renault and a red Fiat. Fatality was in the Fiat."

My heart sank. We didn't speak for the remainder of the drive to the accident scene.

I hastily exited our vehicle when we came on scene.

A Carabinieri officer advised the deceased was the driver of the Fiat.

"He wasn't wearing a seat belt and was ejected from the car."

I checked. He was a heavyset male and not Vincent Catalano.

"The rear passenger *was* wearing a seat belt," said the officer. "She's only got minor injuries. According to witnesses, they were speeding and weaving in and out of traffic."

I walked to the ambulance and was relieved to see Sophie resting on a gurney.

"She'll have some bruises," said an attendant, "but she's going to be fine. She's sedated, but you can check on her."

I stepped into the rear of the ambulance, sat, and held her hand. There was no need for words.

I saw bruising and marks on her wrist from duct tape or restraints.

She gave a slightly loopy smile. "I'm so happy to see you, *Raggio*. I'm so scared."

The attendant helped me sit her up. We slowly escorted her to the police car.

Val was anxious to return to the helicopter, to get Sophie off the island.

"She's not safe here."

We cleared the scene and raced with lights and siren to the airstrip.

Sophie was intermittently weeping and shaking. I explained we'd be traveling by helicopter to Rome, for a flight back to San Francisco in the morning.

The thought of going by helicopter, after losing Mercedes in an airship, was unsettling.

We boarded the Italian AgustaWestland helicopter, a light-weight eight-seater on loan from the Carabinieri for extraction.

After we landed in Rome, we were rushed to a safe house close to the airstrip. At Val's insistence, DIA provided full protection throughout the night, including expedited customs' clearance and early boarding for the flight back to the U.S.

I'd forever be in her debt.

- 89 -

NOT THE VACATION I'D HOPED FOR

We sat together for the fourteen-hour flight to San Francisco, with a two-hour layover in Zurich.

I bought books, magazines, and snacks in Zurich Airport to help pass the time on the plane. For fun, I bought Swiss chocolate bars to eat and give to friends.

Sophie showed little interest in much of anything but enjoyed a spicy Bloody Mary with me in a swank airport bar.

"Look," I joked, "celery sticks, onions, olives, and all those veggies! This is so good for us. I feel like a health food nut. Let's have another!"

Eventually, I got her to smile.

Sadly, back on the plane, the flight brought back memories of the trip from Dubai, less than a year ago. Mercedes, another abused and traumatized soul. *That* journey seemed like a lifetime ago.

After we reboarded the plane for the long haul, Sophie raised the armrest between us, apparently to lean into me while she slept. She said she was cold, so I grabbed a blanket from the overhead bin and covered her. She moved slowly and looked exhausted with dark-gray circles under sad eyes. Her glow and youthful aura were gone, at least for now. She'd been traumatized and robbed of her youthful innocence, and I had every intention of making the sonofabitch pay.

423

Sophie immediately fell asleep, and I ordered another Bloody Mary—for nutritional purposes. I was more interested in the vodka than the tomato juice and eventually dozed off.

I slept for a couple of hours then became restless when nature called. I tried to prop Sophie up so I could go to the lavatory but ended up waking her.

"Sorry, Sophie, I've gotta pee."

She squeezed my hand and adjusted her sleeping position.

After taking care of business, I slowly walked the aisle to get my circulation going and to get some water. The overhead lights had been dimmed, and most passengers were sleeping or taking in a movie.

As I walked toward the rear galley, I sensed I was being watched. Something was off, and as someone who's been hunted for years, I have a sixth sense for threats. I had an enemy on the plane, and we were only four hours into the flight.

I headed back toward the cockpit and squeezed past an attractive woman as I walked past my seat. Sophie was sleeping, and with just two of us in the three-seat section, she was stretched across two of the seats, leaving me the aisle seat, which I preferred.

It felt good to move, so I slowly walked back to the galley. As I turned to go back to my seat, a woman stood.

"You look so familiar. Were you in a magazine? Or Hollywood news, or something?"

Just as I was about to tell her it was possible, I looked past her and, in the area where Sophie and I were seated, I saw her arm raised and flailing. I knew it was her because she was wearing a bright orange sweater over a white blouse.

I excused myself and pushed past the woman to see what was going on. When I got to my seat, the other woman, who a minute earlier I squeezed past in the aisle, was choking Sophie from behind with some type of garrote that looked like thick fishing line. I yanked her off her, twisted her arm behind her back, and forced her to the floor.

A flight attendant ran over.

"I'm a police officer! Get me handcuffs, or restraints, and tell the captain. And get first aid supplies!"

The words were no sooner out of my mouth when I was kicked in the face and attacked by the woman I'd been talking to back by the galley. She kicked me several more times and tried to pummel me.

The captain trotted down the aisle with handcuffs and shoved the woman aside.

"Get back to your seat. Now!"

We quickly secured the first suspect and kept her facedown.

"We need a doctor or a nurse!" I yelled.

A woman came forward and said she was a registered nurse.

"She needs help now," pointing to Sophie. "She's been choked with that fishing line."

I could hear Sophie's raspy and labored breathing.

The *other* Ray had arrived, and the second suspect was about to be introduced.

A fellow passenger—a young, muscular guy—stood up.

"I'm a Marine. I'll watch her, sir. She ain't going nowhere."

I fast-walked back toward the galley and saw the second suspect, the one who kicked me, assuming a martial arts stance, so without a second to waste, I powered my full two-hundred and ten pounds into her, swinging nonstop, battering her head and face. I grabbed a handful of her shiny chestnut-colored hair and slammed her face into the lavatory door until she dropped.

A flight attendant handed me another set of handcuffs, and I cuffed her and sat her down.

The nurse told me had I arrived seconds later, the fishing line would have severed Sophie's carotid artery and she would have bled out. She cleaned the neck areas that were sliced and wrapped her neck in gauze. She held Sophie's hand and found a sedative for her in her purse.

"Thanks so much," I said. "Can you sit with her, while I secure the two women that attacked her?"

"Of course."

The captain explained that an emergency landing wouldn't be possible, as we were on a very northern route over the ocean, but he could radio for an emergency landing somewhere in Canada, or the northeast U.S.

"Thanks, Captain. No need right now. I've got these two secured pretty good.

"If you've got duct tape or additional restraints, let me secure their ankles as well. We should set them apart and close to where I can watch them."

"Right," said the captain. "I'll have the flight attendants ask for assistance from passengers. We've got a lot of open seats, so we should be able to get this done. Let me know if you need anything else. I'll get clearance for you to use a cell phone to notify SFPD airport police prior to our arrival at SFO, so they can be taken into custody."

I checked on the Marine standing watch over the prisoners, and he gave me a thumbs-up. I told him we'd be moving them shortly, so I can keep an eye on them.

"All good, sir."

I went back to my seat and told the nurse, "Thank you. I'll sit with her for now. They're going to be moving our seats shortly, so I can keep an eye on the suspects."

As I sat, Sophie began to tremble and cry. I embraced her, kissed her forehead, and whispered, "I'm so sorry. No one's going to hurt you again. I won't let them."

"I've got seats for you in first class," said a flight attendant.

He escorted Sophie, and I followed with our belongings. After I had her situated, I asked the attendant to have the Marine walk the suspects forward to their new seat assignments.

"I'll be watching," I said. "If anything breaks out, I'll be right there."

The Marine removed the leg restraints, so they could walk forward and be reseated.

"When you get them seated," I said, "let's get the restraints back on their ankles."

They were quickly relocated to bulkhead seats facing me. I made sure that Sophie faced me as well, so she wouldn't have to look at them.

The Marine stood over them while I placed the restraints back on their ankles.

The second attacker I pummeled looked like she'd gone face-first through a windshield. The other suspect had rug burns on her face, like she'd been used as a vacuum cleaner.

Not sorry on either count. If there weren't so many witnesses, I might have killed them both without an ounce of regret.

They were sent to kill Sophie, and me as well, because we were witnesses and victims to Vinnie's offenses.

Assassins, my ass! Vinnie must have sold these two bimbos a bill of goods.

There was an empty seat adjacent to the suspects, and the Marine, whose name I learned was Jack, agreed to help keep them under close surveillance. Without providing too many details, I explained the gravity of the situation, that they were under arrest for conspiracy, attempted murder, a host of FAA violations, and federal RICO statutes, too.

Jack asked, "You a sky marshal?"

"Nope, I'm a cop."

He nodded in acknowledgement.

I couldn't sleep the rest of the flight and asked the flight attendant to keep the coffee coming. I kept a watchful eye on the suspects and tried to keep Sophie occupied with food, small talk, and movies. Her throat was sore, and she was having difficulty swallowing.

I told her, "When we land, I'll see if we can get paramedics to check you over at the gate. It's going to be a little chaotic because I've got cops meeting us there to take custody of the assholes who attacked us. We'll need to write out statements so the suspects can be charged."

She looked out the window and, in a hoarse, barely audible voice, said, "Okay." She clenched a tissue in her hand, occasionally wiping her nose.

About ninety minutes from our destination, the captain came out to tell me that, as requested, SFPD officers, the FBI, and paramedics would be meeting us at the gate. I also asked the captain to contact the airport police and ask them to notify

Inspector Nia Thomas and Deputy Chief Potente, as the incident is part of an organized crime investigation. I handed him their names on a piece of paper.

Upon arrival at the gate, four SFPD officers boarded the aircraft to take custody of the two suspects, who were being guarded by Marine Jack.

After they exited the aircraft, the crew suggested Sophie and I deplane first. The gate area was blocked off with crime scene tape to contain passengers until they could be cleared by police to leave. It would be a long night.

I walked Sophie over to the paramedics and explained the trauma she'd been through. The paramedics wanted to examine her in a private area, so two SFPD officers and I accompanied them. I identified myself to the officers and explained the criminal charges. I also gave them the garotte used to assault her so it could be booked into evidence. I first photographed it with my phone, for additional evidence.

I told the officers not to handle it without gloves and to place it in a paper envelope, as it contained blood and DNA evidence in an attempted homicide.

The captain, who witnessed the arrests, spoke with an SFPD police inspector and an FBI agent.

The paramedics re-dressed Sophie's wound and gave her a sedative. We were transported to SFPD's airport bureau station to provide statements and so Sophie's injuries could be photographed and documented.

Two of the FBI agents that met us at the airport took us to a safe house in a rural part of the Livermore Valley, east of San Francisco.

Special Agent Walter Heil said, "The safe house is a precaution until we complete a threat assessment. Your deputy chief insisted on it, so we'll be hanging with you guys for a while."

We drove along a precarious dirt road with no shoulder that climbed a mountain for at least thirty minutes before arriving at a house that was in total darkness.

"It's not bad inside," Heil said and handed me a gym bag with new SFPD tee shirts, BDUs, socks, duty boots, a holster, along with a .40 caliber Sig Sauer 226 with boxes of ammunition and magazines.

"Compliments of Deputy Chief Potente. He thought you might need these things."

After we got situated, I began loading magazines. It gave me some peace of mind.

With a team of six tactically outfitted FBI agents on overwatch, I assured Sophie we were safe.

She asked me to lay on the bed with her until she fell asleep. Her once-beautiful olive skin had dulled and her eyes were lifeless and droopy, like I'd seen with drug addicts. The trauma and abuse she'd endured had a toxic effect, and her sadness reminded me of the victims of sex traffickers I'd encountered overseas as a SEAL.

I lay next to her, clothed, and drifted off to sleep. Sometime during the night, she pulled the comforter over me. I felt a soft kiss on my face and moisture from her tears.

- 90 -

WHERE TO NOW?

fter two boring days of lockdown in the safe house, SA
Heil took me aside.

"Based on what we've learned so far, we think Miss Rossi
would be safer in WITSEC for the foreseeable future. Her life is
in danger until we get Mr. Catalano in custody. Even after he's in
custody, he can send assassins after her, like he did on the plane.
Why don't you talk to her and feel her out?"

The Witness Security Program, known as WITSEC, was serious business and I felt bad for her; she'd been through so much
already. Still, it was probably the right move in the near term.

Sophie was sitting on the steps of the back porch overlooking
a canyon, sipping tea.

In a hoarse voice she said, "I'm scared, Ray. What should I do?"

I sat beside her and she started to cry. I was reminded of what
she'd just been through by the white surgical dressing and gauze
wrapped around her neck. I put my arm around her.

"Let's take it a day at a time and look at the next month or so.
Do you have any friends or relatives you can stay with? Someone
who other people won't necessarily associate you with? Someone
you can trust? Out of state? The more remote, the better."

She paused, then said, "I've got an aunt, my father's sister,
who lives on a ranch in Paicines. Do you know where that is?"

"Nope. Never heard of it."

She explained it was east of Monterey in a mountainous area in San Benito County.

"My aunt said less than a thousand people live there."

"Tell me more," I said.

"You can't find their *exact* location with GPS. You can find Paicines, but not their ranch, because it's so remote. There's an old cattle gate they keep locked, off a dirt road, and you have to call them to come down the mountain in their old Army Jeep to bring you up to the house. You leave your car at the gate. The road to the ranch regularly washes out. It's ruddy. They're twenty minutes up the side of the mountain, and they say the house has no real address, at least one you can google. They use a post office box as their address in town and keep to themselves.

"They have a nice cabin with a huge porch that my uncle built, and it overlooks mountain ranges and canyons. At night, the sky is filled with stars. It's beautiful up there.

"They do some ranching, and have chickens and stuff. My uncle is smart and has an engineering job with the City of Salinas. I think he drives to Salinas once a week for meetings. They have a spare room and might let me stay there for a while. He hunts wild boar and quail and has lots of guns. I always feel safe there."

"Well, call them first, to see if it's even a possibility."

"What about my job?" she said.

"If you want, when I return to work, I can talk to them and ask if you can be granted a leave of absence. I can explain the situation, without telling them too much. I'll ask them if you can work remotely, too. A lot of people are doing that now."

I spoke with DC Potente, and he seemed satisfied with the proposed solutions. He also said he was sending Inspector Thomas to our location to take statements regarding Sophie's disappearance and her captivity before she's relocated to the next safe house.

I was anxious to return, to get back to work and have some sense of normalcy, even if I still had a target on my back. This shit was getting old, and the hunted was about to become the hunter. I'd had enough.

Sophie's aunt and uncle agreed to an extended visit, so she was happy about that.

SA Heil said, "If we can get Catalano and more of his crew in custody, she can get her life back."

DC Potente said OCTF were making real progress in the lateral academy.

"We picked a great team. Amato said the team even speaks Sicilian among themselves. I guess trying to stay in character. They eat together at night at the apartments where they're staying. They're adjusting. As soon as they graduate, we'll get them in the field to start acclimating to the environment. We'll ease them into it, so they don't get burned. Keep them undercover as long as we can. We've got to start making RICO cases and get these guys off the street."

"Sounds like progress, Chief."

"So, when are you coming back to Central, Ray?"

"How about next week? I want to get Sophie Rossi situated first. She's staying with relatives in a remote location. At least until Catalano's in custody and things settle down. You okay with that?"

"Take the time you need, and I'll let Captain Choo know you're out for another week on paid leave.

"The department appreciates what you've been through and your efforts to rescue Miss Rossi and bring her home. Above and beyond. What you did . . . a really big deal. You'll be receiving a commendation for this."

"Thanks, sir. I'm anxious to get back."

"Good. We also plan to honor Val Andresini and her team. Incredible cooperation and bravery on their part."

- 91 -

PAICINES, POPULATION: 729

Sophie was interviewed the following morning by Inspector Thomas and SA Heil. I sat in on the interview. It was important that we all hear her story from start to finish. It was disturbing to hear the details and the fear and emotion in her voice. I was reminded why that sonofabitch Catalano had to go.

After the interview, we left Livermore in a tactical caravan to relocate Sophie to her aunt's ranch in Paicines. She wasn't joking, this place was in the middle of nowhere. Only Agent Heil and I accompanied Sophie on the jarring ride to the top of the mountain.

Her aunt and uncle were gracious and surprised when I spoke to them in Sicilian. Sophie pulled me aside as we were saying our goodbyes.

"Will you come see me, Ray?"

"Of course, I will. As soon as I can."

SA Heil reviewed safety precautions and how they could reach him—day or night.

We left, and Heil drove the two hours to drop me at the Daly City apartment complex. I didn't have the heart to ask him to cross the bridge and drive to Fairfax.

I offered to buy dinner for his trouble, but he lived an hour away in the East Bay and hadn't seen his family in a couple of days.

He seemed like a decent guy for a fed, and I told him I'd make the trip down to Paicines to check on Sophie in a few days.

"You like her, huh? I think she likes you, too."

"Complicated," I said.

- 92 -

THE BITTER AND THE SWEET

bought a burner at a CVS store in Greenbrae on my way to work to call Sophie. She had given me her aunt's phone number earlier, which I preferred to use.

Her aunt answered, *"Bon jornu!"*

She said Sophie had a restful night, then put her on the phone. The conversation was brief, and I asked if she'd like me to visit on my next days off.

Her voice brightened. "Yes! Come see me, *Raggio!*" She had started calling me that as a term of endearment.

We made plans, and it lifted my mood. The call was brief, and I told her I planned to stop at Café Trieste, where I'd first seen her, on my way to work for an espresso.

"Aww. That's so nice. I wish I could be with you."

It felt good to be back in uniform, behind the wheel of a radio car. I savored the local smells of salt air, coffee beans, and roasted duck in Chinatown, against the squawking of the police radio. It was exactly what I needed to reset.

It was early, so street activity was light. I drove to Aquatic Park to watch the swimmers freezing their asses off. Better them than me. At least for today.

I was desperate to get back to my routines. I wanted to ease into the day and hoped there'd be no A-priority calls, at least for a while.

I planned to visit Gina at Carmine's later, if possible, to see what she knew about Vinnie's whereabouts, if anything. Most likely she, too, was in the dark. If she wasn't, or seemed to be hiding something, that would be a problem.

As I sat with the window down, enjoying some tranquility, I was startled when the dispatcher sounded a radio tone telling all units to stand by for an important "all" broadcast.

After a pause, she said, "Our city is mourning the loss of one of our own today, Sergeant Joseph Amato." She paused, "CHP reported Sergeant Amato was killed this morning in a traffic collision westbound on the Bay Bridge. Sergeant Amato was a member of the 232nd Academy class and was promoted to sergeant in 2015. Prior to joining SFPD, Sergeant Amato served with San Mateo County Sheriff's Office for seven years. Sergeant Amato was assigned to both Southern and Mission stations and most recently was chosen to head the new Organized Crime Task Force. Throughout his career, Sergeant Amato distinguished himself and received numerous commendations and honors for exceptional service and bravery in the line of duty. He is survived by his loving wife Jill and two sons, Joseph Jr. and Anthony. We will miss Sergeant Amato, and we're eternally grateful for his sacrifices and service to the City and County of San Francisco. Rest in Peace, Sergeant Amato, we'll take it from here. KMA 438."

I was stunned, in disbelief.

I'd only met him once in the chief's office, but it was still a terrible loss for his family, the department, DC Potente, and the members of the newly formed OCTF.

I called DC Potente on his cell, but it went to voicemail.

"Chief, sorry to hear about Sergeant Amato's death this morning. I'm back on patrol in the Central. Let me know if there's anything I can do. Terrible loss."

About an hour later, he called me back.

"Sorry, Ray, I've been tied up dealing with Sergeant Amato's death. I have a big favor to ask. Can you go to the academy and touch base with the task force guys? I know you have the skills and experience to help them deal with it. I also wanted to ask you to give them direction for the next forty-eight hours or so. This is their last week in the academy. Their world just got turned upside down. We've got to keep their heads on straight. I'll let Captain Choo know he needs to give you flexibility this week to help us out. For the time being, you're their acting supervisor. They've got to have some oversight. I'll let the academy staff know, too."

"I've got it, Chief. I'll call Captain Choo and roll out there now."

He thanked me and ended the call.

As I pulled into the academy lot, I saw them standing outside the classroom, talking. The mood was somber. They collectively expressed their individual sense of loss.

"We didn't know him well, but he seemed like a good guy. We never had the chance to roll with him."

Nardo had told Luca and Jack about Sophie's rescue with DIA in Sicily, so they congratulated me.

Pivoting the conversation, Nardo said, "Nice work, Ray. We're glad to see ya. What'd ya think of Val?"

I smiled. "A blonde in Italy? She's great, Nardo. Certified badass. I like her a lot."

They brought me up to speed on their studies and what was left to complete. They were anxious to graduate and go to work.

"Chief Potente asked me to make myself available to you guys to get things wrapped up. Here's my cell number. I'm available twenty-four seven. Just call me for anything you need. You've got tests coming up, so stay focused on your studies. Only a few days left. This is the home stretch. I'll be checking in with you."

No surprise, they all successfully completed the lateral academy, and a private ceremony was planned in Chief Castillo's office for 2 p.m. that Friday. DC Potente invited me to the ceremony as an honored guest and said my help had been invaluable in the selection process. I sensed *the touch* wasn't far behind.

It was a low-key ceremony, considering Sergeant Amato's passing. The funeral service for him was planned for the following week. We all planned to attend.

After the ceremony, as everyone was dispersing, DC Potente pulled me aside.

"Ray, as you know, a lot is riding on this unit, and now the team is without leadership. I know you've said no in the past, but I'm asking again, as someone who has tremendous faith in you. Will you join the team? I'd like to put you in the leadership role as the acting sergeant. No one is better prepared for that role than you. Give me a year and if you don't like it, I'll send you back to Central, or wherever you want to go. If all goes according to plan, you'll be eligible by then and can take the sergeant's test and get additional consideration for placement on the list. I'll make sure of that."

Personally, and professionally, I had to do it.

"Okay, sir. I'm in."

"The assignment starts now. Thank you, Ray. I'll put the transfer paperwork in today, so empty your locker at Central Station, and let's assemble the team first thing Monday morning, in my office. Congratulations, Ray. I won't forget this."

I called Sophie. "I'm thinking about coming to see you Saturday. You up for company?"

"I would love that!" she lowered her voice. "It gets a little boring up here and I'm starved for some fun."

"What can I bring?"

"Just you, Raggio. That's all I need right now, just you."

"Okay, that one's easy."

I planned to bring Italian cookies and cannoli from my favorite Italian bakery in North Beach and some good wine. Maybe a couple of paperbacks, too, to keep her mind occupied and off her troubles.

I called her when I was thirty minutes away, so they could drive down the mountain in the Jeep to pick me up.

They were on time, and after I handed her flowers and the pink bakery box and bag full of goodies, I earned a very tight hug and sweet kiss. I enjoyed both, and it was delicious to smell her again. I knew she was coming back from a very dark place.

I had the bakery box filled to the lid and told her family to help themselves. Sophie packed a picnic lunch and blanket and wanted to go on a hike.

"As long as there's a nice bottle of vino in that picnic basket," I said.

We took a well-worn trail into the hills, and at some point during our journey, a mangy dog joined us for the hike.

He resembled a coyote but wasn't.

He reminded me of the lost, roaming dogs we'd see in villages in Afghanistan. No home, no family, nowhere to go. They just scrounge around, looking for food scraps.

He snarled, probably out of fear, when I approached him, but later let me to touch him. He was slowly accepting me.

We found a flat, grassy spot to spread the blanket and enjoy our lunch. Our friend—who I nicknamed Buddy—stayed close, inquisitively leering at us. He eventually relaxed and lay prone. Probably didn't have a lot of human contact up here in the middle of nowhere.

Sophie had packed an assortment of cheeses, meats, and sliced fruit. She'd carefully packed everything in plastic containers, along with the cannoli and cookies I brought. I made sure she packed the Sangiovese with a couple of plastic cups.

She wore a soft, pale-blue turtleneck sweater to cover the medical dressing on her neck, but aside from that, her radiant skin was coming back and the sparkle in her pale-blue eyes. The dark circles under her eyes were disappearing, too. It was a relief to see her looking better. On her worst day, she's the most beautiful woman I'd ever seen.

We kept the conversation light, and I avoided talking about her ordeal or my new role as the head of the OCTF.

I was concerned with the mental trauma she'd just been through. "I bet you sleep good up here with all this fresh air."

"Sometimes."

"It's not unusual to have bad dreams and restless sleep after what you've been through," I said. "I still dream about stuff that happened in the Navy and probably always will. I've learned to live with it. It's not real, so I keep it in perspective."

I moved closer to hold her. We lay back and made out for a good while.

Without saying a word, she pulled the blanket over us and removed her jeans and brassiere. I was sure she kept the sweater on to protect her neck. I pulled her sweater up to kiss her beautiful breasts. She unzipped my jeans and gently pulled them off.

We made love, passionately kissing and embracing like we'd never get the chance to again. She tasted as good as she smelled. We stayed locked in the embrace and fell asleep.

For the longest time, I wasn't sure we'd *ever* be together, but it felt good. This changed everything. When we woke, I poured some wine, and we sat and talked. We talked about things we'd never talked about before, and I admitted how, from the day I first saw her, I wanted her. She smiled and seemed embarrassed.

I didn't want to get ahead of myself so I added, "It's probably too late to say we should take it slow, but I don't want you to feel there's pressure from me."

"I wanted this to happen, and I want you, Ray. I've been pretty messed up, and things have been coming too fast, and I've been frightened; but I'm willing to try if you are."

I paused. "As you know, I recently lost Mercedes, so I'm not in the best shape either. Let's just be there for each other and see what happens."

She smiled. "Deal."

She kissed the top of my hand, then my mouth.

We dressed and packed for the trek down the mountain with the lonesome stray following from a distance.

We had an early dinner with Sophie's family, and though they asked me to stay the night, I needed to get back and prepare for my new responsibilities as head of OCTF. I also didn't want to overstay my welcome.

After dessert with coffee and Italian cookies, Sophie's aunt said she'd do the honors and drive me down the mountain. Sophie insisted she come, too.

We had a long embrace and kiss at the gate, and I promised to call when I got home, so she'd know I got in okay.

The stray followed the Jeep on the slow four-wheel crawl down the mountain.

Gesturing toward the dog, I asked, "Can you feed him for me? He's all skin and bones. I'm thinking I'll take him home, if he'll go with me, the next time I come to visit."

I missed her as soon as my wheels hit the hard pavement.

On my way to work on Monday, I received an incoming international call. It was Val from DIA.

In her straightforward, deliberate style, she said, "We got him, Ray. Vincent Catalano is in custody."

"*Mamma Mia!* That's great news, Val. You just made my day."

I brought her up to date on the sad news of Sergeant Amato's passing and my new role with the OCTF.

"I'm so sorry to hear about your sergeant. That's terrible. I never met him."

She hesitated, then said, "If it's not inappropriate, I am glad to hear that you've been chosen to lead the Organized Crime Task Force. That's wonderful. Congratulations! Then, hopefully, we'll get to work together again."

"I hope so, too. I'm assuming you'll be prosecuting Catalano in your country?"

"Of course. We'll take the first bite." Then she laughed. "I'm sure we'll be coordinating with you and the U.S. Attorney's Office regarding RICO charges."

"If you can send me what you've got," I said, "I'll review it with my boss and the U.S. Attorney. I'll be in touch. Can't thank you enough. I'm on my way to a meeting with the deputy chief as we speak. He'll be happy to hear this great news."

I immediately called Sophie to share the news with her.

"He's in custody in Sicily!"

There was a long pause, then sniffling and tears. It took her a moment to compose herself.

"Thank you so much, Ray. I am so relieved. Do I still have to be in hiding?"

"I just found out, so let me get more information and direction on this. I'll call you later today."

"I'm sending you a kiss," she said. "We can talk later. Oh, your friend Buddy hasn't left our front porch. I feel so sorry for him. He's sad. I think he misses you, *Raggio!*"

In Sicilian I said, "Well, I need to bring him here, so I can take care of him. Two old lonely souls."

She laughed.

"I'll call you later."

Luca, Jack, and Nardo were waiting in the lobby and we went to the DC's office together, as a team.

The chief had coffee ready and treated us to some sweet rolls.

"Don't get used to this!" he said.

We laughed and I said, "Well, Chief, you might want to take us to lunch, too, when you hear this news."

I had his full attention. "Val Andresini just called from DIA, and said they just took Vincent Catalano into custody in Sicily."

The whole team clapped and high-fived.

"Sergeant DeLuca, you're off to a *very* good start."

"Thank you, sir, but a lot of the credit goes to Nardo, who activated DIA and brought Val into the mix. We've got a lot of work ahead of us, but Vinnie was the boss here in San Francisco, so this is a major setback for them, and a good start for us."

We all congratulated Nardo, who shrugged his shoulders, but appreciated the acknowledgement.

We spent the morning creating a plan to get the team into the field. We had RICO training first, then meetings with the U.S. Attorney, the FBI field office, and U.S. Immigration and Customs.

It was coming together, and it was exciting.

Our spirits were dampened, though, with funeral services later in the week for Sergeant Amato. We decided to attend the services as a team.

As we'd say in the SEALS, "All-in, all the time."

- 93 -

HOW DID I GET HERE?

I *ate at Sorella Caffè* before going home for the night. In a relatively short span of time, my life had taken a new course, and not one I planned or expected.

I suffered losses I'd never recover from: Mercedes and Billy.

I was suspended then fired by SFPD.

With my father's help and influence, I got my job back.

Two of my closest friends at SFPD, Hank Lau and Lily Leung, betrayed me. They turned their backs on me when I was at my lowest.

Hank's failure to be honest and transparent about his connection to the Ghost Boys, at least in part, cost Billy his life.

His allegiance was to his Ghost Boy cousin, a career criminal. He almost cost me *my* life as well and made the past year a living hell. I've got the scars to prove it and may never recover from the emotional costs. I'll never trust another partner.

Hank betrayed me, his profession, his wife, and kids, all for his cousin and a piece of ass. He pulled the pin on his life.

Because of Lily's frustrations with *our* relationship, when it failed to materialize—especially after I met Mercedes—her anger and frustrations led to two Use of Force complaints and an affair with a married man. She lost her moral compass and entered an impossible relationship with Hank.

In my travels there was some good. I met Marine Mike, always faithful . . . *Semper Fi!* Now, friends for life.

I met Joe through Billy at Blackhawk and formed a trust and bond that will unify us forever. A salt of the earth green bandito.

I've had a bounty on my head for the past six months, and I've been repeatedly attacked at remote safe houses from the Bay Area to Southern California. I could never get ahead of the Ghost Boys because of Hank's leaks to his cousin. That threat remains, though it's been reduced with the deaths of more than ten Ghost Boys.

I've had little refuge or relief from unrelenting stress and worry due to these attacks, except for fleeting moments with Mercedes.

I lost a woman I was madly in love with, in a freak helicopter accident. I'd planned to spend the rest of my life with her. I'll never get over it.

For the past year, I've lived with death threats and attacks and had my new career and livelihood threatened by Lieutenant Flynn, who never believed in me. Not from day one.

On vacation in Sicily, I was kidnapped and beaten, but escaped and lived to fight another day.

Sophie Rossi disappeared from San Francisco and emerged in Sicily—an unwilling *goomah* of Vinnie's.

Through Nardo's connections with his former employer, Val at DIA, we got the help we needed to rescue Sophie and move us both to safety.

Carmine Vaccaro's death remains classified as a "suspicious circumstances" case, but probably not for long. I have a feeling that with Vincent Catalano in custody, his admission to participating in Carmine's death will be a bargaining chip for him to avoid the death penalty.

Gina Vaccaro is enjoying the fruits of her brother's estate, but there's still a veil of suspicion over her because of a previous relationship with Vincent Catalano. That will be explored, and the facts will come out. From the bottom of my heart, I hope she's cleared.

Sophie was rescued, but almost lost her life on the commercial flight home from Zurich when she was attacked by Vincent Catalano's assassins. I guess he thought if he couldn't have her, no one should, especially me.

My parents only know half of this, and I hope it stays that way.

Sophie and I have a complicated relationship, but I think there's a flicker of hope for me, Sophie, and a dog I plan to rename "Billy."

My name is Ray DeLuca, proud son of mob boss Anthony DeLuca and my best girl, Rose.

▪ *The End* ▪

ABOUT THE AUTHOR

oseph Cariffe is a writer and radio broadcasting executive. He grew up in the shadow of La Cosa Nostra in Newburgh, New York, and his early years were heavily influenced by his Italian American heritage and organized crime. He served in the U.S. military as a military police officer and held sworn positions with the FBI and San Francisco Police Department. He divides his time between the San Francisco Bay Area and the pine forests of North Carolina, where he resides with his family.

Made in United States
North Haven, CT
22 October 2022